The BIZARRU
STARTER KIT

AN INTRODUCTION TO THE BIZARRO GENRE

BIZARRO BOOKS
Portland * Seattle * Baltimore

Bizarro

www.bizarrogenre.org

BIZARRO BOOKS
205 NE BRYANT
PORTLAND, OR 97211

IN COOPERATION WITH:

WWW.ERASERHEADPRESS.COM
WWW.AFTERBIRTHBOOKS.COM
WWW.RAWDOGSCREAMINGPRESS.COM

ISBN: 1-933929-00-6

TABLE OF CONTENTS

DEFINING BIZARRO

1. Bizarro, simply put, is the genre of the weird.

2. Bizarro is literature's equivalent to the cult section at the video store.

3. Like cult movies, Bizarro is sometimes surreal, sometimes goofy, sometimes bloody, and sometimes borderline pornographic.

4. Bizarro often contains a certain cartoon logic that, when applied to the real world, creates an unstable universe where the bizarre becomes the norm and absurdities are made flesh.

5. Bizarro strives not only to be strange, but fascinating, thought-provoking, and, above all, fun to read.

6. Bizarro was created by a group of small press publishers in response to the increasing demand for (good) weird fiction and the increasing number of authors who specialize in it.

7. Bizarro is:

Franz Kafka meets Joe Bob Briggs

Dr. Suess of the post-apocalypse

Japanese animation directed by David Lynch

8. For more information on the bizarro genre, visit Bizarro Central at:

www.bizarrogenre.org

D. HARLAN WILSON

LOCATION:
Bowels of Michigan

STYLE OF BIZARRO:
Irrealism

BOOKS BY WILSON:

The Kafka Effekt
Stranger on the Loose
Irrealities
Pseudo-City
Dr. Identity (forthcoming)

DESCRIPTION: Formerly a town crier in an anonymous Welsh village, D. Harlan Wilson is currently a professor of English at Michigan State University. His fiction is a dark, absurdist, dreamlike exploration of the postcapitalist condition.

INFLUENCES: Franz Kafka, Nikolai Gogol, Jorge Luis Borges, William S. Burroughs, Fyodor Dostoevsky, Russell Edson, Deleuze & Guattari, Jean Baudrillard, Philip K. Dick, Kurt Vonnegut, Rene Magritte, David Lynch, Albert Camus, Airplane!, Airplane 2!, Nascar enthusiasts, Elvis impersonators, and Ben Affleck.

WEBSITE:

www.dharlanwilson.com

AT THE FUNERAL

It's been a week already and the funeral isn't over yet. For seven days and nights we've been roaming the hallways of Frinkel's Death Emporium whispering in each other's ears, massaging each other's elbows, politely trampling each other as we ransack the hors d'oeuvre table, which is replenished with a fresh round of fruit punch and cold Swedish meatballs at noon and sundown every day. The Emporium's staff consists of two short, round men in bird costumes. When they're not setting out provisions and cleaning up after us, they wobble around on their big yellow feet and make bird noises.

Seven days and nights of walking around a funeral home is enough to make anybody tired, and yet nobody seems to be tired but me. I start asking people why they don't sit down for a while, maybe take a nap, but everybody just smacks their lips and waves me away.

Annoyed, I decide to look for a bed and take a nap myself. I find one in a secret room. The bed is king-sized and made out of Queen Anne's lace. On the far side of it, my sister Klarissa is sitting there playing with a doll.

In the middle of it, The Deceased is laying there dead.

The upper half of The Deceased's body is hanging out of a black, halfway unzipped body bag. He isn't wearing any clothes and His skin is absolutely colorless. His eyes look like they're on the verge of popping out of His head.

I sit down next to Him and frown at Klarissa. "Did you unzip this body bag?"

She shakes her head.

"You're telling me you didn't unzip this body bag? Is that what you're telling me?"

She nods her head.

"Well, I guess the thing unzipped itself. I guess that's what happened, isn't it?" This time my sister doesn't respond to me. She whispers something into her doll's ear and giggles.

I use my feet to try and stuff The Deceased back into the body bag, but it doesn't work, and when I'm about to lay my hands on Him, my mother walks into the secret room, scolds my sister and I for being there, sits down on the bed and places The Deceased's head in her lap. She strokes His curly brown hair. A few seconds later . . . He coughs.

"Holy moly," I say.

My mother closes her eyes. "No, no. That's just a reflex."

"Reflex? He's been dead over a week."

My mother begins to massage The Deceased's neck. The Deceased coughs again. Then, purring a little, He mumbles, "That feels good."

Before I can say anything my mother shakes her head. "Reflexes. It's all reflexes."

I stare at her.

My mother says, "Listen, I have to go. Aunt Kay's been feeding meatballs to the spiders and I have to try and convince her to feed them to herself instead. You two can stay here, but not for long, okay? Be good." She removes The Deceased's head from her lap, gets off the bed and leaves.

The Deceased flexes His jaw. He coughs again, and again, and again. He keeps on coughing until a rotten apple flies out of His mouth. It sails across the room and shatters an antique lamp. Klarissa and I leap off the bed as The Deceased starts gesticulating like an angry worm. "Get me outta this damn thing," He says.

"I don't think that's such a good idea," I say. Klarissa adds, "We might get in trouble." Then, under her breath: "Is this a reflex, too?"

I purse my lips.

The Deceased gives us a dirty look. "Fine. I'll get out myself. And I'll never forgive you two for being so crummy to me."

Klarissa and I glance at each other. After a brief struggle, The Deceased manages to unzip the body bag the rest of the way. He climbs out of it. He stretches His wiry, naked limbs, rearranges His genitals, and strides out of the secret room without a word. Klarissa and I watch Him go.

Then we leap back onto the bed and fall asleep on either side of the open body bag . . .

Out in the hallways The Deceased approaches the attendants of the funeral one at a time. He taps them on the shoulders and asks if they can spare some clothes and if it's not too much trouble a meatball and a cup of fruit punch. "I'm very cold and undernourished," He says, eyes fixed on his toes. Everybody frowns and pretends they don't understand Him, except for my Aunt Kay, who, in response to His plea, spits a mouthful of tobacco juice on Him and then shoots up into the ceiling on a thread of spidersilk attached to the back of her neck. The Deceased breaks down and cries. My grandfather threatens to have Him hanged. "We'll string you up right here and won't even think twice about it!" he twangs. The Deceased snarls at him. My grandfather signals the Emporium's two bird men and they all chase The Deceased back to the secret room and tell Him not to come out again unless He wants to die.

"I'm already dead," says The Deceased as my grandfather slams the door on His face.

Klarissa and I don't wake up. The Deceased shuffles over to the bed. He stares at us and thinks about what He should do. Should He kill us? Should He maim us? Or should He leave us alone? Since He dislikes us so much, the most sensible thing to do would be to kill us. But He can't make up His mind. He tries to wake us and ask us what He should do. No luck—we're sleeping like dead things. No matter how hard He pokes our shoulders and screams in our ears, we won't open our eyes.

The Deceased sighs. Then, having nothing else to do, He crawls onto the bed and back into the body bag, and zips Himself up as best He can.

COPS &
BODYBUILDERS

A bodybuilder in a purple spandex G-string snuck into my home and started to pose. His tan seemed to have been painted onto his skin, and his muscles seemed to twitch and flex of their own volition. His grin was as white as the image of God.

I reached underneath the couch cushion I was sitting on. Pulled out a crowbar. "I'll teach you to invade a man's privacy," I exclaimed, and made like I was going to swing at him. He didn't flinch. He went on posing, turning his broad back to me and tightening up his gluteus maximus.

Impressed, I couldn't help making a comment. "Nice gluts," I said. The bodybuilder thanked me, straightened out one of his arms and exhibited a sublime tricep muscle. I made a frog face. "That's pretty nice, too. But could you leave please? My wife will be home soon and if she sees us here together she might get suspicious. Anyway you're breaking the law. You can't just sneak into somebody's house, start posing and expect everything to be all right. Please go."

The bodybuilder shook his head. "I'm sorry but I can't do that. Once I start posing, there's no stopping me." He placed a foot out in front of him and mockingly jiggled his profound thigh muscles back and forth. "I may take five now and then to shoot up an anabolic cocktail and fix myself a protein shake, but otherwise, you're stuck with me. You're stuck with me for a long, long time."

I called the bodybuilder an asshole. Then I called 911. "You're going to jail for what you've done." The bodybuilder shrugged. The shrug was as much a pose as it was a gesture of indifference.

In light of the severity of the crime I reported on the phone, the police didn't bother knocking on my door when they arrived. They simply crashed through my door like a stampede of psychotic oxen. There were three of them, each equipped with a bushy handlebar mustache, each wearing two articles of clothing: a ten-gallon police hat and a purple spandex G-string. Their tans seemed to have been painted onto their skin, and their muscles seemed to twitch and flex of their own volition. Their grins were as white as the image of God.

"What seems to be the problem here, sir?" asked the cop in charge, and struck a pose. It was an impressive Front Double Bicep pose. Following his lead, the rest of the cops also struck it.

I said, "This bodybuilder is an intruder. Take him away."

"We weren't talking to you," replied the cop in charge. He and his colleagues synchronously shifted into an equally impressive Side Chest pose. "We were talking to the bodybuilder."

Confused, I glanced at the bodybuilder. He nodded at me. "This man is inhospitable," he said. "Take him away."

The cops made belittling, sniggering comments about my less than rock hard body as they frisked me, cuffed me, and led me out to the squad car . . .

HAIRWARE, INC.

One day I woke up and decided it was time to get a job. "Jobs are delicious." I smacked my lips.

I rolled over and went back to sleep. Later I woke up again.

After taking a shower, bleaching my teeth, sitting on the toilet, drinking my morning coffee, eating my morning hard-boiled egg, reading an out-of-date newspaper, and allowing Good Sense to sink Its teeth into me, I realized that a job might not be the best course of action. Not a regular job anyway.

I decided to start my own business.

Having no business experience, I wasn't quite sure where to begin. Best sleep on it, I told myself.

I had a dream about a room full of naked fetuses squirming on the pavement in silence . . . I woke up again and scrambled into the bathroom. I inspected my face in the mirror, one cheek at a time.

"Adios," I said to each of my sideburns and then mindfully cut them off with a straight razor. I primped their bristled bodies with a fine-toothed comb, sprinkled a little aftershave on them, and tied leashes to their necks.

I left.

The street was full of men in capes, top hats and Lone Ranger masks. A few of the men accidentally stomped on my sideburns as I walked them to the nearest fire hydrant. By the time I reached the fire hydrant, the sideburns were very flat-looking. I did my best to make them look presentable again.

I climbed on top of the fire hydrant. "Pets for sale," I announced. I struck a pose that conveyed an aura of relaxed confidence.

Nobody paid attention to me.

I said, "Bargain prices guaranteed."

Bodies froze, ears pricked up, irises opened . . . A gaggle of cape-wearers converged on me and started bidding on the sideburns. "Five dollars!" one of them spat. Another exclaimed, "I'll give you a hog, a cow, and two wiggers for the both of them!" Not being a big fan of the barter system, I made approving frog faces only at the men who offered me money.

I ended up letting the sideburns go for $40 apiece. The buyer wanted to pay me with an I.O.U. I demanded cash. He gave me a $100 bill and told me to keep the change.

There was no end to my excitement. A Cheshire permagrin overwhelmed my face as I raced to a bar and spent $90 on overpriced martinis and scotches. I used what was left to buy a hot dog, a pickle and a dirty magazine from a kiosk.

A homeless man raised an eyebrow at me as I stumbled over to his cardboard box and puked in it. I apologized and gave him an I.O.U. for the cleaning bill.

I went back home, toppled into bed, slept, dreamt, woke up, winced at my hangover, swallowed a handful of aspirin, guzzled a gallon of tap water, went back to sleep, dreamt, woke up, stared at the ceiling, blinked, got out of bed, took a shower, bleached my teeth, sat on the toilet, ate a hard-boiled egg, read an out-of-date newspaper . . .

I didn't say "Adios" to my eyebrows and mustache before slicing them off.

This time I didn't even have to tantalize potential buyers with a guarantee. The moment I set foot on the street, dragging the three pieces of facial hair behind me by their respective leashes, I was besieged by wisping capes. As I haggled and dickered and quibbled over prices, I spotted the man who had purchased my right sideburn out of the corner of my eyes. He was leaning up against a lamppost across the street, petting and whispering babytalk to the hairpiece.

The mustache sold for considerably more than the eyebrows, despite the fact that all three hairpieces were more or less the same size and accompanied by sizeable handlebars . . .

I walked away with $350. Not a bad day's work. Business was really starting to take off.

I spent $300 on a prostitute and gave her a $35 tip. I used what was left to buy another hot dog, pickle and dirty magazine from a kiosk.

As I lunched and read, I realized that I needed to hire somebody to manage my money; so far I had been less than frugal with my earnings. Either that, or sell enough products so as to not have to worry about how much of my earnings I spent.

My armpits, I thought. And my pubic region . . .

But I was no whore. Those hairy places were not meant to be shaved and sold as silly, loveable companions.

A nap would surely clear my mind and help me figure out what to do. I took one.

I dreamt of a room full of grouchy fetuses wearing dirty diapers and five o'clock shadows . . .

I woke up. An idea was sitting in the waiting room of my mind. It greeted me with a wet kiss.

I waited until the sun went down and the city was crawling with shadows. I became one of the shadows.

Bums, vagrants, tramps, gypsies, hobos, nomads, vagabonds, itinerants—I started out with them. As they lay sawing logs in their respective boxes, trash cans, park benches, curbs, subway stations, alleyways, fire escapes and roofs, I snuck up on them and relinquished their faces of any and all embellishments, which mostly consisted of unkempt unibrows and nappy, dusty beards.

A garbage bag full of booty hanging over my shoulder, I climbed down every chimney that would accommodate my creeping body and stole a wide variety of facial hair from a wide variety of apartment owners as they snored the night away. I did this until my bag was absolutely stuffed. Then I skulked home, got drunk, went to sleep, dreamt, woke up, went back to sleep, dreamt, woke up, lay in bed, got out of bed, took a shower, bleached my teeth . . .

Later I set up a lemonade stand in the city center.

Village idiots gathered in the city center daily to perform a *cirque d'idéotie* of feats and wonders that ranged from nude trapeze artistry to Elvis impersonations to ultraviolent, gladiator-like battle royals. It was a prime location for any business. There was always a healthy crowd of consumers looking for diversions from being oppressed by the spectacle of the village idiots' idiocy.

It was a hot day. Muggy, too. Surely consumers would be looking for something to quench their thirst.

In addition to thirst-quenchers, I sold pets.

The stand was an assemblage of cardboard boxes I had stitched together with coat hangers to look like a kiosk. On top I painted the title of my business:

HAIRWARE, INC.

I placed a sweating, refreshing-looking pitcher of lemonade on the counter of my makeshift kiosk. Next to it I placed a pair of sharp lambchop sideburns and a Fu Manchu. I stroked the hairpieces with a pinky finger, combed their hides with a toothbrush . . .

"Pets for sale at bargain prices," I announced, tantalizing the public right off the bat.

Nobody minded me. It was the usual throng of men in capes and top hats. But there were some wearing colorful zoot and goodbody suits, and a motley few were dressed up in stonewashed Mexican tuxedos. The village idiots, if they weren't flying through the air naked as torn open clams, exhibited bright white disco outfits with giant collars that flared out over hairy inverted chests. The idiots weren't doing anything special. Nothing out of the ordinary anyway. But clearly they had more appeal than me.

I removed ten more pets from my garbage bag and positioned them on the counter. I attached them to leashes and arranged the leashes in such a way that they were accessible to passersby who may or may not want to take them on a trial walk.

"Pets," I repeated.

Still no response. There were too many distractions. Apparently good idiocy garnered more public interest than a good commodity. The battle royal was the biggest distraction of all. It was taking place in an oversized boxing ring on the far side of the city center. Inside of the ring village idiots were punching one another with brass knuckles, machinegunning one another with uzis, cutting off one another's heads with samurai swords. Blood and viscera erupted out of the ring in a soaking volcanic bouquet as heads bounced like basketballs into the crowd of onlookers surrounding it. I couldn't compete with the mayhem.

There was a village idiot not far from my place of business who had a zipper that ran from the top of his forehead to the butt of his chin. He was entertaining a circle of children by repeatedly opening and closing the zipper and exposing them to his skull. Some of the children were crying and calling out for their mothers. Others merely stared and blinked.

I hung up a sign that read: OUT FOR LUNCH. I walked over to the village idiot, pardoned myself, glanced down at the children, smiled, grabbed the idiot by the neck and strangled him to death. It didn't take long. The idiot didn't even put up a fight— he stood there with a bored expression on his face, waiting to turn purple and die.

The bored look dissolved into a blank look and the idiot collapsed. I turned to the children and said, "Well then. Wasn't that exciting? Hello. My name is blah blah blah. Can I interest any of you youngsters in a pet?"

The children who had been crying and calling for their mothers began to stare and blink at me. The children who had been staring and blinking began to cry and call for their mothers.

"There there," I told them. "There there, there there . . ."

It was at this point that a drove of irate, bald-faced freaks stormed the city center.

There were hundreds of them, all from different walks of life, from the highest caliber of bourgeois yuppies to the lowliest pieces of crumpled up white trash. Spectators and village idiots alike threw their arms over their heads and emitted high-pitched shrieks as they poured into the city center like a swarm of killer bees, annihilating everyone and everything that lay in their path. A pastiche of bodies, body parts and entrails bloomed into the blue sky in slow motion . . .

It didn't take long for the mob to spot the objects responsible for their mania.

Since I had made their acquaintance, the hairware had been acting rather lethargic. They had in fact shown no evidence of being functional organisms. Now, however, they leapt to attention, vaulting out of the garbage bag and quickly lining up in front of me like a regiment of British soldiers. Beards and goatees filled out the front ranks while sideburns and eyebrows brought up the rear. Behind it all, mustaches flowed back and forth as if riding on horses.

The mob froze. Everybody did. Even the mangled and the dismembered victims of the mob's lunacy stopped moaning and twitching and groping for their lost limbs. I cocked my head. The entire population of the city center was pointing its attention in my direction.

The village idiots frowned.

The spectators stared at me indifferently.

The mob stared at me intensely.

There was a long silence during which the village idiots' frowns deepened, the spectators' blank expressions persisted, and the eyes of the mob grew wider and wider as their chins slowly rose higher and higher in the air. Except for the roving mustaches, the hairware stayed in formation and didn't flinch. I calmly, repeatedly checked my watch to ensure that I would not miss taking the nap I had scheduled for later that afternoon.

"We know who you are, and we want them back," the leader of the mob finally trumpeted. He had a bald, fat head and was wearing a nineteenth century Murdstone suit with a frilled white shirt, long chocolate tails and knee-high equestrian boots. His tone was both assertive and tentative. He waited for me to say something. I checked my watch again. Gaining confidence, he shouted, "I said we want them back! Give them to us, sir! Those appendages belong to us, sir!"

The hairware began to growl. A handful of goatees barked. They had been relinquished from the faces that once bound them, yet they continued to be treated like extremities by their former masters, like parts of the faces rather than individual, capable entities. Additionally, it was obvious that they had been mistreated. Very few pieces of hairware were properly groomed, a number of sideburns had dandruff and lice, many of the mustaches had chunks of vegetable soup hidden in their bushy depths, and a few beards had been moonlighting as bird's nests. They were less than pleased. And they were clearly unwilling to return home. As pets and commodities, at least they had a chance to manifest authentic identities.

The mob could see that the hairware didn't want anything to do with them anymore. They still felt entitled to the hairware. The leader said to me, "Call them off. Tell them to lay still. What's ours is ours. Do you think this is funny? Our faces look like deserts of vast eternity. Be a gentleman and return us our property. Otherwise we will be inclined to take them from you. You may also expect us to flog you and perform distasteful public sex acts on you. Am I clear? Do as I say."

The rest of the mob nodded at me in dark affirmation of their leader's will.

I had seen what people who have

had their hairware stolen could do to other people, but I had not yet seen what the hairware itself could do. I sized up both parties, wondering whether it would be in my best interests to consent to the mob or stand behind my product.

I decided to stand behind my product.

I said, "I don't want any trouble. I'm just a businessman. I'm only trying to make a living. There's no harm in that. I suggest you go away. Go home and grow new hairware. I can't even see fit to sell you back this batch for a bargain price in light of how poorly you treated it before I confiscated it from you. You have my answer."

There was an obscene pause . . .

"So be it," seethed the leader. He raised an arm over his head and discharged a shrill Indian warcry . . . The warcry lasted for over three minutes. As it elapsed, the members of the mob stood there patiently gnashing their teeth, fists clenched at their sides.

Shortly after the first minute of the warcry, the village idiots and spectators grew bored. If they were wounded, they went to the hospital. If they weren't wounded, they went home or to the nearest sandwich vendor.

Shortly after the second minute of the warcry, I grew bored. I also grew anxious, realizing it was time to take my nap yet I was nowhere near a comfortable bed.

Shortly after the third minute of the warcry, the hairware grew bored.

It attacked.

The usual macabre exhibition unfolded—hot gore sprayed the ceiling of the sky like an abstract drip painting as bodies were ripped apart as if hurled *en masse* into a gigantic meat grinder. I was surprised by how swiftly and efficiently they took apart their enemies.

When it was over, the hairware retreated to the garbage bag. They filed into it in organized ranks, leaving large piles of steaming carnage in their wake.

Eight foot janitors wearing neon jumpsuits climbed out of manholes and solemnly began to clean up the mess with industrial brooms and waterhoses.

I sighed.

I picked up the bag, slung it over my shoulder.

I walked home. Distressed. I hadn't sold a single pet. My pockets were empty. No money to buy any fun, let alone to buy something to eat and read.

Things were much simpler when I was a small businessman, I told myself. Big business is the pits.

Best sleep on it . . .

This time, the fetuses were in better moods. Their diapers were clean, and they had all shaved . . .

THE MAN IN THE THICK BLACK SPECTACLES

Before opening the door and entering the conference room, the man in the thick black spectacles removed a wad of chewing gum from his mouth and, after glancing in every imaginable direction, stuck it into an unassuming, seemingly clean crack in the wall. He would retrieve the gum from the crack later, after the meeting, which would take no more and no less than five minutes. He knew this for three reasons:

1. This morning the man
   in the cubicle next door
   had told him so.

2. There was a neon billboard hanging from the ceiling of the office that read:

MEETING TODAY
5 MINUTES LONG
NO MORE, NO LESS

3. Of the countless meetings he had attended before, he could not remember one of them being more or less than five minutes.

So there was no reason why this meeting should be any different, and no reason why the man in the thick black spectacles should be worried.

And yet he was worried. Five minutes was five minutes, after all.

He placed a fingernail between his teeth and began to chew on it. What if, say, a fly landed on the gum while he was gone? He would have no way of knowing what the fly had done to the gum in his absence. For all he knew, the fly would crap on it, meaning that the man in the thick black spectacles, in the not-too-distant future, might very well be chewing on fly dung. This was not a pretty thought so he tried not to think it, or to think thoughts like it. He couldn't allow himself to. To allow himself to think that way would be distracting, and this meeting, while short, was, like all of the other meetings, an important one. It required that he be sharp as a tack.

Removing the fingernail from his teeth, he opened the door . . . and hesitated, unable to help himself, despite himself.

Five minutes, he thought. Sometimes one minute seems like an eternity, especially when you're thinking about that minute. It's one thing to handle one minute, or rather, one eternity. But can I handle *five* of them?

Eyeing the gum, he ground his teeth and stroked his brow. He sighed. He closed the door and looked back over his right shoulder, his left shoulder, his right shoulder. Then he looked between his legs, underneath his shoes . . .

Hardly satisfied, but more anxious now about hesitating and being late for the meeting than abandoning the gum, the man in the thick black spectacles walked in at last, closing the door behind him slowly, guardedly, without a sound, pulling his beaklike nose inside just as the door clicked shut.

Immediately the man in the silver handlebar mustache unfolded his appendages and snuck out from behind the water cooler. Giggling, he crept over to the crack in the wall. He stretched out his long neck, rolled out his tongue and began to lap at the gum as a thirsty dog might lap at a bowl of water.

At the same time the man in the neon zoot suit wormed his way up from out of the soil in the pot that contained the office's largest rubber plant, using the branches of the plant for leverage, but still, this worming took a while, and by the time he was free of the soil and had dusted himself off, the man in the silver handlebar mustache was fully engaged, his tongue lapping at high speed. The man in the neon zoot suit would have to wait his turn. Being the impatient sort, he couldn't stop himself from cursing, albeit he did so in an undertone. But after a while the man in the flamingo pink top hat fell through a ceiling tile with a crash and at least the man in the neon zoot suit had some company now. He stopped cursing . . . until the man in the flamingo pink top hat started cursing, first because he had fallen, second because of the man in the silver handlebar mustache, who was taking too long, far too long, who was hogging the wad of chewing gum all too himself!

Not a moment passed before the man in the neon zoot suit joined his estranged colleague in blasphemous harmony. "Why not give us a go, you filthy bastard?" they bitched. The man in the silver handlebar mustache promptly sucked his tongue back into his mouth, stood upright and about-faced. To his aggressors he replied, "If one wants something, all one has to do is ask. That's all one has to do."

The sarcasm in the man in the silver handlebar mustache's tone of voice was flagrant enough but neither the man in the neon zoot suit nor the man in the flamingo pink top hat had ever cared enough about sarcasm to be able to detect it, even if it slapped them across both cheeks. Muttering hasty thank yous under their breath, they attacked the crack in the wall at the same time, smacked into each other and collapsed to the floor. They got to their feet and blinked. Following a brief, woozy exchange, they played rock-paper-scissors to see who between them got to lick the gum first.

The man in the flamingo pink top hat won.

"Balls!" exclaimed the loser; he ripped the peacock's feather out of his tando hat and stomped on it as the victor, with the tip of a sharp tongue, began stabbing at the gum, again and again, growing more excitable and outrageous with each snakelike stab. The man in the silver handlebar mustache, now leaning up against the wall with arms crossed, sniggered, then began moving his tongue around the insides of his mouth so that his cheeks poked out. He smacked his lips, too, each time glaring derisively at the man in the neon zoot suit out of the corners of his eyes.

Finally the man in the neon zoot suit had had enough. Being twice as tall and twice as strong as the man in the flamingo pink top hat and the man in the silver handlebar mustache combined, but always hesitant to resort to his brawn until the last straw had been drawn, which it had, which it most definitely had—he backhanded the man in the flamingo pink top hat away from the wall and sent him sliding down the hallway on his spine, his arms and legs and sharp tongue waving in the air like the extremities of an overturned beetle. Then he pointed an angry warning finger at the man in the silver handlebar mustache, but all that man did was whistle a quiet tune and feign a reverie. This irked the man in the neon zoot suit. Not enough to lead his one-track mind astray, though; he just pressed a finger to one nostril and out the other nostril blasted out an ornery little snot ball and then he opened up his shark mouth and turned and made for the gum that the man in the thick black spectacles had stuck right there in the crack in the wall . . . but too late, too late. The door to the conference room was being opened up, slowly, guardedly, without a sound, and in a flash the man in the silver handlebar mustache folded himself up behind the water cooler again, and the man in the flamingo pink top hat both rallied from the backhand and leapt back up into the ceiling, replacing the tile he had fallen through with a fresh one. So the man in the neon zoot suit was all alone. And when the man in the thick black spectacles emerged, it was he and no other that would be to blame, despite his innocence. For while the man in the neon zoot suit had certainly wanted to lick the gum, and would have licked it if he could have—and the gum had clearly been licked, a forensics expert wasn't needed to figure that out—the truth of the matter was: he had not licked anything.

At this point the man in the neon zoot suit asked himself three simple questions. He would have asked himself more, but time wouldn't permit it.

1. What is to become of me once I get caught?

2. Will the man in the thick black spectacles attack me or give me the opportunity to explain myself?

3. Given the opportunity, how will I explain myself?

The man in the neon zoot suit was about to

ask himself a fourth question, but something overcame him, something that, when he reflected on it later during a water cooler conversation with the man in the silver handlebar mustache and the man in the flamingo pink top hat, he described as an "impulsive burst of energy" that allowed him to spring up and across the hallway, dive back down into the soil of the rubber plant and cover himself over just enough so that nobody would take note of his stealth. "It was a brilliant move," he bragged.

"And yet quite unnecessary," smiled the man in the silver handlebar mustache.

The man in the flamingo pink top hat added, "Yes. Quite unnecessary."

The man in the neon zoot suit said, "I don't get it."

The man in the flamingo pink top hat, who had seen everything through a mouse hole in the ceiling, told him. "As it so happened, the man in the thick black spectacles, after slipping out the door that led into the conference room, was apparently so preoccupied he forgot all about his gum. He stood there in the hallway a moment, nervously fingering an ear lobe and flexing his jowls. Then he spent some time making these sickly croaking noises. I suspected he was either about to faint or have a heart attack and die, but just as this suspicion crept into my mind he bleated like a sheep that's been sat upon by a fat man and then, finally, he scurried off, down the hallway, talking to himself in a worried voice. And that's that."

"That's that," repeated the man in the neon zoot suit in a dull whisper, then turned with a quick jerk, like a man that wants to be alone with his dread.

CLASSROOM DYNAMICS

Situated between floors 863 and 924 of the Ameliabedelia Spacescraper are the offices and classrooms of Pseudofolliculitis State University. Roughly 20,000 students attend the university per year, and exactly 200 professors teach there. Most of these professors are more concerned with their scholarly output than they are with pedagogy. Most of them, in fact, could care less about their students' intellectual well-being, preoccupied as they are with churning out criticism and theory that absolutely nobody (including the professors themselves) reads and that has no bearing whatsoever on the social, political, cultural or economic condition of Pseudofolliculitis City. Fortunately, not all of the professors at PSU practice this brand of absurdity. Dr. Bobby Lee Beebody, for instance, cares so much about his students that he can barely sleep at night. He worries about their intellect. He worries about their emotional disposition. The thought of one of his students being depressed or saddened depresses and saddens him. Even if they are irretrievably idiotic.

One day Dr. Beebody decided to start hugging his students hello and goodbye.

He waited for them at the door of his classroom with a friendly smile on his face and his arms wide open. As the students trickled in, he wrapped his arms around them and gave each of them a warm, loving squeeze. He did the same thing after class as they trickled out. There were no sexual undertones to these hugs, and at no time did his hands slip out of place when he was hugging one of his more attractive lady students and grab or spank a piece of ass. Not that most of his lady students would have minded. Dr. Beebody was a tall, dark, handsome drink of water. He had an aquiline face, bright white teeth, immaculately groomed obsidian hair and a keen fashion sense. He was the complete antithesis of his PSU colleagues, who, for the most part, looked and smelled something like giant balls of tumbleweed. Still, there were a number of his students who were less than excited about being hugged by their professor, especially the frat boys. Dr. Beebody embraced them and they stood there as if something uninvited had just been shoved up their asses—frozen stiff, eyes wide, lips twisted, arms flush against their sides as they breathed in the scent of his stylish cologne. Every now and then a student would try to sneak past the professor while he was hugging somebody else, but he always managed to get his hands on the would-be escape artist. If it was before class, he would simply waltz over to the student's desk, lean over and give him his due, whispering things in his ear like "It's alright" and "I know, I know" and "Everything's going to be okay." If it was after class, he would chase the students down the hallway until he caught them. Once he chased a frat boy half-way across campus, from floor 864 to 892, and when he finally caught him, he hugged him so tightly and for so long that the little bastard passed out and died in his arms. It was a devastating blow, a terrible tragedy. Dr. Beebody was just trying to be nice. The last thing he wanted to do was kill a student that didn't deserve it. But accidents happen. And anyway it is a professor's right to exterminate a student whenever he wishes. In the meantime he would grieve the frat boy's passing and continue to administer as many hugs to his students as possible, making sure not to squeeze their fragile bodies with an excess of verve and tenderheartedness.

Killing a student is one thing. But hugging one? That's quite another. It wasn't long before Dr. Beebody found himself sitting in front of Dean Dingleblazer.

The dean exhibited the pot-bellied physique and the old school fashion statement exhibited by all of PSU's deans. For additional effect, he had also surgically reconstructed his face in the graven image of James Dean.

The two men stared at each other across the dean's untidy desk for half a minute of silence. It wasn't an uncomfortable silence. It wasn't a comfortable one either. In the background was a Muzak rendition of a Daryl Hall & John Oats ballad.

"Hello," Dr. Beebody finally said.

"Hello," Dean Dingleblazer replied. Both men spoke in dull monotones—the only way plaquedemics are allowed to speak to one another according to *The Official PSU Faculty & Administrator Rulebook.* "Personality" can only be exhibited in or near the classroom and in select public zones.

"Stop hugging your students," said the dean squarely.

"Why?" said Dr. Beebody.

"Do I really need to justify that question with an answer? That question doesn't deserve an answer."

"Maybe it doesn't deserve one. But it wants one. All questions want answers."

"What about rhetorical questions?"

"Them, too. They just won't admit it."

A bitter, annoyed expression tried to weasel its way onto Dean Dingleblazer's face, but he nipped it in the bud before it had a chance to flourish so as not to break the Law. "Please refrain from that sort of nonsense, sir. Please make an effort to not bring that sort of assholery to this table. Now then. You're freaking out your students. Stop hugging them. Leave them be. Don't touch them. Don't lay a finger on them. Am I being perfectly clear?"

Dr. Beebody nodded his blank face. The nod did not signify obedience. It signified a simple acknowledgment of a piece of information that had been conveyed to him. "I see," was his response. Ten seconds of dead air followed.

The professor said, "The thing is, I

think my students need hugs. They don't work very hard and most of them are complete morons. But that doesn't mean they don't need a little sensitivity and, dare I say, love. In fact, I think giving them hugs will make them more inclined to transcend their idiocy and take at least a moderate interest in cultivating their mongoloid intellects. My students need help, and I'm in a position to help them. That's the score. I've got hugs to give, Dean Dingleblazer, and I aim to give them."

The dean stared vacantly at the professor. "You're fired."

"Really?"

"If you hug another student, yes, really. That's the end of this retarded conversation. Please get out of my sight. Please do that, sir."

Dr. Beebody ruminatively twitched his lips. He nodded and said "I see" again, obediently this time. He puckered up his lips, widened his eyes, said "Well then," stood up, cleared his throat, glanced absentmindedly around the office, smiled pleasantly, said "Goodbye," nodded again, and left.

Later that day, in Dr. Beebody's NH (Novels about Hitler) 410E course . . .

"Good afternoon, studentry," announced the professor from behind his podium. He spoke in a detached voice, his chin titled up a notch. "Thank you for showing up. You may have noticed that, on your way into our classroom this afternoon, you did not receive your usual warm greeting. It has been brought to my attention that said warm greetings are, in so many words, neither well-received, nor productive on an emotional level. Whereas I tend to disagree with this notion in every respect, I have no choice but to respect and acknowledge it in order to avoid being skidrowed. Hence there will be no more of this touchy-feely hoo-ha. FYI."

Dr. Beebody's students blinked at him. A few of the frat boys sighed in relief, albeit guardedly. To sigh too conspicuously during a class was an indication of boredom, no matter what the sigh actually indicated,

and if they spotted it, professors had every right to murder the guilty (or, possibly, not guilty) party in any way he or she saw fit.

"Right," said the professor. He folded his arms behind his back and walked out from behind the podium. "Right," he said again. "Well. Well then. Let's get right to it, shall we? Okay then. Yesterday we were discussing the psychodynamics of Hitler's desire for his young niece to squat over and urinate on him. Let's begin today by thinking about this enchanting act of perversion in Lacanian terms. I am particularly interested in the way in which the phallus manifests itself here. Who can explain to me what constitutes the phallus according to Lacan?"

None of the students raised their hands.

"Anyone? Can anyone tell me how Lacan defines the phallus?"

The students blinked at him.

Dr. Beebody stroked his square chin. He buried his face in his hand and, with his thumb and middle finger, stroked his temples. He stroked them for over half a minute, praying to God that somebody would speak up of their own volition. Nobody did. So: "Mr. Bitchslapper? Care to fill us in?" He released his face from his hand and stared pointedly at the student.

Pendleton Bitchslapper III (a.k.a. PB3) was one of six frat boys in NH 410E. A ninth-year senior at PSU, he was president of the Phi Gamma Dipcup fraternity, the proud owner of a 1.8 gradepoint average, and a pothead extraordinaire; he had been high for so long, in fact, that his eyes has devolved into two small Xs that seemed to have been carved into his bloated head.

When Dr. Beebody asked his question, PB3 had of course not been listening. He had been daydreaming about having an orgy with the harem of sorority girls he kept as slaves in his bathroom closet. Dr. Beebody repeated himself. "Excuse me? Mr. Bitchslapper? Answer the question if you please."

PB3 snapped out of his daydream.

"What question?" His X-eyes cringed like sphincters.

"Wrong answer." In one fluid motion the professor reached inside of his pitch black zoot suit, removed a large throwing star, wound it up and winged it at PB3. The weapon nailed the frat boy in the eye. The eye exploded in a gruesome potpourri of blood, brains and bong resin. PB3 screamed uncontrollably in his seat, his body twitching and gesticulating, then abruptly clammed up and died. The killing took place in slow motion except for when the throwing star was just about to strike PB3 in the eye, at which point things slipped into ultraslow motion. After the killing, a hulking janitor in a neon orange jumpsuit crawled out of a trap door in the back of the room, picked up and stuffed PB3's corpse in a trash bag, and disappeared back into the trap door.

Dr. Beebody closed his eyes and rubbed them with a thumb and forefinger. He sighed dramatically. To say the least, he wasn't a big fan of killing his students, despite their being allergic to being educated. But the Law was the Law, and if a student wasn't holding up his or her end of the bargain, it was incumbent upon all PSU plaquedemics to do away with them, ideally without apprehension or remorse. Dr. Beebody almost always experienced apprehension and remorse, but he never let on to his colleagues that he did. Still, his colleagues knew he was a big softy. After all, he had murdered fewer students at PSU than any other plaquedemic in his department.

He stopped rubbing his eyes. "Right," he said. "Now then. Where were we? Yes. Lacan. The phallus. Who has the answer? It's not a difficult question if you're willing to not be a difficult person. How does Lacan define the phallus?"

His students were stone sculptures. On average they witnessed five, six deaths a day. They were no strangers to death, but that didn't mean they wanted to be death's friends.

Dr. Beebody cleared his throat.

Nothing. He cleared it again. Nothing.

"Boy," he said. "I despise calling on people. I wish somebody would just answer the question so I don't have to call on one of you. Why won't somebody just raise their hand? That would make me happy. It might make you happy, too, if you give it a try. So. Who wants to be happy?"

No response at first. The students sat there with forearms and hands flat on their desks and eyes locked on their laps. The professor unleashed a series of long, melodramatic sighs. Then a hand rose into the air. The hand contained long, thin fingers and belonged to Ms. Gretchen Blase, an average-looking young woman who wore average-looking outfits and hairdos and was, generally speaking, an average student. Her fingers trembled in fear. Dr. Beebody wanted to walk over to those fingers and hug them with his hand, assuring them that everything would be all right if only Ms. Blase managed to respond to the question that had been posed to the class without making a complete ass out of herself. "Ah!" he exclaimed. "Ms. Blase! That's a good thing, raising that hand of yours. Please tell the class what's on your mind."

Ms. Blase slowly lowered her hand. She used her pinky finger to push her not unfashionable (but not entirely fashionable) spectacles up her forgetful nose. In a voice that was not too loud yet not too soft, she said, "For Lacan, the phallus is s-s-slippery. I mean, it's not a fixed thing. I mean, it has the, uh, power to change. Uhm. To change by itself."

Dr. Beebody's made a satisfied frog face. "Fine, Ms. Blase. That's just fine. That wasn't so hard, was it? Lacan's phallus has the power to change by itself. Yes indeed. Now that you've set the scene for us, we can begin to flesh this matter out. You're a good person, Ms. Blase. I'm not just saying that. Actually I am just saying that, because you're more than a good person. You're a great person. A spectacular person. I love you. I love you madly. And I will continue to love you until the end of time, if that's all right with you."

Ms. Blase smiled a quick, confused smile.

Throughout the class, Dr. Beebody told a number of other students he loved them. He told a few of them that he was *in* love with them. Some didn't even respond intelligently to a question; the professor just thought they looked sad, so every now and then he would point at them at random and announce, "I am in love with you, Mr. or Ms. So-and-so." And when the class was finally over, he stood by the door with his arms folded behind his back and told each individual student he loved them as they passed him by. This behavior flooded over into his other classes and lasted two weeks before he was sitting across a desk from the visage of James Dean again. In the background was a Muzak rendition of a Quiet Riot ballad.

"Hello," monotoned Dr. Beebody.

"Hello," monotoned Dean Dingleblazer.

"Is everything all right?"

"No, it's not."

"Is there a problem?"

"Yes, there is."

"Really?"

"Yes, really."

"Really, you say. Well. I hope it's nothing serious. Serious problems are often problematic. I wonder what it is. Does it have anything to do with me?"

The dean glared at the professor with blank eyes. "Quit telling your students you love them, goddamn it."

"What? I don't know what you're talking about."

"Yes you do. Quit it."

"Quit what?"

The dean glared at him again. The professor glared back, nibbling on his lip. Finally the professor said, "Why can't I tell my students I love them? I'm just trying to make them feel good. What's the harm in that? Most of my students probably never hear anybody say they love them. Who loves

people nowadays? Love is an outmoded concept. That's one of the reasons young people are such imbeciles, in my opinion. Nobody loves them. Nobody loves them, I say."

Dean Dingleblazer resisted the temptation to flex his jaw. He reached into a big tin can of lard sitting on his desk and scooped out a handful. As he dutifully ran it through his lustrous hair, he spoke to the professor in a perfectly candid, perfectly sedated voice. "Dr. Beebody, I hope you can hear me. It doesn't matter if anybody loves your students. What matters is that you're acting like a fucking weirdo. Students don't want their professors telling them they love them. They want their professors to treat them like the pieces of rotten meat they are. You know this, Dr. Beebody. I don't understand why you're attempting to disrupt the system. I imagine it stems from personal problems. But that's none of my concern." Having spread the handful of lard across the entirety of his hairdo, the dean removed an oversized comb from his desk drawer and began to brush his hairdo into place with long, slow strokes. "Get your shit together, sir. This is your last chance. I realize you have tenure, but as you and every other plaquedemic at PSU knows, tenure doesn't mean a goddamn thing. Its purpose isn't to provide security, it's to provide the illusion of security, and while all professors are aware of this, all professors naturally disavow it in order to maintain a relatively congenial disposition. Point of fact: if I so desire, I can dismiss you at the drop of a derby hat. You're not a bad educator. I wouldn't go so far as to call you a good one, but you're not a bad one. You need to deal with this infantile emotional crisis of yours and put it to sleep. No more hugging, no more I love yous. No more emotional outpourings of any kind." The dean paused to apply another helping of lard to his hairdo. This time he combed it in with more flair and enthusiasm. When he spoke again, however, it was in the same anesthetized tone. "Bottom line: you have issues, Dr. Beebody. Issues that need to be worked out. The best course of action you could take, in my opinion, is to go on a minor killing spree. Weed out every last sub-par student under your liege. I know there are a number of sub-par students in your classes that continue to live and breath, not to mention that you own the lowest murder rate in the department. End that, if you please. I promise you you'll feel a little better. Additionally, it's about time you produced a piece of worthwhile writing. If I'm not mistaken, the last thing you published was some short story in some obscure magazine published by some middle-aged wacko who lives in his parent's basement. What was the name of it? It doesn't matter, it was atrocious and embarrassing. You need to write something that matters, and that isn't atrocious and embarrassing. You are, after all, a representative of this university. Start acting like one. Fiction is the stuff of village idiots. Write a piece of decent literary criticism, for once, and become a productive member of society. Do it, or get lost. What do you think?" The question was both in reference to the directive and to the glistening pompadour that was now sitting on top of Dean Dingleblazer's head like a crouching, well-groomed vulture.

Dr. Beebody blinked innocently at the hairdo. He smiled. He nodded. He smacked his lips. He said, "Well." He smacked his lips again. He nodded again. He smiled again. He blinked innocently at the hairdo again.

He rose out of his chair, cleared his throat, tipped his head, cocked his head, cracked his neck, scratched his overlip, made a shrugging gesture, freeze-framed the gesture for three seconds, waved his finger in the air, said "Very well," said "Goodbye then," nodded, nodded again, nodded again, and left.

Dean Dingleblazer shook his head and returned to the copy of *People!!!* magazine he had been reading before Dr. Beebody had interrupted him.

The next day, Pseudofolliculitis

State University was shrouded in darkness; a black cloud of towerfog had wrapped itself around the upper portion of the Ameliabedelia Spacescraper. Dr. Bobby Lee Beebody gazed listlessly out a restroom window at the darkness, admiring the flashes of electricity that periodically sparked up. He thought he saw the visage of his frozen, screaming face in one of these electric flashes. Then he realized that he was not looking out the window, but in the mirror . . .

. . . Dr. Beebody walked down the hallway to his IS (Introduction to Scatology) 220 course in slow motion. He was wearing a pinstripe gangster suit, a fedora with a wide brim, and a plastic press-on handlebar mustache. He walked with the simulated grace and purpose of a dandy. In one hand he carried a black briefcase, in the other a black Tommy gun. The students that passed by him either made an effort not to look at him or looked at him with wide, trembling eyes. The music playing in the background was a souped-up, techno version of Tom Jones' *Delilah*. It was playing so loud, the Ameliabedelia Spacescraper quaked from head to toe . . .

The scene slipped from slowtime into realtime as Dr. Beebody emerged into his classroom. As always before class began, his students were acting like a bunch of mental patients. Most of them were bitching at each other at the top of their lungs about various trivialities. A few of them were standing on top of their desks impersonating syphilitic apes. Others systematically banged their heads against the classroom's whitewalls. Two took turns slapping each other across the face. When the professor walked in, however, everybody shaped up, shut up, dove into their seats, sat up and stared straight ahead. Dr. Beebody was all business. He didn't even look at his students out of his eye corners as he goose-stepped over to a podium and situated himself behind it.

"What's up his ass?" the yuppie mouthed in silence to the skaterat sitting next to him. Too scared-stiff to acknowledge him, the skaterat pretended that she didn't hear him. She pushed out her pierced lips and rolled her eyes to the ceiling, as if experiencing a deep thought.

The estranged yuppie mouthed, "Can you hear me?"

"I can read lips, Nancy boy," intoned Dr. Beebody, and aimed a stern, willful gaze at the troublemaker. Unlike the smaller NH 410E, IS 220 was a seminar course that accommodated 150 students and the professor knew very few of their names. He generally identified and addressed them in terms of their social image. Whenever he called on somebody to answer a question, for instance, he would point at that somebody and say things like "Can you fill us in, wigger?" or "How about it, butch lesbian?" or "Would the piece of white trash sitting in the back row be so kind as to give us an answer?"

The classroom darkened and an unseen spotlight fell on the yuppie like an anvil from the sky. He winced. He glanced in every direction at high speed. "I'm sorry!" he exclaimed.

The professor shrugged. "It's too late for that. Die, scum." He dropped his briefcase on the floor, pointed the Tommy gun at the yuppie and fired a round of shots in slow motion. The yuppie was shredded to pieces by the gunfire. So was the hillbilly sitting behind him. Blood splashed all over the students sitting in their vicinity as if thrown at them out of large buckets. Sound of slung mud and choking gasps . . .

The spotlight slowly grew in size until the classroom was entirely illuminated again. The janitor appeared, cleaned up the mess, disappeared.

"Oops," said Dr. Beebody in reference to the accidental murder of the hillbilly. He shrugged again. "Oh well. That's the breaks, I suppose." He carefully placed the smoking Tommy gun on top of his podium and folded his arms behind his back. At least ten of his students had hot gore dripping down their faces; a few of them dry-heaved

in disgust, some twitched psychopathically, but they all kept their composure, and they all kept their seats. "Good morning, studentry. I apologize for the seemingly off-the-cuff murders, but lately I haven't been feeling so hot. It seems that I've got a kind of a problem. The problem is, well . . . *you*. More specifically, the problem is that you're a bunch of retards, and I don't understand you dumbasses. That's the problem, in a nutshell. Please don't take it the wrong way. There is no doubt in my mind that each and every one of you is a worthless douche bag and always will be, but that's not to say that I don't like you all very much. I do like you, and I want you to be happy. That's all. That's all I wanted to say, for the most part. Actually I wanted to say a lot more. But what's the point? All words do is confuse people. The more words that come out of your mouth, the more you are apt to cause a miscommunication. People should stop talking to each other, I think. The world would be a much saner place to live in, I think. Well then. I guess that's all for today. Any questions?"

The professor raised an eyebrow. Most of his students stared at their laps, but some raised their hands. One student's arm writhed like an electrified snake as she went, "Me! Me! Me!"

Dr. Beebody ignored them. "Okay then," he whispered. He picked the Tommy gun back up, inspected it briefly, sniffed, pursed his lips, blinked, smiled a crooked smile, blinked again, sniffed again, cleared his throat, said "Yes indeed," clicked his tongue, sighed, and fired.

. . . realtime slipped into slowtime slipped into fasttime slipped into slowtime slipped into . . .

Later, as the janitor busied himself with a mop, a waterhose and a chainsaw, Dr. Beebody removed a pen and a piece of paper from his briefcase. He placed the paper on the podium, clicked the pen open, and stared cockeyed at the ceiling for a moment while chewing on his tongue. Then he began to write.

"The postmodern body is always-already a desiring-machine produced and controlled by the schizophrenic mediascape that encompasses it," he wrote . . .

DIGGING FOR ADULTS

A little boy clicked his jaw. He did it to annoy a little girl. He was in love with her. She had pretty red hair, nice skin, and the freckles on her nose . . . well, he wanted to lick them off her face. He sensed the perverse nature of this desire, but he was too young and unfamiliar with the character of his impulses to think twice about the desire: one time was enough, and then the thought was gone . . .

As he continued to click his jaw, he could almost taste those freckles. He had to have them in his mouth right now! But he couldn't just walk up to his love and start lapping at her nose like an excited puppy. He had to get her to fall in love with him first. And the best way for a little boy to get a little girl to fall in love with him is to make her hate him by annoying the crap out of her.

Click! went his jaw. *Click! Click! Click!* His mouth opened wider and wider each time he did it, and drool began to flow down his chin.

The little girl pretended he didn't exist.

The little boy pretended that she wasn't pretending he didn't exist, and went on clicking and drooling.

Crouched down on their knees, the two children were digging for adults in the soil of the neighborhood playground. The adults in the neighborhood had disappeared a few days ago; sick of always having to take care of the children, they made a communal decision to bury themselves underground in hopes that, after a while, the children would get the hint that nobody liked them and go away. So far the endeavor was ineffective. Not only were the children not going away, they persisted in trying to find the adults and dig them out of the ground. The adults were frustrated. But they had promised themselves to stay put for at least a week, dreaming of and praying for a neighborhood that was not subject to the cries and whines and whimpers and demands and threats and maligns and freakery and demonism and pathology of Young Life.

The ground beneath them was very soft and brown. They had dug up over two feet of earth a piece, but they hadn't uncovered any adults yet. They would dig for a little while longer and then move to another spot.

Click! Click! Click! Click! Click!

Eventually the little girl said something to the little boy. She didn't want to say something to him, but his jaw was driving her up the wall.

"Stop doing that," she said. "It bothers me very much. You're a very bothersome person, do you know that?"

"What?" replied the little boy, playing dumb. He clicked his jaw especially loud, so loud the group of children digging for adults on the other side of the merry-go-round heard it. They stopped digging and looked in his direction with dazed and curious expressions, as if they had just woken up from being knocked unconscious.

The little girl looked at him with an embittered expression, as if somebody had just dunked her head in a pot of garlic water. She sat back on her knees and put her tiny fists on her hipless hips. "Stop that, I said. Stop making that noise with your mouth. It's distracting me. I'm trying to concentrate. I'm trying to find my mom and dad so I can ask them if I can stay up past my bedtime. How am I supposed to do that with you doing what you're doing? You're drooling all over the place, too. You're gross. You're ugly. Go somewhere else. I was here first."

"I was here second," the little boy responded matter-of-factly, not looking up at her, continuing to dig, drool and click.

"What's that supposed to mean?"

"Nothing."

"It means something. Nothing means nothing."

"Except nothing."

"What?"

"Nothing. It means I was here second and you were here first and it doesn't matter one way or the other, okay?"

"I don't get it. I don't get what that means."

"That's because you're a girl and girls don't get anything. Dig your hole, whyncha?" *Click!*

"Oh!" said the little girl. "Oh! Oh! Oh!" She wanted to say something clever to the little boy, something that would make him feel as retarded as she felt right now, but she couldn't find the words. So she said "Oh!" one more time.

"Stop saying 'Oh'," said the little boy. "It's really starting to bug me and I'd appreciate it if you'd shut up. Thank you."

A deranged, wide-eyed glare overcame the little girl's face. How dare that creep! Her lips began to twitch with rage. They got to twitching so intensely that the little boy could actually hear them.

"You're lips are making a funny sound," he said. "Tell them to knock it off."

The lips pinched together. A long, tense pause followed . . . Then the little girl calmly leaned over, as if she was going to whisper a friendly secret into the little boy's ear, and yelled, "I HATE YOUR GUTS, FREAK!!!" When she yelled, the kids over by the merry-go-round glanced at her. She cast an evil glance back at them and said, "MIND YOUR OWN BUSINESS, NERDS!!!"

Being nerds, the kids obeyed.

The little boy smiled. The little girl had told him she hated him—*that* meant she loved him. He may have been young and idiotic, but he wasn't young and idiotic enough to not know that saying you love somebody and saying you hate them means the same thing. His plan had worked. He could now lick her freckles without feeling guilty about it. Just a few more louder-than-hell clicks to make sure his lover genuinely hated him, and wasn't just saying that to make him behave . . .

The little girl stood up and threw her fists down at her sides. "I'm going over there. You stay here. Don't follow me, or I'll scream. I hope you die!" She waited for a response. Didn't get one. She stomped away.

Proud of himself, the little boy snickered under his breath. He would give the little girl a minute or two before disobeying her command and allowing true love to run its course. He scooped another handful of dirt out of his hole.

And exposed the face of an adult. The face pretended to be asleep, but he knew otherwise: it was the face of his mother and she always pretended to be asleep. Ever since his father left them and moved to Gary, Indiana . . .

"I know you're faking it," he said. No reply.

He clicked his jaw once . . . twice . . . a third time . . .

The eyes of his mother opened. They were red, worn, sickly eyes that looked like they had been crying for years. "Keep it up young man," she said, "and your jaw will fall off. It'll fall right off of your face. Then what the hell will you do?"

The little boy shrugged.

"Don't shrug at me. Listen to me. I want you to stop acting up and mind your goddamn manners. Do you understand?"

The little boy shook his head no.

"Yes you do. You understand me perfectly. Now be a good boy and bury me. Bury me, and don't ever try to dig me up again. Pack a bag and move to a different country, too."

The little boy blinked at his mother. She blinked back at him.

Then: *Click!*

Maddened, his mother ordered him to go to his room. He refused. She told him to get a handkerchief and wipe the drool off of his face. He refused. She called him a bastard. He called her a bitch. They continued to bicker until a ball of dirt fell in her mouth and she choked on it. Her face convulsed, and her eyes rolled back into her head.

The little boy knocked on his mother's forehead. "Anybody home?" he asked. But he knew the answer to that question.

He pushed all of the dirt he had dug up back into the hole, then stood and patted it down with his feet. When he was finished, he stared down at the grave and worried, for a fleeting moment, about his own mortality. But then the moment was gone . . .

The dizziness of freedom washed over the little boy as he quietly slunk towards the little girl, who was digging another hole, this one beneath the colorful bulk of a tall spiral slide.

CARLTON MELLICK III

BOOKS BY MELLICK:

Satan Burger
Electric Jesus Corpse
Sunset With a Beard
Razor Wire Pubic Hair
Teeth and Tongue Landscape
Steel Breakfast Era
The Baby Jesus Butt Plug
Fishy-fleshed
The Menstruating Mall
Ocean of Lard (w/ Kevin L Donihe)
Punk Land
Sex and Death in Television Town
Sea of the Patchwork Cats
The Haunted Vagina
War Slut (forthcoming)
Ugly Heaven (forthcoming)

LOCATION:
Portland, OR

STYLE OF BIZARRO:
Avant Punk

DESCRIPTION: Carlton Mellick III writes trashy child-like novels set in surreal versions of modern or future day Earth, with an emphasis on nightmarish absurdities, punk perversions, and social satire.

INTERESTS: sideburns, razor sausage, Japanese punk, vodka, Jesus porn, zombies, retard music, bald tattooed girls, hamburger sculptures, Live Action Role Players, and Aqua Teen Hunger Force.

INFLUENCES: Dr. Suess, Kathy Acker, H. R. Giger, Jan Svankmajer, Kurt Vonnegut, Brothers Quay, Shinya Tsukamoto, David Lynch, Franz Kafka, John Waters, Roald Dahl, William Burroughs, Russell Edson, Luis Bunuel, Kathe Koja, Mr. T, Japanese cult movies, and Troma movies.

WEBSITE:
www.avantpunk.com

THE BABY JESUS BUTT PLUG

CHAPTER ONE

We adopted a baby jesus only a few months ago and it has already grown accustomed to our butt holes. Normally it takes close to a year before a baby jesus will go fully inside of its owner's rectum, but ours can do it on command. Mary—my current wife who has sausage-colored hair and a tattoo of a famous basketball player on her right eyeball—calls it a *super* baby jesus because of this. But the ad in the newspaper said nothing about him having super powers at all. I don't think he would have been given away for free if he did. Super baby jesuses are worth a fortune!

The ad was placed by an elderly couple giving away a litter of baby jesuses to anyone who could provide them with a good home. And when they said "a good home" all they really meant was they didn't want to give them to anyone who would stick them in their butts. But that was no surprise to us. We were well aware that most older members of the community believe it is socially unacceptable to use the baby jesus as a butt plug. They always shout "Jesus is the son of God, not an anal probe!" to people at the adult shops downtown. We decided not to buy a baby jesus at an adult shop. They charge way too much and it can be quite embarrassing to walk out of the store holding a wiggle-crying baby jesus in your arms, trying to keep it quiet inside of its plastic bag. Everyone stares at you in disgust, their mouths dropped open in shock and their eyebrows curled in anger. They know what you're up to. They know you're planning on taking the baby of God home to put him in your butt. That's why most people get them through baby jesus breeders. It's cheaper and more private.

Mary was the one to find an ad in the newspaper for a litter of baby jesuses. She ruffled the paper excitedly in my face, screaming "Let's get a baby jesus! Let's get a baby jesus!"

I groaned with horse hair. All year she had been wanting to get a pet baby. She didn't want to get a baby version of either of us, though. She wanted a baby version of somebody famous.

I meek-responded, "W-why do you want to get a baby jesus for anyway? D-do you want people to know we put things in our butts?"

"But they're FREE!" Mary screamed. "And I'm sick to death of borrowing the neighbor's baby jesus all the time!"

"W-why can't we just get a normal pet baby like we agreed?" I asked. "What happened to that litter of john lennon babies that your boss was selling?"

Mary crossed her arms pouty-faced. "They weren't full-breeds. They were john lennon/andy warhol mixes. But they looked more like andy warhol/ulysses s. grant mixes."

"Well, w-what about the elle fitzgerald baby that your sister was giving away?" I ask.

"Do you know how old that baby is? She's had it for ten years! It's ready to collapse."

"How long do elle fitzgerald babies live?"

"Ten years if you're lucky."

"But baby jesuses only live to be eight years."

"I don't care," Mary cried. "You've been promising me a baby all year and I want one now!"

"Well, I guess it would be okay," I told her. "But we shouldn't go around telling everyone we have a baby jesus. They're just going to think we use it for a butt plug. I can't handle people calling me names. Maybe we can tell them it's just a baby version of me."

Mary smiled and kissed her arm lightning-fast at me. "Yeah, we can do that! I think it'll work! . . . But you know jesuses perform miracles at unpredictable times. He'll give us away if he starts walking on water in the middle of a dinner party. Or what about how he raises the dead all the time. What happens if he raises a bunch of people from the dead when we have guests over? We'll have zombies running around the living room eating people's heads!"

I touch her shoulder lightly. "Oh, I'll make sure to lock him in the bedroom when guests are over."

"Maybe we can also get its vocal chords removed so it won't disturb us with its crying all the time . . ."

I nod my head in agreement.

CHAPTER TWO

We got him that same day, met with the old woman on the other side of town. She looked almost younger than Mary, but she was over a hundred years old. I could tell by the way she was dressed and the style of her copper hair.

Inside the woman's kitchen, the baby jesuses crawled over each other like greasy blubberroaches, squeaking and biting at each other.

"Which one's the mother?" Mary asked.

The old woman pointed to the baby jesus lying in the center of the baby pile. "That's the mother, the one with the swollen teets."

We looked at a baby jesus with six large breasts lined down its ribcage. The other baby jesuses were fighting each other to suck the nipples.

"Well, which one is the father?" Mary asked.

"The father's dead," the old woman responded with a painted on eyebrow. "He bit one of the neighbor's kids and had to be put to sleep."

"I thought jesuses were pretty mellow babies," I say to the old woman.

"Baby jesuses are a strange breed. Sometimes they are very affectionate darlings and other times they can be nasty."

"That's too bad you had to put him to sleep," Mary said. "Was he cremated?"

"No, my husband wanted him stuffed. It was our first baby, so we were pretty attached. Once we get it back form the taxidermist, we will put it over there by the fireplace."

"Oh, that will be a lovely place for it!" Mary said with a big cherry-flavored smile.

"So do you want a boy or a girl?" asked the old woman.

"They all look alike," I said. "H-how can you tell them apart?"

"From their belly buttons," the woman said, picking one of the babies up by its leg. "See this one is a boy because it has a frog-shaped belly button. If it were a girl, the belly button would be nose-shaped."

"I don't understand," I told her. "How do they reproduce?"

"Well, they lick each other's belly buttons until the female's nose-shaped belly button flares its nostrils and the male's frog-shaped belly button opens its mouth and releases several sperm-like creatures that look kind of like wolf spiders."

"That's disgusting," I told her.

"Well, nature can be disgusting sometimes."

"Let's get a boy!" Mary screamed. "I always wanted a baby boy."

"Well," said the woman, "they are all baby boys in a sense."

"I don't care," Mary said. "I'd rather have a male baby boy than a female baby boy!"

"J-just don't touch his belly button," I told Mary. "I don't want any wolf spiders in the house."

Mary picked the one she wanted and wrapped it up in a blue blanket. Her face was brighter than it was the day we married.

"One more thing," said the old woman. "You're not like those weirdos who use baby jesuses for sex, are you?"

Mary and I looked at each other. My left eye twitched a little.

"No, we hate those people," Mary said.

"Yeah, those people are perverts," my words rattled out.

"Well, I hope not," said the old woman. "You know what will happen if you mistreat them don't you?"

Mary kissed the baby on the forehead.

"God will punish you," she continued. "God doesn't stand for people making a mockery of his son just because he is in the shape of a baby. If you stick this child in your butt, you'll damn yourself to hell."

"Don't worry," Mary said to the old woman, holding the infant tight to her chest. "I know exactly what you're talking about. There are all kinds of horrible people in the world these days. It just makes me sick to think of what they are capable of! I can't believe that some people actually have the nerve to use the holy powers of the messiah on anal expeditions! Sometimes I can't even sleep at night."

The young-looking old woman nodded in agreement at Mary. You could tell by the look in her eyes that she was thinking Mary would be a great mother to that baby jesus. Mary would provide it with a very-very good home.

CHAPTER THREE

Once we got home, we immediately took turns inserting the baby jesus into each other's rectums. And then we fucked on the top shelf in our bedroom closet, Mary's back grinding into all the dusty boxes of clothes and cobwebs, my butt cheeks smacking against the ceiling. And with each thrashing movement, I felt the unbelievably refreshing pain of the butt plug/son of God as it squeezed against the interior walls of my defecation hole. And as I came, I thought about robots made out of wood and soil traveling across the garbage landscape of central Wyoming.

We lay still for some quiet moments up there in the closet. Mary shifted her hips a little to prevent a high heeled shoe from digging out her lower back.

"What are you thinking about?" Mary's voice came from the shadows.

". . . Robots," I answered.

CHAPTER FOUR

When we removed the baby jesus from my butt hole, he was covered in blood. At first, I thought it was my own blood because it was streaming down my legs for several minutes after he was removed. But then we noticed something different about its appearance. Looking closely, we noticed the baby jesus was nailed to a tiny cross.

"What is this?" Mary cried.

"A crucifix," I said. "He must have crucified himself while in my butthole."

"Ohhh, how cute!" Mary said. "His first crucifying!"

Mary smiled with a stupid dazed face. She wrapped her arm around me and put her head on my shoulder.

"Let's name him Bobby," she said.

"Y-yeah," I replied. "Bobby is a g-good name for a baby jesus."

CHAPTER FIVE

That was the only time lil' Bobby ever cruci-fied himself. And nothing seemed out of the ordinary with him at all until yesterday, when I noticed a small wooden doorknob growing out of the skin above his left nipple.

"What is it?" Mary whisper-asked, wearing a blue plastic-wrap dress and a self-created black eye.

"It's a doorknob," I told her, look-ing down at the sleeping pet baby.

"It looks like a normal growth to me," she whispered. "I mean, doorknobs are supposed to grow on doors not babies."

"It must be some kind of mutant baby jesus."

We watched the sleeping baby with cardboard faces, unsure what to make of it.

CHAPTER SIX

Later that night, we noticed the growth was now a full-grown doorknob.

"What should we do?" Mary asked. "Should we call the vet?"

"No," I screamed at her. "What if people see us with a baby jesus? Th-they'll spread rumors!"

"Well, we have to take him to the vet sometimes. What if this is serious?"

Bobby cooed and gurgled and played with the knob on its breast.

"I told you it was a bad idea to get a baby jesus."

"You promised me a baby!"

"Why did you even want a pet baby? They're useless pets and hardly worth the hassle."

"I wanted us to be more like a fam-ily!" Mary screamed.

"Well, why didn't we go down to the copy shop and get ourselves a real child, one that would actually make something of itself?"

Mary didn't say anything. Her eyes and face were burning red. She couldn't talk. I waited for a response, but didn't get even a glance in my direction.

Once she calmed down, Mary turned the doorknob on Bobby's nipple and opened him up, causing two things: One, it turned a light on from inside of the baby jesus, quite like the opening of a refrigerator door. And two, music began tinkering out of its chest, quite like the opening of a music box.

We bit each other's lips when we saw his insides. There weren't any internal organs at all. Not a lung, a heart, or even bones. It's insides seemed to be made of wood rather than meat. And the only object occupying the empty space inside of our pet baby was a tiny plastic ballerina, spinning in circles to the metallic harmony.

"W-w-what is this?" I screamed at Mary, blood dribbling from my lip into her mouth.

"A music box," she replied with a big happy bloody smile.

CHAPTER SEVEN

Before we went to sleep:

"Do you think baby jesuses have souls?" Mary asked in a green voice.

"I don't know."

"Do you think they go to Heaven? Do you think God uses them for butt plugs too?"

"I don't know."

She was smiling in bed, the blan-kets cuddled all the way to her chin.

"Mary?" I whispered.

"Yes?" she whispered back, still in

her excited voice.

"I'm scared to death of it," I told her.

"Scared of what?"

"Of the baby jesus."

"What?"she screamed, throwing the blanket off of her.

"How can it still be alive without any insides?" I cried.

Now I was cuddling the covers up to my chin.

"How dare you say that about my son!" Mary screamed.

"It's not your son, it's the son of man-made clones of God's son."

"How can you say he's scary, he's sooo cute!"

"Cute? It has a ballerina instead of a heart. Do you think that's normal?"

"Ballerinas are sooo pretty!" Mary screamed.

"I know they're pretty, but it's just not natural. That baby jesus is some kind of mutant freak."

"You're not taking my baby away from me!" Mary screamed. "It's not a freak just because it has a music box instead of internal organs! You never wear matching socks. That's pretty weird. But I never call you a freak!"

"I do that because it's good luck," I told her.

"Well, maybe our baby jesus has a music box chest because it's good luck."

"You don't understand me at all do you?"

"You'll understand me when I knock your lights out!"

"Look," my voice went calm. "It just seems a little funny to me, that's all."

"I'm not talking to you anymore," she said, turning out the light and wrapping the blanket around her head.

"I'm sorry . . ." I said in the dark.

"Go to sleep," she hissed, shoving my knees out of the way with the back of her heel.

Back to the present . . .

CHAPTER EIGHT

I have been avoiding the baby jesus all day today. It's my day off and I was supposed to be spending it in relaxation, but I am scared to death of that unnatural *thing*. Mary went to her sister's house and left me alone with Bobby. "If anything happens to it, I'll kill you," Mary said to me on her way out. But all I can think about doing is breaking its head open with a rock. I don't want to take care if it. I don't want anything to do with it.

It's been crawling after me all afternoon, making horrible gurgle-noises at me. I think it's trying to get inside my butt hole.

At this thought, I look down at the baby jesus and see a little evil smile on its face, thinking of doing something terrible to me. I dash across the rubber-tiled floor and lock myself in the bedroom. My head is leaking pieces of brain instead of sweat. I pull on a second pair of pants and strap on a thick rawhide cowboy belt, tightening it two notches smaller than usual, and I tuck the pants into a pair of garden boots.

That better work.

When I turn around, the baby jesus appears behind me with a crooked head. Its eyeballs have mutated into balls of blood-red and razor-sharp wires grow out of its skull. It makes some squeaking sounds and then jerk-crawls up the door and onto the ceiling above me. It just looks down and drops a line of drool into my nose.

I scream/stumble-flee from the room, hearing the creature's chest open and tinker music fill the room. At that moment I recognize the tune is that Christmas song, "Oh Holy Night," which Mary once sang in church a long-long time ago. It's been awhile since either of us have been to church . . .

When Mary gets home, she finds me hiding under the kitchen sink with wet circles on my knees and elbows.

"What are you doing?" Mary asks, bouncing the creature in her arms.

"It's evil," I tell her. "That *thing* is like the devil!"

"What are you talking about?" Mary says, kissing the baby on its wiry head and stepping away from me.

CHAPTER NINE

I spend the entire evening avoiding the baby jesus. Mary is playing marbles with it. They are somewhere in the living room under a shadeless lamp. She has its belly open and is singing the words to Oh Holy Night with the tinker music and patting the tiny ballerina on the head. The tinker music is not as lively as it was before. The gears seem rusted, creating a zombie-machine sound.

"Mary?" I call from a safe place.

She turns to me with a wrinkled face, and gives me an eyeing of disgust. The baby jesus also turns to me and angry-stares with beady black eyes. The skin on the pet baby seems to be turning crusty-green. It is becoming mold-rotten.

I shiver wire spiders through my hairs and my voice comes out cracked, "W-we need to talk."

Mary ignores me, turns back to clacking marbles, kisses the little ballerina inside her pet demon baby.

I walk away and go to bed, curl up into a deep blue dream.

When Mary finally enters the room at three in the morning, I can hear her from inside my head. I look out of my brain at her. When she crawls into the covers, I immediately sense the muffled tinker music issuing from between her legs ...

CHAPTER TEN

I leave for work lightning-fast: rip some clothes on my body, eat a bruised apple outside the front door as I pull on my shoes, wash my face with acid water on the bus ride to Nomax.

Nomax is a data entry company located in an eight story building at the edge of town. It is the seventh largest data entry company in Seattle. I take the elevator all the way up to the second floor and take my seat in the forty-third row of cubicles.

Papers are piled out of the inbox, stacked higher than the monitor. Green lemon bugs are eating the dirt off of my keyboard, smiling and waving at me. I brush them away and begin working. For the first five hours of work, I copy a stack of paper into the computer. The papers read "Nomax is the seventh best data entry company in Seattle" over and over again. Normally, I only do this data entry work for two hours a day, but I need to catch up for taking yesterday off.

"Hey Joe, try to finish this for me by lunch, okay?" My smooth-featured manager says, dropping a stack of papers on my desk.

The assignment is important, obviously. I look it over and see that I have to hold the "Q" button down on my keyboard for 90 minutes and then switch to the "K" button and hold it down for 120 minutes. After I am finished, I save it in a file and send it back to my manager.

I go to lunch with my work-friends, Peaceful and Hairy.

Nomax, like many other companies, does not allow us to leave the building until after the day is over. Nor do they allow any outside food inside the office. So for lunch the only choice we have is to eat in the company cafeteria, where the food quality is worse than fast food, but the prices are higher than the best restaurant in town. In fact, half of our daily income goes to lunch.

Unless you let yourself starve, as

Peaceful and I do. We just drink loads of tap water and sometimes swallow pieces of napkins. Hairy always buys lunch, though. He thinks food is what makes life enjoyable. He'd rather spend all his money on it than not have it at all.

"So how was your day off, Joe?" Hairy asks between greasy bites.

"Not that good," I tell him.

"Yeah." He chuckles to himself. "Well, it'll be a long time before you get another one."

"I don't know why you take your days off anyway," Peaceful says. "I mean, if you work through them you get time and a quarter! Don't you want the extra money?"

"Yeah," Hairy says. "Think about it. If you work through all four vacation days, you'll get a free day of pay every year! How can you beat that?"

"I think I'd rather get extra money from ditching lunch rather than giving up my days off."

"You need to grow up," Hairy tells me.

"So how's Mary doing?" Peaceful asks.

"She's okay," I tell him. "She doesn't talk to me anymore. All she ever does is play with our pet baby."

"You actually got her one of those pet babies?" Hairy said with his angry beard. "That's pure immaturity!"

"Yeah, Joe," Peaceful says. "In this day and age, there's no room for babies. We're born into this world as full grown adults. There's no time to be children let alone raise children."

"I know, I know," I tell them with my face in my fingers.

"You're such a wimp, Joe," Hairy says. "Why can't you just stand up to her for a change?"

"I know, I know."

CHAPTER ELEVEN

After lunch, I find my cubicle has been overrun with thousands of green lemon bugs, crawling over each other and biting each other's limbs off. I try sitting down and wiping them away, but there are too many of them. I stand up and tell them to go away, but green lemon bugs are the most disobedient of pests.

My manager pats me on the back, admiring the insects devouring my work station.

"Excellent, Joe," he tells me. "Excellent, excellent work."

I turn to the smooth-featured man and stutter-nod.

"There's a call for you on the seventh floor," he says. "Why don't you go take that."

My eyebrows curl. "Where on the seventh floor?"

"Where do you think?" The managers face sinks downward, upset with my question. He returns to his office.

I've never been on any floors higher than the second. There's never been a need to. The company prefers that employees move very little while in the building. It is rare to see anyone get on the elevator at all.

In the elevator:

A woman with purple lipstick and plumpcurls is outside the elevator, staring at me.

"I'll get the next one," she says, wiggling her nose hairs.

I always see this woman near the elevator, but I've never seen her get on. As if she has work to do on another floor but hesitates to go anywhere.

I half-smile at her as the glass doors slide shut. She continues to stare at me through the glass as the elevator goes up-up.

THIRD FLOOR:

A more populated version of the second floor. As cluttered as a toy box. Cubicles are stacked on top of each other in all directions, all the way to the ceiling. Some people are forced to stand on shoulders to reach their monitors. Others are lying on the ground underneath desks at feet level, getting kicked in the face by accident sometimes. One man's computer station is nailed to the ceiling and they have him strapped into his chair as he types upside-down. He half-waves at me as I pass by, trying to smile but his face is too blood-rushed to make pleasant expressions.

FOURTH FLOOR:

A chaos of wires and computer panels. I see a few technicians wearing full body protective suits, as if they are working with radiation. The room is split by giant circuit boards and engines. It seems as if the room is one big computer and the men are inside of it. There is no sound coming from within. Perhaps they are working in a vacuum. They stare at me through haunting google-masks.

FIFTH FLOOR:

A white-white room. No walls or cubicles. Unlimited space. There doesn't seem to be electricity here. The room is lit by candles. Papers are scattered across the field of carpeting like ghosts. Is it abandoned? No, over there at the end of the room there is an old woman in a tiny desk, sleeping. And over there are two children running in circles with toy airplanes chasing each other. Children? Aren't children only in movies and television shows these days? Aren't they extinct? I get on my knees and press my face to the glass to see if they really are children, but they disappear into the background.

SIXTH FLOOR:

The elevator light buzzes dim. There doesn't seem to be electricity this high up in the building. The sixth floor doesn't have any lights at all. No windows to let the sun in. The room is flooded with a blackish-green fluid. It is about four feet deep. I can look into the liquid through the glass door, but it is not very clear. There is bubbling porcupine movement in the distance.

SEVENTH FLOOR:

The elevator comes to a stop and the doors swing open.

This floor is very quiet. It looks similar to a library, an intricate maze of records and filings. A little girl of about ten years steps out of a nearby office to me.

"Hello, Joe," she says to me. "I've been expecting you."

The girl has short black hair and purple eyes, wearing a silvery dress with leather straps.

"Who are you?" I ask the girl.

"I'm Tia Ki," she says, quick-bowing. "The vice-president of Nomax. Surely you've heard of me?"

"No, I haven't . . ."

She takes me by the hand and leads me down a hallway of filing cabinets and shelves.

"But you're only a child . . ." I tell her.

"I'm 243 years old," she says. "How old are you?"

"I've b-been alive for eight years . . . How can you be 243? I thought life expectancy was 150 years at best."

"150 years applies only to adult bodies. But they say children can live for five to seven hundred years. Nobody knows for sure, though. A child has yet to die of old age. We could very well live forever."

"But you're just a little girl. Surely a child brain is not capable of understanding the world as adult brains do."

"All the leaders in the world happen to be children," she tells me with an annoyed tone. "We are the oldest and therefore the wisest."

"Why was I sent here?" I ask her. "They said I had a call, but I don't understand."

"I told them to send me a new assistant. The last one I had was inadequate and had to be let go immediately. You are his replacement."

"My manager said nothing about this. He just said I have a phone call."

"Yes, there is a phone call for you in my office. But first we have to do some quick business."

"I'm not sure if I'm the right person for this j-job . . ."

"Nonsense," the girl tells me.

She takes me to the end of the cabinet maze to a large room. Inside I discover a city of dolls and dollhouses, toy buildings designed to match the neighborhood.

The little girl picks up two dolls from a pedestal and holds them to me. "This one is me and this doll is going to be you. It was my old assistant's but we can get it modified to look more like you. For now we'll just have to pretend."

"What is all this?" I ask the girl.

"It is important business. You are the boy and I am the girl. Now hurry up. Every afternoon at 2:00 we get married at the church and we are almost late for the ceremony."

She kisses my doll with her doll.

"They are in love," she says, smiling.

"This is insane," I tell her.

"You should see the CEO of the company's train set! It is even more insane than this!"

"This is d-disgusting," I tell her, squeezing fists and inching away from her. "This is a professional company, not a playground."

"This is how we conduct business here . . . this is how all business is conducted. There is nothing unprofessional about it."

I shake my head at her.

She says, "I know better than you. I am the vice president. Now get this doll ready to marry!"

I turn and walk away from her. "I need to talk to my manager about this."

I run through the maze of cabinets and slip into the office by the elevator—

There is a naked man tied to a chair in here, wearing leather bondage gear with a gagball in his mouth. He is overweight and similar to a doll with a mustache. He also has superglue holding his eyebrows together.

"I need to use the phone," I tell him, wheeling him into an office closet filled with fairy costumes and closing the door.

"What do you think you're doing?" the little girl screams at me from the doorway, holding the two dolls in her hands like pistols.

"I'm going to complain to my manager about this," I tell her. "I am declining this position."

"You don't have a choice," the girl shrieks.

I pick up the phone and hit a blinking button:

There is heavy breathing on the other end . . .

"Hello?" My voice echoes. "Hello?"

There is a scattering sound and then a sobbing voice.

"Joe?"

It is Mary. She is crying and her voice is cracky.

"Mary?"

"You were right," she tells me. "The baby is . . . It's trying to kill me."

"Hang up that phone this instant, young man!" the girl screams, tugging on the phone chord.

I grab her by the back of the neck and squeeze it hard. She shrieks at me as I shove her out of the office and lock the door.

Back to the phone: "Mary?"

No answer.

"Mary? What's happening?"

"Joe . . . I've been hiding here all afternoon. I think it knows where I am. I think it's playing with me."

"Mary, just hold on. I'm coming with help."

The little girl screams through the door. I see her red face pressed up against the glass, whine-crying.

"I'm calling the police on you!" the girl screams.

"I'm calling them first," I tell her.

I go back to the phone, "Mary?"

No answer.

"Mary?"

I hear some gurgling baby noises before I hang up the phone.

"Go ahead and call the police," the little girl screams, slamming the dolls against the door. "Do you think they'll believe a low class eight-year-old like yourself over a 243 year old little girl that is vice-president of Nomax?"

"I'm not the one with a man tied up in my closet," I tell her.

"He's nothing but a cockroach," the girl screams.

A burst of whines wail out of the girl and she smashes her face against the office door. I see an explosion of blood spray across the glass of the door and the girl stops screaming. Her body crumbles to the floor.

When I look through the window, I see the girl has a ripped and swelling face. Blood and meat are in pools beneath her. She must have a concussion.

"I don't have time for the police," I tell the girl. "I need to get help elsewhere."

I pick up the phone and dial an information number. They slowly put me through to the closest copy shop in the neighborhood.

"I need as many male c-copies of myself that my credit can afford," I tell the female employee on the other end.

"It is for emergency reasons . . . A one-day expiration will be fine. I need them

sent to my home address as quick as possible."

The woman says it'll be quicker to make both male and female copies, because they have separate machines for each gender. I agree. With my credit, I can afford to buy nine plus delivery to my house.

"I want them to have my full memory," I tell her.

She puts me on hold so they can scan my brain through the phone. It has a funny electric feeling and poppy sound. It is almost as if they are sucking the brain out of my head.

CHAPTER TWELVE

When the bus finally gets me home, I can tell the clones have already arrived. The door has been forced open, windows broken into, and there is a body with its guts torn out on my front lawn.

The neighbors do not seem to care. They go on watering their flowers, walking their dogs, waving at passersby on the sidewalks . . .

Upon entering the house, I am transported to another world.

The interior of my home is now a giant museum of fleshy electric walls, skeletal patterns creeping the ceiling. Crab and snail shells have replaced the floor tiles. Everything has been stretched and distorted into an insecty alien landscape. But I can still tell it is my home. I know that the living room is through the passage straight ahead of me, and the kitchen and hallway to the bedrooms are to my sides.

Another dead clone, a female, lies on the ground at my feet. The front of her torso has been torn off. I can't recognize any resemblance to me.

I go straight ahead towards the living room. The passageway is a giant ribcage, and I feel as if I've been swallowed into a whale-like creature. The path opens into the living room, a long auditorium. It is made of giant fire-beetle shells and steel icicles.

I choke on my breath as I see someone seated on the tar-wiry couch. It is sitting with its back to me, watching bubbling metal liquid swirl-dance on a mirror-like object which used to be the television set. By the color of its hair, I can tell it is not a clone of myself. It must be Mary. But I get a strange feeling when I look at the back of her head. She seems to be enjoying the television casually, like nothing is wrong with the appearance of the house.

"Mary?" I call to her.

She ignores me.

I step through the muddy floor and reach out to her. A noise like popping/cracking bones echoes through the room. "Mary?"

I grab her hard and shake her. Her hair slips out of her head, piling on her shoulders. A plastic-smooth white skull.

"Mary!" I race around to her front and collapse to my knees as I see her face.

It is gone. Her face is blank. It is smooth like her bald scalp. The only facial feature still attached to her is the left ear. Everything else is as smooth as an egg, but made of flesh.

"Mary . . ." sobs burn my voice. "W-what did it do to you?"

I rub her ear. It is the only part of her body I can still recognize. I lick my finger and rub it through its curves.

"I love you, Mary," I tell her.

I turn the ear like a door and open her face. There isn't a brain inside. Only a tiny plastic ballerina spinning in circles to tinker music, to Oh Holy Night.

Before I can cry—my neck bubbling with red pain—I notice the little ballerina's face is Mary's. Her beautiful features have been transferred from her real head to the little plastic music box figurine. So besides holding back just my tears, my anger, I now have to hold back a loving smile . . .

CHAPTER THIRTEEN

I hear some screams. They come from where my kitchen should be. I step away from my wife and run in the direction of the kitchen. Entering a twisted room of melted counters and devices, where a crowd of clones have gathered. Some of them are holding knives and forks and pointing them at each other.

"What's going on?" I ask the copies of me.

I get dizzy as they look back to me. They are like mirrors that can walk and talk.

"There you are!" says a male clone. "We need to get out of here!"

His voice is strange, unfamiliar. Do I really sound like that? Do I really move so mechanically?

Something is wrong. I examine the situation.

. . .

Not all of the people in my kitchen are clones. Many of them look like . . .

"Z-zombies!" screams a female copy of me, running out of the kitchen.

There are two male copies and one female copy. One male and the female are naked, but the other still has its orange wrapping provided by the copy shop. The rest of the people in the kitchen are ex-clones. They are ripped apart, bloody. Mutilated versions of myself. Intestines drip out of their bellies and drag on the floor as they stagger toward us.

The clothed male drags me away, screaming, "The b-baby jesus killed them and then raised them from the dead! They are mindless undead flesh-eating jesus s-slaves!"

We race down the spidery hallway of gray flesh and metals, the corpses shambling after us. We dump ourselves into the master bedroom and slam a greasy lard door, pushing bookshelves in front of it. Zombie arms squeeze through the flesh-door and seize hold of the naked copy of me.

My eyes curl backwards as I see

the clone torn to shreds by the creatures. His chest opens up, his neck twists, popping bones. I am so flabby and out of shape. I look disgusting naked.

CHAPTER FOURTEEN

"It killed her," cries the female clone, crying thin tears. "My sweet Mary is dead."

I almost feel offended when I hear the female me say this. It was *my* Mary, not hers. I can hardly tell the woman is a copy of me. She is totally unfamiliar. I see her hair color and birthmarks are the same as mine, but she is still different. She is so much better looking than me. Her body is like mine, not at all muscular, but she carries her flab in a sexy way. Her breasts are large with weight, nipples darker and wider than mine. She is also a little shorter and doesn't have my thick ugly neck.

"How come you're naked?" I ask my clone.

She stops crying. "I was hiding in the pantry with that copy." She points to the dead clone on the sludgy floor, rubbing her tears. "I don't know why . . . we started fucking. We only have one day to live, that is if the zombies and demonic baby jesus don't kill us sooner. We decided to make the most of our time."

The remaining male is hitting the zombie hands with a barbell that has a large weight attached to the top. He breaks their arms and fingers against the book shelf and door.

"Your goal in life was to save Mary!" I tell her. "That's how you were supposed to make the most of your time!"

She begins to break into tears again.

"Now your life's goal is to avenge her death. That creature has g-got to die."

She nods her head at me, understands me completely. She knows that I will also be spending my last breath killing the demon baby. I have nothing else to live for.

We go back to barricading the door. The female uses butcher knives to cut the zombie hands off. She stabs one through the fingers with a fork, pinning it to the side of the shelves.

"What are we going to do?" the female screams, slicing the door.

But I was just about to ask her the same question.

CHAPTER FIFTEEN

We are lying on the lizard bed together. Playing cards. Solitaire. The female has put on Mary's blue pajamas and has her hair greased back. She doesn't fit very well in Mary's clothes. Her boobs are too big for them. Her flabby belly hangs out as we nervously move the cards.

"Maybe we should make our move soon," says the male. "We're just going to end up falling asleep at this rate."

"Yeah, maybe we should," I tell him.

We continue playing cards.

CHAPTER SIXTEEN

I awake to a commotion of yells and growling. The two clones are up in the closet, screaming at me to wake up. I look up at them.

"What's going on?"

They don't have any clothes on. Probably in the middle of masturbating/masturbating.

"Behind you!" they cry.

I feel a claw-hand caress the back of my neck. Then it tightens its grip, a sharp lightning-pain, digging fingernails into my flesh. A splash of blood sprays out of me as the zombie cuts the side of my neck. The pain becomes dull. I look down and see my chest and arms and the bed sheets are covered in blood. The zombie version of me eats into the back of my neck. Again, I can hardly feel this. I fall against the bed and become like a dream. My jugular has been cut. I watch my clones up in the closet as they screw each other. They glance down at me a few times, but are more interested in having orgasms. I begin to admire the stitchwork of the blanket I am lying on as my consciousness wanders away from me.

CHAPTER SEVENTEEN

I awake in the closet with a warm body pressed against me. A woman.

"Mary . . ."

Breasts squeezed hard against my chest and my penis inside of her.

When my brain clears, I discover that Mary isn't on top of me. We are in the shadows, but I can tell that it is my clone fucking me and not my wife. I turn my head to look around. I am up on the top shelf in the closet. Boxes of dusty clothes and high-heeled shoes are stabbing into my back. My clone's butt cheeks are smacking against the ceiling. But she is trying to screw quietly, slowly. My hands squeeze her fleshy ass, and my knuckles grind into the ceiling as she pumps up and down.

I look out of the closet to see a zombie eating a copy of me on the bed over there. I watch it ripping flesh from his body, slurping skin from his neck. It gazes up at me and snarls.

But I don't want to stop fucking. I am almost ready to come. Her hole is much bigger than Mary's, deeper, with long flaps of skin. She has a variety of fluids dribbling out of her, different colors and textures it seems. Sliding against me. She knows exactly how I like it. She knows what I'm thinking. Mary never knew what I was thinking. I

wonder what her name is . . .

Her motions are slow, rubbing me inside her in places that make my nerves coo. The weight of her breasts smothering me as I come, ejaculating into her, and my member pulsates in a way that brings her into orgasm. The female collapses on top of me, her cheek resting on my forehead.

I watch the zombie on the bed. It ignores us, more interested in eating the clone.

"That's me he's eating," I tell her.

"The zombie is you too," she says. "So am I."

"No . . ." I tell her. "I mean . . . That clone is me. I remember being on the bed and getting attacked from behind. I remember it killing me."

"That's impossible," she whispers. "You have been up here with me."

"No, I think somehow my mind transferred to this clone after I died."

"You are not a clone," she tells me. "You are the original. He was the clone."

I'll take her word for it. I don't understand how anything happens anymore, but I don't have time to argue with logic.

"It's time to kill that thing," she tells me.

I nod my head in the shadows.

CHAPTER EIGHTEEN

We are both shaking. The sweat on our bodies is turning ice cold. The female takes her knives from the adjacent shelf and lets me have one. Then we drop down to the floor. The female leads. She walks casually out of the room. Her ass is so wet it is shiny as it moves, approaching the zombie who is gnawing on the clone's leg muscles.

"Let's go," she says, and we charge the zombie. I run to jump on its back, but the female beats me to it. The zombie screams and thrashes at her, but she is holding it down. We stab at its head, but the knives won't penetrate the skull. I plunge my knife into its neck, the weak spot, remembering how easy my neck was torn apart with fingernails. The blade goes all the way through. The zombie's growl-noises stop as I cut through the voice box. I force it up and down, ripping the hole larger. And I saw at the neck, blood sprinkling our naked flesh, covering our legs, our breasts, arms, stomach.

The woman pulls the creature by the hair, scratching the neck muscles in such a way that the edge of the knife pops right through the front of its throat. And the female me is able to rip its head from its shoulders.

When it stops moving, we shift away from the bed. I can hear zombies in the hallway. They are still growling out there, but I am getting used to them being there. They are like white noise.

"We'll never be able to kill all of them," I tell her, but she isn't listening.

She is in a paralyzed stare at the dead zombie.

"What is it?" I ask her.

She grabs my arm and constricts it, pointing at the zombie's ass.

The baby jesus's face is squeezing out of his asshole. The little baby head is deformed, its eyes crooked, making gurgling baby noises as it emerges.

When it opens its mouth, snotty strings extend from its lips. And when it giggles, the female screams and stabs her butcher knife through the baby's head and leaps away.

It is silent.

We stare at it lying there with the butcher knife hanging halfway out of its face.

It doesn't move. Frozen with its crooked eyes split by the blade.

The woman steps forward and retrieves the knife in its head, pulls on it. But the pet baby comes with knife. It slips out of the zombie's rectum, stuck to the blade. She screams at it and slams the baby against the wall. Forces the knife out of its head and

nails it through the baby's hand into the wall.

She steps away from it. The tiny corpse hanging on the wall, dangling by its hand. Then she takes my knife away from me and spikes it through the baby's other hand. She steps away from it again.

We watch it in silence. Standing here, expecting the crucified body to do something. But it just hangs there. Bleeding. It looks pretty dead. Crucifying must kill demonic baby jesuses like silver bullets kill vicious werewolves.

"I'm going to rip that fucking ballerina from its chest," I tell her.

I approach it quickly and turn the knob on its torso.

Intestines and internal organs pile out of the little door, sliding down the wall. There isn't a ballerina inside. It doesn't play any music.

CHAPTER NINETEEN

I wake up naked on the bathroom floor covered in peach goo. I rub the sticky substance between my fingers as my head clears. It is the remains of the female clone. I remember going to sleep on the bathroom tile with her wrapped around me—me wrapped around myself. She must have expired in her sleep, melted down to muck as temporary clones are designed to do.

Stepping into the bedroom, the bodies here have also dissolved to a peach film covering the sheets. The baby jesus is no longer hanging from the walls, but its little innards are still piled on the floor over there. The bedroom door has been torn open, but there is only silence in the hallway. The house has returned to its natural appearance, but it hardly feels like home.

My bare feet squish into the sticky peach substance in the hallway where the zombie clones had melted down. I don't wipe it off, sticky goo between my toes, shambling through the hallway.

I freeze.

Listening.

I can hear tinker music coming from the kitchen.

Oh Holy Night.

I don't bother going back to the bedroom to get a butcher knife. I am too worn and tired to fight if the baby jesus is still alive and wants to kill me. I will let it do what it wants.

Staggering into the kitchen, I see Mary standing there. She is holding the corpse of her pet baby in her hands, cradling it. Her hair and features are still missing, smooth like a flesh-egg, and her head-door is open to the little ballerina and the tinkering music.

Mary has her shirt unbuttoned, pressing jesus's mouth against her breast. She rocks the tiny dead baby in her arms to the music, comforting it.

"Mary?" I step to her.

The music in her head stops. She stops moving.

I approach her, put my hand on her shoulder, caress her neck. She turns to me. The tiny ballerina face—her face—stares longingly at me.

"I'm sorry . . ." the tiny plastic head says to me.

She wraps her free arm around my waist and hugs me tight to her. And I press my mouth through her skull door and kiss the tiny ballerina inside.

She says, "Once Bobby resurrects, we can be a family again."

I nod at her.

We sit down on the living room couch and hold each other, gaze out of the window, waiting for the infant between us to wake up from death. After a couple of days, it begins to smell. The flies are getting to it. The sun is setting in the wrong direction.

JEREMY ROBERT JOHNSON

LOCATION:
Portland, OR

STYLE OF BIZARRO:
Tweeker Lit
(aka Crackhouse Rhapsodies)

BOOKS BY JOHNSON:

Angel Dust Apocalypse
Siren Promised (w/ Alan M. Clark)
Extinction Journals
Skullcrack City (forthcoming).

"A dazzling writer..."
- Chuck Palahniuk, author of *Fight Club*

DESCRIPTION: JRJ writes freakish (and often experimental) cross-genre stories about people, or people-like things, or thing-like people. These are stories with teeth and tentacles and purple fingernails with glitter on them. And inevitably, despite JRJ's protestations, someone in these stories is always ingesting a shit-ton of drugs and "wyling out." JRJ's fiction is high in cathartic strangeness but low in poly-unsaturated fats.

INTERESTS: Anthropology, chemistry, parasites, forensics, physics,-isms, evolution, lucid dreaming, non-ironic humor hats, high fantasy metal, running, Burning Man, sharks (particularly the still-existent carcharodon megalodon), not being eaten by sharks.

INFLUENCES: Ellroy, Rand, Selby, Wallace, Burroughs, Vonnegut, Welsh, Williams, Palahniuk, Barker, King, Cronenberg, Miike, Romero, Lovecraft, Jodorowsky, Dali, Bosch, Methylchloroisothiazolinone, Thompson, Noe, Hafiz.

WEBSITE:
www.jeremyrobertjohnson.com

EXTINCTION JOURNALS

CHAPTER ONE

The cockroaches took several hours to eat the President.

That much Dean was sure of. His buggy business suit had a severe appetite. Anything else - life/reality/desire - came across secondary and suspect.

Although Dean *was* fairly positive that World War III had begun.

Extent of the carnage- Unknown.

Nations involved- Unknown.

Survivors he was aware of- One.

There were two, originally. The President *had* been alive when Dean found him out here by the base of the Washington Monument. The guy was nearly catatonic, pacing a small circle, slack-jawed, but breathing. Still, he never had a chance. When a man in a suit made of cockroaches meets a man in a suit made of Twinkies- well, that's about as easy as subtraction gets.

As scenarios go, Dean branded this one Capital L Lonely. He'd choked out the President as an act of mercy, to save the man the sensation of being eaten alive. That meant that at present Dean had not a soul to talk to.

He tried to address the suit.

"Hey, roaches. Are you guys full yet?"

Nothing. Or maybe they thought it rude to respond while eating.

Instead, Dean's Fear, that nagging voice that he thought he'd snuffed out by surviving the bombing, decided to chip in.

Yeah, that's reasonable. Talk to the insects. How cracked is your mind at this point? Are you even sure you're alive? I mean, we're talking full-fledged nuclear war here. You absolutely should not be alive. It's ridiculous. How do you know that you weren't vaporized in the first blast? That's more likely. And this is some sort of nasty purgatory that you'll be forever condemned to, all alone, stuck in this ugly place with your ludicrous bug suit...

"Shut up." It felt better to Dean, saying it out loud. Quieted the ugly part of his brain for a moment at least.

Dean was pretty sure that he was alive. He couldn't imagine a metaphysical plane where he'd feel so damn hungry.

I need to pee. There's no way they kept urination in the afterlife.

Dean was also pretty sure that the world, or at least his continent, was getting darker and heading towards deep-sea black. It was already beyond dusk at what was probably three in the afternoon. Nuclear winter was spreading its ashy chill through the air, fed onward by black smoke and blazing nouveau-palace pyres in the distance. Fat flakes of glowing grey floated in the air.

Dean shivered and tried to move the heft of his weight into the radiant heat coming from the bodies of the cockroaches beneath him. There were tiny pores in the suit's fabric at each point where he'd delicately sewn each roach's thorax to the outfit. He imagined heat seeping through, but didn't really feel it.

Dean received little comfort or consolation. But he didn't demand those things either. The suit kept him alive here at catastrophe central and Dean felt guilty for wanting more.

Relax. Let the suit take the lead. Let instinct kick in. They've had millions of years of training. They're ready for this.

But why are they eating so much? They never needed this much food before.

Dean blanched. This level of consumption was totally un-natural. He'd guessed they'd stop feeding when they finished with the toasted yellow sugar cakes the President had been coated in.

Back when Dean had lived in the slums of DC, as he was creating the suit, he'd woken many evenings and found the creatures nibbling at the dead skin around his eyelashes and fingernails, but he'd never seen them go after new, wet meat like this. What, he wondered, had he strapped onto his body?

Maybe they'll turn right around when they're done with El Presidente here and they'll keep on eating. Could you fight them off Dean? The leader of the free world couldn't stop them. What makes you think you could? You think these roaches know you? That they give a petty shit about you and your continued existence? They're filling up Dean. They'll eat you slow...

"Fuck that fuck that fuck that." Dean had to say this out loud, and quickly, to clear his mental slate. With nowhere to go the Fear could run rampant if he didn't run containment.

The rolling sheet of hunger Dean had clothed himself inside of just kept eating. It took in a million tiny bits of once stately matter and processed President in its guts.

Could they taste the man's power, Dean wondered, like an Iroquois swallowing his enemy's heart? A fool's question, but he had little to do but think and adjust while his handcrafted cockroach suit stayed true to its sole purpose- Survival.

Here, amid the ash of the freshly destroyed capital, hunkered over an ever-thinner corpse in the shadow of a blackened obelisk, Dean's suit was fueling up for potential famine/war/voyage. The legion of bugs sewn into the front of his suit jacket and pants clung tight to the supine body of the recently deceased world leader, forcing Dean into a sort of lover's embrace with a man he'd once feared and despised more than any other. And there were so many mouths to feed. A multitude of mandibles denuding bone, sucking skin off of the fingers that had presumably launched the first volley of nuclear arsenal earlier that day. Cockroach jaws chewing away at the kingly lips which had once taunted foreign dignitaries and charmed the breadbasket into submission with phrase like, "HOO BOY, and good morning to you!"

Despite the largely unappetizing sounds of insect consumption beneath him, Dean felt a low grumble in his own gut.

Will they let me eat? Do they have to get their fill before I can find something for myself?

He pushed down on the cold, dirty ground with his bare hands, again regretting his oversight during the design phase. His cockroach suit, completed with the addition of blast goggles, an oxygen tank and mask, a skull-topper crash helmet, and foil-lined tan work boots, was totally lacking the crucial support that a pair of nice woolly gloves could provide. Dean cursed himself and pictured surging blast rads sneaking into his heart via his exposed fingertips. He felt gamma ray death in the grit beneath his tightly-groomed nails.

You won't make it a day, Dean-o. You're probably dead anyway, right? This is your hell, Dean. You'll be here, right here, forever. You'll keep getting hungrier and hungrier while the radiation makes you puke your guts out and you'll feel every...last...second...

"Quiet!"

Dean shifted his legs against the tugging movements of the roaches on their prey and managed to get the toes of his boots planted firmly behind him. Now all he had to do was push up and away from the ground and hope he could break the masticating grip of the ravenous bugs sewn to his suit.

Jaw clenched tight/teeth squeaking with stress/thin muscles pumping at max output. Still, no give. The thick cloister of bugs that covered Dean's chest had dug deep into the corpse. Dean could tell from the stink of half-digested lobster bisque that the bugs had breached the President's belly. Worse, the smell only made him hungrier.

Cannibal. Beast.

"Shut it shut it shut it."

Dean readied himself again, flattening his hands, fingers wide, anxious to assert his own need to survive. He and the roaches had to learn to live *together*. If not in total symbiosis, then through equal shows of force- a delicate balance between Dean and his meticulously crafted attire.

They'd be a team, damn it.

Dean pushed, exhaling sharply, goggles fogging up with exertion, sweat pooling at his lower back.

Come on. We can take the body with us. I just need to get some food in my belly and you greedy little fuckers can return to your meal. Just let go...

Dean pushed and felt a shift. He realized that his full-force push-up had only served to elevate him *and* the body stuck to him, just before he realized his shaking right hand was edging into a patch of blood-spattered Twinkie filling.

Quick as a thought Dean's hand slid out from under his newly acquired girth, and he thudded back to the ground. The weight of the landing was enough to compress a stale breath through the lungs of the President's body.

And Dean would swear, to his last day, that the impact of his weight on the President's chest forced a final "HOO BOY!" from the dead man's half-eaten lips.

It was upon hearing this final and desperate State of the Union Address that Dean allowed exhaustion, un-sated hunger and shock to overcome him.

He rested deeply, cradled by a suit that slept in shifts and fed each of its members a royal feast.

This was the first day of the end of human existence.

CHAPTER TWO

Deep belly grumbles/acidic clenching. The light pain of an oncoming hunger headache made mostly unimportant by the stranger sensation of being in motion while in the process of waking.

Dean opened his eyes and rubbed accumulated ash from his blast goggles. The suit was moving, quickly, away from something. He couldn't shake the God-like sensation he got when the roaches carried him across the ground.

Overlord Dean. The Great One To Which We Cling. The Mighty Passenger.

Dean would have been more amused by his invented titles had he not noticed what the suit was fleeing from.

A thick bank of radioactive fog was rolling in behind them, moving in the new alien currents created by a global weather system blown topsy-turvy. It had a reddish tint at its edges that read cancer/mutation/organ-sloughing. Dean imagined each of the nuclear droplets must be nearly frozen inside the fog. The temperature was cold enough to sap the heat from his fingers and face. Thirty-five degrees and dropping, easy.

But the roaches could handle the sort of deep level radiation that filled the fog. Were they moving in order to try and preserve *him*? Ridiculous. So they must have exhausted their food source and were just moving towards the next step. A dark place to hide. A place to nestle in and lay eggs.

Should I just let them keep leading me along? The way they'd treated their last meal... if I don't take over now they'll never let me eat. They'll just keep moving and consuming. Hell, with it this dark outside, they won't even feel a need to hide. This is their world now. I've got to show them I deserve a place in it.

Carefully, so as not to crush any of the suit's communal members, he lowered his heels to the ground and then got his feet beneath him. Within seconds he was standing, lightheaded and waiting for the blood to catch up. The few Madagascar cockroaches he'd sown to his pants, amid all the Germans and Smokybrowns, jostled at the disturbance and let loose with high-pitched hissing.

"Come on you guys. Take it easy."

Dean ignored their susurrant complaint. He respected the suit, but now it was time for the suit to respect him. He felt the roaches' legs bicycling in the chill wind, seeking purchase, trying to stay on target with wherever they'd been headed.

Maybe I should let them take over. They got me through the overpressure of the blast. They got me through the radiation, so far. They found food instantly in a dead landscape. They're almost happy, it seems. Vibrating. Thriving. Do I have that same instinct?

I have to. No choice. Assess the situation.

Dean ignored the motions of his suit, took a few breaths from his oxygen mask to try and clear the chemical taste from his throat, and realized that he really should have hooked up a gas mask instead of his portable breather unit.

But he couldn't subject himself to that level of suffering. Dean had a severe aversion to having his entire face enclosed in rubber; an extraordinarily rough time with a dominatrix in Iceland had forced him to forever swear off such devices. He could barely even tolerate the tiny respirator.

Now, though, he couldn't help wonder about what this tainted air was already doing to his lungs. And he thanked the collective gods for whatever miracle had prevented the small oxygen tank on his back from exploding when the first bomb sent out its terrible heat-wave.

I can't fucking believe I'm still alive.

It was quickly becoming a mantra, but a useless one which distracted him from the act of actually living.

He shook away the thought, surveyed his surroundings.

Black rubble. Fire. Ash. Nothing remotely human or animal in any direction. Whatever bombs were employed- fission/fusion/gun-triggered/dirty bombs/H-bombs-

they did the job to the Nth degree. The view triggered Fear.

Last man standing, Dean-o. Look at the world you've inherited. All the nothing you could ever want. You're either stuck in this till the end of time or...

"Enough. No."

It was night-time. Maybe. Or the sky born debris had completely blocked out the sunlight. Regardless, still-flaming buildings were the remaining source of illumination. Dean figured anything that depended on photosynthesis was torched or starving at top speed in the blackout.

He couldn't assess his distance from the ground zero hypocenter but he guessed he was within fifty miles of an actual strike.

That's good, Dean. Pretend you know what's going on. Pretend you aren't a man coated in cockroaches and that you can make sense of the world. But remember that if the world makes sense, you're dead. Are you dead?

The black clouds above rolled over each other with super-natural momentum, colliding and setting off electrical storms that flashed wide but never struck the ground. There were few high points left to arc through.

Dean felt strangely honored as a witness. For all he knew, his were the last human eyes taking in a vision that royally outranked Mt. St. Helens or Pinatubo, and surely even went beyond what the first people to emerge from tunnel shelters at Nagasaki saw.

Don't drift. Think. Take action.

He ran down research, looking for a plan. He spoke the details aloud to his suit, and hoped that somehow they were paying attention. Teamwork would remain crucial.

"Okay, guys, here's what we're looking at. Assuming bombs haven't hit every single inch of the U.S., we might be able to clear the fallout ground track by heading out 30 miles past the central explosion. Rain and fog this close to the blast will jack the fallout up to intolerable levels. If we can find a safe place for now, and hole up for three to five weeks, then our travel options should open wide. The radiation will drop by then. Decontamination requires things we don't have-flowing water/backhoes/man-power. We're going to have to soak up some rads no matter what. Not that you guys are worried about that."

No response.

Were you expecting one, Dean-o? Are you that gone?

But Dean didn't expect any response. What he didn't tell his Fear, what he didn't want to say or even think, really, was that the loneliness was already making him feel sad in a way that was dangerous. Dean had never spent much time talking to people in the months just prior, but there'd been some interaction each day. The mailman. Fast food clerks. Small vestiges of human interaction. Faces that reacted. Voices that weren't his.

Dean continued to lay out the game plan.

"We can access emergency drinking water by filtering contaminated H20 through more than ten inches of dirt. But that dirt had better be from below the topsoil, which is toxic in and of itself right now. Access to a supply of potassium iodide could mitigate some of the effects of the radiation on me, not that you guys care about that."

He almost hoped for a response to that last part. Some sign from the roaches that they did indeed give a shit. But there was nothing.

"The top new symptoms on my watch list will be-nausea, vomiting, diarrhea, cataracts, and hair loss."

Of course, Dean's constant exposure to the cockroaches and their profusion of pathogens meant he was often riddled with the first three symptoms, but if they got much worse than usual....

And what about the suit itself? Dean decided to skip talking to them about these details.

He'd expected the roaches sewn to him- at least the females- to survive for two hundred days or so. As long as they had food and water they'd get by. Perhaps, within that time span, the Earth would find some new equilibrium in its atmosphere and Dean could survive without his living fabric.

What the hell kind of plan is that? Did I even believe, deep down, that this suit would have actually kept me alive? Maybe it was just something to do to keep the Fear away until I died. Like old folks playing bridge.

No. Somehow I knew this would work.

And I lived. I'm living. Now I have to keep things that way.

Dean wasn't sure how to feel about the ever-worsening nuclear winter growling around him. He dropped the roach edification because he was a bit confused on the whole issue.

Best I only speak to them in a confident tone, or not at all.

Back in the Seventies nuclear winter had been declared humankind's endgame by Sagan and the Soviets. But in the Eighties Thompson and Schneider played that off as Cold War propaganda. So the weather was either headed towards the colder and darker spectrum, or was hitting its worst and soon to wane. Better to error on the side of Sagan and hook up some Arctic gear in case the temperature went negative. Easier to strip that stuff off if it turned out that the long-lasting dinosaur-and-human-ending nuclear winter was just a big Russian bluff.

Food. Dean's main mission until his belly became quiet, and something he figured his pals would like to hear about.

"Listen up, guys. Assuming not *everything* was vaporized, there should be enough in warehouses and stocks to feed the entire U.S. for sixty to ninety days. The rest of the world will be worse off. Maybe thirty three days of food before they run out."

And will they be able to get to the U.S. at that point? Would they be coming for your food, Dean, those starving pirate citizens from small countries deemed Not Worth Bombing but still dependent on the global infrastructure for grub?

He shook off the doubts and tried to inject his voice with renewed poise.

"What about cows? There should be cows around. Somewhere. A non-irradiated bovine could supply us with food, milk or even an extra layer of leather protection."

Not, Dean realized, that he would know how the hell to go about starting that process. He'd never touched a cow that wasn't already sectioned and shrink-wrapped.

There was never enough time to learn the tools needed for surviving the apocalypse. Too many ways for a planet to go rotten.

Dean laid out a plan. And as plans go, it was on the lackluster end of things. The problem- he'd spent so much time thinking and chatting up the roaches that his hunger had crept full force into his brain.

Now all he and his belly could coherently put together was the following:
Get Food.

Dean asserted himself. He trekked on foot, away from the blast center and the noxious red fog bank that seemed to keep rolling inland. His fingers went numb. He wished he hadn't sewn the pockets shut on his jacket and pants, but had needed to in order to ensure every inch of his outfit was roach-ready.

His headache pushed inward, its own fog rolling through the crags of his cerebellum.

He cursed the extra weight of the oxygen tank on his back. He junked it.

He'd adapt to the new air like he'd adapted to the roaches. He'd press his limits. Couldn't stomach that mask anyway. It conjured up flashes of too-long ball-gagged seconds at the hands of his Icelandic ex-mistress. The smell of vomit trapped between skin and rubber. A pressure behind the eyes.

His mouth tasted of the burning tenements that flanked him, of dried cat shit

under a sun-lamp. He knew he was wasted if his thirst outgrew his hunger.

Water. Food. Now.

No one to talk to. Nothing to see but burning buildings, gutted cracking skeleton structures that might once have held sustenance.

Depression hit quick, ran through Dean's whole body like a low-grade fever that only served to slow him further as he slogged onward.

So. You lived. What now? Why keep going? Daddy Dean Sr.'s money doesn't matter any more, you little trust fund bitch. You don't really know how to survive. What were the odds your numb-nuts roach suit experiment would have worked? Why do you deserve to keep going when millions just died? You manage to survive a nuclear blast, and kill the President, the man you thought had a personal hard-on for your death. In one day you conquered both your greatest fears. Victory was yours, right? And now you'll die because you didn't think to pack a loaf of bread and some bottled water in that suit. You're letting a bunch of shit-sucking insects dictate the flow of your life.

Shall I go on?

Water. All Dean wanted was some water. He was cold, but if he stepped closer to the smoldering buildings his lips cracked and his thirst grew. It was a head-fucker.

You don't have any reasons to stay alive. The man who kept you going- the man who gave you something to fight against- is turning into plastered pellets of roach shit all around you. What are you going to do? Find a woman? Re-populate the Earth? You never really liked people before. Empathized maybe, but never really felt any communal love. Women wouldn't talk to you before, Dean. You think you'll be a big charmer now, Roach Man?

One foot in front of the other. Twelve slow, slogging miles. The edge of the city. What *was* the city. What would now be referred to euphemistically as a "site."

There- the empty field that bordered

the suburban intersection. A small tin shed. Not black. Not burning.

You'll be like them soon. The roaches. Just living. Thoughtless. You'll be sterilized. Your guts will blacken. The end of you. But they'll breed. They'll keep going. And you'll be dragged with them to the end, shoving carrion and rotten plants into your mouth if they'll let you.

Finally, a vision. Might be an oasis.

Dean stumbled forward and gently crouched before the shapes that leaned against the western side of the building. The nagging voice in his head fell away as he bent down beside the tiny metal shed and picked up the sealed jar of water and single pre-packed cup of chocolate pudding.

CHAPTER THREE

Pudding beats sex, big time. Of course, having had little sex, most of it running the gamut from earnest/mediocre to awkward/ugly, Dean found this comparison easy to make.

He tried to eat slow, to let the tiny chocolate heavens loll on his tongue before gulping the gel down, but it wasn't easy.

It's just so...goddamned...GOOD!

He nearly choked on a runny cocoa dollop when he tried to pull a breath through his nose while swallowing. But he held the cough. Kept the pudding in his mouth. Every little drop of it. He licked the last bits from his unwashed fingers and ushered untold levels of bacteria into his gut. He knew it. He just couldn't stop himself.

Then he had to rinse it down.

Get some water in my system. Get my head on straight.

The Fear seemed to be gone, chased away by sugar to the brain and Dean's new sense that he was truly alive and breathing.

Somehow I'm... here.

He unscrewed the lid of the Mason jar, which gave a satisfying pop as its seal ruptured. He already had three quarters of

the pudding-tinted water down his throat before he remembered.

Shit. They need water too.

Dean hesitated. Felt the water rushing through his body, his headache already distant. Those terrible voices quieted. He thought about how much better he'd feel with the rest of that water running down his gullet. Thought about how the suit had denied him even a hint of food when it had access.

No, that's not right. Maybe if I give them water now, they'll learn. They didn't survive this many years without being able to quickly adapt to new scenarios. Maybe I can establish trust.

As silly as the thought felt in his head, it also had a weird ring of truth. Lions and hyenas learned to share in their own brutal environment. Maybe even the bug's cutthroat existence didn't have to be all or nothing.

Dean realized that hand feeding was not an option. To find a way to apply water to each of those tiny mouths would be ridiculous even if he had the time/energy/patience. This was never a problem before. The suit had always fed solo, safely stored within a lock-box in Dean's rat-trap apartment. He wasn't sure how to hydrate them in the present since he didn't dare remove the outfit. They were absorbing who knows how much radiation right now, shielding Dean's fragile skin and organs from invisible rays.

How would they get the water if I wasn't here?

With that thought, Dean walked into the small hollow tin structure and gently poured the remaining water out on the concrete floor. Luckily it was poorly laid and the water puddled at a concavity in the center of the cement.

Dean eased himself onto the ground, lying prone.

"Drink up, little guys."

They took to it like pros, the most robust sections of the suit contorting to the puddle first and siphoning up their own tiny portions of liquid life.

Dean's right arm was drinking from the pool. He peered upward at the ramshackle lid on the structure and noticed that it was starting to lift up, as if a wind was catching beneath it. The hairs on his neck popped rigid.

The shack's lid raised and slapped back down twice, shaking the whole building. Then it simply disappeared. No tearing away at creaky hinges and rusty nails. The thing was just *gone*. Dean's skin ran wild over spasming muscles.

Another blast? A second volley? Who was left to launch this one? Was New Zealand armed? Did the Maoris have missiles, half-etched with tribal paint, striking down on U.S. soil?

No. There was no heat this time. No terrible pressure.

The roaches had stopped drinking. They began to crawl, frantically, out of the shed and into the open field. They did circles, unsure of where to go, Dean riding their agitated wave.

Dean had seen this type of motion in roaches before, prior to figuring out how to rig his apartment with UV lights. The bugs were steeped in negative phototropism, it was a key to their continued existence. Allowed them to function out of sight of their predators.

And what they were doing now was exactly what they used to do when he'd arrive home and switch on the overhead lamps.

But where was the light coming from? All Dean could see was the steady wavering light of fires succumbing to the increasing chill of nuclear winter.

Dean pushed off of the ground and stood up, halting the flight of the cockroaches against his better judgment. He had to figure out what they were running from. What if it was an airplane? Something else? Another survivor?

Dean craned his neck and pushed his blast goggles up into his hairline to make sure he could see as well as possible.

It was then that Dean's pupils began to fluctuate in size and his stomach threatened to surrender its precious pudding.

Because, as Dean looked skyward, he saw a great chariot of fire and aboard that chariot, the shape of something like a man.

Trumpets sounded, a terrible multitude of them, a great shrieking air raid that threatened to cave Dean's eardrums had he not shielded them with chocolate-streaked hands.

The chariot, and the shape it carried, were headed straight for him. Bearing down at top-speed. The figure in the chariot was definitely humanoid, with a head, two arms, and a torso, but the skin shimmered with silver and hints of the full spectrum. The thing had but one great eye at the center of its head.

Dean felt no heat from the chariot but noted that the roaches coating him were frantically trying to escape to anywhere, to be free of that brilliant light.

Then the chariot halted, perhaps fifty feet from where Dean stood with his mouth agape.

Then the chariot just disappeared. Gone. Poof. Like the top of the tin shed.

That was when Dean decided to turn and run. Anything that can make matter disappear- majestic though it may be- was dangerous.

"HALT!"

Dean halted. That *voice*- part insect/part trumpet/part his father's.

He turned to face the creature.

It hovered there for a moment, where its burning chariot had stood, and then floated slowly towards the ground before Dean.

Dean nearly lost his legs. His teeth squeaked against each other. Sweat popped along his forehead. But he stood strong- falling now meant the roaches would continue their frantic escape.

The shape landed just three feet from Dean, and though it didn't radiate heat, Dean suspected that the ground beneath the thing would have ignited had it not already been charred clean.

Thunder rolled in the purple/black clouds above them.

The thing stared through Dean with its one huge eye.

Dean surveyed the creature. It returned the same. From what Dean was seeing he could think of only a few words.

Ergot. Mycotoxin.

Whatever was in that pudding, it's driven me mad. Is there grain in pudding? Could it go bad all sealed up like that? Was the pudding full of gamma rays?

Have I finally snapped?

He remembered the rough times after his father had passed away in a brutal deer/Slurpee straw/airbag-related auto accident. Dean had chased a new life then, thought he could find it through drugs and rituals and chants and smoke ceremonies. Instead he'd only found Fear, the same cold gut feeling that had inspired him to build his cockroach suit.

But in all his travels, all those long nights of the soul, chasing demons on the dirt floor of some shaman's hut, he'd never seen anything this wondrous.

The creature stood at the same height as Dean, the exact same, although this felt like an illusion to induce comfort. It had the limbs of a human, although Dean could perceive no joints. It appeared, in fact, to be liquid, with a skin of entirely separated translucent scales floating over the shifting eddies and rivers and storming oceans of its surface. Each scale cycled through the spectrum, every color that Dean's eyes could perceive. He felt as if his brain was learning to interpret new shades with each second, colors without names. A painter, Dean thought, would be in tears right now.

At the center of the thing's chest a thin pink light shone through the scales as they whirled from torso to limb to face to back.

The great eye regarded Dean without any clear emotion. Human facial expressions would, Dean knew, appear petty across this surface.

The thing emitted a low, nearly subsonic noise and the roach suit seemed to dive into a comatose state. The feelers and legs stopped their incessant clawing at the air.

Eight long tendrils of light unfurled from the creature's back, straightening themselves out in direct opposition of each other, their points forming a perfect circle behind it.

Dean had been without God, without wonder, for years since Daddy Dean Sr. had passed, but he was about to weep when the creature spoke. It had no mouth. Rather, the voice, *that voice*, appeared directly in Dean's head asking:

"Where did everybody go?"

Dean was unsure how to respond, or if he even should. Was this a test? What revelations were about to occur?

"Where did everybody go?"

The creature wanted a response. But surely something this wondrous would already know the answer.

"No. I don't know what's going on. Something has changed. Today was supposed to be the time of my manifestation."

"Your manifestation? I'm sorry, I'm just so…"

"You don't have to use your mouth to communicate right now. I can speak inside of your mind, but cannot see through it as much as I need to. Please open it up to me. I'm going to emit a frequency, and once you do the same, we'll have an open line."

Dean had no idea how to "emit a frequency" but the creature began to vibrate and a low humming noise came from its center. It rattled through Dean's bones and he found himself humming until his throat was producing the same tone.

"There" the thing said, "We're in line with each other now. I can tell from your colors that you are confused. So much grey."

Dean had experienced the hucksterism of aura reading before. He began to think of ergotism and bad pudding again. Nothing was making sense.

"I can help you," said the thing.

"First, I'll share my wisdom, then I'll ask for yours. Does this sound okay?"

Dean nodded Yes inside of his head and kept humming.

A thin purple lid dropped over the creature's color-shifting eye and it began to tremble. A lower hum rattled through Dean's ribcage, and he feared his heart might collapse. The pressure continued to build and then there was a thumping sound and the creature's knowledge came pouring into Dean's mind. Dean struggled against the flow and tried to hum back questions when he was lost.

"The creatures of this planet have called me down to unite them. They have abandoned their earliest forms of energy transmittal, what some call religion. The disparate forms of energy they've since adapted and harnessed have fractured the colors that float around their sphere."

"Sphere. You mean Earth?"

"Yes, you could call it that. These new energy systems ran thick with dark currents and were quickly poisoned. Even once noble ideas collapsed under structure and hierarchy and the presence of the human identity. Possession. Power. Control. Life was bridled. The focus was shifted towards the individual bits of matter that made up this sphere."

"Bits of matter. You mean the living things."

"Sort of. But most of those things stayed pure. The parts of the sphere that called themselves 'I' were the source of the poison. But something inside their replicative code recognized the sickness and began to create me."

"So humankind's DNA recognized that religious systems were pulling the species further and further away from some lifeforce that drives our existence?"

"Well, sort of. How much do you know about super-strings? Whorls? Vortex derivatives?"

"Oh, god, nothing at all."

"Okay, that doesn't help. Is there someone else around here that I can talk to? This is much easier if I can speak in your mathematics. I mean, I know you people understand this. All I am is a gradually amassed energy force that your being created. I don't exist beyond the scope of the power that already runs through your body."

"My body?"

"Yes, your body. The infinite spaces in between the atoms that compose you, and the matter itself."

"I'm really lost now. Are you sure you're making sense? Maybe we're humming at different frequencies or something… hold up… no that hum sounds about right. Listen, I've had a really rough day and I think maybe I got a hold of some bad pudding and I'm hoping you can just amplify your powers and give me all this knowledge at once, in a way that encapsulates it so that I fully understand."

"That's not how it works. Unearned realization does nothing to shift the colors. There were supposed to be billions of you when I arrived. The collective unconscious would have ignited, all religions would have fallen. Time as you know it would have ceased its passage and all human matter would have lost its identity and returned to its source, where a new lifeform would have been created, one properly coded for continued existence and evolution."

"The Rapture?"

"We were going to allow you to call it that. Your belief gave that concept power. And all the energy systems, even those that did not espouse it, found the idea enchanting, so it would have been very effective. Those with the slightest vibration of the old energy at their core would have floated up and merged with me, bathed in my energy. Any others would have softly ceased to exist, floating away in a warm surge of white light."

"So what now?"

"Exactly. I'm lost. I exist, and am present, so something of the old belief must still exist. Something on this sphere, other than you, is alive and believes that I should be."

"So, are you going to wash me away in soft light now?"

"No. Everything has changed. I must adapt. Which means I need your help. Please tell me, *where did everybody go?*"

"They're dead. All of them, so far as I know. The President was still alive a while ago, but my suit ate him. It's really hard to explain."

"I have nowhere else to go. Neither do you. You may have noticed I've halted time."

Dean had wondered why the roaches were so still.

"Okay. I'll give it a shot."

Dean let loose what he knew through a series of modulated hums. He waxed as poetic as he could about the Cold War, the Iraq wars, Sierra Leone, the fall of Russia, nuclear proliferation, his country's tyrannical hillbilly puppet leader, Wal-Mart, peak oil, the internet, pandemics, suburban sprawl, the ultimate fallibility of the President's Twinkie suit (although Dean admired it in theory), colonialism, plastics, uranium, fast food, and global conflict. But when he got to the end of the story it felt like the whole thing was a colossal waste of time because the punchline, no matter what, was this:

…and then we killed ourselves.

Which, Dean felt, was a terribly down way to end his story.

The creature agreed. It shook its beautiful mono-orbital head and retracted the long whips of light that had extended from its back.

"So what" Dean asked, "are you going to do now?"

"I'm not sure. Without your species, I doubt I'll exist much longer. I'll probably just fade back into the ether. The worst part is, I think I know why I was finally called down, why the energy was strong enough to bring about a change."

"Will I understand it if you tell me?"

"Probably. When the bombs started dropping, I think people forgot all of the dark systems that might once have ruled over them. And I think, for a moment, they found their way back into the old energies."

"You mean they were all praying before they died?"

"Not exactly. Sort of. It's not really prayer. It's this state the mind goes into when it knows it's about to die. There's a lot of power there."

"But it was too late?"

"From what you've told me, yes."

"Shit…"

Time must have started to flow again. Dean felt the bite of hot tears in his eyes.

"Does that make you sad?"

"I guess. I get this feeling when I think about people dying. Mostly, I just feel bad that *they're* so sad about it happening. And that sadness is strong. I'm afraid of it. So what I do is ignore them and just focus on staying alive. Because as long as I'm here, as long as I'm living and fighting off death, then I feel alright…I don't ever want to feel as sad as those people."

"But death is natural. It's part of how your particular energy stays in existence."

"Yeah, people always say that, but lions eating people is natural, too, and I'd chew my way through a room full of boiled shit to avoid ever ending up in the jaws of some giant cat, even for a second."

"You still don't understand."

"No, you don't understand. I'm here and I'm *alive* and that's the one thing I've ever known for sure since I started breathing. I understand just fine."

The creature sighed, and began to turn.

"You're going then?"

"Of course. No reason to stay here. You're dead already."

"Oh, c'mon. Don't be like that. Maybe I can learn from you. Will you at least tell me your name?"

"Had I needed a name during my time here, you would have called me Yahmuhwesu."

"That's a terrible name."

"I thought so, too. It's not my fault you've got an ugly language. But it would have worked. The floating horseless fire chariot wasn't my idea either. But according to the vibrations from the hive mind, it would have been the most impressive way to appear."

"Probably. Can I ask where you're going?"

"Sure. I can still feel a pull here, so I'm going to look for other humans. If I find another, perhaps something will come of it. If not...."

"Well then, Yahmuhwesu, goodbye. Wish me luck."

"Despite knowing better, I will."

His feet lifted from the black floor of the Earth, floating just inches above it.

"And by the way, Dean, I thought you might find this amusing. For a man with such a singular obsession with death, you are *hugely* pregnant."

CHAPTER FOUR

Pudding doesn't taste as good on the way back up.

Dean noted this as he wiped a string of bilious chocolate drool from his lower lip and surveyed the sad pool of snack treat that sat beneath him in the charred soil.

Pregnant? What the hell is he talking about? You can't just tell a man he's pregnant and then disappear from existence like that. It's too much.

Dean couldn't fathom the idea of licking up the pudding off the ground, so he eased himself into a supine position and let the suit have at it. They deserved a little sugar. God knows what being frozen in time did to the poor things.

Dean's body rotated slowly over the ground as the roaches took turns feeding on the regurgitated confection.

I hope they hurry up. We need to keep moving inland.

It had to be a coincidence, but as Dean had the thought he felt the bugs beneath him pick up their pace, shuffling quicker through their arcane feeding system.

Weird. I must be in shock. First I'm talking to some sort of scaly god, now I'm imagining that roaches can read my mind.

Pregnant. What could that have meant?

Then Dean realized what Yahmuhwesu was talking about.

The roaches. They'd been attached to the suit for a few weeks now. Long enough for some of them to reproduce. Especially the German ones. They didn't even need sex to breed.

When choosing the different types of roaches for his suit, Dean had put them through a rigorous series of survival tests. The Smokybrowns and Orientals had done well, extraordinary paragons of genetics really. But the Blatella germanica was in a class of its own.

He'd cut the head off of a German and watched it navigate through tubes back to its preferred spot by the baseboard molding in the corner of his bathroom.

Then he took the headless roach and put it in an airtight jar so see how long it would keep going. Ten days later the decapitated juggernaut was not only in motion, but had sprouted an egg case from its abdomen.

A week later there were thirty nymphs in the jar. They looked healthy. And full, since they'd eaten their headless mother.

Right then Dean had made the choice. His suit was going to be seventy percent German. It upped his odds. You just couldn't kill the damn things.

Dean slid his goggles down and cleared them of deposited ash. He tilted his head forward. He lifted his right arm off of the ground, anxious to see if any of his roaches were reproducing.

Yahmuhwesu was right. Dean wasn't just pregnant, he was completely covered in life. An egg case for almost every German. Even the ones he could have sworn were male a week ago.

Shit. That's a lot of extra mouths to feed.

Dean gave himself a week, maybe two before they hatched.

And what if they think of you as their headless mother, Dean-o?

Shit.

He should have thought of this. New sweat surfaced in a sheen across his body. He was back to the same old agenda, the Find Food and Water routine, but now it was doubly important. He had babies to feed. Thousands of tiny new bellies to fill, along with his now empty gut.

I can't just sit here. The clock is ticking. I've got to get moving. And NOW!

With that thought, quick and urgent as it came, the suit abandoned the remains of its pudding and began to crawl west, towards the heartland. Dean couldn't help but acknowledge this second instance of collusion between his desires and the actions of the roaches surrounding him.

And while this fact made him strangely proud, something at the back of his mind recoiled. Because communication was a two way road, and roaches must certainly have desires of their own.

CHAPTER FIVE

Time played tricks. Could be decompressing. Could be redacting. Dean had no watch, and day and night were old memories. Kid stuff. The new grown up reality was this: darkness/food/water/fire. Stay moving.

Primal shit.

Days passed. At least, what *felt* like days. Dean tried to calculate mileage, to figure a way to gauge time by distance traveled.

It was a waste. His internal atlas was non-existent. His last score on a geography test- Mrs. Beeman's class, 5th grade- was a D minus.

Even if the road signs weren't blazed or shattered, Dean would barely have known where he was. Sense of place wasn't part of his make-up. But he felt that the best plan was to keep moving inland. Pick a major road and stick with it. Keep walking.

The upside being that sleep didn't halt his progress. When he was on the ground- snoring, twitching through his REM state- the bugs kept moving. They were relentless in their drive.

Dean was awakened once, by the sensation of his crash helmet sliding against a surface with more yield than the roadway he was used to being dragged along while resting. The roaches had veered off into a field- they'd hit farm territory just hours before- and found the crispy remains of what might have been a baby goat. Dean managed to tear off a chunk of it and sequester it to the wide top of his left boot. He'd need to wash it off before he could eat it. Couldn't just dive in like his insectile friends. If he got desperate he guessed he could just peel away most of the outside of the meat and maw down its center. Maybe the fallout didn't get in that deep.

The temperature seemed to have leveled out around a chilly forty-or-so degrees. It pulled the moisture from Dean's face and hands and left his skin feeling tight and chapped. He guessed his face was stuck in a sort of permanent grimace. A charming look, he was certain.

Thirst was always nagging him. He made do with the occasional thin puddle of water that either hadn't been vaporized or had resettled, and once he found a decent batch, maybe a gallon, still tucked inside a fractured chunk of irrigation pipe. With nothing to contain it in he was forced to gulp down what he could and make sure the roaches took the rest.

I could always eat some of the bugs

if I got too hungry. I'm sure there's some water in their bodies, and they'd understand. They'd be eating each other right now if my sewing job didn't have them all in assigned seating.

But the thought felt wrong. Mutinous. They were working together now, or at least it seemed like it. He'd stopped short of giving them each names, but he felt an attachment to the bugs. They understood him. They shared his motto: Do Not Die.

No. They'd survive this together.

But why?

Dean was giving up whatever marginal hope he'd had of finding either a rich food source, other living beings, or both. When he traveled through cities, or whatever was left of them, he was able to acquire a few things. A sturdy hiking backpack from the remaining third of a ravaged outdoor store. A thick plastic bottle for water. Remnants of cloth and thin tinder wood (usually partially burnt) to make torches for lighting the way as the un-natural winter worsened. He'd edged around a still-flaming gas-tank crater and found a small fridge with three diet sodas inside. It was hideous shit but Dean knew he couldn't afford to be picky right now. He used one of the diet sodas to clean the radiation from his stashed chunk of toasty goat meat. If the cola could remove the rust from airplane parts, it ought to be able to deal with a little nuclear waste.

It was *not* fine dining, nowhere near pudding-good, but Dean wolfed it down and kept moving. He couldn't wear the backpack for fear of disturbing his suit, so he tied it to his waist with a length of twine and let it drag behind him, whether walking on foot or traveling by roach. The pack was pretty sturdy and helped him keep his motley assortment of goods in one place. And if it started to fall apart Dean figured he could use the sewing skills he'd learned constructing his outfit to fix it.

Finally- at the borders of a suburb Dean had named Humvington for its sheer numbers of blazed-out SUV frames- he made

a valuable find. There, inside a half-melted tackle-box, Dean found a pair of thick gloves with leather across the palms and the finger tips cut off. It was a blessing, and for a few hours Dean felt a renewed sense of vigor. He was semi-equipped, alive, and heading places.

But the further he went the more he realized his efforts might be pointless no matter which direction he hiked. As insane as it seemed, no one else was alive.

The global imaging satellites and tiny computer chips guiding the missiles that hit America had done a *flawless* job. Every time Dean reached some new urban center he was confronted by fresh blast craters. Instead of clearing the radioactivity he'd tried to leave behind, he was charging into new ellipses of damage, places that would take much more than weeks to be livable again. And whenever Dean dared venture into buildings or homes in search of life he was greeted by the same thing:

Death. Unrestrained and absolute.

Exposed finger-bones pointing accusations at the sky.

Baby replicas composed of ash, mouths still open in a cry.

The bodies of a man and his dog fused together, skin and fur melded. Nobody wanted to die alone.

WWIII was less a war than it was a singular event. A final reckoning for a race sick of waiting for the next pandemic to clean things up. And since Dean never saw any sign of invasion, or even recon, he guessed that most of the other countries were now sitting in the same smoking squalor.

Each new region was the same. Crucial buildings, city centers, food stores- all dusted. He had much better chances of productive forage at the outskirts of cities, and then it was back into the blackness and the road to the next noxious burg.

It was during this seemingly timeless stretch of travel that Dean started to find *them*. The other ones like Dean.

He understood the zeitgeist, and

how the media had allowed the entire planet to experience the same set of stimuli. So Dean shouldn't have been so surprised that others would have tried to protect themselves like he had.

But their ideas- their suits- were so bad. Crackpot, really. At least Dean's knowledge of entomology, passed down from his Ivy League father, had given him some viable theory to work on. And he had to assume that the President's Twinkie suit was based on top-level Pentagon science that didn't quite hit the right calculations. But these poor folks, they'd just been guessing.

Styrofoam man had surrounded himself with customized chunks of beverage coolers. Most of the enterprise had melted right into the guy's skin. Hadn't he ever tried to cook some sweet-and-sour soup leftovers in the microwave?

The cinder block guy had a better idea, but it appeared that the pneumatics that were supposed to give him mobility had burned out in the first wave of fire. Dean had crawled up on the suit to check and confirmed that the man had died of heat exposure and dehydration. Without being able to move he'd spent his last days trapped inside a concrete wall, right there in the middle of the street.

The lady Dean found who was wearing two leather aprons and steel-toed work boots on each of her four appendages? He couldn't even force that to make a lick of sense. But she appeared to have died from exposure. She was missing great swaths of her hair and was face down in a pool of black and red that was probably a portion of her lungs.

This was the response of the populace. Madness in the face of madness.

Dean found one man who was actually breathing, although it didn't look like that'd be going on much longer. His body was laid out in a splayed X in the yard of a smoldering duplex, next to the melted pink remains of a lawn flamingo coated in grey ash. The man's eyes had gone milky white

with cataracts and the smell on the body was bad meat incarnate. But the chest was rising and falling ever so faintly.

Could be my eyes fooling me. A flashback from that bad pudding.

Dean squatted in closer to the man's body and noticed how loose and wrinkled his face was. He'd never seen skin so rumpled, like one of those fancy dogs they put in motivational posters at work.

Dean gently pressed the middle and forefinger of his left hand against the man's neck to check for a pulse.

It was this motion that caused the man's face to slide off of his head.

Not only that, the man changed colors. His first wrinkled face was stark white. His new face was light brown. The same cataract-coated eyes peered out at the heavy sky.

As if from the shock of losing his first face, he stopped breathing.

God damn it! I finally find someone and now they're gone.

Dean couldn't take it. Everyone he'd met since the bomb dropped was either dead or potentially imaginary.

Maybe it's not too late.

Unsure of what exactly he was doing, Dean attempted to perform CPR. But his hands kept slipping from side to side and it was hard to center over the man's chest. This man's surface was so *loose....*

He must be wearing someone else's entire skin!

Dean ripped open the man's shirt. Dean freaked. Stitches up the center of the abdomen and chest. Industrial floss or fishing line, Dean couldn't tell. Skin dry and puckered at the puncture points. Horror-show shit.

Dean tugged at the sutures/got a finger hold/got them to slip loose. He laid back dead white skin and uncovered brown slicked with blood and Vaseline. Tried to swipe the goop off the guy's chest. Succeeded. Started compressions without the slippage.

Dean wished he had paddles. Wished he could just yell "Clear" and shock this guy back into the world of the living.

The compressions weren't doing much. Dean moved north and started blowing breath into the man's mouth, fighting back the nausea induced by the smell of lung corruption.

A hand at Dean's forehead, pushing up and away. A moan. He was trying to speak.

"…the fuck are you doing, man? Get up off me!"

"What? Okay, just stay calm."

"Tell me to stay calm. I'm just lying here in my yard and you think you can molest my ass. That's fucked up, man. Fucked up. For real."

"I wasn't molesting you. You had stopped breathing. I was doing CPR."

"Seriously?"

"Yeah."

"Well, alright then. I've been confused. Didn't mean to snap at you, man. I'm not feeling right. Haven't been for a couple of days. Name's Wendell."

Wendell strained to raise his left hand, still coated in dead pale skin. Dean took the hand, felt slippage.

"I'm Dean. Wendell, I think you might be very sick."

"No shit, genius. You a doctor? Part of a rescue team?"

"No. I'm just a guy."

"Just a guy, huh? Maybe you can tell me what's going on. I mean, I know the bombs dropped, I was ready for that, with my mojo and all… but do you know if the whole U.S. got hit? Is there someplace we could get to better than this joint?"

"I don't know much, Wendell. I know I've been traveling for a couple of days and haven't seen anything but destruction. I was starting to lose hope, but now I've found you and I guess that's a good sign. Maybe there are more people like us who survived the first wave."

"What about…hey… what about…

do you know if they got our president? Is there somebody out there with rescue plans, working on rebuilding."

Dean realized the real answer to this question might just shock Wendell right back into the grave so he opted for a simple out.

"The president's gone. There are no plans that I know of."

"Wish you had better news, but I can't say I'm going to miss that stupid cracker motherfucker. Hell, I figure he's a big part of why I'm laid out here right now."

"Yeah…hey, you called him a 'cracker.' Do you hate white people? Did you think the 'white devil' would live through the bombing? Is that why you're wearing this guy's skin?"

"What skin? You mean my Mojo? Oh, no, that's got nothin' to do with color. I've had plenty of white friends and now they're just as dead as anybody. No, my Mojo is all about good luck. See, my friend Peter, he lives…pardon, used to live… three blocks down from my house and I swear he was the luckiest motherfucker I ever met. Never saw a lotto ticket he didn't recoup on. Lucked into not one but *two* boats at the expo raffle last year. The odds were always in his favor."

"So you skinned him?"

"Patience, man. Don't jump ahead. You got somewhere to be?"

"Not really, I guess."

"What about food or drink? You got somethin' for me? Might as well ask since you busted in and interrupted the flow of my story."

"I've got a couple of packets of fruit snacks and two diet sodas."

"Diet soda? Goddamn! That gunk is terrible for you. Full of aspartame. You know the guys that work with that stuff have to wear biohazard suits?"

"I hadn't heard that, Wendell. Do you want one? It's all I've got."

"Normally I wouldn't, but I'm pretty parched. I'd probably still take you up on it if all you had to offer was a bucket of cat piss."

Dean cracked a can. That pop and hiss of released carbonation was comforting somehow. Familiar. An old sound from what now felt like a whole different age.

He handed the can to Wendell.

"Thanks, man." As Wendell was bringing it towards his lips, the soda slipped from his hand and hit the ground rolling. Dean snagged it and tipped it back upright, trying to save whatever he could.

"See, Dean, my goddamn Mojo ain't worth a barbecued shit. It's too lose. I thought Peter and I were about the same size, but I guess he wore slimming clothes. Maybe his good luck always made him look skinnier than he really was. Who knows?"

Dean helped Wendell tip the soda can to his lips. He took a deep slug and winced.

"Hurts going down. Can't be good."

Dean didn't offer any solace. He was amazed this guy was talking at all.

"Okay, back to my story. The deal is, Peter's got more luck than sense. And his one big mistake, I guess, was thinking he'd be lucky enough to get away with fucking my wife, Gladys. But maybe something in his good fortune shifted. I don't know. And this is about a week and a half back, when the news got all crazy and the President disappeared and nobody would answer any questions for nobody about what was going on. You remember that feeling in the air? Like we were all dead for sure? Like it was just a matter of time?"

Dean nodded.

"Well, I think that feeling made some people do the things they always wanted to. So Peter, who'd always had an eye for my wife- I mean, I'd seen him looking at her at church no less- he decided it was his time to take a poke at her. And I caught 'em, right in the middle of their rutting, under the laundry line in the back yard. They were biting each other, and…um… smacking each other. Pulling hair and shit. You could tell this was

something they'd wanted in about forever. I had a little flip-out gator knife on my belt. And, uh, I guess I jumped right into the same pile of crazy they'd been rolling around in. The rest I'm sure you can figure."

Another nod from Dean.

"But the thing I should have thought of was that things had *changed*. We'd entered our end-times. The rules were different. They had to be. Otherwise Peter's lucky streak would have continued and I never would have known any better. So I should have figured that all that good luck was gone, and never tried to wear it over me. I wished this thing…" Wendell pinched at the dead face that lay next to him, a thick fold of it in his fingers, "would protect me, but it didn't. It wasn't really the Mojo I'd hoped for. It was just some dead asshole's skin. And now… now I'm dyin' in it."

There were tears in Wendell's cloudy blind eyes. Dean wanted to give him a hug, but the roaches hadn't eaten in a while, and the last time he'd wrapped his arms around someone they'd been eaten whole. Call it a non-option.

The best Dean could do was take off his gloves and hold the man's hand. But not for long. This man would die soon, and Dean didn't want to be around for that.

So, as Wendell's breath slowed and he seemed to float into some layer of sleep, Dean released the man's hand. Then he let the roaches hit the ground and begin their steady westward crawl, leaving all forms of bad mojo behind them.

CHAPTER SIX

Three more days- maybe four- passed. Dean and his suit made good time. In another, less nuclear world this whole ambulatory clothing thing might have sold great to people who wanted to conserve fuel. The ASPCA and PETA would have complained, sure. That was what they did. But the rest of the world didn't give a damn about insects. Get them past their initial revulsion, make it look pretty and clean, and you've got a best-seller.

During his travel Dean acquired two loaves of rye bread, one jar pureed vegetable baby food, one scarf with the words "Winter Fun" embroidered on it, three gallons unfiltered water in various containers, and one overall sense of crushing ennui.

To keep busy and clear his mind he handled a lot of the footwork himself and periodically checked his suit for birth-signs. So far the host of egg cases adorning him remained in gestation, but they looked darker. Soon the nymphs would be here, demanding sustenance.

He kept the "Winter Fun" scarf wrapped- very lightly- around his face and crossed his fingers. He had to keep breathing but guessed that the air quality around him would petrify even coal miners.

So far, though, there were no signs of the cellular corruption that had taken Boot Lady and Wendell to their graves.

A day ago he'd woken from his sleep to the sound of flowing water. He'd popped up quickly enough to run down to the river's edge and fill the containers he'd amassed in his backpack.

Could have been the Ohio River. Could have been the Mississippi. He cursed his D minus geography skills and wished he knew. But since then he'd been heading south, probably a few hundred yards from the river at any time. It seemed crazy to abandon a water source, but it also seemed crazy to stay still when they were certainly in a dead zone. Besides, if he made it to the gulf perhaps he could find a boat and head south to a less ravaged continent. Who would bomb Peru? Somebody who hated llamas?

The clouds overhead remained black as ever, but also seemed to emit a low luminescence that coated Dean's path like filthy moonlight. Maybe his sight was just adjusting.

Any longer in the dark like this and I'll be pure white with pink eyes, finding my *way with echolocation. Interplanetary spelunkers will find me and call me a wondrously adaptive creature. Look at how he works in concert with the roaches that surround him!*

That was the other thing bothering Dean. When he wasn't fighting off a sense of weary resignation and trying to chase away the self-destructive worries that paralyzed him, he found himself experimenting with the seemingly stronger link between his desires and the actions of the suit.

He could make patches of the outfit skitter faster than others. He executed circles and vertical rolls. He could choose which group of clustered mouths would drink from his carefully poured puddles of water. Most disturbing, he found that if he concentrated hard enough he could get them to twirl their feelers in clockwise or counter-clockwise directions. The sensation that ran through his mind when this occurred wasn't anything he recognized. It was a thin, high-pitched buzzing and he could swear he felt it in his bones and at the spot where skull and spine met. It made his skin itch a bit, but it wasn't totally unpleasant. In fact, the sensation was seductively mind-clearing. No more doubt. No more concerns over the *meaning* of being alive.

It was the *feeling* of being alive, and nothing else. Existence without thought.

Dean tried not to engage in this sort of thing too often, but there was little else to do, especially when he took feeding breaks. No TV's to watch. No magazines to flip through while noshing down veggie mush on rye.

It was after one of these enchanting culinary pit stops that Dean noticed the tiny moving lights in the distance.

They were slight at best, damn near microscopic from this far away, moving across his path in the direction of the river. Each of them was uniform distance from the other and moving at a quick pace.

Dean closed the distance, slowed

slightly by the water-heavy bag he was towing.

The closer he got, the more familiar the motions of the lights seemed. Like something from one of Daddy Dean Sr.'s bug documentaries. They had to be glowing insects of some sort. No other animals moved that low or that orderly.

When Dean was within inches of the line of shuffling light he crouched down and removed his goggles to try and see more clearly.

What the hell is this?

As hard as Dean focused his eyes, all he could see were tiny sections of leaves, each with a faint sort of phosphorescence.

Then he felt the buzzing at the tip of his spine. He honed in on it, cultivated the sensation until he picked up its tone.

Fear. He could feel the roaches' legs twitching a hundred yard dash through the cold, damp air.

A glow to his left. Before he could turn his head- a voice. Female.

"Don't move. The bugs are panicked because you are surrounded. There are thousands of soldiers on every side you."

"Soldiers? Where?"

"Look down."

Dean tilted his head towards the ground. There, aided by the glow coming from the woman, he could see them. Ants. Big ones, thick enough to make a popping noise if stepped upon. An armada of them, crawling over each other, maintaining a tight circle around the space he was crouched in.

"If you reach out to touch the foragers you will be swarmed by soldiers. This is what they do. This is *all* they do. I can try to stop them but their instinct will likely rule out whatever control I have."

Dean believed her. There was an earnest and concerned tone to her voice that reminded him of the time his father warned him not to get too close to his prize bombardier beetle. *He'll blind you without a thought, Dean.* That's what his father had said.

"So what do I do now?"

"Stand up. Slowly. Then take a few very wide steps back from the forager's trail. They'll no longer perceive you as a threat."

Dean did as he was told. His knees felt loose and shaky with each step he took, but soon he was ten feet from the steadily marching troop of leaf-bearing ants and their protectors.

"Good. That was good. You got too close."

She sounded exasperated. How much danger had he been in? What the hell was going on?

Dean turned to face the woman.

Holy shit...now the ants are swarming her...they're everywhere...

"What can I do? How should I help you?"

Dean ran over to his back pack and fumbled for the zipper.

I'll get my water and douse her with it. I'll wash those little fuckers away.

"What are you doing?" she asked. Her voice was now perfectly calm. Post-sex mellow. Almost amused.

"I can get them off of you. Hold on just a second..." his hands were shaking but he had a grip on the zipper now. "I've got something that can save you."

He felt her glow coming towards him. Caught graceful strides from his periphery.

"My dear man, I'm not looking for a savior." The voice was confident, with a hint of laughter behind it.

Dean let go of the zipper and looked up at her. She had a thin hand outstretched in his direction. It was free of ants but had a coat of... something... over it. The rest of her was covered in ants of various shapes and sizes, hundreds of thousands of them shuttling around, touching each others antennae, carrying bits of shining wet plant matter.

She was, aside from the ants, entirely nude.

"I'm Mave," she said. "Now you.

Who exactly the hell are you? And where did you get that fabulous suit?"

CHAPTER SEVEN

She had a place of her own, a tattered tarp lean-to backed by a portion of white picket fence. Where she rested, it used to be the backyard garden of some family that no longer existed.

She said she'd always wanted a white picket fence. Corny, but true.

Dean had shaken off his initial shock and introduced himself back at the roadway. He'd told her a very abridged version of his own story-omitting the appearance of Yahmuhwesu, who he still believed might have been a hallucination- as they walked back to her current digs. She had questions along the way.

"Twinkies?" and

"Goat marinated in diet soda! That tasted hideous, right?" and

"The guy really thought Styrofoam would work?" and

"Did you check Wendell to see if he wasn't wearing a couple more layers of skin? Maybe there was a Mexican or Asian guy deeper down?" and

"Do you know how close you just came to being killed?"

And she smiled every time she questioned him.

How can she be so happy at a time like this? Isn't she afraid the ants will get inside her mouth.

Dean knew she wasn't. Whatever rudimentary mental link he'd founded between himself and the roaches, she blew that out of the water. The ants- she called them Acromyrmex or leafcutters as if the names were interchangeable- never crossed her lips. They never scuttled into her eyes. They did crawl through her shoulder length black hair, but didn't mat it with the bright fungus they were growing on her skin. And although he tried not to look, they didn't appear to hover around the folds of her vagina.

She walked carefully and avoided resting her limbs against her body. Didn't want to crush any of the Acromyrmex. Couldn't stand the lemony smell they made when they died.

Here, at her new garden, the ground burst upward with miniature rolling hills.

"The rest of the colony. They can produce a certain amount of fungus on my skin- my perspiration actually seems to speed its growth, which was unexpected- but it really requires a more total darkness to produce the gongylidia. That's the key part of their harvest. The stuff they feed to the babies."

At the mention of the word "babies" Dean felt a sudden need to inspect his suit. So far, so stagnant. The tiny eggs remained whole. Thank goodness.

"Oh, that's right." Mave smiled, watching him. "You're the pregnant one! Yahmuhwesu told me about you."

"Pardon me?"

"Yahmuhwesu. The collective unconsciousness guy. Fiery chariot and all that... Oh, come on. Don't make that face. I know you know exactly who I'm talking about. He met you before he appeared in front of Terry and I. But when he spoke with us he figured you'd die before you ever had a chance to give birth."

Dean tasted vomit and goat in his mouth. This was too much all at once. His shock must have shown on his face because Mave had furrowed her brow.

"Shit. It's a bitch to take in this sort of info, isn't it? And here I am just dumping it all over you... sorry. Listen, when he met you he taught you how to do that humming trick, right? The tonal language. If you can lock into my tone I think we might be able to communicate better. Something about the nature of speaking like that that cuts out a lot of the filters."

She didn't wait for him to respond. She simply straightened her spine, closed her eyes, and started humming.

The sound was lullaby-beautiful. Dean couldn't help but move closer to it.

He started to hum in return, closing his eyes and listening as hard as he could, trying to find the exact range in which she was vibrating.

He hit it. They locked in. Their eyes popped open. He took in grey pupils with flecks of gold in them. Her eyes were gorgeous. He couldn't look away.

Is she even human?

"Of course I'm human."

"Oh, yeah. You're in my thoughts now." He blushed, heat blooming across his face.

"And you're in my thoughts, too. And since we don't have too much time, we need to start figuring things out."

"Wait. Why don't we have time?"

"I'll get to that. Soon. But for now I just need to know that we're thinking in line with each other so we can make the right plan."

Thunder cracked in the dust-heap clouds above.

"Mave, have you noticed that this process seems to stir up the clouds?"

"Uh-huh. I wonder if lightning will strike us if we stay like this for too long... Doesn't matter. Stay with me here. I've got a couple of things to tell you.

"First- Yahmuhwesu is real, or at least, he's as real as anything else on this planet. He- at least I think it's a he- visited you. He visited Terry and I. And I'd imagine that if anyone else managed to live through this ridiculous nuclear fuck-up, Yahmuhwesu's visited them too. And I think, as far as gods go, that Yahmuhwesu is a bit on the crazy side. Or at least, he's *confused*. So he's playing with us. I'm sure you've noticed some changes in yourself recently."

"Yeah, I have. The roaches have been listening to me. To my thoughts. Doing what I want. And I think I'm listening to them a smidgen too. There's this buzzing sound at the back of my head that I used to create by thinking at them, trying to communicate. But now it's just... there. It's very quiet. And it makes me itch."

"And, Dean, you're not dead. *You're not dead.* Didn't you wonder why Wendell's lungs had ruptured but you're able to traipse around drinking atomic water and sleeping in ash? I think you, and me, and Terry, we'd all be goners right now if we hadn't been visited. Sure, that suit may have helped you survive the blast by some ridiculous miracle, but it can't be *only* that."

"You think Yahmuhwesu did something to us?"

"Look at me, Dean. I wasn't born the world's biggest walking anthill. This is something fresh, something I woke to just as Yahmuhwesu disappeared. He definitely made this happen. You may have grown up with comic books, Dean, but in real life you've got to know that gamma rays toast people. They vomit until they taste their guts. It's terrible. So if the nuclear explosion didn't do this, I can guarantee our vanishing deity did. There are no other feasible answers. It's an Occam's Razor scenario... Do you know what I used to do, Dean?"

"Ballet?" It wasn't an intentional compliment. Dean had never been that smooth. But he had noticed how strong and sleek her legs looked. Spring-loaded.

"No, not ballet. I was never that coordinated. I was an entomologist, just like your father. Just like Terry. And I'd devoted my life to these ants. Acromyrmex. The leafcutters. They're truly beautiful creatures, easily the pinnacle of social and technological expression in ants. That's what I said in my papers when I was working out of U of M. Cultivated my own nest mounds using a queen and fungi shipped up from the Guanacaste province of Coast Rica.

"I watched that queen every day and saw how hard she worked to grow a culture. Tending to the fungus and her eggs. Aerating soil. Creating a whole new world on her own. It was the most incredible thing I'd ever seen, and I felt something then, something far beyond myself. It faded, but when I saw Yahmuhwesu appear it came back again, and fierce. And whatever that feeling was, he filled me up with it, to the brim. Everything seemed clearer, the interconnectedness of all life, matter, energy, everything. He told me I had a new purpose here, among my 'subjects.' That was the word he used. And when I woke up from whatever fugue I was in, I had become the new queen.

"I could feel them in my brain. Calling to me. Like that buzz you describe. Only it didn't make me itch. It made me... wet. I could feel waves rolling through my belly. I got gooseflesh. My breath ran short. Panting. I buckled twice on the way to the lab and the nest. Because I could hear them. They were still alive. The university's lab was underground and somehow intact. And they needed me. I didn't even think of how I'd abandoned Terry back at the shelter."

"Wait, who is this Terry guy? You were with him when Yahmuhwesu appeared to you?"

"Yeah, but I need to finish telling you about these ants. I think it's important, somehow, that you understand them. Because they are part of me now. They have been ever since I managed to crawl my way through the rubble and get access to the nest mound."

She related the rest of it then, how she'd dug down through the soil and found the existing mother queen and swallowed her whole. How the future mother queens-fledgling tribe-bearers who were meant to eventually carry eggs and fungal spores outward to start new nests- had all crawled to her then, running up her legs, crawling inside of her and resting against the walls of her uterus, triggering orgasms that left her shaking for hours. And after that the rest of the tribe had filed out- tiny food workers/minimas/foragers/soldiers- each finding their place on her body and immediately starting to do their jobs however they could.

"I'm still me. Still Mave," she said,

"but now I'm also this colony. My mind contains their hive mind.

"What I don't understand, yet, is what this new fungus is, or why it glows, or why it grows so goddamned fast. Even a hint of it on the jaw of a forager will instantly attach itself to a cutting. That's why the fragments you saw crossing the road were already bright.

"This fungus didn't originate with any of the queens inside; they came to me with nothing other than their instinct. So... I think the new fungus is coming from *me*. But I don't know how, so I've been holed up here to try and study it. Some of the ponds and riverbanks near here have vital plant life right at the edge of the water. We need it to really make the colony grow."

"We?"

"Yes, I told you that I'm their queen. I guess I'm using the royal we. And we're the ones who need your help."

He looked at her then, this strange new woman and her legion of tiny ants and her grey/gold eyes. The leafcutters were everywhere on her now, most holding little glowing slivers of plant matter that swayed in the winds and gave her an appearance of profound life, of a majesty that made him want to serve her despite the buzz at the base of his head that was screaming "Run- we can survive best alone."

"What am I supposed to do?"

"That what I'm not quite sure of. I know that we can't stay here much longer, though I'd like to."

"Picket fence?"

"Yeah. That and the nest. But the plant life here was scarce to begin with, and we've already processed most of what remains in the area. Plus, I think Terry might find us."

"Why is that bad?"

"Terry was an entomologist too, before the bombs hit and made everyone's job titles obsolete. That's how I knew him. We both worked out of the university. We were lovers in a purely pragmatic way. We understood the need. The pheromones.

"He was renting an old house in the suburbs south of campus. It was Cold War equipped- bomb shelter in the back yard. We screwed down there for kicks. He wore a gas mask. We passed out holding each other in an army cot and didn't wake up until we felt the concussion of the first bomb exploding. Total dumb luck that we lived.

"Then, when we crawled out a few days later, there was a glowing god waiting for us. Terry could barely handle the shock of all of it. He was crying one second, furious the next. Unstable. Then Yahmuhwesu hummed his way into our heads and changed us. I haven't seen Terry since.

"That's why I'm afraid. Because if Yahmuhwesu affected Terry the same way he did with us, then right now Terry is hunting down a hive of his own."

"More leafcutters?"

"I wish. Terry's bug of choice was the *Nomamyrmex*, Dean. Army ants."

"That's bad?"

"It's terrible. If he manages to find a hive in nature there will be millions of them. And if his mind is as fragile as I believe it to be then Terry will become an instrument of the hive instead of the other way around."

"You don't think he could control them?"

"I don't think he'd even try. He was always so clinical. His brain wasn't equipped for this sort of metaphysical shift. I grew up with hippies in a commune and started meditating with my imaginary friends when I was four years old. I've always desired a more mystical reality, despite my chosen field of work.

"And you, your single-minded drive to stay alive appears to usurp any need for reality.

"But Terry, his brain probably split in two the moment that first bomb dropped and he realized he wasn't ever going to have a cup of Starbucks coffee again."

Dean wanted to laugh, for a moment, but he saw how serious the look in Mave's

eyes was. This was dire. The leafcutter ants that covered her were frantic, almost disorganized in their movements.

"Dean, if Terry does unearth a Nomamyrmex colony they'll be *starving*."

"So they'll eat Terry?"

"If we're lucky. But, assuming he's still conscious by then, they'll know what he knows. That there is a veritable smorgasbord waiting for them in the basement of the U of M lab. And when they don't find them there they'll be able to follow our scent trail."

"They eat leafcutters?"

"For centuries the Acromyrmex has been the favorite food of the army ant. Particularly the queens. They'll sacrifice thousands of their fighters in battle to get a good chance at a fat, juicy mother ant. They'll drag her, still living, all the way back to their tunnels, and then slowly pull the eggs from her body and eat them until she collapses and dies. She is consumed last. A victory feast."

Dean saw Mave recoil at this, felt a scared tremor enter the cross-tuned vibrations relaying thought between the two of them.

"Dean, I *am* the Acromyrmex now. I and the colony might be all that is left of us on Earth. And if we can't find a way to move from this place soon, we'll be eaten alive."

CHAPTER EIGHT

The long stretch of internal communication had wiped them out but left them wary. Exhausted, they shuffled over to the fence and agreed to sleep in shifts before figuring out how they could travel.

Dean lay near Mave in the lean-to for a few hours, watching the sleepless march of the ants as they moved over her and traveled back and forth to their garden nest. She had been right about the beauty of the creatures. While Dean admired the tenacity and strength of the cockroach, they lacked the grace and civility and immense complexity that made observing the leafcutter such a pleasure.

The roaches knew how to stay alive, but for what? He tried to cut the question off in his mind, knowing the sense of existential dread that was sure to follow any attempted answer.

Dean's father had built up a life for himself. He had done much more than simply "get by." An esteemed figure in his field. Research papers published in all the right magazines. A loving son who helped him through his years as a young widower. But in the end a ridiculous auto accident took his life. His papers and ideas were replaced by newer ones that failed to credit him. His son flipped out and traveled the world squandering the money the father had saved up for years. No, Daddy Dean Sr. had existed for nothing. And now the last of his bloodline was surrounded by semi-empathic roaches and trapped in a wasteland, lying next to a fungus-coated woman with exotic ants in her womb.

Actually, Dean thought, his dad might have been really intrigued by that last part, but it wasn't what you necessarily hoped for when you had a kid.

After a while Mave opened her eyes (those *eyes*) and within seconds Dean allowed himself to drift into a shallow sleep.

He dreamed- army ants marching/ his face consumed by baby roaches/Terry chewing his way through Mave's vagina. He woke screaming. Mave placed her hand on his forehead, the smell of her fungus rich and almost sweet near his nose. He calmed. He caught another hour of shut eye. This time real slumber.

But at waking the dreams still chilled him. They lingered. From the look in *her* eyes, she'd somehow shared his fear.

They hit the road within hours.

Travel time moved on the following agenda:

Head back north, then west when the river branches. Stay close to the water.

More likely to find some sort of plant life there. Get far enough west and Mave knew of a place where there might be safety. A military liaison to the university had once been sweet on her and spilled post-coital secrets to impress, including the general location of a military stronghold they'd built out of a natural cave system.

The place was supposed to have some degree of sustainability. Which meant flowing water and clean air. Which could mean weapons with which a person or persons could effectively stave off an invasion of army ants. Which *might* mean a self-contained bio-system that she and Dean could adapt their insectile selves to.

Travel time was a bitch.

They tried to drag part of the Acromyrmex nest behind them on top of her old lean-to tarp. That meant slow-going. That meant frenzied waste workers cleaning out dead ants/collapsed tunnels/reduced gongylidia output. That meant confused foragers hunting dead land for any plant life at all, coming back with empty, ashy mandibles. The fungus across Mave's skin began to lose its luster without new plant life to culture on. The crumbs and trash they tried to adhere to her made her look diseased.

The new queen was upset. Dean would hear her humming, but not in a frequency he could even try to reach. He guessed she was calming the colony; asking them to endure. He knew the sound of her excited his roaches. Their cerci swayed to the sound.

He watched Mave's movements, the sway of her hips, the way her feet seemed to keep moving without real exertion.

For some reason her beauty pitched him double lonely. She would never have a guy like Dean, would she? He considered running ahead, leaving the queen and her dying colony and heading west to the Pacific by himself. She'd only slow him down, maybe even bring a horde of ravenous ants with huge jaws his way.

He could be free. A lone wolf. He'd finally tattoo his knuckles with his motto, four letters across each fist:
DONOTDIE

But was that all he really felt now? He wasn't sure. Those grey/gold eyes kept him unstable.

Maybe we could spend the rest of our time together. Maybe we can find some place with a white picket fence and forty acres out back for nesting.

So for now Dean kept things left foot/right foot/repeat and followed the queen of the dying leafcutters along the river.

CHAPTER NINE

"It's getting warmer, don't you think? Brighter, too."

Mave had demanded they sit by the river for a while to let her ants search for some plant life and harvest proteins from their collapsing nest.

Dean thought she was right about the warmth. He hadn't worn his "Winter Fun" scarf for the last fifteen miles or so. He'd guessed he was heating up from exertion- dragging a backpack full of water and a tarp full of dirt was a gut-buster- but maybe Mave was on point.

He hoped she *wasn't* correct for a few reasons:

1. Dean was sure the cold was all that'd kept the now fantastic number of eggs on his suit from hatching. Currently he and Mave were located nowhere near a worthy stash of baby roach food.

2. The Nuclear Summer theory- Following nuclear winter the ozone layer and stratosphere are effectively destroyed. UV light would torch any remaining territory that wasn't already turned to desert by the lack of photosynthesis during the blackout. Anything that had a harsh time with UV light before would really feel the burn. Genetic defects galore. Polar ice caps would melt. Continental flooding. The greenhouse effect in fast fast forward. Even sea life would go stagnant, except for those weird things that live off of gas vents at the bottom of the Marianas Trench.

3. As much as he would welcome a bit of light, it freaked his suit out and ravaged the leafcutter's fungus. They'd both be in even more of a pinch with the sun blazing overhead.

However, he was enjoying the increased sensation of warmth in the air, slight though it was. He laid back against the gentle slope of the riverbank and watched the cancerous clouds churn overhead. He thought, even at this distance from her, that he could smell Mave's fungus. It calmed him. He relaxed his neck, allowing his crash helmet to sink its heft into the ground. His shoulders dropped.

The sound of the river water running seaward formed a constant white noise soundtrack. He let himself float with it, pictured himself as a drop of water, incapable of death, unknowing, yet immensely important and powerful.

He closed his eyes and let his head tip over in Mave's direction.

The smell of her was sort of like lavender mixed with fresh coffee. It invigorated as much as it soothed. Were there spores of it, he wondered, working their way into his brain right now? He hoped so.

She was sovereign. Let him join her subjects, enthralled.

Two sensations:
Movement without control.
The scent of lemons and hot metal. The smell of ruptured ants.

Dean opened his eyes, instantly awake. He was no longer on the riverbank. The roaches were moving at full-out speed, autonomous of his control, heading towards a nearby copse of charred tree stumps.

A scream in the distance, explosive, and then suddenly cut off.

Mave.

Dean forced his hands and feet to the ground, churning up hardened earth, leaving tracks. The roaches were not stopping. Whatever they had sensed, they wanted to get as far away as possible.

Go with them, Dean! The roaches got you this far. You can keep living.

You can survive.

Their pace never flagged. Now they were just feet from a low hiding spot.

Another shriek. Crunching sounds that rolled Dean's stomach even at this distance.

You know what's happening, Dean. It's Terry. He's found you. He's found Mave. But he wants to eat her first. A big fat juicy mama ant. Now is your only chance to run!

The suit kept crawling, more cautious now, looking for a way to crest the next hill without being seen by anything down below.

Dean dug his heels in harder but couldn't get traction.

Shit shit shit! Mave's dying. Stop this. Do something.

Dean began to hum. He focused his thoughts on the tight space at the back of his skull and tried to bring the sound as close as he could to the buzz that flourished there.

The roaches began to slow. He let the hum drop to a low drone at the back of his throat. The hive mind buzz locked in.

we are scared we are scared predator scared predator scared distance dark distance quiet scared escape distancehidehidehidehidehideprotecthide

Dean didn't hear actual words, but this was the message he received in a language older than any man had ever created.

The language of survival.

It was a sound for animals. It ensured a thriving planet. It was old and powerful and he was sure that a hint of that audible pattern echoed inside of every atom of his body.

But it wasn't anything Dean wanted to listen to anymore.

There was something stronger working through his mind now. A brighter sound at the front of his head. A siren's call.

Her spores really did get into my brain.

Dean tuned into the sound. It felt nearly as ancient as the desire to run, to live at all costs. But this sound had a beauty to it. A nobility.

And as he found the right tone in his throat to harmonize there was only one word at the front of his thoughts:
Fight.

He could smell her and the colony on the poison wind. Sweet fungus. Acidic death. Adrenaline. Pain.

There was another smell in the air, and whether he was pulling it into his mind via his own nose or the roaches receptors he was unsure.

It was the smell of hunger. Desperation.

Dean charged toward it face first, his own feet pushing him onward, workman's boots rubbing his feet raw.

Go in without hesitation. Strike first and then don't stop until she's safe.

He held in a roar, though it raged at the inside of his chest. He let its energy carry him faster.

There- two hundred yards south. A man stood over Mave. Watching her face twist in agony. Her body was covered in moving black shapes, thick ropes of them, orderly lines of assault tearing away at her face/belly/legs.

Nomamyrmex was on the march.

Dean screamed then, hoping the sound would somehow distract even the bugs which were eating away at Mave.

The man- it had to be Terry- rotated to face the sound. He looked right at Dean. One of his eyes was missing. His nose was also absent, replaced by a jagged black triangle bisected by exposed bone.

Despite these obvious deformities, Dean could tell the man was smiling.

Why would he be smili

The earth fell out from beneath Dean and he felt something long and sharp bore through his right leg before he even realized he wasn't running anymore.

"We're diggers. You cah see that ow. It only took us a few hours to displace over six meters of dirt alog this ehtire perimeter. Quite astoudeeg, really."

Terry had approached the pit. The noseless fuck.

"We couldit fide as mady sharp sticks as we'd hoped for, but you do what you cad with what you've got, right? Guess we've lucked out that you hit that particular spike as square as you did. Providess."

Dean said nothing. What good would rage do now? He surveyed his surroundings. Narrow dark rift marked by a million ant trails. A chunk of fractured tree branch jammed through his upper thigh, a few slaughtered roaches hanging from its tip. Wound not bleeding too badly. Must have missed the femoral.

"She told us your name is Dee."

"It's Dean."

"That's what I said. I caht quite make all the sowds I used to. I must admit that we were quite huggry on the trip to fide the Acromyrmex. We had to eat pieces of my face. Other parts too."

At that Terry's remaining eye went wide with fear. Absolute panic.

He emitted a cough, a bark of a low tone. His eye snapped back to empty.

His human brain is still trying to assert itself. Jesus, he's scared. He's so scared, the poor bastard. Those ants are inside of his mind and they've been feeding on him for days.

"Listen, Terry, I know you're in there somewhere. I know you're scared. I know they are hurting you and you're confused and the whole world seems wrong right now, but if you can push to the front of your brain and take control you can stop this. They're just ants."

"Quiet!"

With that Dean noticed the black surge cresting over the lip of the makeshift pit. Thousands- no, hundreds of thousands of them. Thick fingertip-sized ants with bulbous split red-horned heads, each meaty half as big as two whole leafcutters. Their jaw musculature visible from feet away.

Pain is coming, and it will not be brief. If nuclear fallout couldn't kill me how long will it take these ants to end it?

Then he heard the sound. A new tone, from up above. Weak, but coming from Mave.

She's still alive.

He felt, instinctively, that he must try and match her sound.

The first wave of ants was on him. At his earlobes. Sinking their mandibles into the roaches that covered him. Tearing away at his fingertips. Trying to get *into* his fresh wound.

He cleared his throat. He pulled in as much air as he could. Ants bit into his lower lip, sought the meat of his tongue.

From the bottom of his lungs Dean let out his matching tone. It found hers. The sounds merged and became a terrible bellow.

This was a call to war. Dean felt it in his bones.

There was a crackling noise- the sound of thousands of dry distended roach eggs tearing open at once.

Dean's delivery day was here. Within seconds he was the proud father to a seething multitude. The tiny nymphs were too small to be crushed in the huge jaws of the Nomamyrmex, over whom they flowed heedlessly.

They washed up out of the trench,

a hungry flood with one target.

Dean stood up, shaking loose hundreds of army ants from his frame. His right leg held. A thick cast of roach nymphs had formed around it, bearing the weight of his broken limb.

He kept his mind focused on Terry. On Terry's face. Those open holes.

Roaches adored dark wet places like that.

Terry turned to run. The nymphs were already halfway up his legs. He made it one stride before the babies had covered his good eye and were piling in to his blasted orbit.

Terry opened his mouth to scream but the only sound Dean could pick up was the rustle of tiny roaches rubbing against each other on their way down the man's throat.

Dean looked away. He hoped they'd kill him soon. He'd tried to focus the nymphs' movement towards Terry's brain but he wasn't sure how long it would take them to chew through to grey matter.

There was a man inside there somewhere. Confused. Violated. Alone.

Shit.

Dean couldn't take it anymore. His suit helped him crawl up out of the pit and over to Terry's twitching body.

Dean shoved one of his gloves in his own mouth. He bit down. He made a two-fisted grab for the sharpened branch that was rammed through his leg. Twisted left. Twisted right. Wailed through a mouthful of wool and leather. Bit down again. Gripped tight. Pulled up and away. Scoped the point of the stick, dripping his own blood, bits of roach still stuck to it.

And then he swung that same spear down into Terry's empty eye socket as hard as he possibly could.

CHAPTER TEN

This is the way Dean looked at it, much later:

One day you go to bed happy. The next day your dad dies. In a stupid, stupid way.

And maybe you give up on the world. Maybe the world forgets you ever existed and you're okay with that. Because you're alive. Not dead. Not anywhere near that sadness again.

Things are easier alone. Nothing to lose = no loss.

But what if *you* die? Isn't that the biggest loss of them all? You're the only one who will ever truly know you were even alive.

So you protect yourself, with a nod to the esteemed Malcolm X, by any means necessary.

But Malcolm, at the moment he'd said that, probably never guessed one of those means would be covering yourself in nasty, nasty insects.

Probably never even came near being a thought in his head.

His loss. Because he's dead now. And you, you just keep living, no matter what the world throws at you. Nuclear weapons, crazy presidents, toxic fallout, man-made gods with nothing better to do than alter the genetic code of the remaining humans on Earth.

Fucking army ants.

Oh, and loneliness. Lots of loneliness. You always have to fight that one. But maybe everybody does.

At least that was a problem when you were human.

But that's not exactly the case anymore, is it?

Back up.

Start again.

One day you fall asleep happy. Next to a river under a dark sky. Then you wake up and everything has changed. Including you. You changed so much that for the first time you actually *risk* your life.

For what?

Love? It's as good a word as any. It'll do.

And you've gone so crazy with this feeling, call it love, that you find yourself in an absurd situation, humming and moaning at telepathic bugs and killing brainwashed entomologists.

I know.

It sounds silly.

But it feels important at the time. So important that you nearly die from blood loss lying there in a desolate field next to a corpse filled with baby roaches.

Again, you fall asleep. Or perhaps you pass out from blood loss. But you're happy. Not totally happy, but feeling like now maybe your life was really a *life*. Something more than rote respiration for as sustained a period as possible.

Then you wake up and everything has changed so goddamned much you think you're in heaven.

But you're not dead, and neither is she. The one you love. Sure, her original right arm is missing (eaten by army ants you guess), but it appears that some enterprising leafcutter ants have assembled her a new one out of radiant fungus.

These same enterprising bugs have healed up your sundry cuts and wounds and even staved off the infection in your leg with a Streptomyces bacteria that lives on their skin.

A woman once told you these were the best ants on Earth. You now believe her 100%.

As great as those ants are, you might miss your cockroaches.

"I've set them free," she tells you. "They're up there doing what they're meant to do. Making babies and eating death and putting nutrients back into the soil for when the nuclear summer passes and things can grow again."

It's a lot to absorb at once. Losing your friends like that. Finding out the whole

Earth has gone Death Valley for the time being. Trying to figure out how this miraculous woman managed to drag your nearly dead/coma patient ass all the way out west to these secret caves. But you accept it all after a while.

You might explore your new home. Filters. Generators. Tunnels and tunnels and tunnels. You guess one of them might run right to the center of the Earth, but you never find that particular path.

The woman you love, her favorite place is the sustainable eco-sphere. She can even farm there, next to her ants. But they do a pretty great job without her.

All those rooms- the ones that were supposed to house the soldiers and U.S. officials who weren't ready when the bombs hit- they start filling up with the glowing fungal tufts the ants produce. Aside from that it's dark down there, wherever you want it to be.

One day (or night-who can tell down here?) you fall asleep lonely. Then you wake up the next morning and the woman you love is on top of you. She's lifting her hips and putting you inside of her and making every other Best Moment of Your Life seem pretty pale. And when she's done and you're done you hold each other tight and watch as three luminous Acromyrmex queens emerge from between her legs and crawl up to her belly.

Their wings dry. They shiver/ shake/touch antennae.

They take flight.

You can tell that they're headed to the surface- nuclear summer bound.

Their movement through the air is heavy with theft.

This makes the woman you love cry. But she is smiling through the tears.

Beaming, really.

For she believes, as you do, that she has just given birth to the first strange children of that terrible new sun.

KEVIN L DONIHE
(aka Sir Edwin Walri IV)

LOCATION:
Kingsport, TN

STYLE OF BIZARRO:
Walronian Fiction

BOOKS BY DONIHE:

Shall We Gather At The Garden?
Ocean of Lard (w/ Carlton Mellick III)
The Greatest Fucking Moment In Sports
Grape City
House of Houses
Voluptuous Sunrise (forthcoming)
Bugaboo (forthcoming)
The Bonville Bones (forthcoming)
The Flappy Parts (forthcoming)
Fuck Apocalypse (forthcoming)

DESCRIPTION: Kevin L Donihe often writes about things that explode or come apart in big and/or freakish ways. Circus midgets may or may not appear in his books. A feeling of agape love may or may not manifest as a consequence of reading the work of Mr. Donihe.

INTERESTS: Walruses (walri), reading, writing, fine cheeses, alien mind beams, agape love, antiques, silent/weird/awful movies, travel, mountains, the woods, Lionel Richie.

INFLUENCES: Pugnacious Jones.

WEBSITE:
www.myspace.com/kevindonihe

THE GREATEST FUCKING MOMENT IN SPORTS

Who is Oscar Legbo?:

Renowned Insectarian, role model, and now 7-time winner of the *Tour de Saucisse-Dommages*, Oscar Legbo is the reigning king of the sport of competitive bicycle racing; his popularity stretches across most, if not all, demographic lines. It is even rumored that a particular terrorist admires Oscar Legbo and has posters of him plastered upon the walls of his cave.

Something to Know About Legbo:

As a child, Oscar enjoyed killing bugs in borderline psychotic ways. If ever there was a Hitler-figure amongst the bug kingdom, it was surely Mr. Legbo. He filled bb guns with ball bugs (otherwise known as "rolly pollies') and shot them into snails. He also peeled bagworms from their cocoons and held their lower bodies with leaves intended to mimic bathtubs. Often, he would construct off-the-cuff monologues and pretend the bagworms were saying these things, usually before getting a thorn rammed through their heads as though they'd been murdered by a jilted lover, like some character out of a mystery novel, or by an assailant, like the unfortunate Frenchman from the painting.

If a bagworm survived long enough,

he put a dramatic death soliloquy into its mouth.

In his early teens, after he built up the courage to experiment with gasoline, Oscar realized that a sardine can full of gas wouldn't explode when lit, and so he drew terminal baths, usually for snails, as their protective slime evaporated gradually and, for a short time, offered a buffer from the flames.

Eventually, Oscar grew to hate himself for the things he'd done, especially after digging a series of grave-pits in which he left fuzzy caterpillars to rot, covering the hole with a twig roof and mud so they smothered and baked rather than being crushed by dirt, and some survived for weeks before finally turning into thick and smelly goop.

One night, after stirring a particularly deep and noxious pit, he felt caterpillar souls scrape at him as he tried to sleep, wiggling beneath his covers and begging for surcease. The next morning, when he contemplated the food he ate, he imagined heat-softened corpses were layered inside it and, when he stirred his potatoes, a familiar decomposition smell arose from them.

Oscar threw his food away and vomited, off and on, for almost an hour.

In the end, it had been fuzzy caterpillars that inaugurated his transformation, but they were no different from the bagworms, the slugs, the rolly pollies, and other insects he'd murdered. To kill any bug, he realized, was unacceptable, if not a crime.

It was after reaching this epiphany at age 19 that he devoted his life to the sport of competitive bicycle racing. At first, it was a simple diversion that kept him from doing what he sometimes still wanted to do, but, with the constant aid and support of Coach Fernardo de Papa, racing supplanted killing bugs as the crux of his day-to-day existence.

To this day, Oscar wears a uniform that features a five-pointed star, and upon each point sits a different bug: a camel cricket, a caterpillar, a bagworm, a katydid, and a June bug. Below them, a lone snail coils around a sprig of ivy. He also wears a pair of floppy antennae while racing, and last year added a dark spot on his uniform right above his heart.

It, of course, signifies a bb pellet wound.

Preparation for the 89th Annual *Tour de Saucisse-Dommages*:

Oscar pedaled with not one, but two cinderblocks strapped beneath his feet. His hands were wrapped in barbed wire and, just for added effect, handcuffed to the handlebar. He wore nothing but an antique loincloth that Coach de Papa had personally chosen for him.

The coach had outfits, too – a series of costumes that accompanied seven alternating dioramas that were hoisted atop a high school homecoming float, which was then tied to the rear of Legbo's bike.

Coach de Papa was known for his unusual training techniques. Some days, he was a chariot racer, and Oscar his mechanical, wheel-legged horse. Other days he was Satan himself, and Oscar just another lost soul forced to serve a master. Today, however, he was King Neptune, replete with trident and flowing sea foam green cape, though he still wore the same little red running shorts that he'd worn, nonstop, for the last twenty years. He also braided his beard for the occasion and wove a small starfish into its center. Life-sized plastic dolphins, positioned to look as though they were leaping from the sea, bracketed Coach de Papa.

Oscar was likewise a dolphin – a sleek, aquatic slave – and would remain so for eight-to-twelve more hours. Sometimes Coach de Papa demanded that he create dolphin sounds, and, if they sounded phony, would lash him with his ever-present whip.

Legbo International paid for the costumes, the dioramas, and the float. The company didn't mind because Coach de Papa's excesses inspired results.

"I am Neptune!" he roared. "How dare you not give me 100%!"

Coach de Papa cracked his whip against Oscar's naked back.

"*Faster*! You're a dolphin, not a manatee for Christ's sake!"

"Yes, Coach de Papa! I am a dolphin!"

"Not Coach de Papa! *King Neptune*!"

"Yes, Neptune!"

Coach de Papa threw a conch shell at his head. "*King*! King Neptune!"

"Yes, *King*! *King Neptune*!"

He cracked the whip again. "You only need to say 'king' once!"

Oscar trudged on. Fifteen miles had passed, but thirty-five more loomed ahead. He hung his head briefly, an attempt to center and relax himself. Bringing his gaze down to the road, he saw a bug – a large, black beetle with pinchers – less than a foot away, crawling into the path of his bike.

He turned the handlebar sharply, sparing the bug. Oscar let out a sigh, but then heard a loud *creak* behind him. He turned to see the float, tilted at a 45-degree angle and keeling fast. Atop it, Coach de Papa struggled to maintain his balance.

It pained Oscar to see such a great man stumble; he straightened the path of his bike, but the float continued to lean, Coach de Papa clutching the Styrofoam representation of a mermaid until it broke in two. Then he tumbled out onto the road, and the float fell atop him.

Oscar jumped off the bike and slid out of the cinderblock shoes. Still, he dragged the bicycle behind him. Coach de Papa had the only keys to the handcuffs.

He ran to the overturned float but couldn't make himself look to the side of it. Coach de Papa had never fallen before; Oscar didn't even know the man could fall. Finally, he looked, and, at that moment, had to make himself breathe.

Coach de Papa's legs were pinned by the float and his trident – which was real and not a prop – had impaled him straight through the chest.

Oscar leaned over his body. "Coach de Papa?"

"Oscar." He coughed up a blood-gout.

"Don't talk." Oscar tilted Coach de Papa's back in an effort to remove the trident.

He scowled. "Please don't do that."

"Quiet, coach. If you just let me—"

"*Don't touch the goddamn trident! When you wiggle it, it hurts like a fucker!*"

"Sorry Coach de Papa, but there has to be something I can do!"

"There's nothing you can do."

"Please, just let me do *something*!"

"Oscar," he finally said, his voice a groan, another blood-bubble in his mouth. "Just – just tell me one thing, okay?"

"Anything!"

"Why did you do this?"

"I – I did it for the bug, Coach. It would have been crushed!"

Coach de Papa gritted his teeth. "What the fuck, Oscar."

"I didn't know that this would happen! I never meant to hurt you. I – I love you, Coach de Papa!" Then Oscar had to turn away; he couldn't stand the way his coach stared at him.

"I mean, really. What the—"

And then he was gone.

The Press Room, Just Before the Race:

Oscar was attired in bright, skin-tight racing gear, his hair slicked back and his teeth finely scrubbed with tiny loofah brushes just minutes before by a team of handlers. His body was lean and taunt, and reporters – male and female – oogled his physic for longer than necessary, amazed to find no indications that the Ebola virus had traveled through his system the summer beforehand. He had been the first to survive the disease, encountered on a wild safari tour with two young American men, both of whom had pledged to a fraternity. They died horrible, painful deaths,

and it appeared as though Legbo would as well – until he didn't. Medical professionals viewed his recovery as miraculous, but Oscar neither confirmed nor denied the supernatural. His reply: "What happens, happens."

He took to the stage, and the press corps fell onto each other, a mound of writhing humanity.

"Oscar! Oscar!" one shouted. "How do you feel about racing so soon after the death of your long-time coach, Fernardo de Papa?"

Oscar spent a moment in thought. "I loved my coach – loved him like no other man – and his loss hangs heavy on me, but he would have been very disappointed had I failed to race today."

"And is it true that you caused his death?"

"It was an accident, a horrible, horrible accident." He exhaled slowly. "But, in the end, Coach de Papa died so that another might live."

"By 'another' do you mean a bug?"

"Yes. Specifically, I mean a big black beetle."

An elderly reporter stood: "What's your opinion of the German rider, Helmut Starb?"

Oscar's bottom lip twitched. "I'd rather not talk about Helmet, thank you very much."

"But he's your strongest competitor; some commentators have predicted his victory."

Now his left eye twitched. "Yes. Yes, I know this."

"Surely, you want to say *something* about such a bright and rising young—"

"*I said I'd rather not talk about him*! Next question, please!"

That reporter sat and another stood: "If you win today, whom will you do it for? God? Country? Family? Coach de Papa?"

He did not hesitate. "I do this not for God, or country, or family, or even Coach de Papa, though I love him more than the last three combined." He slammed his fist against the podium. "No! I do it for bugs!"

His passion shot across the room and made all the journalists in attendance buckle, hitch, and waver in their seats, or fall from them and do what Oscar now thought of as *the electric salmon* across the floor. He didn't know why this happened at every press conference since his return from Africa. It had concerned him at first, but he didn't mind now. He found their display weird but touching, and it stroked his ego.

One, an Asian reporter, finally recovered enough to speak, though she remained in a supine position:

"Do you realize, Mr. Legbo, that most Americans willfully and without remorse kill as many bugs as possible on a given day, and that there's a certain fetish that involves the stomping of insects by nubile women for voyeuristic, sexual pleasure?"

"Yes, I am aware of these things, and it irks me to no end. People can have whatever quirks and kinks they want, but leave the fucking bugs out of it!"

Intersplice:
The Office of Standards and Practices:

"He didn't just fucking say *fucking*, did he?"
The man nodded.
"Run the eight-second delay!"
"Already on it."

Press (*cont.*):

The press lady cowered in the corner, her hands over her face. Oscar looked down, recognized her fear, and, in an instant, came back to himself.

"Oh, sorry."

The woman did not – could not – respond.

"When I get worked up about bugs, I sometimes black out." Oscar smoothed creases in his racing uniform, drew in a series of deep breaths, and returned to the podium.

"I don't imagine it'll happen again, at least not today."

He continued his answer as reporters dusted off their clothes and rose slowly from the floor:

"But yes, I am aware of our society's indifference to bugs. And maybe they're right. Maybe a bug's death doesn't matter, not in the long run, but this is my personal battle, so let me wage it in the way I see fit."

Another reporter: "And what was it that made you believe the way you do? Was it some grand epiphany, and, if so, what was the nature of this epiphany?"

"You know my story; I've never been less than honest with you. I used to be an evil, evil man who did evil, evil things to bugs, but I don't want to say any more than that because I know children – millions and millions of them – are watching right now."

"Do you ever think you're being too hard on yourself?"

"No. This burden is mine to carry, so I carry it." Oscar drew in a deep breath, held it in for a few seconds, and exhaled slowly. "But it is a sweet, sweet burden, indeed."

"And why is it sweet?"

"Without it, I would have committed suicide long ago. My guilt was strong, but my love and my sense of duty were stronger, and they brought me back. Once this happened, I realized that love and a sense of duty can bring *anyone* and *anything* back, if both are pursued with the right heart."

"And that's why we love you!" screamed a man on fire in the back row. Yet another fan – doused head-to-toe in gasoline – had slipped into a press conference with the desire to self-immolate.

Oscar left the podium. He didn't even realize he had done so until he was standing by the man, his hand atop a flaming shoulder.

"Self-immolation is not recommended, sir."

At that moment, the fire receded. The man looked at his hands and slid them down his face. There was no charred or bloody skin.

"Wait," he said. "Shouldn't I be dead?"

"Probably, but why are you fussing when you're not?"

The man did not reply, at least not audibly. He nodded his head back and forth, too lost in Legbo's eyes to notice the angry-looking men who stalked up behind him.

* * * *

Once the fan had been escorted away by armed security, the barrage of questions surged anew.

One: "How did you touch him?"

Another: "Are your hands coated in fire retardant?"

A third: "Are you the second coming?"

Oscar shook his head. "Sometimes I don't know what I'm going to do until I do it or what's going to happen until it happens. It's the power of agape love working through me, and, and, hopefully, it shall soon work through you, too."

A reporter piped up from the second row: "And how will that be done?"

"This win – this monumental and historic win – will return the love that's now missing on this planet. These words may sound like candy and rainbows to you, but such is the intended nature of my working." He took a hearty chug from a water glass.

"And how do you know that this – uh – *working* will work?"

Oscar smiled winsomely. "Because you love me, and because I love you."

Parts of the room erupted in applause. Two or three more people went up in flames.

"Now, if you'll excuse me, I must prepare for the race."

Legbo's Pre-Race Ritual:

Oscar dressed for the press conference, but couldn't perform his pre-race ritual with clothes on, so he lost them.

First, he touched the plushy, stuffed ladybug that crouched on his dresser. He'd named it Charley. On the road, he slept with it. At home, it had a permanent place on his sofa, joining him each night to watch TV after a long day of practice. Oscar's eyes rolled back into his head as he made contact with the thing, feeling as though an electric pulse had been transmitted through the stuffed bug and into him.

His synapses now prepared for the experience, he contorted himself into the lotus position and, with his index finger, touched his nasal chakra. An old Hindu had told him that nasal charkas didn't exist, but that man was a fool. How could they not exist when he was touching his own and feeling it radiate through all the subtle pathways of his body?

When the time was right, Oscar recited his customary incantation: *"June Bug! June Bug! Skitterbug! Ra! Atman! Ra!"*

At that moment, all the bug souls he had ever freed from Earthly bodies enveloped him, stretching outward from his core in a massive spiral. They stared at him without approval and without dismay. Then they began to spin, emitting colors and lights until, with a sound like a vacuum, they were sucked into his body where the memory of their Earthly pain and hate could fuel him for the race.

When the ritual was over, Oscar relaxed in a corpse-pose until he'd be late at the starting line if he didn't get up and get dressed.

He slipped back into his racing uniform and placed the floppy antennae – an item he only wore from racing, as it functioned as a special receptor – on his head. Oscar then looked into the mirror and gave himself a grin. It was now time, time to go out and show the world what it meant to love.

At the Starting Line:

Oscar allowed his body to fuse with the bicycle as he awaited the starting gun. He imagined flesh becoming steel and steel becoming flesh until there was no real separation between the two.

He was returned to himself by the words of a Belgian bastard whose name was Decker *Something*. Oscar couldn't remember his last. Decker was red-haired and stockier than most riders and had a tattoo of a bicycle stretched across his face, with his eyes serving as the center of the wheels. "Nice antennae, Oscar," he said. "Know where I can get a pair?"

Oscar admired Decker's devotion to the sport, but was tired of his taunting, school-bully ways. "Oh, go to hell," he whispered under his breath.

Helmut Starb, future racing champion and friend of the Belgian, snickered. Oscar turned and scowled; he hated even looking at him. His nose was reminiscent of a bratwurst and his stringy hair of a pile of sauerkraut that hung out over a wrinkly brown skullcap. Oscar didn't know what purpose the skullcap served, or what it was supposed to signify, if anything.

"Hey, Oscar," he said. "Look at the bottom of my shoe!"

Then Helmut showed him his sole where a large grasshopper was smashed yet twitching. Oscar felt sympathetic pain, and then irrational, all-encompassing rage. He imagined ramming an oversized thorn into the man's head, shooting his unresponsive body into that of another bug killer via cannon, or dumping him down a personal death-pit, sealing it, and then stirring his muck after a few months had elapsed.

"You like this, no?" Helmut then looked to his left. "Oh, a cricket, too!"

"Don't you—"

Helmut smashed the cricket, grinding it into the pavement with his heel for a few more seconds than necessary. When finished, he raked his shoe clean, leaving a black smear on the road.

Another rider – a too-thin Frenchman with a spiky unibrow who Oscar sometimes saw alongside Helmut and Decker – smirked, but said nothing. Oscar remembered neither his first nor his last name, and didn't care if he ever found them out.

"I can't believe it," Helmut said, and both the Belgian and the Frenchman turned at the sound of his voice. "An ant!"

Oscar couldn't take it anymore. "Bug killing motherfuckers!" he screamed to an international audience of millions, as there was no eight-second delay.

The Race Begins:

It had taken him a while to calm down, up until the moment the starting gun fired. Finally, his hands were able to become vices and his legs pumping pistons. Sometimes, he imagined his penis was likewise a piston, but that was too distracting to visualize during important races.

The terrain was so familiar that he could negotiate it with his eyes closed. Every bend and every curve were like the supple contours of the women he could never quite convince himself to touch. *The bitches – the evil, horrible bitches!* His mind screamed. *Oh God, I love them still!*

Oscar forced himself to snap out of it; he looked up at the sky. It was overcast, gray, and threatening, and the air around him was chilly.

Perhaps the weather wouldn't change for the worse, but change seemed inevitable. Though he had raced in less than favorable conditions, those races hadn't been 48-hours removed from the death of his coach. Usually, he was able to toss distractions aside and get into – if not become – the race. Today, however, felt different and *wrong*.

Maybe that Helmut bastard really had what it took to become champion. Maybe it was time for him to retire, anyway.

Maybe it was *past* time.

He made himself snap out of it again. *Oscar Legbo was a winner, is a winner, and shall be a winner*, he thought, and applied pressure to the radial axle bar.

Another Thing to Know About Legbo:

The part to which Legbo had applied pressure was not a 'radial axle bar' – bicycles don't have such a part.

During his early training, he called the axle a *dum-dum* and spokes *ree-dees*. He had equally nonsensical names for all the other parts, too. Oscar's immaturity drove Coach de Papa to the brink of madness, but he suffered through it, for he knew he had a racing prodigy on his hands.

As Oscar got older – in his late 20s – he started calling parts like the steering system 'radial axle bars,' thus trading in a few (but not all) of the baby sounds for names he imagined were more sophisticated and scientific-sounding. Still, he refused to call any of the parts by – or even learn – their actual names.

This is a tightly kept secret no one but Oscar and those closest to him – and, of course, the CEO of *Legbo International* – know.

The Race Continues:

Earlier, it had appeared as though the sky might crack open, but things had changed. The temperature had risen, becoming warm without being hot, and, for the last ten or so miles, there hadn't been a cloud in the sky.

Maybe these were good omens.

Oscar felt silly for having worried. Helmut didn't stand a chance, and Coach de Papa – God bless him – was surely smiling down upon this race, beaming with post-mortem pride.

Perhaps, Oscar thought, *it was he who cleared the skies...*

Then he noticed something in the road in front of him.

At first, he thought it was a bunch of loose gravel; perhaps some had slid down from the opposing hill during the last rainstorm. Then he noticed that the things moved, skittering around on the ground like ... like ...

Bugs.

Oscar ground his bike to a halt just in time. He looked out over the mess of writhing insect life before him – crickets and rolly pollies and katydids and June bugs and fireflies and praying mantises; there were far too many – in terms of both number and variety – to have gotten there on their own volition, and the fireflies and June bugs had all had their wings clipped.

He jumped off his bike and leaned it against an incline on the side of the road, scowling as he thought of Helmut, Decker the Belgian, and the Frenchman. He didn't suspect the other riders had anything to do with this, as they weren't assholes, at least not to his face.

"I'll save you, my babies!" he shouted, picking up a handful of bugs and placing them, facing away from the road, in the grass. "I won't let bad wheels crush you!"

But they kept returning, like the pavement had been sprinkled with pheromones.

"No!" he shrieked. "Don't go back there! Bad bugs! *Bad bugs!*"

Oscar heard the sound of approaching bicycles and looked up.

Helmut waved at him. "See you at the finish line, Oscar!" As he passed, he made sure to smash as many bugs as possible.

"Rot in Hell!" Oscar screamed, shaking his fist until he could not longer see Helmut.

Then Decker the Belgian and the smirking Frenchman passed him, followed, in time, by all the other riders in the 89th annual *Tour de Saucisse-Dommages.*

And Oscar wove in and out of traffic; saving as many insects as he could and screaming while others were crushed.

In the Channel 5 Newsroom:

Anchorlady Jane (*clutches a handful of papers from which she is clearly not reading*): For the first time in the history of his involvement with the *Tour de Saucisse-Dommages*, Oscar Legbo is dead last.

Anchorman Tim (*takes a quick gulp from a coffee cup emblazoned with Oscar Legbo's head*): This is a sad moment for America. Oscar, listen to your fans when we say, "lay off the bugs, just lay off them."

Anchorlady Jane: Everybody needs a mission, Tim. It's what makes life worth living.

Anchorman Tim (*flushes red*): But not if it costs him the race! Look, I respect and admire Oscar's dedication. Hell, I even quit stomping bugs for a year because of him!

Anchorlady Jane: Why don't we take a look at what went wrong?

(*Cut to pre-recorded video of Oscar dodging bikes and leaping to the ground, saving bugs or shrieking like a girl when they splatter at his feet.*)

Anchorman Tim: See what I mean? That's just pathetic! (*He gets up and looks about the studio, first beneath the desk, then on the walls, then on the floor. Finally, after almost a minute, he arises with something in his hand.*) Hah! Found one.

Anchorlady Jane: Found what, Tim?

Anchorman Tim: A bug, Jane. (*He brings it over to the camera, so close now that his face fills the frame. Then he takes the bug and smashes its guts across the lens.*) See that, Oscar? See the first bug I've killed in a frickin' year? (*His gaze becomes distant.*) This is my sacrifice to you.

Anchorlady Jane: Now, Tim, we don't want to upset the members of our audience. You know many of them have adopted Oscar's non-violent stance toward bugs.

Anchorman Tim (*comes to himself*): Forget about them! And forget about the bugs, too! Get your head in the race, Oscar, before you lose it!

Helmut Starb:

Helmut had the strength and dedication to defeat Legbo; he knew this. The stars just hadn't aligned yet. But he was sick of waiting on them, so he paid his cousin 100 Euro to collect a bunch of bugs and dump them on the raceway.

Besides, it was time – *past* time – for Oscar to fall. In the past, even he had liked Lebgo, but now saw him for what he was: just another glory hog. And to what end? *Bugs*? Helmut scoffed at insects. They were pansy; they were gay. The walri, however, were different.

Helmut was a proud walri-man.

He knew the plural of *walrus* was *walruses*, but he nevertheless thought and said *walri*. Though grammatically incorrect, he felt that the word better encapsulated their spirit. Walri were big and strong and had large brown phalluses and even larger ivory tusks. At times, he went out to his patio late at night and made sensual walri mating sounds; fuck a bunch of neighbors.

He wore the walri-skin skullcap to get in touch with the most admirable walri qualities: their toughness, their steadfastness, and, most of all, their ability to survive in harsh, arctic conditions. There was also something vaguely mystical about them, something that made it seem as though they knew something that humans did not. Helmut felt on the verge of groking this *something*, and it would only be a matter of time until the mysteries of the walri were revealed in full. He didn't feel their spirits surge through his skullcap, though; he wasn't a bona fide kook like Legbo.

When not riding bicycles, Helmut rode walri at the aquarium in his hometown, ostensibly for the amusement of children, but really for his own. At times, he considered sneaking in late at night to have carnal relations with one or more walri, but all the walri at the aquarium were male, and he was heterosexual.

The Belgian understood his singular passion, and so Helmut converted him, made him a *Walrite*. He'd given him a skullcap identical to his own and led him through an elaborate initiation ceremony involving a dagger and a golden chalice brimming with walri semen. He had accepted this offering, but Helmut was disappointed to see Decker not wearing the skullcap at the starting line; he had told him to put it on, but not before meditating for at least an hour beforehand.

The Frenchman was more stubborn than Decker; he refused to even partake from the cup or carve the image of *The Grand Tusk* into his chest. Helmut wasn't ready to let him back down, not yet anyway. He would just have to take things slowly with Pierre, just as he would have to take things slowly with the world once his popularity eclipsed that of Legbo, thus paving the way for the Age of Walri to begin.

On Mile 18 of the *Tour de Saucisse-Dommages*:

Oscar realized that the last bike had passed him. The bugs were in no further danger, but he was in danger of losing the race.

There was only one thing to do.

He got onto his bicycle and prepared to enter the Zen state, or what he liked to call the *nobody-can-touch-me-not-even-myself* state. It was a dimension he discovered, accidentally, during his third running of the *Tour de Saucisse-Dommages*. In it, time and space became meaningless, and, if he gave himself utterly to the moment, then that moment would carry him anywhere he needed

to go.

He closed his eyes, blanked his mind, and imagined himself far away from the race, perhaps on some enchanted isle, dancing with human-sized rolly pollies amongst daffodils and lady slippers as bugs of various types and sizes looked on. Here, they no longer cared that they had been murdered, for this was a place far beyond caring.

He continued to live in this world until he sensed the presence of another. He opened his eyes and saw that he now raced beside Helmut. Still, he did not exit the Zen state, just its accompanying world.

"Take a look at this, Oscar Bugbo!" Helmut shouted. "It's part of a collection I've had since I was eight!"

Oscar turned to him, but he did not scowl or shout. Such things were impossible in the Zen state. He just looked at and through Helmut, seeing him for the sick, sad, and desperate little man that he was. Oscar would have laughed, had laughter itself been possible.

Helmut reached into a fanny pack tied around his hips and brought out a handful of dry bugs, their bodies still skewered on pins. Then he threw them, most of the bugs either missing or rebounding from Oscar. Others, however, stuck to his racing suit.

Helmut laughed, thinking Oscar might shriek or flail his arms and lose control of the bike, but these poor, abused corpses served as fuel. In the Zen state, he was more receptive to their spirit energy, still clinging to long dead and dried husks. They radiated through him in hard, steady currents and, soon, Oscar perceived these currents as inseparable from his body. He then flew like an insect himself, through the wind, leaving the German clutching a handful of dead and now useless bugs.

In the Channel 5 Newsroom:

Anchorman Tim: This just in: there has been a dramatic change in lead position at the 89th

KEVIN L DONIHE 🍖 82

Annual *Tour de Saucisse-Dommages*.

(Cut to a playback of Oscar Legbo overtaking Helmut Starb, which is superimposed over the image of a flapping American flag.)

Anchorlady Jane: It's amazing that Oscar Legbo can go from last to first place in such short time, but this man is no stranger to breaking the odds.

Anchorman Tim: My god! *(His eyes roll back into his head.)* Think how well endowed this guy must be!

Anchorlady Jane: Yes, Tim, he must truly have a python down there, but Helmut Starb – said to be Oscar's biggest competition – is still 100% in the race, as are Belgium's Decker Rasmussen and France's Pierre LaChaise.

Anchorman Tim *(says beneath his breath)*: Damn foreigners.

In Dreams:

Augmented by swirling bug spirits, the dream world now enveloped him fully. Whether Helmut was still throwing his bug collection at him, Oscar didn't know, and didn't care.

In this world, the rolly pollie suddenly paused its exotic, Eastern-flavored dance and pressed itself firmly against Oscar's torso. Its seemingly hundreds of tiny, almost thread-like legs pulled down his zipper.

It was time for the happy ending.

But, Oscar realized, there would be no time for the usual coda. Zen-ing out was perfect when a quick burst was needed, but not when his physical attributes and conditioning were enough to see him through. He sensed this was now the case, and it was unwise to take advantage of so precious a blessing.

He broke the embrace. "I'm sorry baby, but this'll have to wait. I've got a Tour to win."

The rolly pollie looked sad, but Oscar knew that it understood.

He turned to face his audience: "Bye fireflies," he said.

"Bye."

"Bye June Bugs, katydids, and cicadas!"

They said the same thing as the fireflies.

After everyone had said their goodbyes, the insects and the world they inhabited began to waver. When the scene faded, it did not do so into black, but into a backdrop of squiggly, multi-colored fractals. Once they were gone, Oscar would be back in his old world.

The last fractal fizzled out thirty seconds later, and a black blur leapt into the road in front of him.

Helmut Starb:

Helmut saw the black blob, too, but saw it for what it was: a man in a ninja suit who jumped from dense shrubbery lining the road and chopped off Oscar Legbo's head.

He almost fell from his bike, thinking that, perhaps, the ninja would go after him next. Though over 50 feet away, he was the closest rider to Legbo.

But the assailant didn't as much as look at him, and disappeared quickly into the shrubs.

Helmut also bore witness to the aftermath. Oscar remained astride his bike, his neck shooting a fountain of red high into the air. It was vile, disgusting, and Helmet felt sick right down to his core. He wanted to vomit, but knew that he couldn't – everything would become slippery and he would wreck – so he held it in.

As he waited for his gorge to settle, Helmut came to a certain realization. He smiled at that moment, though he still wanted to throw up.

In the Channel 5 Newsroom:

Anchorlady Jane: What you are seeing is real.

(Cut from the anchor to the replay of Oscar Legbo's decapitation. A man in a ninja suit jumps into the road and strikes at Lebgo with a sword. His head flies off his shoulders and hits a small Ukrainian boy in the crowd. Though he is fazed but unhurt, his mother invokes a curse from her tribal god, but no one hears it. Pandemonium erupts as a blood geyser shoots from Oscar Legbo's neck stump, the flow of it so strong and red that it would be beautiful overlaid against the afternoon sky had it not come from a person.)

Anchorlady Jane (voice-over): Oscar Legbo, America's golden boy of professional bicycle racing, is dead.

(The decapitation replay ends – after looping over for six times, three of those six times in slow motion; cut back to the studio.)

Anchorman Tim: Oh my fucking god, Jane! That blood geyser was pumping from his neck like crazy! It didn't look like it would ever end!

Anchorlady Jane: I don't think you're supposed to take our Lord's name in vain or say 'fucking,' on the airwaves, Tim. (*Eyes widen.*) Oh fuck, now I said it!

(A voice off-stage, perhaps that of a stagehand who has just fallen from a ladder or plugged something into a wall socket while standing in a puddle: "Fuck!")

Anchorman Tim: This is worse than the time North Korea dumped loads of nuclear waste off the San Franciscan coast and laughed and screamed taunting, homophobic insults to those who lived in the vicinity.

Anchorlady Jane: I don't remember that happening, Tim.

Anchorman Tim: The only thing you ever remember is who you had to blow to get this job! (*He composes himself.*) Sorry about that, folks. I'm a diehard Oscar Legbo fan, so this is a very trying time. At any rate, I have been informed that the President is making a statement. We will now go live to that.

(Cut to the President. He sits in a chair in the oval office, looking slightly disheveled, like someone has awoken him from a nap.)

President: Today, the sports world – and America as a whole – experienced a tragedy beyond compare. No words I say will console you; I understand this. (*The president leans in closer to the camera.*) But please – I beg of you – do not allow this one act of cowardice to serve as a catalyst for American-on-Ninja violence. I speak from experience when I say that most ninjas are good, caring people who do what they do out of an overarching sense of loyalty, honor, and decency. Again, please do not riot against or in any way harm these treasured members of our national community. Thank you for listening, America; my heart travels out to you today.

(Cut back to the news desk at Channel Five.)

Anchorlady Jane: I didn't realize we had ninjas in our community. But, if we do, I stand by our President in saying please – citizens of America – do not harm them or torch their residences or businesses. What we need now is *healing*, not more pain.

Anchorman Tim: I say let them burn.

(An assistant – who is also a Lebgo fan and, in fact, wears a Legbo shirt – rushes into camera range. He whispers into the anchorman's ears; Tim's eyes widen.)

Anchorman Tim (*to assistant*): What? He's

still going? Oh my God...

* * * *

Ninja:

Before his head can strike the pavement, I'm in surrounding woods, away from the gaze and energy of the crowd, though I still hear the sounds of chaos – screams and shouts and sirens. I hate such noises, but they are constant companions in my line of work.

I am a ninja, my body sleek and well oiled. Though I function as a killing machine, I do not despise my prey; I respect and honor them. Once dispatched, their blood becomes my own and, as it flows through my veins, strangers become brothers.

My target was Oscar Legbo. I had to track him and slaughter him like a beast of burden. Perhaps, in a different life, I might have met this man over a bowl of miso soup (brown not red) where we'd chat for a while, and, if we were both into it, smoke *heycheeba*, the ninja equivalent of herb. Such was not to be. Rather, my sword separated his head swiftly and painlessly from his body. Such is the blessing – and the power and precision – of my blade.

But something uncharacteristic happened today. Right before I struck, things went fuzzy all the sudden. The ground felt like rubber beneath my feet and there was this little buzzer that went off in my head, and it just wouldn't quit. It was like I had a computer up there, something electrical that churned away and made me think things that I didn't want thought.

"*Do it*!" an angry voice screamed inside my skull. "*Do it now!*"

I refused – a ninja does things when *he* wants – but then what felt like angry, long-nailed hands took hold of me, first via my brain, then via my nut sack.

"Okay, okay!" I head-screamed. "I'll do it now!"

The buzzing faded as I lept from the crowd and into the roadway. Then I let my sword grow wings and fly.

I walk through the woods until I can no longer hear the sounds of chaos; I find myself at a stream. It looks inviting, so I sit at its bank, drinking water and contemplating what I've done.

It is a singularly pleasant environment, but I wish I could sit by Legbo instead. It's only the density of the crowd that makes this impossible. Even in his present condition, we could converse, as I'm sure his head still lives. Such is the magic of my blade.

Once, I sat and talked with a noble farmer for over an hour after his decapitation. We became friends, and I told him about my life and he told me about his. In the end, I hated to see the fire go out of his eyes and hated even more the fact that it was my sword that had snuffed it, but that is the way of things.

With lingering heartache, I trace in my mind the events that brought me here today. I realize, with some confusion, that I don't even know who had ordered me to assassinate Oscar Legbo. I just remember being led into a room and forced into a chair, a big sturdy one with a carved wolf's head on the top. Another man was there, too, my nameless and faceless benefactor. He leaned into me, his countenance still lost in shadow, and said: "Do you or don't you?"

"I do," was my response. I remember this clearly now, though I don't think I was wearing the same clothes or – and this may sound weird – the same face when I said it.

No matter. There's really nothing to gain in thinking about the past, but I do it anyway. Though ninja, I am also human, so I get sentimental at times, or sad. But I never get lost in these emotions; I just suck it up and do what I have to do, and now my spirit and the spirit of Oscar Legbo have bonded. We are one, and I will honor his constant presence as it trails me through this life of shadows.

Inside Oscar's severed head:

I am severed; I am severed and I am dead. I am a deadhead. Leghead dead. Bohead Leg.

Wait. That's not right. That's not what (who?) I am. Not at all. I am Osdead BoLego. Or is it Deadleg Bo or, perhaps, just Leghead?

No, none of those seem right. I am . . . I am . . . I am . . . *Oscar Legbo.* Yes. I am Oscar Legbo – bicycle racer extraordinaire and friend to bugs everywhere – and someone has just decapitated me, ruining both my race and my working. It's odd that I'm worrying about such things when I'm dead. You'd think I might have something else on my mind, namely *nothing.*

But, nevertheless, *something* is on my mind. I'm not entirely sure that it's possible, but, if I can get back in control of myself, I might just be able to finish this race, and maybe even the working, too; I have to focus on the here and now, and make myself win. It doesn't matter how many tours I've completed in the past; if I can't finish this one, then I'm a failure. My body is superb and conditioned, and it knows every twist, turn, and bend of this course, but it can't go on forever without a guide.

At the moment, I see only the landscape in front of me tilted at an extreme angle, but maybe, if I put all my energy into it, I can reach out to and control my body. A kindly old monk taught me how to do this with other bodies once, during one of my travels to Tibet. It was difficult at first; I just stared for hours at the darkness behind my eyelids as my instructor chanted indecipherable words in the background – but, finally, I was able to see, and able to hone in on what I saw, so much so that I was able to spy upon Coach de Papa bathing at home, thousands of miles away. As he sat there, unaware of my scrutiny, I made his hands wash his lower body, slowly and with small circular motions that he seemed to enjoy. He was very clean by the time I finished with him.

No. I'm getting lost in the past. I must pull away from it because it's far too distracting, and there's no time for distractions.

My eyes close. In darkness, I am able to hone my concentration, and I concentrate so hard that veins would have probably burst had blood flowed through them still. Once I feel ready, I grab hold of my essence and project it in eddies so as to locate the rest of me.

Yes! Yes, I think I've found it! But no, it's just another racer, the Belgian bastard with bugs on his shoes. I shiver upon realization and break the connection quickly. Finally, I feel myself: the unique presence of a moving body without a head.

I latch onto myself just in time. If I'd stayed in the dead zone (or was it the zone-before-the-dead-zone?) any longer my body would have lost its ingrained memory of the road. Now, I do not worry about such things happening. I can even feel my legs, pumping away. I sense them in a mode that's different from ordinary perception, but it's perception just the same. Then, I focus on my hands and make pale, almost bloodless fingers clutch the *dee-da* tighter.

I suddenly feel confident, more confident than I have in ages. I can overcome any adversity; I just gotta get my head in the race. That's what Coach de Papa always told me. It won't be easy, being decapitated and all, but I'm up for the challenge – *always* up for the challenge.

If it can be done, then Oscar Legbo can do it.

Helmut Starb:

Helmut's bliss became confusion. Oscar's body refused to fall from the bike, and – weirder still – his feet refused to stop manipulating the pedals.

He wondered how he would have reacted if it'd been his head instead of Oscar's. Would he have kept going like a trooper or shat his pants and fell to the road, twitching and dead?

This made him hate Oscar all the more.

He drew in a few deep breaths, but they did nothing to calm him. He had to slow down, to process everything that he'd seen and was seeing. No rider was close to him yet; he remained comfortably in second place, and Oscar had to fall *sometime* before the finish line; the race had over 40 miles to go.

The slower pace did relax him somewhat, and it helped to be further away from Oscar, to not see the blood geyser, his ragged neck, and the little sprig of spine that sprouted from it.

Soon, he heard the *whizzz* of an approaching bike. Someone was gaining on him. He turned around and saw that it was Decker, who slowed down as he approached Helmut.

"Oh God!" Decker shouted, looking at Oscar, who was, from his perspective, a red-spurting dot. "What happened?"

"Some ninja guy cut off Oscar Legbo's head!"

"A ninja guy?"

Helmut nodded.

"Then why's Oscar still in the race?"

"Fuck if I know!"

Decker turned around to face the road and pumped his legs faster. Helmut did likewise, but the Belgian still managed to slip ahead of him.

I don't think I like that guy anymore, Helmut thought.

Ninja:

I lose myself in birdsongs and the sound of the gently babbling stream – then my goddamned head starts buzzing again: "*You must commit* Hiri-kuku!" The voice shouts. "*Do it now!*"

"What!" I say, aloud this time. "That wasn't part of the agreement!"

"*Oh, yes it was. You just don't remember.*"

I cup my face into my hands; I want to live. Still, *Hiri-kuku* provides the noblest way out for a ninja, and all flesh – I remind myself – must rot away eventually.

Hiri-kuku is accomplished by cramming three large sweet potatoes down ones throat until one chokes to death. Too bad I don't have sweet potatoes handy, but my socks are orange and perhaps they'll suffice. Too bad they're only two of them; guess I'll also have to use my underwear.

I bend down, and, with a heavy yet willing heart, remove my black ninja slippers and pull off my bright orange tube socks.

Bright orange tube socks?

I stare at them, again confused. Shouldn't I be wearing sleek and silky ninja stockings? But these socks have different colored bands printed around their tops, like something an 80s kid would wear.

No matter. I rip them from my feet and stuff them, reeking, into my mouth. (*Are ninja feet supposed to reek? Fuck it.*) Then I remove my sleek ninja pants and see that I'm wearing tighty whities beneath them, and that my legs and thighs are flabby and pasty, like those of an overweight, thirty-something American.

But why would I have this sword and mask if I were not a ninja? I didn't see other people dressed up today. It's certainly not Halloween.

My head starts buzzing again. When the voice speaks, it's positively screaming.

"*Ninjas don't know about Halloween, you dumb ass.*"

I spit the socks from my mouth. "Shut up!"

"*It's a western thing.*"

"I know! I know!"

"*So, if you know this, then you also know there's no way you're a ninja from 16th century Japan.*"

"Fuck you, fuck you, I am a ninja! Fuck you!"

I run behind a tree and beat my head upon nurturing and life-giving ground. When the voices finally stop, my forehead is lacerated and there are twigs in my mask.

In the Channel 5 Newsroom:

Anchorlady Jane: If you are just joining us, Oscar Legbo has not only again proved his stamina and virility by racing without a head, but has also provided the world with a truly unique and amazing moment in sports.

Anchorman Tim: *Amazing* is not the word. Try *ball-staggering*, Jane.

Anchorlady Jane: Why don't I just stick with *amazing*? At any rate, what was once national mourning has become national hope. If Oscar Legbo manages to pull through, not only will he win his eighth *Tour de Saucisse-Dommages*, but he'll also become the first rider to do so while decapitated.

Anchorman Tim: Keep in mind that he has over twenty miles to go before he reaches the finish line.

Anchorlady Jane: If past performance is any indicator, then Oscar Legbo should have no problem.

Anchorman Tim (*bites his bottom lip*): But he had a frickin' head then, woman! Sheesh! (*Draws in a deep, calming breath.*) But if anyone is capable of pulling off such a feat, it's Oscar Legbo.

Anchorlady Jane: And now we go to roving reporter Jake Dallas for another edition of *The Word on the Street*.

(*Cuts to a heavyset young man, standing with a microphone on the corner of a busy city street.*)

Jake Dallas: Thank you, Jane. (*He approaches a smart looking woman in a business suit.*) What do you think Oscar's chances are of winning this year's *Tour de Saucisse-Dommages*?

Woman: He'll win. I have faith in Oscar, and think he'll do America proud next year, too.

Jake Dallas: You think he'll be in next year's race, too?

Woman: Yes.

Jake Dallas (*approaches a middle-aged man in a ball cap and wife-beater*): And how about you, sir? Do you think Oscar Legbo still has what it takes to win?

Man (*speaks while crushing a beer can against his crotch*): Whew fuckin' hoo! A-frikin'merica baby!

Jake Dallas: I guess that means yes. (*He faces the camera.*) So, as you can see, the American public believes Oscar Legbo has what it takes to win this race – and perhaps future races – even without a head.

(*Cut from Jake Dallas to live shot of the Tour de Saucisse-Dommages. Oscar's body is seen, pumping the pedals and controlling the handlebar in such a way that if one were to put a sheet of paper on the television where his head used to be and ignore all the blood on his clothes and bike, one would think that things were still par for the course.*)

Anchorlady Jane (voice-over): The blood geyser is still flowing, I had no idea a man could have that much gore in him, but I no longer see it as a disgusting thing. I now think of it as a red *Fountain of Freedom*.

Anchorman Tim (voice-over): That's very touching, Jane. I'm sorry I said all those bad things about you earlier.

(*Live feed ends.*)

Helmut Starb:

Walri Power Go! He thought, and allowed the strength of the *Odobenus rosmarus* to become his own. Helmut pedaled harder and harder until he was right on Decker's tail.

But, as it so happened, he didn't need the extra get-up-and-go because Decker had slowed down considerably. Once neck-and-neck with Oscar, he now trailed him by at least twenty feet.

Helmut swerved to his left, maneuvering his bike so that it traveled alongside the Belgian's. He shouted: "I don't care if you or I win, just as long as one of us beats Legbo! It's now or—"

Helmut froze. Decker sported the largest boner he had ever seen.

"What the – what the hell are you thinking about?"

The Belgian didn't respond immediately. His eyes didn't even seem to be looking at anything in this world, though they were focused on the red geyser still shooting miraculously from Legbo's neck stump.

"Oh god! Oh god, it's so beautiful!"

"What? *That's* giving you a hard-on?" Helmut crinkled his nose; a fan of Oscar's blood had gotten on the man's pants. "It's not sexy, it's disgusting. And you're a sick fuck, Decker."

"No, not *it*," he moaned. "Look *into* it and see!"

"Excuse me?"

"The *things* – the beautiful twisty golden spirals of eternal agape love! See them!"

"Eternal agape what?"

"LOVE!" Decker screamed, eyes bulging so far that Helmut feared they might shoot out and hit him. Then he noticed thin wisps of smoke rising both from Decker's ears and from his slightly parted mouth.

"Are you okay?" Helmut shouted, his confusion making him say the first thing that came to mind. "Do you need an antacid or something?"

Instead of replying, the Belgian burst into flames.

Ninja:

I've never felt lower or more dejected in my life – but I am *Ninja*; this I must believe. It's the core of my being, my *Upbranahamanan*, my uppermost soul. Evidence to the contrary shall not sway me. I don't care if a million screaming cops descend upon me in Messerschmitt fashion and have me locked in a padded room where I receive Thorazine and enemas for the remainder of my days. These things are *mayanamanana*, illusion. Sweet and green Japanese fields will always be my home, but even they too are illusion. The only thing that is real is me…

… and I am *Ninja*.

Inside Oscar's severed head:

I feel someone try to pick up my head and, judging from the sound of rustling plastic, put it in a bag. I don't know if it's a paramedic or a souvenir seeker, and I don't care either way.

"Leave me alone! I'm fucking trying to concentrate here!" I manage to groan, the sound like water gurgling through a leaf-clogged drain.

The man runs away, screaming.

That particular distraction is gone, but another follows, and it's far more difficult to ignore or brush off. The bugs have returned; I imagine that they are huge and I am tiny, and I am lost in their world. Once again, I am connected to a body, but, if I could, I'd wish it away. Angry souls surround it, bite at it, stomp-tickle it with bristly feet.

"Please stop," I shout at them. "Please leave me alone and let me do what I have to do!"

"You didn't leave us alone, Mr. Legbo," they say, their voice a collective one, high-pitched and nearly sonic. "So why should we leave you alone?"

"Haven't I done enough? Haven't I atoned?"

"You can never atone, not in our eyes, eyes which once saw and enjoyed the world, but no longer."

"I need to win. That's all I ask of you. Let me win this race, please."

"That's not possible. You belong to us, and it's only fitting that you do."

"But I wear your image on my uniform! My severed head has plastic antennae stuck to it! Don't these things count?"

"No."

Rage like I hadn't felt in years builds up inside. "Well, fuck you, then! I was silly for loving you, for caring that I killed you! You're just bugs for Christ's sake! I'm going to win this race and I'm going to do it without you!"

The bug spirits waver and hitch as though their forms have become quicksilver on a hot city street. When they are gone, Coach de Papa appears before me, glistening. Shirtless, he wears the same tiny pair of red running shorts that I've grown to know and love. His look is rugged, and a moustache stretches across the entirety of his aged yet joyful face.

Still, his eyes seem far off: "Oscar, I am so proud."

I can barely speak. "Coach – Coach de Papa is that you?"

"Of course, Oscar."

"But you're dead."

"And you – for all intents and purposes – are, too."

He has a point. "But why are you here? And why are you proud?"

"Because you finally got off your bug kick, that's why. I wish you knew how much it pained me to see such a talented man live his life with such a silly, silly burden. You went far in that life, but you could have gone farther had you been free." Coach de Papa pauses to flex, his seventy-six year old body firm and taunt. "Too bad you had to lose your head before you realized this, but that's the way the world works sometimes."

"Yes, Coach de Papa, I know."

"But you were always stubborn, and you marched to the sound of your own drum, for good or for ill." His eyes sparkle. "And that's why I always admired you, even if that admiration was begrudging at times."

"But I killed you, Coach de Papa."

"I don't worry about that anymore."

I look down at my imaginary feet. "You seemed so angry before you died."

"You're sure as shit I was angry. I didn't want to be messed with, not then. You could have talked to me, that would have been fine, but you had to go and mess with the trident."

"But I couldn't just watch you die."

"Would you want someone messing with a trident if every time he touched it your entire body rippled with pain?"

"No, Coach de Papa. I wouldn't, and I'm sorry."

"I know you're sorry; you have a good heart." Coach de Papa offers a thin smile. "Come to think of it, you remind me of myself at your age, only less gay."

I feel as though someone has punched me. "What!"

Coach de Papa moves in closer and lays a big, thick hand down on my imaginary shoulder. "Be true to yourself, Oscar."

"I – I don't know what to say, Papa."

"Perhaps this the best – if not only – time to figure out what to say." Coach de Papa shakes his head. "You can be the world's greatest bicycle racer and be gay at the same time, you know."

Events that I had forgotten suddenly flood back and, once the pieces come together, they make sense: The times I'd watch Coach de Papa from the corner of my eye in the changing room, the day I pantsed him playfully, but really wanted to see if he wore anything beneath his shorts (which he didn't), and the fact that I masturbated to his picture not once but twice.

"Yes, Papa," I finally say. "Yes, I see. And while I don't admit that I was gay, I admit that I was gay for you."

"That's enough for me, Oscar. Good boy." He rakes his hands across my imaginary chest and shakes away sweat. "That's what I've always wanted to hear."

"It is?"

"Yes, now stop obsessing. Clear your mind and do what needs to be done. Focus. Get your head in the race. Okay?"

"I will, Coach de Papa."

"Win for me. Fuck a bunch of bugs."

"I will, on both counts."

He turns away. "I gotta go now. My time here is through."

"Okay, but it was good seeing you again."

"You, too."

"Goodbye, Coach."

"Goodbye, Oscar." He smiles – widely and warmly, just the way I remember – and then he's gone.

Suddenly, I'm back on the ground, eyes closed and focusing again on the race. I feel that the antennae have slid from my head, and it's a good thing.

My head is in the race like never before.

Helmut Starb:

Helmut fell back and made sure not to stare directly into the red fountain spurting from Oscar's neck. If the Belgian could spontaneously combust, then he figured the same could happen to him.

Pierre LaChaise, the Frenchman, took advantage of this opportunity and passed Helmut without a backwards glance.

At that moment, he decided he didn't much like that guy anymore, either.

Ninja:

The voice in my head: *We're really happy that you feel good about yourself and all, but it's time for* Hiri-kuku *now. Please, do not keep us waiting.*

The buzz that accompanies this voice no longer bothers me, for I now know what I have to do, and have come to terms with it. I delay no longer. I pick up my tube socks from the ground without dusting them. I put them in my mouth, along with my briefs, but cannot swallow these things enough to choke.

I must use a stick, so I take one from the ground beside me and ram it against the wad in my throat until my hands are raw and bloody. The briefs remain stuck to the back of my throat, but the socks, I imagine, are far enough down to get the job done. My skin is sweaty; I cannot breathe, and my heart races. Ninja training had covered *Hiri-kuku*, but it did nothing to prepare me for the actual experience.

I must relax; I cannot freak out.

Once again, my head buzzes: "*A ninja does not use the term 'freak out'.*"

"Shut up!" I think-scream. "I'm trying to die here!"

The voice falls mercifully silent. I collapse into a carpet of leaves. Bringing my hands to my face, I see that they are blue. When I bring them down, a great vortex spins before me, growing wider by the second.

I say in my head: *Oh sweet Brumahumananan, or whatever god Ninjas worship – provided I am, in fact, a ninja and not some overweight thirty-nine year old trucker named Joe – protect me as I pass from this world and enter the next!*

But then the pain goes away. The world for which I'd prayed opens before me, and it no longer matters whether I'm a ninja or not. All that matters is that I visualize myself amongst the corky, twisty trees of the orient, thinking, oddly enough, of a particularly tasty hamburger I'd eaten at a Tulsa, Oklahoma rest stop in 1992.

Inside Oscar's severed head:

Just when I think I'm going to make it, a pleasant haze washes over my brain. It's tempting, and I want to fall headlong into it, but I must hold out. I haven't gone this far just to stop. I didn't beat the bugs and express undying love for my dead coach to fall before reaching the finish.

But I can no longer feel my legs, and can only barely feel my hands. I see them with my mind's eye, still confidently pumping away and gripping, but don't know how long they can maintain such efficiency without 100% of my essence there to guide them.

Focusing on my body is now useless, so I pan my gaze out in front of me, to the road as it unfurls. I'm familiar with this stretch as I'm familiar with all stretches along the *Tour de Saucisse-Dommages*. There's only a mile to go, give or take, but that upstart Frenchman is neck-and-neck with me.

It's almost as though he senses my scrutiny as he turns to my body and extends his middle finger while laughing. Has he no respect for the dead?

In the Channel 5 Newsroom:

Anchorlady Jane: I've just received word that a rider – #4, Pierre LaChaise from Catrombeau, France – is gaining on Oscar and may just take the lead.

Anchorman Tim (*slams fists on desk until knuckles bleed*): Goddamn that asshole! I hope he breaks his neck!

(*Cut to live news-feed from the* Tour de Saucisse-Dommages. *Pierre LaChaise vies with Oscar Legbo for the lead. He smirks confidently as he taunts Legbo, but that confident look turns to one of sudden terror. His eyes grow wide and a pained expression spreads across his face. Then he collapses against the handlebars. Seconds later, the bicycle goes over a ravine, immediately after which the scene cuts back to the news desk.*)

Anchorlady Jane: It appears as though Pierre LaChaise has suffered a heart attack and

may, in fact, be dead. Unless something major happens, Oscar Legbo will surely win the last stage of the *Tour de Saucisse-Dommages*.

Anchorman Tim: Yes! Go, Legbo, go!

Meanwhile, as all this is taking place:

The CEO of *Legbo International* paced across an oak and marble boardroom as he rethought his global strategy. Two other men were in attendance, seated at a long, rectangular table in an otherwise empty room.

"I want to ask you" – the CEO stopped pacing – "if it's possible to effectively market a headless role model."

A sycophant: "I don't see why not."

"Won't the T-shirts appear distasteful?"

"Perhaps, but I've heard that kids go for gore."

"Really?"

The sycophant nodded.

The CEO resumed pacing. "Of course, we'll have to revise our action figure line, too. And we'll have to do more than just remove their heads. Something else needs to be done, something that will give them extra added *oomph*."

"Excuse me, sir, but could they have super squirting action?"

The CEO spent a few moments in thought. Then: "I *love* that idea."

The third wheel: "And you'd need the liquid inside to be red, of course."

"Of course," the sycophant replied. "Do you think we're idiots?"

"No sir. I do most certainly *not* think – under any set of possible circumstances – that anyone in this room today is an idiot."

The CEO leered. "Are you sure about that?"

"Yes, sir!"

The sycophant turned to the other man. "Personally, I'm not so sure."

The CEO laughed.

The third wheel sulked.

Ninja:

I come to and realize what I'd seen wasn't ninja heaven at all. I was just suffering from delusions brought on by panic and a lack of oxygen. Also, the socks and briefs have slipped from my throat and out of my mouth before they could choke me to death.

My head starts buzzing, louder than ever. *"What kind of fucking ninja are you? You can't even commit* hiri-kuku!*"*

I get up, slowly. "I – I'm sorry. I am a bad ninja and, through my failings, have brought a great and everlasting shame down upon my head."

"You can say that again."

I say that again; then sigh and bend down to retrieve my clothing. I put the socks and underwear back on, unnerved to feel their wet stickiness against my skin, but they're all I've got, so they must suffice. Then I slip the bottom half of my ninja gear back on, but wearing it feels wrong, as I may no longer be worthy of the honor.

"You're not, so hold your breath until you die."

There is too much inner feedback for me to hear them the first time: "What?"

"I said hold your breath until you die!"

I try this, but each time my heart starts racing and my face starts turning blue, I exhale with a gush.

"You're not supposed to start breathing again! That's the whole point!"

"But it hurts if I don't breathe!"

"Of course it hurts! It's supposed to kill you, you dumb ass."

"Please, give me another way out!"

"Okay, then. Why don't you swallow your tongue?"

"But that is a *very* dishonorable way for a ninja to die! It will bring shame not only to me, but to my entire community!"

"Do it anyway!"

And so I do, but, again, it fails to work; my tongue just isn't long enough.

The buzzing is now so loud I fear I might go deaf. *"We hoped it wouldn't come to this, but you give us no choice. For failing three times, you must be punished."*

I steel myself, apprehensive yet nevertheless ready to accept the punishment, for I know, in my broken ninja heart, that I deserve whatever I get.

The shouted commands begin:
"Bop yourself in the head!"
I bop myself in the head.
"Stick your fingers in your eyes!"
I stick my fingers in my eyes.
"Say you're a stupid, fairy pansy muthafucka!"
"I am a stupid, fairy pansy muthafucka."

Another voice, usually there's only one: *"Stop it! Now you're just playing with him."*

"Sorry. Where was I?"

"You were punishing me, sir."

"Yes, yes. That's right. Well, we're finished with that."

"Now that I've been punished, can I go on with my life and not commit *hiri-kuku*?"

"No," the voice again roars. *"Commit* hiri-kuku! *How many times do we have to fucking say it?"*

I don't know what to do, so I look around for things that, if used correctly, might prove deadly. First, I try to drown myself in the creek, but it's the same as holding my breath; each time it starts to hurt, I stop. Then, I poke at myself with a stick for fifteen minutes, but it does nothing but irritate my skin. Later, I find a long, green garden snake and try to strangle myself with it, but it bites me and I scream and the thing slithers away.

I try everything in the woods, but nothing there will kill me, or maybe it's that everything around me *is* lethal, but I just don't have the balls to make anything *be* lethal.

"You're fucking hopeless; do you know that?"

"Yes," I say. "Yes, I know."

In the Channel 5 Newsroom:

Anchorlady Jane (*unfastens the top two buttons on her blouse*): Well, it looks like I've come down with Legbo Fever tonight.

Anchorman Tim: That doesn't make you special, Jane. The whole country has Legbo Fever.

Anchorlady Jane (*quickly refastens the top two buttons on her blouse*): You might be right, Tim. At any rate, this is a glorious day for America.

Anchorman Tim: Better than Christmas, the Fourth of July, and a good Tijuana lay, all wrapped into one.

Anchorlady Jane: I wouldn't know about Tijuana lays, but—

Anchorman Tim *(appears as though he might be masturbating behind his desk)*: Take a look at this! Can you believe it, Jane? Oh shit! Oh holy shit! Yes! *Yes!* It looks like Oscar Lego is just seconds away from winning his eighth *Tour de Saucisse-Dommages*!

Inside Oscar's severed head:

I feel bad for what happened to the Frenchman. He was an asshole, but didn't deserve to die. I didn't even know that I could do that. I just projected my anger at him – in the most dark, horrible and drippy corpse-like form I could muster – and hoped he might sense the presence and feel a vague sense of unease. I didn't expect that he would actually see the thought-form and *die*.

But oh well…

With the Frenchman gone, the end is in sight. Ordinarily, I'd feel very comfortable at this point in the race, but now I feel less certain, the prospect of making it all the way no longer guaranteed. Everything is dark and fuzzy before it goes over to gray, then black.

Helmut Starb:

Fuck it. If I spontaneously combust or fall of a cliff, just fuck it. I'll win this race if it kills me.

Helmut concentrated on his skullcap and there found the strength to pump the pedals with *pinnipedal power* – (At that moment, he reminded himself that he should have the phrase 'pinnipedal power' trademarked as quickly as possible) – and, in a matter of seconds, caught sight of Legbo.

"You're mine, bugfucker!" He moved in to usurp the lead, so close now that Oscar's blood splashed on him, turning his white and blue racing uniform red. Helmut found himself enjoying, if not luxuriating in, the hot and sticky warmth, and wondering if this made him a freak.

But the sensation, he soon discovered, wasn't erotic at all. The blood was doing something to him – perhaps on a molecular level – and reminding him of the time he dropped acid at college in Frankfurt.

Maybe, he thought, *I should let Oscar win.*

Then: *What am I thinking?*

And then: *Oscar deserves it; Oscar is great and bugs are great. Better than walri.*

Finally: *No they're not – but they are! Oh God, they are!*

Against his will, Helmut looked deeply into the Fountain of Freedom, past the apparent and into the *real*. What he saw scrubbed his mind, and he could only think, *it's love; it's all love* over and over again. Physically, his hair stood on end; his walri skullcap tumbled off his scalp, and his phallus extended so fast and furiously that the boner snapped his tiny Euro briefs.

Something bubbled inside him; he broke into a sweat that was first hot then cold. Helmut couldn't see his ears, but he knew smoke rose from them. If he didn't release energy soon he would combust, so he jumped off the bike and tore a hole in his racing uniform right over the crotch. Then he got facedown on the road, arched his back, and, with his right hand – and in front of an audience of millions – saved himself from a fiery demise.

No one at the race or in the viewing audience paid much attention, however. All eyes were turned to Legbo, his Fountain of Freedom shooting higher than ever as he crossed the finish line in first place.

Inside Oscar's severed head:

I sense that I have crossed the finish line, but have no way of knowing this. Also, I have no way of knowing how much time has passed, for the void that now wants me seems timeless. No matter. Such things are no longer in my realm of concern. I've done what I needed to get done; now I can rest.

At the very last second, my perception returns, like a personal slideshow that I'm able to tune into from afar. My headless corpse is now being carried, held aloft by countless loving hands.

I also sense that my working has been successful; I feel a presence around me now, one that I've never felt outside the meditative state. Still, I don't know how long the working can be sustained without me around to guide and nurture it; I fear it will fade as I do, but maybe a taste of agape love is all the world needs to satiate itself..

I want to smile, but cannot. I couldn't have asked for a better scene with which to end my life, so I allow my inner eyes to close. As my mind begins to unfurl, I again scream out to the only man I have ever loved.

Coach de Papa, Coach de Papa, be my guru and infuse meaning into my soul. In my last thought, as a gift to you, I will think of a dee-da as a handlebar. That was another thing you always wanted, and I know this

now. Coach de Papa, Coach de Papa – forgive me for my blindness, and, most of all, forgive me for killing you when I should have squashed the bug.

His voice returns, booming in my head: "I forgive you, son."

He called me 'son.' I can die now. I can die. I die.

Where am I?

The Outpouring:

(*So many reports and updates have come into the studio since Oscar's victory that Anchorman Tim has had no time to celebrate. Stagehands constantly cycle by the desk, throwing small white notes onto it. The surface is covered, but they throw still more. Both anchors scramble to keep up with the influx, but are drowning.*)

Anchorlady Jane (*passes out briefly, unable to withstand the volume of reports, updates, and newsflashes*).

Anchorman Tim (*pauses to catch his breath*): This is truly the greatest fucking moment in sports.

Anchorlady Jane (*lifts head briefly to read from a note, and then drops it again*): Yes, Tim. People are spontaneously combusting. Fire is everywhere, but the fire is said to be beautiful beyond words.

Anchorman Tim: And for every person on fire there is another masturbating in public, but no one cares because even the police are doing it.

Anchorlady Jane (*arises for the long haul and picks up a report littered with pie charts and diagrams*): And it is predicted that, twenty years from now, Oscar will be the legal name of approximately 876,040,530 people worldwide.

Anchorman Tim: Also, the CDC has declared Legbo Fever to be the first ever *epidemic of joy.*

Anchorlady Jane *(picks up yet another note, appearing to have been rendered in orange crayon)*: A litter of alien atomic kittens (or AAK, for short) was discovered wrapped up in a basket near Hyde Park today. It is unknown whether these creatures were alive or dead at the time of their discovery. We will keep you updated as to how this story develops.

Anchorman Tim (*is handed another sheet of paper, but this time the stagehand shoves it directly in his face, like it's very, very important and must be read* now): This just in: there is no more war; there is no more famine, and the dead are no longer dead. Rejoice, America; your loved ones return!

Anchorlady Jane (*receives her own urgent message and reads it on-air*): Crackbabies are no longer crackbabies!

Anchorman Tim: The national debt has vanished!

Anchorlady Jane: And hospitals and mortuaries have closed down!

Anchorman Tim (*sweeps notes to the floor and gets atop the desk and rends his clothing)*: There is nothing but love, shooting, spurting gouts of effervescent love, covering the nation – in *love.*

(Anchorman Tim *and* Anchorlady Jane *lose focus. They dart their eyes about the studio and swat their arms around in the air as though fending off something that the viewing audience cannot see.*)

Anchorlady Jane: It's too big, too big and righteous. I can't let it into my body!

Anchorman Tim: It's too strong, Jane! You can't fight it!

(Nevertheless, they continue to fight for another minute, after which time they finally give in to the moment. Violent seizures rock their bodies; their eyes roll in ecstasy. Minutes pass before Anchorman Tim *and* Anchorlady Jane *regain consciousness. When they do, their eyes look different, glassy.)*

Anchorlady Jane *(turns to Anchorman Tim)*: I want you inside me.

Anchorman Tim: You're already there.

Anchorlady Jane: Am I?

Anchorman Tim: Yes.

Anchorlady Jane: And have I always been there – *(pupils dilate suddenly)* – coiling inside your soul?

Anchorman Tim: Yes.

Anchorlady Jane *(looks at her hands)*: Am I tripping out?

Anchorman Tim: Relax. Just go with the flow.

Anchorlady Jane: Am I going to die, Tim?

Anchorman Tim: No Jane, you're going to live.

Anchorlady Jane *(goes with the flow)*: I am Love, Tim.

Anchorman Tim: And I am Love, Jane.

(They lift their hands and touch their palms together and stare into each other's eyes.)

Anchormanlady Timjane: We now are Linked; we are United; we are One. God is with us. We are with God. God is with us. We are with God.

(They repeat these two lines twenty-five times before saying anything new.)

Anchorladyman Janetim: It is *void* that I see; it is Nirvana. We are here. Radiate with us. Radiate with our splendor.

(They babble for fifteen minutes before falling silent. With vacant expressions, they stare at and into the camera for another fifteen, sometimes reaching arms out as though to touch something. No one in the studio cares, nor does anyone in the home audience, either, because they're all doing the same thing.)

The Ultimate End:

The crowd at the finish line carried Oscar's body for nearly ten minutes, hooting, hollering, and enveloped by the sheer joy that was Legbo. They imagined they carried him not atop the ground, but in space, atop a blanket of exploding, Technicolor stars. By the time they dropped him by the winner's platform, the hallucinations had ended, and the red *Fountain of Freedom* had gone dry.

Still, the press corps gathered around a now garland and tinsel draped Legbo, often having their pictures made with him or contorting his body into suggestive or alluring poses. Someone else shook a bottle of champagne, opened it, and, in the spirit of celebration, sprayed its contents all over Legbo. Yet another approached Oscar and rubbed his hands up and down his cold chest and, in an entirely different spirit, groped Legbo's package repeatedly. No one stopped the man from doing this, so quite a few others soon joined in.

"Speech! Speech!" someone said.

But Oscar made no speech.

Everyone waited for him to get up, thinking, perhaps, that he was just tired from the race, but he never did.

When realization set in, hooting and hollering turned into lunging and slobbering.

In the Channel 5 Newsroom:

Anchorman Tim *(sits with his head on the desk and his fingers laced in his hair, down from his sudden agape love high and feeling very hung over. Just seconds earlier he had been animated, coming out of his love trance and spraying various fluids all over the newsroom and the people in it. When he finally speaks, his voice sounds lifeless)*: It's now official; Oscar Lebgo is completely and utterly *dead*.

Anchorlady Jane *(feels separation anxiety due to her sudden soul-split with Tim, but maintains composure for the camera's sake, though her bra still hangs half-on/half-off the desk)*: That's true, and it's also been reported that numerous fights have broken out amongst the crowd at the *Tour de Saucisse-Dommages*. It is uncertain at this moment whether fatalities are involved, but I've been told that these skirmishes are especially brutal and involve most, if not all, of the spectators.

Anchorman Tim: Whoop de shit.

Back in the Boardroom:

"Damn it! Damn it all!" The CEO of *Legbo International* reached into a desk drawer and removed a box of capsules. "I never thought it would come to this." He turned to the sycophant. "Give one capsule to every worker here today, and then take one yourself."

The sycophant arose from his chair and gave a salute. "Yes, sir!"

"Good. Now take the box; do what you have to do."

The sycophant disappeared quickly from the office, box in hand.

"And you" – he turned to the third wheel – "I want you on corpse detail, and don't forget to take *your* pill afterwards."

"Must I?"

"Of course; you know the drill." The CEO smiled. "And I'm taking mine last just to make sure you take yours first."

Ninja:

As much as I might want to, I cannot stay here. If I cannot die, then I must return home and face the wrath of my community. But then I realize that I don't know where home is or if I'm even part of a community.

And what will I do once I get wherever it is I'm going? What *can* a one-time ninja do in the real world? Work fast food? Wash cars? It's not as though I have money to go back to college.

My answer is suddenly clear: I must become a wanderer; I will have no brothers or sisters, and a staff will be my constant companion.

* * * *

I walk for almost twenty minutes before I again hear the sounds of chaos. Instead of dying down, the noises have gotten louder.

As I begin to see the road, I realize things are hanging from the trees that line it. I can't see what they are until I get closer: people dangling without pants, for their pants now serve as both ropes and hangman's nooses. A few of the bodies still twitch, though most are still.

I wonder what caused this, and then hope that whatever did wouldn't cause the same to happen to me, especially since I'm wearing tighty whities and would hate to be caught dead in them.

But I am *Ninja*; I must be strong; I must ready myself for any possible assault against me. In preparation, I reach down deep to locate my chi, but it's nowhere to be found.

I exit the woods anyway, and then enter into madness. At first I think monsters are ripping at each other with teeth and hands like claws. Then I realize these monsters possess human forms, which makes me think they're zombies – or, as we ninjas call them,

gualangas – but the absence of decaying flesh tells me this cannot be so.

An ugly, misshapen man passes close by, though he does not turn in my direction. It takes some time for me to realize that this isn't a man at all, but a woman wearing a freshly shorn skin suit.

Then a voice interrupts my thoughts, but it's not in my head: "Hey, ninja-man," a young, crew cut guy in an Oscar Legbo t-shirt mumbles as he lurches towards me, something hanging from his mouth that looks suspiciously like a severed penis. "Wanna *rumble-ahhaha* with me?"

I do not know what this person is talking about, so I say nothing.

He gets closer. Now I see that the thing is undoubtedly a penis and, judging by the growing red stain on his pants, it's his own. "I said, do you want to *rumble-ahhaha*?"

This man won't leave me alone, so I humor him: "I'll gladly *rumble-ahhaha* with you, provided the taste of my sword is to your liking."

I look down, and realize that I've left my sword in the woods. "*Fuck*," I say under my breath and run away, but barely go two steps before encountering another bunch of crazies. These bastards are all committing variations of *hiri-kuku*, successfully, and in mass numbers. And they aren't even ninjas, just stupid flabby Americans and Europeans. I hate them. I hate them so much.

My head buzzes: "*Face it, you're just jealous because they can commit* hiri-kuku *and you can't!*"

And it is then that I realize – truly realize – that the voices in my head have always been right, and that I do suck – and suck hard – as a ninja.

In the Channel 5 Newsroom:

Anchorlady Jane: And we again go live to reporter Jake Dallas for perhaps the most important segment of *The Word on the Street* ever.

(*Cuts to the same heavyset young man, standing with a microphone on the corner of the same city street.*)

Jake Dallas: What do you think our chances are of surviving until tomorrow?

Man #1: (*Dressed like a TV repairman.*) Slim to none. The Fuck Apocalypse has arrived. It's so bad outside now that all we can do is go inside and fuck.

Jake Dallas: I guess you better get going, then. Sorry to keep you. (*Turns from the man and approaches a woman dressed as a bohemian poet.*) Now, I'd like to ask you that same question.

Woman: It's all death and death and gray and gray. It's all thunderstorms, cloudbursts, and rainy days.

Jake Dallas: Indeed, and how about you, sir?

Man #2: (*dressed like a total retard*): We're totally plungered, dude.

Jake Dallas: And you? (*Turns to a man dressed head to toe in entrails. Otherwise, he is naked.*)

Man #3: Skidee-haha! Skidau alpo-mennyhanah! Skidoo delap-nahanaha! (*He attempts to lick Jake Dallas, his hands leaving deep red stains on the reporter's suit as he clutches it.*)

Jake Dallas: Please, you're upsetting me, and need to back away.

Man #3 (*rediscovers his human tongue*): You didn't say 'the fuck.'

Jake Dallas: Excuse me?

Man #3: For me to have taken you seriously you would have to have said 'and need to back *the fuck* away.'

Jake Dallas: I'm sorry. Can I – say it again?

Man #3: No, too late! Skidaa hoffa-nomenklatta! I'm going to rip your heart out with my teeth! (*Then he does just that.*)

(*Cut to the news desk at Channel 5.*)

Anchorlady Jane: We hope the best for Jake Dallas.

Anchorman Tim: Fuck him. (*He leaves his desk with a lumbering gate.*) And fuck everything else for that matter.

Anchorlady Jane (*is very confused*): Well, I guess the show has to – uh… wait, I'm receiving word that people – perhaps hundreds of them – are throwing things at our downtown office.

(*A blood-leaking stagehand staggers up to Jane and hands her a note before collapsing.*)

Anchorlady Jane: Oh, my God, if what I'm reading is true, then that man Jake interviewed was right. The Fuck Apocalypse has arrived as people – if I can even call them that – throw severed human heads and various other freshly carved parts at our downtown office. Please stop doing this. Please stop rioting. No sports figure is worth a single life lost. I'd even say no god is worth it. Please stop. There have been reports of cannibalism. Don't do this. Please go home now; tend to your families. (*Her eyes widen and her mouth becomes a wide O.*) Oh my God, Tim!

(Anchorman Tim *is presently off camera, biting an unresponsive stagehand. Then he chows down, ripping away and then consuming half the man's face in a single bite. Tim notices her attention and lunges in her direction, a piece of gristle hanging over his bottom lip.)*

Anchorlady Jane (Spoken off camera, while running): And now we go live to an emergency address from the President!

(Cut to the President, again sitting in a chair in the oval office. He too appears to have something hanging over his lip.)

President: Oh Glory *Hallelujanamarah* – or however you people out there say it – we, as a nation, have gone from the heights of expectation to the heights of sorrow to the heights of joy and back again in a single day. Oh *God-Narharmarhar* – this is too much for us, myself included, to take.

    My Fellow Americans, we have long feared its arrival, but *Apocalypse Fuck* is finally here.

Intersplice: The Office of Standards and Practices
would do something, provided people there weren't busy fucking and/or killing each other.

President (*cont.*):

Fellow nations, please don't look down on Americans or America as a whole; you can't expect us *not* to break down, to break down and cry, if not scream and rend things, breaking the intact and annihilating the already broken; nor can we be expected not to put things in our mouths or other cavities that were never intended for such ingress, or not to run naked and screaming through the dark and sticky passageways of a night that will never end.

    I'm sorry – so terribly sorry – but there's no magic pill to swallow that will return us to our previous state. It is a paradise lost. And so – beginning with this proclamation – Oscar Legbo supplants the eagle to become America's new symbol, one that our beautiful dead and dying nation can get behind as it takes that great and final leap into the Forever Beyond.

    Ladies and gentleman, I've said all that I can say, and now must leave you. (*President removes a small caliber revolver from his coat and blows his brains out on national TV.*)

(Cut back to the newsroom, but there's no one there, and the camera is slightly askew.)

GINA RANALLI

LOCATION:
Seattle, WA

STYLE OF BIZARRO:
Chunky Absurd

BOOKS BY RANALLI:

Chemical Gardens
Suicide Girls in the Afterlife
13 Thorns (w/ Gus Fink) – forthcoming

DESCRIPTION: Gina's stories are absurd and bizarre, with a twist of the dark side. She will take you down some unexpected roads and leave you in the dust, crying for your mother. Sometimes there is a fair amount of swearing and that kind of shit in her books. Well…more than sometimes. Her stories might piss some people off. In fact, she hopes they do.

INTERESTS: environmentalism, feminism, eco-warriors, animal rights, veganism, metal and punk bands, guitars, Halloween, zombies, skulls, horror flicks, tattoos, stacking books so high around the room that they are a crushing hazard.

INFLUENCES: Tim Burton, Jackson Pollock, Kerouac, Vonnegut, Rosa Parks, Dorothy Parker, Basquiat, Kurt Cobain, trazodone dreams, lava lamps, lots of caffeine.

WEBSITE:

www.myspace.com/ginaranalli

SUICIDE GIRLS IN THE AFTERLIFE

CHAPTER ONE

Tramping through the electric forest on a rainy night is suicide.

All around me, tin-foil trees glow silver-white, lightning branches scratching the belly of the black sky which thunder-purrs its pleasure and promises a newborn baby downpour.

Still, the night birds are unfazed by the threatening weather. Back and forth, they sing static to each other and occasionally I get a glimpse of their comet eyes gazing down at me as I pass.

I'm searching for the river of ice. I increase my pace, knowing that the instant rain begins to fall, I'm fried. The entire forest will connect to itself and become a web of electricity, impossible to move through without catching more than a friendly volt.

Tuning out the cacophony of the woods and listening *beneath* it, I at last hear the *clunk clunk clunk* of the river. Almost there.

Already, I can feel my hair coming alive, sizzling on my head and reaching for the sky. Moving too fast to avoid a low branch, my shoulder grazes it and I yelp as a jolt shoots all the way down my arm to my fingertips.

Fuck.

My foot catches on a Brain tree, some of its skeletal roots dancing blurs above the river and I am airborne, grasping the longest vine and flying out over the ice just as the forest goes super-nova and I burn blind.

CHAPTER TWO

"Upsy daisy."

I ignore the male voice, comfortable in my slumber.

"Ms. Pogue Eldridge," the voice announces loudly. "Your immediate presence at the Sterling Hotel is humbly requested."

It's daylight now and all around me the forest still sputters here and there, happy in its afterglow.

"We need to get you out of there," says the man gripping my arm. He's an older guy—sixties perhaps—handsome and dressed in an immaculate white suit that matches his hair and trimmed beard exactly. "Have to get you checked in."

"Am I dead?" I ask.

"You're dead weight, I can tell you that." He continues pulling at me.

"I don't feel cold. I'm dead right?"

He pauses in his struggle. "What do you think?"

I shrug. "I hope so. I tried to kill myself last night."

Ignoring the statement, he straightens up, crosses his arms and clucks disapprovingly. "Suicides are a classless bunch. Now, get yourself out of that ice. We don't have all day."

Without thinking about it, I obey him, climbing out of the river and standing on top of it, facing him.

"That's better," he says. "Now, allow me to introduce myself. My name is Salvadore. I will be your escort to the Sterling Hotel and I suggest we get a move on. You have a reservation."

"I do?"

"You do." He offers me his arm. "Shall we?"

CHAPTER THREE

Salvadore leads me through the electric forest until I'm completely disoriented. East, west? I don't know, and Salvadore isn't saying. Behind us lays a vast white emptiness, a new canvas without borders. No left, no right. No up, no down. Just white nothing, snug up to our backs.

My heart stammers. "What the hell...what's going on?"

Indifferent, Salvadore reaches into an inner pocket of his pristine white jacket and pulls out a small roll of candy. He pops one into his mouth and offers me the roll. "Life Saver?"

I stare at him.

He shakes the candy. "It's green," he says temptingly. "Fungus flavor."

"Salvadore, where did the road go?"

Deciding he'd like the green candy for himself, he deftly flips it from the roll and into his mouth before returning the Life Savers to his pocket.

"Salvadore?"

"Now is all there is," he tells me with a small smile. "It's best not to give it much thought. Just come along. We need to get you checked in."

We resume our journey but I've only gone five or six steps when I sneak a glance back and see the white again. Fascinated, I turn around and retrace my steps, peering into the nothing for some sense of...*something*. There's a moment when I think I see movement in there, in the nothing, and I stop, straining my eyes. And then I see it again, a flickering flash, white on purest white and I reach out my hand, wanting to touch the motion despite a sudden and distinct chill that surrounds me.

"No!" Salvadore has come up beside me once more, swatting my hand aside. "You don't want to do that, Pogue."

"Why not? What's in there?"

He opens his mouth as if to speak, then closes it again. "Come on. We need to—"

"Get me checked in, I know, but..." I look at the wall of white and then back at him. "You're not going to tell me?"

"There's nothing to tell. Now, come. Look, we're almost there."

We come to the top of a hill and and I see a blinding light bouncing off the tall buildings of a great city.

"Welcome to the Virgin City, Pogue," Salvadore says. "Spectacular, isn't it?"

Nodding, it takes a moment for the name of the place to register with me. When it does, I look at him. "Did you say *Virgin* City?"

"I did. You've heard of it?" He seems stunned.

"No...but why *virgin*? Is that one of the prerequisites for getting into heaven? Because if it is, you definitely brought me to the wrong place. I haven't been a—"

He hushes me by holding up his hand and shaking his head. "It's nothing like that. Look."

My eyes follow his pointing finger to the sky, to the sun, which it turns out, isn't a sun at all but the gentle smiling face of the Virgin Mary. She is gazing down at us with a pleased expression beneath her baby-blue shawl, nodding her approval and giving me a wink.

Salvadore raises a hand and waves to her, nudging me to do the same. I do and her grin becomes wider, all teeth, white and blinding.

I look away, blotches of light dancing on my retinas. "Damn," I say. "She sure is bright."

"She's happy to see you," Salvadore says.

Rubbing my eyes in an attempt to see again, I say, "What's up with this anyway? I'm not even Catholic."

Ignoring my question, Salvadore places a hand on my elbow and says, "Come on. We have a bus to catch."

"A *bus*?"

CHAPTER FOUR

Sure enough, after we descend the hill and enter the city, we walk down an impossibly clean street to the corner, where there is a bus stop and a bench. Salvadore sits down and pulls a hanky out of an inner jacket pocket and blows his nose.

"Where is everyone?" I ask. I can't help but notice that we are the only people within sight. And not only are we alone on the street, but neither is there any traffic. Absolutely nothing moves anywhere, except us. Not even a single candy wrapper blows by. "This is kinda creepy," I say.

"Maybe they all have the day off," Salvadore says, returning the hanky to its pocket. I start to reply but the appearance of an immaculate city bus distracts me. It appears to be brand new, sparkling clean, like the buildings themselves.

"Here we are," Salvadore says, rising from the bench. "That wasn't too long of a wait."

The bus door hisses open and Salvadore gestures for me to board first. I climb the steps cautiously, eyeing the black female driver with more than a little suspicion. She smiles cheerfully at me as I look around for a coin box that isn't there.

"No toll," Salvadore says from behind me. "Just take a seat."

I do as I'm told, choosing the first bench on the left, and slide over to the window. Salvadore sits beside me as the door closes and the bus pulls out onto the deserted street.

"Almost there now," he says.

Frowning, I look from him to the view outside the window just as the bus is pulling over at what must be the next bus stop. Before I can make any reaction whatsoever, he has risen from the seat and is exiting the bus again. I leap up, hurrying after him.

Once more on the sidewalk, I say, "Was that even half a block? We could have just walked."

Salvadore isn't listening though. Instead, he is smiling up at the building before us. As I turn to follow his gaze with my own, I notice that it is no longer day but night here in the Virgin City. A comfortable, breezy night, late summer or early fall by the feel of it.

And we are no longer alone either. People are everywhere; happy people, every last one of them. Milling around, talking, laughing, smoking, joking. Some of them are dressed to the nines while others appear to be homeless and in rags. A good number of them I hear commenting on the beautiful evening, the stars and the moon.

Glancing skyward, I once again see the Mother Mary smiling, replacing the moon as she had replaced the sun. Her countenance is more than just the moon though. Peering closing at the stars, I can just make out her blue shawl on each and every one of them. A billion Marys hang above us, twinkling and joyful and I have to look away quickly, suddenly feeling a bit queasy.

"Overwhelmed?" Salvadore asks, placing a hand on my shoulder. Without waiting for my response, he continues and gestures at the building before us, "Why don't we go inside."

For the first time, I focus my attention on the grand white structure lit up as if for a debutante's ball. "What is this place?"

"This," Salvadore says, "is the Sterling Hotel."

CHAPTER FIVE

We move through the crowd and begin ascending the hotel's two dozen marble stairs to the revolving glass doors that allow us access into the elegant building and its beautifully refined lobby.

Despite all the bustling outside, the lobby is relatively calm. A few people are seated on lush white furniture, speaking in soothing tones and smiling and nodding at each other.

"This is too weird for me," I say, stopping in my tracks. "Why does everyone seem so nice?"

Salvadore shrugs. "They're mostly pretty nice, I suppose."

"Is this the afterlife? A fancy hotel? Because if it is, I have to tell you, I'm kind of disappointed."

He stares at me, looking vaguely annoyed. "We have to get you checked in. As I think I mentioned, I have other appointments."

"Are most people happy to find out this is the afterlife?" I glance around again. "I can't believe they're happy about it."

Salvadore sighs. "This isn't quite the afterlife, Pogue."

"It's not?"

"I'm not supposed to say anything about this. But, frankly, you're getting on my nerves. You were *supposed* to go to the seminar."

"What seminar?"

"The seminar that would explain all this to you." He gestures at our surroundings. "This is just where we have to put you up for a while. Free of charge, of course."

"Put me up? What are you talking about?" I am beginning to suspect that I'm not actually dead at all. My suicide attempt must have failed and now I'm in some loony-bin, probably imagining all of this. Salvadore is probably a head shrinker. Unless I'm imagining him too. "I'm not really dead, am I? Fuck! I *knew* I'd manage to screw it up somehow." I stand there shaking my head, disgusted with myself.

"You're dead all right," Salvadore says.

I look at him, skeptical. "You're just saying that to make me feel better."

He holds up a hand, his thumb and pinky folded down. "Scout's Honor, Pogue. You are indeed dead."

It takes me a second to decide whether or not I believe him, but then I smile.

He does seem like an honest old coot. "Oh, thank God. I was sick of my life. You have no idea."

Rolling his eyes, he says, "Can we get back to business, please?"

"Oh, right. Sure. You were saying something about a seminar?"

"Yes. But never mind that because you won't need to attend it now."

"Why not?" For some reason I feel slightly jilted.

Salvadore is starting to look extremely distressed and impatient, so I just forget my last question and resign myself to let him tell me whatever it is he needs to tell me. Which turns out to be this: "Both heaven and hell are undergoing some renovations right now. Everyone who's already there is fine. But we have nowhere to put up all the newcomers, like yourself. You have to understand, both places—but particularly Hell—are growing in scope and size every day. So, every few millennia, we have to make renovations here and there. Spruce the place up, if you will."

I listen to all this, nodding like I know what he's talking about. When it seems like he's finished, I say, "So, you put everyone in a hotel?"

"That's correct, yes."

It's my turn to sigh and I let out a huge one. "Wow. That's pretty fucked up. When will the renovations be complete?"

He smiles, like he's finally on familiar ground again. "Any day now." He holds out a hand to me. "Shall we get you checked in now?"

I think about it, regarding his outstretched hand carefully. "I guess so," I say finally, taking his hand and allowing him to lead me to the front desk where a clerk with a pencil-thin mustache awaits, smiling happily like he has the best job in the world.

"Check in," Salvadore says. "Eldridge, Pogue."

The clerk nods and types something into his computer. "Ah, yes. Suicide. Electrocution was it?"

Frowning, I say, "What does that have to do with anything?"

Pencil-mustache's smile widens. "Only everything," he says.

"Electrocution," Salvadore confirms and Mustache bends down, rummages beneath the counter for a minute and comes up with a keycard. "You'll be on the fifth floor. Room 658."

I take the card and look at it. One side has the picture of a hippie guy, grinning and giving the peace sign. I flip it over and the other side shows a pouty Goth, wearing black eyeliner and looking sullen. "Who are these guys?" I ask.

"Well," Salvadore says. "My job here is done. Good luck to you Pogue." He holds out his hand to be shaken.

"You're just gonna leave me here?" I say. "I thought you were my escort."

"I was. And I escorted you. Now, if you'll excuse me—"

"You should at least escort me to my room," I interrupt. "That would be the gentlemanly thing to do."

"Actually, Pogue," he says. "Truth be told, I wasn't even supposed to be your escort. I was just filling in for someone else."

I fold my arms across my chest. "Who?"

Turning around to face the doors, Salvadore points and says, "Her."

I look and see a big black woman just spinning out of the revolving door. Once inside, she turns to the person behind her, just entering. "Get your scrawny white ass in here, bitch," the black woman bellows. "Do I *look* like I got all day?"

The person she's yelling at—a teenage girl—looks pissed. She's dressed like a street kid, in ratty clothes that are too big for her and her hair hangs to her shoulders in long greasy strips.

The black woman, dressed in a big purple dress with swirls of green and orange all over it, grabs the teenager by the arm and starts pulling her over to the check-in counter.

"This is Katina," the woman tells Mr. Mustache. "Another damn fool who went and offed herself before she's even old enough to vote."

"I told you," Katina says, trying to pull free of the woman's grasp, "I didn't off myself. At least not on purpose."

The black woman releases the girl and puts her hands on her hips. "Uh huh. Did you or did you not stick a needle in your arm?"

Katina looks at the floor and says nothing.

"Uh huh," the woman continues. "And did that needle contain enough smack to drop an elephant or did it not?"

Again, Katina makes no reply.

"Uh huh," the woman repeats, turning back to the desk. "Suicide."

"It was an accident!" Katina cries.

Beside me Salvadore shakes his head sadly while watching this exchange.

"Honey," the woman says to Katina. "There are no accidents. Almost every-damn-body is a suicide when you get right down to it. Those are just the rules. You smoke and die of lung cancer? The big boy upstairs says suicide. You eat at McDonald's every damn day of your life and your heart turns into a little ball of cement? Suicide. You get drunk and drive into a tree or turn your liver into jelly? Suicide. Don't matter how long or short it takes people. Fact is, most people kill themselves and it's no use arguing about it. Like I said, those are the rules."

Katina looks at me, her eyes pleading.

I shrug. "I did it on purpose. Sorry."

Salvadore clears his throat and addresses the big black woman. "Ms. Stardust, I'd like to introduce you to Pogue. She was supposed to be *your* pick-up."

"Is that so?" The woman gives me the once over. "Well, sorry I missed you, sweetheart, but as you can tell I've had my hands   full."

It's only when I'm looking at her face to face that I notice the Adam's apple bobbing up and down in her throat. And now that I'm thinking about it, her voice *is* an octave or two too low.

The fact that she's really a dude is only of passing interest to me. "Nice to meet you…uh…Ms. Stardust."

"This sucks," Katina blurts abruptly. "It's not fair! I have to go to hell for killing myself, even though I didn't really kill myself?"

"I don't make the rules, sweetheart," Ms Stardust says, examining her long red fingernails. "I just follow 'em."

"Hell?" I say, alarmed. I look at Salvadore.

"What is she talking about hell for?" He looks down at his watch. "Would you look at the time? I can't believe how far behind I'm running!" And before I can stop him, he walks briskly through the lobby and out through the revolving doors.

I stare after him, my jaw hanging. "That son of a bitch."

Ms. Stardust barks a laugh. "Honey, you're lucky he took time out of his busy schedule to escort you over here. He almost never lowers himself for the suicides."

"What do you mean?"

"Oh, that Salvadore. He usually does the rich white people who died old. Or sometimes young ones, if they were in tip-top condition and had nothing to do with their own deaths, which according to the rules, amounts to pretty much the same thing."

"I'm not following you," I say.

"Look," Ms. Stardust says, addressing both Katina and I. "Pretty much everyone is considered a suicide. The only ones who aren't, are the ones who could afford to take care of themselves, you see what I'm saying? Rich folks that could go to their fancy-ass gyms, buy the best organic foods, get the best medical care. Those are the folks that are in the luxury suites right this very minute and those are the folks old Sally escorts over here. You were just a fluke, honey."

I try to absorb what she's saying and can't quite make it work in my head.

Katina says, "So, in other words, the rich people own fucking heaven too? What the fuck is up with that? That's not right!"

Ms. Stardust says, "Umm hmm. Death is no fairer than life, sweetheart. Don't let anybody tell you different." The she turns to Mustache Man and starts getting Katina checked in while Katina and I eye each other with morbid curiosity.

"You really offed yourself then, huh?"

I nod. "But I had my reasons."

"No reason is a good enough reason," Ms. Stardust says over her shoulder.

Katina reaches into the pocket of her gray hoodie and pulls out a pack of gum. Juicy Fruit. Thoughtfully, she unwraps a piece and then offers me the pack. I accept and by the time Ms. Stardust has returned her attention to us, we are both merrily chewing away and not talking.

Ms. Stardust hands Katina her keycard. "You're on the sixth floor. Room 544."

I pause in my chewing. "I'm on the fifth floor."

Arching an eyebrow at me, Ms. Stardust says, "Is that right? Honey, I'm surprised you're not on the first or second."

"Because I killed myself on purpose?"

"That's right."

"And Katina here killed herself by accident, so she gets to be on a higher floor."

"Now you're catching on. And you know what? I'd love to stay here and chit-chat with you lovely girls all night long, but my shift isn't over yet and I got more junkies to claim."

Still chewing her gum, Katina asks, "Are you a grim reaper or what?"

Ms. Stardust puts her hands on her hips and looks down at Katina, her face scrunched into a frown. "Now, why would you want to go insult me like that? Do I *look* like a grim reaper to you?"

"Well, no, but. How should we know

what a grim reaper looks like? It's not like I've ever been dead before."

"Umm hmm," Ms. Stardust says, still looking perturbed. "Anyway, you ladies enjoy your stay here at the Sterling Hotel. If you need anything, just dial zero on your room phones and Louis over there will see that you get it. Okay, then? Good. Bye-bye."

Katina and I watch Ms. Stardust sashay across the lobby and out into the night, both of us chewing our gum much louder than we have to, as if the normal act of chewing gum will rub off on this extremely strange situation.

Once she's gone, we look at each other and shrug.

"Guess I'll go find my room," I say.

"Yeah, me too."

Together we make our way over to the elevators, Katina snapping her gum every few seconds. I push the up button and the door immediately opens. Inside, a young pale guy stands there, just watching us.

I say, "Are you like, the elevator guy?"

"The elevator guy? No, I'm Ago."

"Pardon me?" By now Katina and I have entered the elevator and the shiny silver door has slid shut.

"That's my name," the guy says. "Ago."

"Ah."

"That's a pretty stupid name, you ask me," Katina says.

Ago gives her a wounded look, so I quickly say, "Don't mind her. She's pissed because they're saying she's a suicide."

"Pretty much everyone is a suicide," Ago says.

"Not me!" Katina snaps her gum angrily and pushes the button for the sixth floor. "Hey," she says. "There's a button here that says 4 ½."

"That's my floor," Ago says. "You don't want to go there."

"Why not?" Katina asks.

"Because it doesn't really exist."

Katina and I both look at Ago as if

he slipped a groove. Finally, I say, "I don't know. Now you have me curious."

"Me too," says Katina. "I'm getting off on your floor."

Ago sighs. "I knew I shouldn't have told you."

The elevator stops at every floor but no other passengers get on.

We arrive and leave the fourth floor without incident and then the elevator lurches violently, causing all three of us to lose our balance. Katina and I fall down, but Ago is holding onto the rail, obviously expecting it.

"You could have warned us," I say, getting to my feet.

"No, shit," Katina agrees, standing up. "I swallowed my gum."

Ago ignores us and begins trying to pry open the elevator doors with his fingers. He grunts and groans with the effort, occasionally swearing under his breath. "Can one of you give me a hand?"

"Sure," I go over and start to yank on the doors. A minute later, it budges and we can clearly see that we're stuck between floors. Forcing the doors wide enough for a person to be able to squeeze through takes another few seconds and then I stand back to admire our handy work. "Looks like we'll have to climb up."

"Always do," Ago says and begins to do exactly that.

Outside the elevator, there is nothing to be seen. Just darkness.

"Is the power out on your floor?" I ask.

"There's never any power on 4 ½," Ago says, hauling himself up and clambering into the darkness. Then he disappears out of sight, as if the darkness has swallowed him whole.

"Ago?" I call. "Where did you go, Ago?"

As if from very far away, his voice drifts down to us. "Just be on your way. This is no place for you."

Of course this does nothing but

make me want to check out floor 4 ½ all the more. "Give me a boost," I say to Katina.

For a second she looks like she may protest, then she shrugs and makes a step out of her laced hands.

Using my elbows for leverage, I pull myself up and exit the elevator into nothing but thick blackness. I turn around to see the inside of the elevator, though it is no longer directly behind me. It's a long ways off, a skinny rectangle of light that seems to be receding even as I watch. "What the hell…"

"You made a mistake," Ago says, his voice beside my ear now.

"How can you stay on this floor? You should definitely ask to be moved someplace else."

Ago chuckles. "I wish. But this is Purgatory."

"Purga—wait. What?"

And it's as if the word being spoken aloud has triggered some kind of limbo switch, because my body flattens and stretches and twists in a way that the human body is definitely not meant to do. Or maybe it's the darkness that is actually changing shape, but if that's the case then that would mean that I have become part of the darkness and the thought—in addition to the ceaseless shape-shifting—suddenly makes me feel like vomiting, which I almost certainly would have done if I'd been able to determine where my stomach was or if it was even still part of my body.

"Are you guys okay?" Katina. From very far away. "Guys?"

I try to respond that I'm most definitely *not* okay but I have no words. I'm not even sure if I have a mouth or vocal cords. I decide that if I ever get out of here, the hotel management is going to get an earful. They'll wish they'd never even heard the name Pogue Eldritch. Maybe they'll even realize that this whole Purgatory thing was a bad idea. A *very* bad idea.

I'm just starting to compose a letter of complaint in my mind when I feel something like a boot plant itself firmly in what I suspect is my ass, but I can't really be sure. It's more of a mental push than a physical one and the next thing I know I'm falling down into light.

I crash with a grunt and look up to see Katina looking down at me. "How was it?" she asks, snapping a new piece of gum, her expression bored.

For the second time, I pick myself up off the elevator floor and say, "I don't want to talk about it."

Katina gives me a snotty look and says, "What*ev.* Help me get this stupid door closed."

CHAPTER SIX

Together we manage to close the elevator door and then we're rising again, but only for a few seconds. Then the door *whooshes* open and we're looking out into what appears to be an average hotel hallway.

"Fifth floor," Katina says, watching me expectantly.

"I see that! Don't you think I see that?"

Katina waves towards the hall. "Well, fucking go."

I clear my throat. Take a deep breath. Gingerly stick my foot outside the elevator and test the floor of the hallway. Seems solid, so I step out and then turn back just as the elevator door is sliding closed. I raise my hand to wave goodbye to Katina but then she reaches out, stopping the door from closing. "Fuck this," she says, getting off the elevator to stand beside me. "I don't want to do this shit alone."

Who can blame her? She's just a kid after all.

I pull my keycard out of my pocket and say, "Room 735. That's funny. I could have sworn it was a different number before."

"Isn't 735 kind of high too?" Katina asks. "This place doesn't seem big enough to have that many rooms."

We consider this for a moment and then shrug in unison. "Oh, well," I say, looking up and down the hall. The nearest room is numbered 737. "I guess we're pretty much here already."

At 735, I slip the keycard into its slot and a little green light flashes. I open the door cautiously, unsure of what to expect.

When I flip the light switch, however, the room appears to be completely normal. A carbon copy of a million other hotel rooms across the globe.

There is a double bed, a floral pastel bedspread across it, a small desk, a lavender lounge chair, a little table with two straight-backed chairs tucked neatly beneath it. A closet with a wooden sliding door. A night table with a white ceramic lamp and that's it.

"This is so not how I pictured Heaven to be," Katina says.

"It's not Heaven," I remind her. "Heaven is under construction, remember?"

"Whatever," she says, plopping herself down onto the bed. "I can't believe you don't even have a mini-bar."

"Yeah," I say. "That sucks."

I go over to the one window in the room and pull back the pink drapes. Outside, there is a mountain range, gray with snowy peaks. Quite beautiful, except that it's moving. Rolling past the window as if it were the backdrop of a movie. "Shit," I mutter. "The mountains are moving. How messed up is that?"

Katina comes over and looks out. "The mountains aren't moving. We are."

"Really?" I look closer at the mountains. "It doesn't feel like we're moving."

She sighs loudly and moves away from the window. "Well, we are. The hotel is flying or some shit."

I watch for another minute or two and determine that Katina is correct. Though it can't be felt, the hotel is indeed flying. I wonder where we are. The Rocky Mountains? The Andes? My stomach lurches and I have to turn away from the window.

Katina is sitting at the table, looking at a menu. "Are you hungry?" she asks. "I'm starving."

Sitting down across from her, I ask, "Is there room service?"

"Surprisingly, yes. At least according to this there is, but the menu is kind of…uh…sparse."

"Give me that." I lean over and pluck it from her fingers. Studying the menu, I say "What the hell? 'Floors six and lower (excluding floors one and lower) can choose from a wide variety of our house baked pies, day or night, free of charge.' "Pies? That's all we get? I was hoping for nice plate of pasta in white sauce."

"Yeah, and I could go for a nice bloody steak but it looks like we're SOL." Katina leans back in her chair and puts her feet on the table. "Did you look at the *kinds* of pies they have?"

I look down at the menu again. "What's *rock* pie?"

"Beats me. Probably made with rocks, is my guess."

I get up and go over to the phone on the nightstand. I dial zero and wait for someone to pick up. It takes them several minutes, but when they finally do, I recognize Mustache Man's voice right away. "Hi," I say. "Yeah, this is room…uh…" I look at Katina and snap my fingers, pointing to the keycard on the table. She picks it up and says, "631."

Frowning at her, I repeat the number into the phone. "We're kind of hungry up here and noticed that the menu says we're only allowed to have pies."

"The pies are excellent, I assure you madam," says Mustache Man.

"I'm sure they are, but you know…we're hungry for something a little more substantial than pie right now."

"House rules," he says crisply.

"House rules," I repeat, trying to sound indignant.

Katina jumps out of the chair and barrels over to me, grabbing the phone out of my hand. "Listen, buddy, we think your house rules suck, so why don't you just send us the menu that all the rich people on the upper floors are getting?"

I sit down on the edge of the bed and watch as she listens. It seems like she listens for a long time. Then: "Okay, fine. Whatever. But it better be good." Then she slams the phone down into its cradle. "Fucking wanker," she says to it.

"Are they sending us another menu?" I ask.

"Nope," she replies, heading towards the bathroom. "He said he was sending up pie."

Groaning, I flop back on the bed and look at the ceiling. Oddly, it's covered with tire tread marks of all shapes and sizes. Thin treads that could have been made by a little wagon of some sort, bicycle treads, all the way up to treads that could have only been made by an SUV. I make a mention of it to Katina who lies down beside me and points. "I think that one is from a grocery cart," she says. "I used to work in a grocery store."

"Hmm," I say.

Someone knocks on the door and Katina jumps up to answer it. I don't move. I'm pretty I don't want to know who it is, but nevertheless, Katina says, "It's room service with our pie."

"Great," I say sarcastically.

"I'll just put it over here on the table," says a new female voice.

I sit up to see a strange alien/human hybrid in a tuxedo shirt and black trousers crossing the room and carrying a silver tray with a covered dish, plates, and silverware on it. She smiles at me, big black alien eyes blinking slowly. "Hi. I'm Jane 62," she says with her tiny slit of a mouth. She puts the tray on the table and uncovers the pie. It looks like a regular pie but it sounds like there's music coming from it, very faintly.

"Is there a Jane 63?" Katina asks.

"Not that I know of," Jane 62 replies, cutting into the pie with a huge knife.

I get off the bed and go over to the table, leaning over to listen to the pie. Jane 62 dishes out a slice and suddenly the room is filled with loud opera music, a woman bellowing in what I think is Italian.

"Opera pie," she says, handing me the plate. "It's quite delicious."

Crinkling my nose, I say, "I hate opera." If I could, I'd crinkle my ears as well.

"Guess we should have gotten the rock pie after all," Katina says, taking her plate.

The pie looks like cherry, but I have no intention of eating it. It's giving me a headache and I hand it back to Jane 62. "I'm not hungry right now," I say loudly, to be heard over the music.

Katina decides not to eat it either. "Let's try to get up to a higher floor and find some real food," she suggests.

"Good idea," I say. I turn to Jane 62. "Will you get this out of here? I really can't stand opera."

"We also have a nice country pie," she says pleasantly. "Apple flavored and not quite as loud. Would you like me to bring one up?"

"No!" Katina and I say together.

Jane 62 looks hurt but starts stacking the plates of pie back onto the tray and covering them. Immediately, the volume of the music becomes at least tolerable. "You'll have a hard time getting to the higher floors," Jane 62 says. "It would be much easier to go down than up."

"Why is that?" I ask.

"It's just the rules," she replies.

"Fuck!" Katina blurts. "I'm so sick of hearing about the rules."

"The guests on the upper floors have entitlement issues," Jane 62 explains. "Most of them are not very pleasant."

"Rich people," I say. "Why am I not surprised?"

"I don't care," Katina says. "I just want to
get out of this room. I'm bored."

"We could go check out your room," I suggest.

She nods. "Maybe I'll have a better menu."

Jane 62 asks what floor Katina's room is on, then shakes her head. "*You* can go up there," she says to Katina. "*You* can't," she says to me.

"That's retarded," I say.

Katina starts bouncing around. "I'm *bored!* I don't care where we go. Let's just *go!*"

We follow Jane 62 out into the hall, me patting my pocket to make sure I have my keycard on me.

Outside my door is a cart filled with covered trays and it sounds like a dozen different radio stations playing at once. Jane 62 starts pushing the cart down the hall and the tangled music starts to recede a bit.

"Why don't you come with us?" I ask when she pauses at the room next door to mine.

She turns back. "Upstairs? I'm not allowed up there either."

"Why not?"

"This is my floor," she says. "We're all assigned our floor and we're not supposed to leave it."

"That's bullshit," I tell her. "Why would you let anyone tell you what to do like that? What is this, a prison?"

Jane 62 looks uncertain, the gray-green skin of her forehead wrinkling slightly as though she's worried. "I have always wanted to see other parts of the hotel."

"Hey!" Katina says suddenly. "We should go back to that limbo floor and get that guy too. What was his name again?"

"Ago," I say.

"Yeah, him. What do you think? Party in my room?"

"Sounds good to me." I look at Jane 62. "You only live once. Fuck the rules."

She stays where she is, so I shrug and Katina and I head for the elevator. Just as I'm pushing the button, Jane 62 jogs over and says, "I hope I don't get caught."

"Will you get fired or something?" I ask.

"I have no idea. I don't even get paid."

For some reason this strikes me as funny and I start laughing. Katina cracks up too, but Jane 62 just stands there looking thoughtful.

The elevator opens and the three of us climb in. I push the button for 4 ½ and when we get there, we have to pry open the doors again.

"Ago!" I yell into the darkness. "You in there?"

"Get your ass over here," Katina shouts. "We're having a mutiny!"

I laugh again and together Katina and I scream for Ago and finally he shows himself. He has to crouch down and stick his head into the elevator so we can see him. "What kind of mutiny?" he asks.

"We're gonna explore the hotel," I tell him.

He seems puzzled. "Why?"

"Why not?" I counter.

"Well, we might run into Lucy for one thing."

Jane 62 lets out a little gasp that might be fright.

"Who the fuck is Lucy?" Katina demands.

His face deadly serious, Ago says, "Lucifer."

CHAPTER SEVEN

"Lucifer," I say. "As in, the devil? *That* Lucifer?"

"The one and only," Ago says. "But, from what I heard, it's best if you don't call him the devil to his face. He's pretty sensitive about it."

I purse my lips, carefully considering this new information.

Beside me, Katina is laughing. "I'm gonna get to meet Satan in the flesh? This is too awesome! I don't even believe in him!"

"You will soon enough," Ago says and climbs down into the elevator. "But, what the hell. Purgatory is getting boring anyway."

Clapping him on the back, I say, "Great. One more person for our revolt."

The elevator doors slide shut and I push the button for the 6th floor. The box gives a lurch, jarring us all, but then doesn't move.

"See?" Jane 62 says. "We're not allowed up there."

"What about me?" Katina protests. "My room is on the 6th floor!"

"You could go up there if we weren't with you," Jane 62 explains. "But since we are, the elevator won't go any higher."

"It's like a built-in security system," Ago adds.

"Well, that's just great," I say sarcastically. "Why didn't you guys tell us this before?"

"We never tried to go up before," Jane 62 says. "We just heard that this would happen and apparently it's true."

"Great," I say again. "Can we go down to the lower floors?"

"Why would you want to go down?" Ago asks, as if it's the most preposterous idea he's ever heard.

I don't bother answering him and just start pushing buttons. The elevator comes back to life, lowering us slowly.

"Oh, shit," Ago whispers, while Jane 62 makes that gasping sound again.

"What's wrong?" Katina asks them. "Scared of a little Beelzebub are you?" She laughs maniacally, pointing and teasing them.

CHAPTER EIGHT

A second later the elevator comes to a stop and the doors open onto a floor that doesn't look very different from mine. A little more rundown, but that's about it. The four of us tromp out and then split up, knocking on doors and trying to get people to join us in our little rebellion. Mostly people just give us weird looks and politely refuse. A couple times we have doors slammed in our faces. A few of the guests won't open their doors at all, but yell curses at us just the same.

We go down to the next floor and find it to be even more raggedy than the previous one. Here the wallpaper is peeling off the walls and the carpets have stains and cigarette burns and the room doors are all dirty. The lights in the ceiling fixtures flicker sporadically and on more than one occasion we find ourselves in almost complete darkness.

Again, we have no luck and pile back into the elevator, both Ago and Jane 62 becoming increasingly nervous.

When the doors open on the next lower floor, we see that it is in even worse condition than the last. The ceiling leaks and the hallway is strewn with trash. There's shouting coming from behind several of the doors, as well as the sound of people weeping. I go to knock on the door of room 256 and the only response I get is something thrown and smashed against the other side of it.

At the far end of the hall, two guys come running out of a room, one chasing the other with a huge meat cleaver and screaming, *"I'll chop your fucking head off, you prick!"* The first one plows into Katina, almost knocking her over and then barrels down the hallway towards me. I flinch as they race by and then they run into another room, slamming the door behind themselves.

"Maybe this wasn't such a great idea," Katina calls out to me.

I open my mouth to agree, but the door behind me suddenly swings open and I turn to see an older woman standing there in a slinky red robe. She looks somewhat like Marilyn Monroe, if Marilyn had lived to enter her mid-fifties and drank hard liquor every day of her life. She's smoking a cigarette in one of those long cigarette holders and looking at me from beneath eyelids painted a ridiculous shade of blue.

"What's this you're yelling about, honey?" she asks, exhaling smoke through her nostrils.

"Uh…" I hesitate, but then tell her about what were doing. She listens silently, smoking, without expression.

"Sounds like a real gas," she croaks, when I finish. "I ain't got nothing better to do."

By now, the others have joined me and are regarding this woman with blatant skepticism.

"What's your name?" I ask, out of politeness.

She grins at me, showing off her yellowed crooked teeth. "The name's Lithia, darlin'. And who might you all be?"

I introduce myself and everyone else.

"Pleased ta meet ya," she greets everyone in turn. Then: "Yep, I reckon I'll come along for the party. I'm sick to death of this hellhole. You're all from above, eh?"

I tell her that Katina and I are, but Jane 62 is sort of an employee of the hotel and Ago is from Purgatory.

Lithia nods. "Gotta be better than this shit. You see where they put me? Only a floor or two above Hell, that's where. Those fucking bastards. I was a Rockette once upon a time and this is how they treat me! Look at these gams!" She sticks out one of her legs and wiggles it seductively. We all make sounds like we're impressed but, really, it just looks like a leg. A little scrawny if anything.

The two guys who were chasing each other fly out of their room again, this time the previous chaser is now the chasee and his meat cleaver is buried deep inside the back of his head.

We watch them go by, all of us horrified, except for Lithia. "Oh, don't mind those two," she says. "They're just playing."

"Maybe we should get off this floor," Jane 62 suggests. "I think I've seen enough of the lower floors for now."

"Great idea, missy," Lithia says. "Lead the way. I'm right behind ya."

"Don't you want to put something else on?" I ask.

"Nah. This is all I got anyway. What I was wearing when I did the ole…" She points a long-nailed finger to the side of her head and mimes shooting a gun.

"Suicide, huh?" Katina says. "There's a surprise."

"Suicide-*murder*," Lithia says with a tone of pride. "That no good bastard had it coming though, I can guarantee you that."

None of us care to ask her to elaborate, so we just smile and nod and then head back towards the elevator, Lithia bringing up the rear in her bare feet.

When we get into the elevator, though, we quickly discover that it won't go back up. All the buttons to the upper floor remain dark when we push them.

"It's because of her," Jane 62 says, pointing at Lithia. "It won't let us go back up with her in here."

"Well, don't that beat all," Lithia says mildly, dragging on her cigarette. Even though she keeps smoking, the cigarette doesn't seem to be getting any shorter.

"What should we do?" I ask no one in particular.

The elevator suddenly jerks to life, going down.

CHAPTER NINE

"Uh oh," says Jane 62.

"We're fucked," Ago agrees.

Katina starts laughing yet again and everyone looks at her like she's crazy.

"You have a weird sense of humor," Ago tells her.

She makes a face at him, but then bites the inside of her cheek in an attempt to quell her giggling.

The elevator door opens, this time with a strange hissing sound and the scent that wafts inside is unmistakable.

"Oh, man," Ago says, pinching his nose closed. "Brimstone!"

Katina loses her struggle and busts out laughing. She's practically falling over, she's so hysterical.

Outside the elevator, the sounds are not nearly as identifiable as the smell. There is the sound of screaming, but it's hard to tell if it's human. Could be animal.

The hallway in front of us is even more dark and gloomy than the floor above us was. So dark that you have to squint to see anything at all.

"I'm not going out there," Ago says, punching the elevator buttons, trying to get the door to close.

Katina pushes past us, goes out into the hallway. "This isn't real," she yells at us, grinning like a lunatic. "This *can't* be real! Don't you guys get it? It's like…a dream or…"

A shadow—moving fast—slams into her and explodes on impact. At the same exact instant, any meager light source out there is extinguished.

Out of all of us, Ago is the one who screams.

"What in the name of holy hell was that?" Lithia asks.

I jump out of the elevator to the place where Katina just was, expecting to have to run in either direction, either to avoid something or to search for her. Instead, I trip on something and almost fall. I manage to keep my balance but from somewhere in the gloom on the floor, Katina, yells, "Ouch! Watch where the fuck you're walking!"

"Sorry," I say, reaching down to where her voice came from, offering her a hand up.

"Trust me," she says. "You don't want to touch me. Oh, fuck, it smells like….it smells like *shit!* That thing that hit me was made of *shit!*"

The lights flicker, threaten to go out again, but stay on, at least for the time being.

Katina struggles to her feet and sure enough, she appears to be covered in shit.

Smells like it too.

From inside the elevator, Lithia says, "Oh yeah. I heard of those dung devils before. Never believed they really existed but I guess they do." She chuckles dryly, takes a drag off her cigarette and then starts hacking. She coughs so long and loud that Jane 62 exits the elevator with a disgusted look on her face. Not an easy accomplishment, considering she barely has features.

From behind a nearby door, someone lets out a wrenching scream that makes us all jump.

"This is where people get murdered over and over again," Jane 62 says nervously.

Ago cringes in the corner of the elevator and says, "This hotel blows. I'm glad I'm not paying to stay here."

"Oh, you're paying sweetheart," Lithia coughs. "We're all paying plenty."

As if in response to Lithia's statement, the elevator begins to shake violently, bouncing around the two of them still inside. Ago falls down and then scrambles out on all fours, his eyes rolling with fear. Lithia seems less alarmed and manages to keep her balance, stepping out into the hall with the rest of us, a sour expression on her face.

"Piece of shit," she growls at the elevator.

The moment it's empty, the box ceases its shaking and the door slides shut with a clanking thud. Ago immediately begins punching the *up* button and says, "Sorry, ladies, but even Purgatory is better than this."

But the elevator ignores him, refusing to open, and then it is promptly forgotten as a tremendous wind blasts us, blowing our hair and reeking of crap. We all turn as one to see the dung devil, easily as tall as me, round the corner, heading straight towards us.

A shit cyclone, splattering the walls and everything in its path with feces.

"That one is bigger," Katina shouts, turning and fleeing in the opposite direction. It doesn't take the rest of us long to follow suit, bolting down the hall with the dung devil at our heels, stinking of a Hell we never knew existed.

In the lead, Katina abruptly slams to a halt and dashes inside the nearest room, which is, thankfully, unlocked. We all make it inside and slam the door just as the shit twister is passing on the other side.

"Hey, sorry about barging in, man," Ago says turning to face the inside of the room. "We were just—*aw, fuck!*"

The room we've just jumped blindly into is littered with dead babies…or, rather, *pieces* of dead babies. A tiny arm here, a foot over there, various heads, all in different stages of decomposition. Baby parts strewn over the floor, the bed, the desk. There are pieces nailed to the walls and ceiling, like props in some especially gruesome movie. The man standing in the center of the room is naked and holding something in his hands at crotch level, his hips pumping back and forth.

I blink rapidly, certain that I can't be seeing what I think I'm seeing, but Katina's gagging assures me that my eyes are indeed telling the truth: the guy is standing there fucking a baby's head, slamming his dick into the neck stump over and over, his eyes screwed shut and sweat pouring down his face in rivulets.

"Jesus, God," Lithia whispers and Katina starts to scream.

CHAPTER TEN

The screaming is what breaks the man's trance and he opens his bloodshot eyes to look at us, and then he adds to the screaming himself. *"I can't stop!"* He wails as his hips keep pumping, the muscles of his ass clenching and unclenching. *"I can't stop! Can't stoooop!"*

I feel my stomach lurch and reach behind me to open the door. Dung devil or not, I'm getting out of this nightmare.

I manage to make it into the hallway before I puke into a slimy trail of shit that travels up the hall and around the corner. The path of the dung devil.

The others are around me a moment later and someone pats my back. I look over my shoulder to see Jane 62 watching me and shaking her head. "Humans," she says. I wait for more but then realize that that is her entire statement on the subject: just "humans." Her face remains expressionless but her tone sadness and disgust and I can only turn back to the task at hand and continue throwing up my guts.

"We have to get off this floor," Ago says, sounding a little green himself. Katina is freely weeping now, Lithia supporting her with an arm around her waist.

"There has to be stairs," Jane 62 says. "In one direction or the other."

"Maybe we should split up and look for them," Ago suggests.

"No!" Katina and I shout at once. We exchange a glance and know we've both seen all the same horror movies where splitting up is never a good idea.

Ago looks vaguely annoyed but says, "Okay. But either way, we'd better get moving before another one of those shit storms comes around."

"They're the tumbleweeds of Hell," Jane 62 says quietly, almost to herself.

Lithia ignores her and says to Ago, "Before the lights go out again too."

"Right." He looks down the hall, first one way then the other and finally shrugs. "Does anyone have a preference?"

I also look in both directions before pointing to our right. "So far, the dung devils have been traveling that way. I'd rather have them at our back than run into them headfirst."

Everyone agrees that this makes sense, so we start off that way, leaving the dead baby fucker's screams behind us.

We round the corner and pass a few more doors with weird sounds emanating from behind them, but we keep moving until we see a figure approaching from the opposite direction. The distance and flickering lights make the person hard to make out at first, but it quickly becomes clear that it's a tall thin male, walking slowly, his face tipped towards the floor, apparently watching his shoes.

No ones says anything at first, all of us silently dreading whatever it is that we might run into next, but the closer we get to the approaching man, the less threatening he seems until finally he looks up and, seeing us, stops.

"Don't ask me for any favors," he says. "Because I'm fresh out."

Ago and I look at each other warily but continue walking with the others behind us. "Is this the way to the stairs?" I ask the guy.

He makes an irritated sound. "What the fuck did I just say? Are you fucking deaf?"

Now that we're closer, I can see he's just a skinny Goth guy, dressed in a black see-through net shirt and black pants. His hair is jet-black and spiked and he's wearing black nail polish.

We reach him and stop. "There's no need to be rude," I say. "It was just a question."

The Goth snorts at me, then looks over my shoulder at Lithia. "You got another one of those smokes I could bum?"

"No!" she snaps at him with such ferociousness that we all look at her. "Why don't you ask one of your minions?" she asks him. "Or is there no cancer in Hell?"

Puzzled we all turn back to the guy, who looks genuinely wounded. And tired. There are sagging gray bags beneath his eyes, which are emphasized by thick lines of black eyeliner. "Fine." He waves a dismissive hand. "Fuck you too."

"Why don't you introduce yourself to everyone, Lucy?" Lithia says. "No need to be shy."

"Wait," I say, looking the skinny guy up and down. "*You're* Lucifer? As in…" I stop myself, remembering how he doesn't like to be called the devil. "As in, er…the dark prince?"

He makes a face at me and sighs heavily. "Not what you were expecting? My pitchfork is in the shop right now."

I frown. Who would have thought that Satan would be so snotty?

"Wow," Katina says, fully recovered from the sight of dead baby bits. "Damn, you're fucking *hot*!"

Lucifer looks at her and smiles slightly. I'm suddenly alarmed to see that he *is* actually amazingly handsome, if you can get past all the make-up and ridiculous outfit. He looks like a movie star when he smiles.

"You're pretty hot yourself," Lucifer tells Katina. "What's your name?"

"She's *fifteen*," I bark at him, as if he would care.

The smile slips off his face and he regards me with what is obviously dislike. "Who are you? Her mother?"

Pushing past him, I ask "Is this the way to the stairs? We're in a hurry."

Lucy laughs bitterly. "In a hurry, huh? To go where? To do what? Don't you morons get it? You're stuck here now. With me!"

"That's bullshit," I say. "They said we couldn't leave our own floors too, but we did."

Ago gives me a nudge and whispers, "Knock it off, Pogue. You don't want to piss him off. He's the devil, remember?"

"I heard that!" Lucifer pouts. "Oh, screw you guys. This is what I get for trying to be nice." He squeezes by everyone and continues on his way down the hall.

"He was trying to be nice?" I wonder aloud.

Katina chases after him, asking, "So, what do you do for fun around here?"

The rest of us give each other worried looks and follow behind the two, watching as Lucy drapes an arm around Katina's shoulders. "Oh, you know," he says. "A little of this, a little of that. Want to see my room?"

"NO!" I shout, catching up and tugging at Katina's wrist. "She *does not* want to see your room. Come on, Katina. This guy is a loser."

"Not to mention the anti-Christ," Lithia adds from behind me.

Lucifer lets out a huge sigh, as if the weight of the world is on his shoulders. "Don't be jealous. You can come too. All of you can. Besides, we're here already."

A door opens in the wall where before there was nothing, leading into a room lit with a warm golden light.

"Fucking cool!" Katina barges forward, completely fearless, and crosses the threshold. My breath catches in my throat, waiting for whatever horrible thing is about to happen.

But nothing does.

CHAPTER ELEVEN

From the hall, we watch Katina bounce on a king-size bed, exclaiming, "It's a water-bed! Oh my God, you guys have to see this." Then she bounces off the bed and disappears from sight.

Smiling innocently, Lucy says, "See? Nothing to be afraid of. I know I have a bad reputation, but it's really quite undeserved."

"Whatever you say, pal," Lithia snorts as she enters the room in search of Katina.

"Don't go in there!" Ago calls, too late. He gives me a helpless look. "We're screwed now."

"Don't be such pussies," Lucifer says, waving us into the room after him. "I won't bite."

Ago, Jane 62 and I stand in the hall, debating with looks alone until I say, "Well, fuck it. I'm not leaving Katina in there."

I go inside and find Katina gazing out the window on the far side of the room. She glances at me and says, "Check this out."

Joining her, I look out to see the moon. Not riding high in the night sky, as one would expect, but right below us, as though the hotel is *on* the moon. Dusty white craters of every shape and size make up what should have been a lush green lawn lit with garden lamps.

"Like the view?" Lucy asks from behind us. "If not, I can change it."

"That won't be necessary," I say. "We're not staying. Come on, Katina."

By now Lithia is seated at the little dining table, tapping her cigarette into a crystal ashtray while Jane 62 and Ago are examining framed photographs decorating one wall. "Is this when you were little?" Ago asks, pointing to a random picture.

Lucifer peers over Ago's shoulder and grunts without interest.

Curiosity gets the best of me and I join them at the wall. Sure enough, there are photos of a young man who can only be Lucifer, at least how we know him at the moment anyway. "Why are you standing with your arm around that big worm?" I ask, pointing.

"Ah." Lucy has wandered into the bathroom, but now comes out again, shaking pills into his hand from a brown plastic bottle. "That's me with my dad."

"Your *dad?*" Ago balks. "You mean…"

"Yep. The one and only." At our disgusted faces, he says, "Oh, he takes on whatever shape amuses him at any given moment. That day it was a giant worm."

We puzzle over this for a few seconds until the pills draw my attention. "What are those?"

He shakes the bottle at me. "Xanax. Want one?"

"I do!" Katina trots over, holding out her hand.

At my suspicious look, Lucifer says, "Doctor prescribed, I can assure you. Don't look so amazed. Is it so shocking that I fight a battle against depression and anxiety just like everyone else? Do you have even an inkling of what it's like to be me? Of the pressure I am constantly under?" He absently hands the bottle to Katina and then moves back next to Ago to gaze at the photos and shake his head sadly. "I used to be his favorite, you know. He used to say I was his most beautiful angel, and I was too."

"Save the pity party for someone who'll fall for it," I say. I give Katina a worried glance, watching her dry swallow a couple pills, but then I shrug it off. She's already dead. What harm could really come to her?

Which brings me to a question that has been lingering in my mind since I woke up in that river of ice. "Are we ghosts, Lucy?"

He turns away from the wall of photographs, his expression blank. "I beg your pardon?"

"We're either ghosts or zombies, right? I mean, we *are* dead, but at the same time, this feels exactly like being alive."

"I'm not dead," Jane 62 pipes in. "At least, I don't think I am."

"I'm dead," Lithia says. "Deader than ten day old dog shit is what I am."

"How should I know what you are?" Lucy says. "Do I look like some all-knowing, all-seeing son of fucking God to you?"

Lithia makes a clucking sound with her tongue. "Why so snippy, demon beast? Sounds like jealousy to me."

"Don't call me that! And I'm not jealous of anyone!"

"Sounds like you are."

"Well, I'm not!"

"Stop bickering," I tell both of them. "Shit, it was a simple question. Sorry I assumed you would know the answer, Lucifer."

"He doesn't know shit," Lithia says, sneering behind her cloud of smoke.

"Fuck you!" Lucy snaps. He looks furious, but not the kind of furious where you're struggling not to murder someone. The kind of furious where you're struggling not to cry.

"My," Lithia taunts. "So sensitive."

Lucifer ignores her and snatches his pill bottle out of Katina's hands. "Gimmie that. I need it more than you do."

Several seconds pass, all of us afraid to say anything. Except for Lithia, that is. She just goes right on snickering to herself.

Finally, once Lucy has taken a few more pills, he appears to calm down and gives me a serious look. "You'll probably have to ask Jay what you are."

"Jay?" I raise an eyebrow.

"You know.... *Jay!*"

Scratching my head, I open my mouth to speak, but Katina interrupts. "Jesus!" she blurts. "Jesus fucking Christ!"

"You got it, sister," Lucy says, flopping into an arm chair, his face bored. "But I'd leave out the 'fucking' if I were you. You'll ruin his whole day if you say that to him."

"Him?" I ask, not knowing if I'm getting the concept of what they're talking about. "Who him?" Everyone looks at me like I'm retarded. "Okay, fine. I just wanted to be sure."

"Where can we find Jay?" Ago asks the devil.

Lucy waves his hand impatiently toward the ceiling. "He's where he always is, up there somewhere, where else? He would never soil his reputation by coming down here to visit the damned, even though they could certainly use an uplifting word or two now and then. Much more so than those fat old farts sitting pretty in their fucking marble Jacuzzis."

"He's here?" I ask. "In the hotel?"

"Of course! You think he'd miss all this fun?" Lucy laughs dryly at the prospect.

"I want to meet Jesus!" Katina exclaims excitedly, bouncing up and down on her toes. "Can we? Please?"

I look at the others, who all shrug. "I don't see why not," I tell her.

"Sweet," Katina says. She's grinning from ear to ear until her eyes fall back to Lucifer sitting in his chair, numbing out on Xanax. "Why don't you come with us, Lucy?"

Four mouths open, screeching protest, but Lucy sits there calmly, his eyes vaguely amused. He doesn't speak until we're all finished with our objections and then he says, "Why, thank you, Katina. I think I will join you. I haven't seen Jay in quite some time, now that I think about it."

"You're just trying to spite us," Lithia growls at him.

He gives her his winning smile, his black, black eyes flashing with mischief. "That's exactly correct, old woman. *Exactly* correct."

CHAPTER TWELVE

Lucifer leads our little parade out to the stairwell that we never would have found on our own, simply because it didn't exist until *he* wanted to climb it.

We go up several flights in silence, except for Lithia's huffing and puffing. When we arrive at a door marked 8th, Lucy swings it open and gestures us all forward. "After you," he says with a little bow.

I'm a little leery—who knows where he could be leading us—but Katina marches right through like she owns the place. Like it's not the devil inviting her through, but a cute misunderstood boy. I suppose, in his own way, that's exactly what Lucy is.

With thinly veiled trepidation, the rest of us follow Katina out into the hall and I sigh with relief. The place is sparkling and clean, a lush white carpet that looks as though it has never been walked on before beneath our feet. Brass lamps with frosted glass globes sit on expensive mahogany tables, glowing bright and welcomingly. From somewhere, music is playing and the song sounds vaguely familiar but I can't quite place it.

"Come along, my little piggies," Lucy says, starting down the hall. "Follow the big bad wolf."

We oblige, treading quietly, as if we're trying hard not to disturb the patrons of this five-star hotel, lest they discover our presence and have us thrown out like the bums that we are.

The music swells the further along the hall we travel and then it finally comes to me: the Beach Boys, singing "Wouldn't It Be Nice."

Lucy stops directly in front of the door where the music is coming from and raps his knuckles against it loudly. He looks at us and smiles, looks at the unanswered door and frowns. He raps again, harder this time. "Open up, Jay. You have visitors."

The door across the hall opens instead and we all turn to see several nuns peeking out at us. One of them spies Lucy, makes the sign of the cross and hisses something in Latin. Another one immediately begins singing along with the Beach boys, clapping her hands in time with the beat, completely oblivious to us.

"That's the Singing Nun," Lucy tells us. "The Flying Nun is in there too."

"You've gotta be shitting me," I say.

"Swear to *God*," he says dramatically.

One of the nuns pushes past the other two and joins us in the hall. The sight of her makes us grimace: blood flows down her face, streaming from her bloodshot eyes. Lucy jerks a thumb at her. "The Bleeding Nun." Then he pounds on the door with his fist. "For fuck's sake, Jay, open the fucking door!"

The door opens abruptly and a young bearded man peers out at us, followed by a cloud of smoke. I sniff and look at Ago. "Mary Jane," I say and try not to laugh.

"Jesus!" Ago says, his own nose wiggling.

"Hey, how ya doin', man?" Jesus smiles cheerily. I notice his eyes are even more bloodshot that those belonging to the Bleeding Nun.

"These kindly folks would like to have a word with you, Jay." Lucifer says patiently.

"No shit?" Jesus looks at us with his brown cow eyes. "Well, come on in!" He steps aside, taking a toke off the joint he's holding. As I pass him, I can't tell if I'm surprised by the way he's dressed, or completely unsurprised.

He's wearing worn out leather sandals (no surprise), torn dirty jeans (a bit of a surprise) a tie-dye T-shirt with a big pot leaf on the front (a pretty big surprise). His shirt is decorated with various pins: smiley faces, more pot leaves, The Grateful Dead. His wrists are decorated with hemp bracelets and around his neck are several long necklaces, colorful beads glinting in the sunshine of his room.

"Sorry the place is so trashed, guys," he says once we're all inside. Even the Bleeding Nun has come in, trailing silently behind the nearly-silent Jane 62. Jesus starts throwing stuff around the room, clearing off the furniture for us to sit. He tosses clothes, comic books, a dirty pair of sneakers, empty soda cans, pizza boxes. All of it goes straight into a pile on the floor at the foot of the bed, which he promptly sits on, facing the TV. He takes another toke and points at the television which is playing a video game. "Mario Kart, guys," Jesus says smiling, speaking loudly to be heard over the Beach Boys. "Anyone wanna race?"

Lucifer rolls his eyes. "I told you, Jay. These people want to ask you some questions."

But Jesus isn't listening. He's started a new game, racing Mario around the track, trying to catch up to Luigi. After a moment, he says, "Yeah, there's some cold pizza over on the...the..." He trails off, concentrating. When his little cartoon car crashes, he laughs like a child and smokes more of his joint.

Lucy clears his throat and says, "They want to know if they're ghosts or zombies, Jay." He speaks to Jesus as though the guy is a complete idiot and I'm starting to see why. I think he's toasted a few of his brains cells in the last 2,000 years or so.

"Just say no," Ago murmurs.

"Jay?" Lucy says, louder. "Can you please stop doing that for a minute?"

"I'm listening," Jay insists. "Kinda."

"Well, which is it?" Lithia demands.

"Ghosts? Zombies? Spirits? None of the above?"

Jesus looks around the floor for an ashtray to stub out his roach. Once that is accomplished, he looks up at the rest of with those earnest brown eyes and says, "That's a pretty existentialist question. I mean, who are any of us, right, man? Maybe you're not even here. Maybe *I'm* not even here. See what I'm saying?"

Katina has moved to the window and looks out. "Sunflowers," she says softly. "An endless field of sunflowers."

None of us are interested enough to look out with her. Instead, I look down at Jesus and say, "That's not really helping, Jay."

"Or," he continues, as though I didn't speak. "Maybe you're the whole world. The whole *universe*. Did you ever think of that?" He pinches his thumb and index finger together to signify something very small. "Maybe the entire solar system exists only in the pupil of your eye."

I'm beginning to feel a headache coming on and have no idea how to respond to the son of God when he is spewing such nonsense.

"Are you sure you're Jesus?" Lithia asks suspiciously.

Jesus laughs and resumes his game.

"This whole thing is starting to get on my nerves," Ago says. "I think I liked Purgatory better."

"Fuck that," Katina replies, finally turning away from the window. "If I'm stuck here, I at least want to be stuck on one of the higher floors where we can eat something other than opera pie."

Now convinced that our question won't be answered after all, I'm inclined to agree with her. "We may as well see what we can see. Evidently, we have nothing but time anyway."

"I'm in no rush to get where *I'm* going, if you know what I mean," Lithia says in her cracked voice. "They can be renovating Hell till the cows come home for all I care."

"The renovations are almost finished," Lucy tells her with a smile. "I'm looking forward to it myself."

"I've been hearing that for as long as I can remember," Lithia says, clearly not intimidated.

I say, "So, I assume we still have to take the stairs, right?"

"It's not as impressive as you think up there," Lucifer says. "The lower floors are where the fun is at."

"I'm sure you would say that, but why don't you just humor us for a minute."

He sighs loudly and pouts out his lower lip. "Jay should take you. I hate it up there."

We all look at Jesus, who has just lit up another doobie and is stroking his wispy beard in a thoughtful manner. He shrugs and says, "I'm down with that."

CHAPTER THIRTEEN

So, our parade has yet again increased by, this time by two. Despite an endless stream of complaints, Lucifer has decided to tag along and he and Katina bring up the rear, whispering among themselves.

Ago and I follow Jesus up a flight of stairs, while Lithia, Jane 62 and the Bleeding Nun trail behind us. Jesus begins humming "Stairway to Heaven," then laughs uproariously at his own joke. The rest of us chuckle politely but I know the others, like myself, think the messiah is a major dork as well as a hopeless stoner.

Eventually, the stairs end and we all crowd onto the small landing, watching for Jesus to open the door. He places his hand on a highly polished gold knob and say, "Okay, you guys ready?"

There are a lot of groans but I say, "Yep, we're ready."

Jesus opens the door with a flourish and then steps back. Ago and I pass over the threshold first, completely astounded. The others follow us through and I can hear soft gasps behind me. We stare in silence for what feels like an eternity.

And then, Lithia's voice: "What the hell is this? A joke?"

I blink at the vast whiteness of where we are. A bright blinding nothing. Absolute emptiness. When I turn around, I see my companions and not one other thing. We're standing on air, it seems, and the door we just passed through no longer exists.

"I told you it was boring," Lucy says.

"This is it?" Katina asks. Her voice is on the verge of breaking. "This is Heaven, where all the fucking good rich white people go? What the *fuck*?"

Everyone begins to talk at once, except for the Bleeding Nun, who stands silently, the blood on her face the reddest thing I've ever seen against all this white.

Suddenly I remember when I first met Salvadore and we began our trek to the Virgin City. When we first emerged from the electric forest—all that white space that crept up behind us with every step, wiping out the road, the trees, the sky. Everything.

I remember staring into that vast white space and struggling to see something—anything—and then I did. I saw some fleeting movement, too fast, too blurry to identify as anything but a trick of my imagination.

I saw something because I was trying to see something.

Looking around again, I see the faces of my companions and now they're all silent, staring at me expectantly. "What?" I say.

"What?" They all reply at exactly the same time, in one single voice.

My voice.

Stumbling back a step, I shake my head. "What's going on?"

Again, they all repeat my question, all their lips moving simultaneously, all their voices mine.

I look hard at Katina—young Katina, so much like myself when I was her age—and watch in fascinated horror as her head begins to melt like hot wax, her features slipping right off her face and dribbling down her neck and shoulders.

All of them are melting right before my eyes, each one of them a bubbling mass of flesh colored goop, their clothes melting right along with them and puddling on the floor of nowhere.

Jesus is the last to go and as I watch, his face doesn't exactly melt, but morphs into mine. A masculine version of me, but still very clearly me.

"We were all you," the Jesus me says. "Every facet of you that ever was."

"That can't be," I say, my voice undistinguishable from his. "No. No, no."

Jesus me begins to melt just as the others did and I quickly turn away, concentrating on the white. I know there is something in all that nothing, something alive and moving and if I just try hard enough I'm sure to see it. If I just concentrate…

My headache worsens but I see something, a brief flittering of silver light. I screw my eyes shut and open them again, focusing hard on the spot of silver.

The single dot of silver begins to bloom, spreading out and at first I think it may be a star. But then it grows fingers, long and spidery, reaching up and up and then the whole thing resolves into what is unmistakably a tree.

A sparking electric tree.

Once I'm able to see the tree, the rest of the forest is easy to create. I think and it is: it's as simple as that.

I suppose I could have thought up anything. Maybe a city or a farm. A snowy mountain with a big lodge atop it, smoke curling up out of its stone chimney. A vast blue ocean and a warm welcoming sun.

I don't know why I created the electric forest but as soon as it's completed, I know that I made a mistake.

I know I have to try again, go back to the beginning, but I don't know how. Erasing things is not as easy as creating them, though I try hard to do exactly that, to no avail. I can't undo what I've done.

The rain is just starting to fall and there is a river of ice up ahead. I know because I put it there.

It seems important that I reach it before the black sky breaks open and electrocutes me where I stand.

And so I run.

ANDRE DUZA

LOCATION:
Philadelphia, PA

STYLE OF BIZARRO:
Brutality Chronic

BOOKS BY DUZA:

Dead Bitch Army
Jesus Freaks (je-'zus fre-ks), n. see ZOMBIE
Necro-Sex Machine (forthcoming)
Dancing and Stabbing (forthcoming)
SuperNigger (forthcoming)

DESCRIPTION: Author of horrific, bizarre, smart, funny, fast-paced fiction.

INTERESTS: Avid bodybuilder and Certified (junior-master level) Instructor of Spirit Fist Kung Fu. Competes in tournaments from time to time. Also studied Boxing, Tae Kwon Do, Chinese Kempo, Street-fighting

INFLUENCES: Human behavior, angry childhood, politics, James Baldwin, Marcus Garvey, Poe, Bierce, Sergio Leone, John Carpenter, George Romero, David Cronenberg, George Carlin, Wes Craven, Tobe Hooper, Fantastic Planet, Repo Man, the hood, boarding school, Chang Cheh, Lau Kar Leung, Richard Pryor, Unsolved Mysteries, In Search Of, Eric B. & Rakim, KRS-One, NWA, Gangstarr, Zeppelin, psychedelic rock, Goblin, 70s horror, 70s porn, 80s slasher flicks, Frank Frazetta, Frank Henenlotter, fear of mediocrity, blaxploitation, comic books, lurid detective magazines, old school anime (Speed Racer, Battle of the Planets, Star Blazers), ig'nant-ass niggas.

WEBSITE:
www.houseofduza.com

Don't F(beep)k With the Coloureds

FADE IN:

White letters against a black screen:
Generic Films Presents…

DISSOLVE TO:

It is the middle of the night. We open on a wide, three-story, Rundbogenstil-style building set dead center in the frame. The letters carved into the archway above the large front door read: **Harrington House Retirement Center.**

Narrator: Someone is killing the residents of Harrington House...

CUT TO:

A hand wrapped in a latex surgical glove fills the frame, fingers tense and straight. A second hand simultaneously pulls the glove at the wrist to work the fingers in.

Narrator: …someone who promised to care for them.

CUT TO:

A nervous-looking woman dressed in office attire is talking on the phone. Fear colors her voice.

Nervous-looking woman: I think Dr. Everhardt is experimenting on the residents.

She is suddenly startled by someone who enters the room from behind. She turns and sees a distinguished-looking, middle-aged man (Dr. Everhardt) standing there.

CUT TO:

A group of nurses struggle to hold down an elderly man who thrashes in pain on his hospital bed. Heart monitors are beeping. The nurses are talking over each other. The man's eyes are rolled back, veins bulging. His body shoots to a rigid arch as the worst pain hits him. He is foaming at the mouth and shaking his head back and forth in a vain attempt to signal "no." His screams begin to echo.

Narrator: Lifetime Movie Channel presents a film based on a true story. Crystal Bernard, Tracey Gold, and Bruce Boxleitner star in…

There is a sudden distortion.

The narrator's voice recedes to incoherent mumbling. The frame begins to stutter and tear, then finally melt as if the film is burning.

Beneath the celluloid surface, words began to materialize…

Three years ago…

The winding driveway that led up the hill to the wide, three-story, Rundbogenstil-style building (the Harrington House Retirement Center) writhed with activity like a tongue rolling out in effigy of something dead sexy. Sirens screeching like mechanized infant calls, amplified by the dark-matter din of night in the 'burbs. Two police cars raced up the long driveway, which was finger-flecked by branches that reached out on both sides from the semi-wooded land between Route 1 below and the old building at the top of the hill. "Private Property, No Trespass" signs dotted the road.

The first two officers at the scene (McMahon and Shields) were already crouching behind their opened car doors when the first backup car roared up, slid sideways, and stopped a few feet from them. Then the next ones screeched to a halt right up on them.

Officer McMahon waved his hand down to signal Officers three (Simmons), four (Tate), five (Carter), and six (Reilly) to stay the fuck down. The new arrivals crouched in the open night and assumed defensive positions behind their cars' bulk.

"So, what've we got?" Reilly inquired, hungry for action.

This was Cloverleaf County after all. The most that ever happened here was the occasional date rape on campus at the college or a drunken bar fight over a chick between privileged frat boys.

"Nothing yet," McMahon responded. "A neighbor phoned in the complaint. Said she heard gunshots while she was out walking her dog."

"Spotted some movement in one of the upstairs windows," said Shields, pointing with his eyes. "Not sure if it's our shooter."

Sporting a knowing grimace, Simmons grumbled, "Nearest house is half a mile from here. What the hell's she doing walking her dog in front of this place?"

"Looking for trouble… just like everyone else," Shields responded.

"It was a rhetorical question, man. Of course she was looking for trouble."

It wasn't the first time the police had been called to Harrington House. In fact, they'd been around more than they would have liked lately. The old folks had been acting strange lately, running around naked, scaring the locals, and playing mean-spirited pranks on each other and the staff.

Harrington House was a place for well-to-do retirees. The brochure boasted grand ballrooms and suites sporting décor and furnishings from the 1920s and '30s. "Take a trip back to the good old days," the pamphlet claimed, "to a time when gentility reigned, when women were ladies and men were gentlemen." Elegant social gatherings and theme parties in the style of old Hollywood were touted as the norm.

"So, what's it gonna be this time?" said McMahon. "Some old fart who forgot to take his medicine?"

"An old fart with a gun," Shields added.

McMahon rolled his eyes.

"You have a knack for pointing out the obvious, Shields…"

Though generally an overlooked sound, the click of a heavy lock sliding open screamed at them from the front door. Bouncing to ready, the officers trained their guns on the sound, following its echo back from the air around them to the front door as it yawned open and allowed a woman to exit before slamming shut.

Her hips spoke loudly through the thigh-length nurse's uniform that stuck to her ample curves like white on rice. A Harrington House crest was stitched just above her right breast. Her intoxicated state fell upon them secondary to her overall beauty. In fact, it wasn't until she nearly fell down the front steps that they noticed her inebriation.

It was a miracle that she didn't fall on her face. The move that she performed to save her balance, like a retarded step and slide, was the kind of thing that she could have never duplicated no matter how hard she tried.

"Are you all right, ma'am?" McMahon called out, sympathetic, yet stern. "Is there anyone else inside?"

Judging by the look in her eyes, she was somewhere else entirely (and ridin' bareback on some quality shit).

The police, with their little guns and flashing lights, were nothing to the toxic god who violated her sobriety. To her impaired eyes, they were like gnats bouncing around the beacon of the red and blue orbs, swirling and stuttering, making colorful tracers.

"I said, is there anyone else inside?"

Lulled into calm by her drunkenness, the officers relaxed their gun-arms, hands loosening their grips. They traded faces to decide who'd approach her. None of them wanted to come off as overeager, even though they all felt the same tingle in their loins. As indirect an opportunity as it might have been, it was still an opportunity to secure some down-the-road-pussy once this chick was all rehabbed and back in the world.

The way she began to move her hips sparked a lurid curiosity in them, well, five of them anyway. Married with children, Officer Jack Tate was as straight as they come. He had even convinced himself that looking at other women that way was a sin.

The others did everything to get a good look at what was about to happen. Fuck safety.

The nurse writhed as they watched, their expressions adopting a figurative dog-pant, their eyes bulging like the fronts of their trousers in testament to dirty, stinkin' sex vibes.

Hanging onto visions of hinted-at nakedness that enhanced the scene, they gawked like prepubescent boys who were tasting real lust for the first time as the nurse let her uniform fall from her shoulders. It caught and lingered at each curve of her S dance before eventually landing in a soft heap around her dainty feet.

Disbelief made the officers smile at the extended full-frontal shot that she gave them.

Tate, who pitied her behavior, shook his head.

The woman's body was firm; her torso long with subtle curves; her skin glowing sepia, with licks of dark brown around her plump nipples and radiating from her wide eyes. They seemed to shine brighter now that she was naked. The look on her face said "I'm high as fuck," yet behind it was solid confidence.

Tate's first plan—to simply clear his throat—didn't even come close to diverting his colleagues attention away from the naked, writhing woman.

Plan number two—grabbing a blanket from his squad car and approaching her with it held out in front of him—only made the other officers groan, as if he was killing their buzz.

But then…

They didn't notice it all at once, but they all eventually saw it: the impression of subdermal arms and hands caressing and embracing the nurse and causing her to sway euphorically to their slithering embraces.

Tate, who was the closest to her, was the first to see it. He didn't want to touch her from the get-go, mainly out of disgust and some twisted idea of loyalty to his wife, but now he was plain-old scared. They all were. One or two of the men hinted at raising their weapons.

The rhythm of her dance suggested a slow, seductive, yet animalistic melody; the skin-deep appendages proffered eerie strings.

The woman turned her back to them and jutted her tight, round ass outward. The dark valley between well-rounded teardrops of flesh invited ogling eyes to look closer. Subdermal hands teased the teardrops open and let them bounce closed.

When she turned back around, a single blue eye, reddened by anger or maybe hatred, glared at the officers in the place of each nipple. Her navel had stretched into a large mouth that was grinning deviously and leaking saliva from its sepia-toned bottom lip. Her head was slumped to the side, her eyes rolled up under her eyelids, mouth hanging open. Although she maintained her dance, her hands tracing her own curves down her flat stomach and between her legs; she was clearly unconscious.

Diverted by the hands and arms and

the moist slurp-snap as the nurse raised her hand from between her legs, the officers didn't see what it was that she pulled from her vagina until it was too late.

The nurse fired off three shots from the small handgun before they had time to react.

"In-a-gadda-da-vida, baby," quipped the mouth in her stomach in a gravely, Wolfman Jack-like tone. "Donchu know that I lu-u-uv you?"

The first shot caught Tate in the throat and passed clean through. He collapsed immediately, clutching his neck and gurgling out a brief response as he hit the ground and writhed. The blanket he was holding fell over him.

The remaining officers drew their weapons and fired.

Aside from the bang of their revolvers, the night was quiet enough that the smack-smacking of their bullets punching through the nurse's silky flesh could be heard clearly. She didn't bother to wait for the last gunshot before she straightened, tipped over like fleshy Swiss cheese and hit the ground ugly.

When it was all over, Simmons and Carter ran over to the thrashing lump partially hidden under Tate's blanket. Simmons paused, knelt down, and pinched back the edge of the blanket. He could only look at his partner's face for a split-second before it overwhelmed him. Tate desperately tried to breathe as he gagged and choked on his own blood, grabbing at the mangled flesh where his esophagus used to be.

Reilly ran to his car and radioed for an ambulance.

"Officer down!!!!" he yelled into the receiver. "Get an ambulance here. Fast!"

McMahon and Shields approached the nurse's body with caution, stepping tentatively, arms held straight, but pointed down in text book, TV-cop style. She lay with her back, right shoulder and breast to them, twisted in a wildly beautiful pose.

She flinched once... twice...

McMahon pulled the trigger and fired into the ground, then lifted his gun and fired once more at the woman's head.

Instead of blood, the wound drained and spurted colors: reds, oranges, yellows, greens, blues, indigos, and violets. There was blood—real blood—pooling around her abdomen and chest, but from her head there were only colors, thick, frothy, and alive.

McMahon and Shields couldn't believe what they were seeing. Even as they watched the colorful liquid ooze five feet to the manicured lawn and soak into the dirt, their subconscious minds told them that it was impossible, that they must be seeing things, that maybe they were slipping. Each had his reasons for questioning his own sanity, and neither of them knew if the other had seen the colorful liquid. And they just might have seen two eyes and a smile float by in the ooze.

McMahon was going to play it cool until Shields said something. That was the safest way. Shields, however, was planning to do the same thing.

Leaping full-throttle out of the quiet, laughter came at them in varied pitches and volumes, suggesting very large and very small things lurking inside the building, things that didn't sound at all like people laughing, but almost. Whatever they were, they were busting a gut. The sound was flowing from every window and doorway along the front of the building, as if heads with open mouths were leaning out. It contradicted what the officers saw through the lit windows, which was nothing: a lamp, maybe a dresser, a bed, a few paintings of scenery. They could see a few feet into the unlit windows as well. Clearly, there was no one there.

The officers stiffened. The laughter had them ready to shoot first and shoot any-fucking-thing-that-moved. It wasn't as if "What to do when confronted with a gorgeous woman with eyes for nipples and a mouth in her gut" or "What to do in case of disembodied, inhuman laughter" was in the handbook.

Simmons, however, was beyond all that. Watching his partner gurgle and choke and drown in blood left him numb. The laughter tickled his inner savage and gave it an appetite for vengeance.

Carter was the first to snap out of "What the fuck!?" and snap right into panic when he realized that they were standing out in the open, completely vulnerable to… whatever was inside.

"Everybody take cover!" he yelled. The officers scattered. By the time anyone noticed Simmons, he was halfway inside the main doors.

Crouching behind their cars, they watched the door slam shut.

Old cartoon characters reciting trademark phrases was the last thing Simmons expected to hear when he entered the main lobby—laughing woodpeckers, smartass wabbits, a stressed-out Chihuahua in the middle of a meltdown…. It was coming from the door-lined corridor at the back of the lobby. There were three rooms on either side, blue light flickering from the doorways like high beams. All the televisions seemed to be on.

What was going on?

The long corridor intersected with another a few feet from the fifth and sixth rooms. There was an office on the other side, directly ahead. There were letters on the frosted window of the door; some sort of official title, he guessed. He was too far away to read it.

Simmons paid little attention to the lobby he was standing in. He could not have cared less about the antique leather furniture, the Italian chandelier that hung from the ceiling, the brown and white murals of "roarin' '20s" city life that decorated the walls, the wide, winding staircase that snaked upward to darker places.

The voices stopped as soon as his foot crossed the threshold from the lobby to the hallway. Static and pitch-bending radiofrequency noise filled the void. And there was one more thing: the smell of fresh paint. It was a toxic stench, so strong that it stung his eyes. Strange, he thought, but currently it registered about a 4 on his "give-a-fuck" meter. Finding out who was behind what happened to his partner blotted out everything else.

Simmons came to the first two rooms and found nothing but an unmade bed and a television screen filled with static in each.

There were still four more rooms, and the office. He could read the letters on the office door now: Reigert Everhardt, MD. Settling into his surroundings, Simmons thought he saw things on the walls all around him, and the ceiling, too—cartoon characters smiling down on him. Their smiles shook the weight of whatever they were trying to mask. It looked like anger, or maybe disgust.

The characters were born of completely different styles and levels of talent. He recognized a number of them from his youth; back when credits with names like Chuck Jones, Tex Avery, and Hanna-Barbera were burned into his mind. Others reminded him of Ralph Bakshi, John Kricfalusi, and Frank Frazetta—a few favorites from his teenage years.

They have kids here too, he thought. Then he noticed the nudity, both male and female. What kind of fuckin' place is this?

A jumble of sounds indicated movement down the hall. It was coming from the office.

Snapping into position, his gun pointed, Simmons called out, "Somebody inn'ere?"

He turned his ear to the door and listened. The silence spooked him. It wasn't a dead silence, it was a weird marriage of static, emptiness, and feverish pounding.

"Don't make me have to come in there after you… whoever you are," Simmons warned the eyes peeking out from behind the office door.

They disappeared behind the office door in reaction.

From his immediate left came a voice…

"Eh… I don't think he's coming out, bub."

Simmons whipped left and ended up face to face with the things on the wall. Only now, he saw frowns; pink lips peeking out from black faces. It gave him a jolt. He backed away and spun to check the wall behind him. Same thing.

"What's goin' on in there, Simmons? Talk to me, man!" MacMahon said into the front door.

Simmons suddenly felt ambushed, closed in. Somehow his eyes found their way back to the office door. The eyes were back. They were watching him hard.

He started to back away when paint from the walls rained down on and around him as if an invisible levee had finally been broached.

McMahon and Shields fell into the lobby and right on top of each other. Carter and Reilly followed them and planted themselves into position, their weapons aimed at the "thing" that coughed and flailed at the air in the middle of the door-lined corridor. From its feet up to its waist, it looked like a man wearing police blue.

Simmons? They wondered in unison.

From the waist up, the man was animated—a weird, elongated caricature of Officer Simmons. Whatever it was that had painted him to look like some bastard lovechild of Stephen Gammell and Peter Chung was creeping down his body and coloring the rest of him.

Simmons reacted to the commotion at the front door by blindly firing. His eyes were stung closed by the paint so he couldn't see who it was. And he couldn't see the makeover that the paint was giving him. The toxic smell burned the inner lining of his nostrils. The taste caused him to gag. His gun was big and fat, like a child's toy. Three bullets literally screamed out and bore down at the men with determination. From the side view, an anime blur indicated just how fast they were moving.

"Let's git dat mutherfucker," the bullet in the middle said.

"Get down!" Carter yelled, and the officers scattered.

The three bullets chased Carter to the floor and swarmed around him like angry bees. They were frowning and baring teeth.

McMahon, who was the closest to Carter, crawled away on his side. Reilly and Shields watched dumbfounded as the first bullet tore into Carter's left hand, which he held in front of him to defend. The others found his arm, shoulder…

Carter leapt to his feet and batted at himself with his good hand as he stumbled and bounced from wall to wall. He ran in circles, screaming bloody murder.

Shields took a chance and fired at the animated bullets. He hit Carter instead, three, four, five times.

"Shields!" McMahon scolded.

The animated bullets had just eaten Carter's head and were on their way down his torso and right arm. His body slumped to the floor, knees first. He leaned forward and began to fall.

There was nothing left to hit the ground, only tiny ribbons of flesh and fabric floating where Carter knelt. The three bullets disintegrated when they were done ravaging Carter's remains.

"Oh my God! What happened to me!?!" Simmons screamed. He was staring at his strangely drawn hands. He lifted them to his face and felt both sides of it. His fingers translated the distortion perfectly. To his own ears, his voice sounded fine. However, all McMahon, Shields, and Reilly heard was static and pitch-bending radiofrequency noise coming from his mouth whenever he spoke.

They aimed their weapons at him.

"Is that… Simmons?"

"Can't be."

Realizing that he had fired on his colleagues, Simmons said, "Oh shit! I'm so sorry! I thought… I didn't know."

McMahon led the backwards retreat toward the door. They stepped blind, holding their aim on the Simmons-thing who talked like a bad transistor radio lost between clear signals.

"No guys, wait," he hurried toward them as he spoke. "It's me. It's Simmons."

"Don't come any closer!" McMahon demanded.

"It's me, Mac." Simmons pleaded. "I swear it is. I don't know what's going on but the paint… it fell on me and…"

"I said don't come any closer or I'll…"

"Jesus Christ, Mac!" Shields added. "It looks like Simmons!"

Somewhere in the lobby, a woman screamed. Her voice had an otherworldly echo.

The roarin' '20s' street scene came to life on the wall that bordered the stairs. A young blond nurse ran through the two-dimensional crowd of boys in knicker suits, men in pinstripes and bowler hats, ladies in tea dresses and beaded gowns. The white of her nurse's uniform stuck out in the dull brown and white mural that held her. From her upper right breast, a Harrington House logo called out in bright red letters.

A few of the men in the crowd tried to grab at her but missed. She continued to lurch through the pedestrians. Judging from the look on her face, she was running for her life. She seemed to be getting away until a lamppost with teeth reached down and snatched her up by the head. As she dangled,

kicking and flailing, the street surrounding an open manhole below her turned pliable. The manhole stretched up from the ground, human teeth poking forward until they resembled those of a great white shark. The manhole bit down on her waist and tore her in half, then settled back into the street where it chewed and swallowed with a loud "GULP."

Simmons was jogging toward them now, looking over his shoulder at the wall alongside the stairs.

McMahon and the others found themselves flabbergasted once again.

Simmons was almost on them when he tripped and fell into McMahon, who put his arms up at the last minute. He braced himself for the approaching weight, but there was only liquid.

Simmons had literally splashed all over McMahon and soaked him to the bone.

"What the hell?!?" McMahon spit through the harsh-tasting sludge. He squeezed his eyes shut at the burning sensation and wiped himself feverishly. "Fuck! What is this shit?"

He reached out to Shields and Reilly. They quietly backed out of range.

"Shields… Reilly… I can't see. What is this stuff? Where's Simmons, er…"

The paint slithered over McMahon's torso and under his clothing.

"C'mon, guys. Gimme a hand!"

The paint around his chest began to stretch outward away from his body and into the shape of a cartoon character from the waist up—a rabbit that was familiar to all of them.

"Saaay, you need a hand, doc? How's this?" it said, cocking its arm back and slapping McMahon off balance with its oversized hand. He felt his jaw shatter and tasted his own blood swishing around the inside of his mouth along with a few of his teeth.

The rabbit just as quickly sank back into the living paint.

"Ahh," MacMahon shrieked, rubbing the paint away from his eyes. He opened them to a blur.

An infant wearing a fedora tipped to the side and clenching a stogie between his teeth emerged on his shoulder. "Or this!" it said, as it jabbed two tiny hands deep into McMahon's eye sockets and retreated into the paint.

McMahon screamed in response to the pain and pressurized pop as the soft tissue splashed from his crushed eyeballs. Blood stole the voice from his throat.

The characters continued to come and go, emerging from random spots on his upper body. "Or this," each said in a voice as unique as the styles in which they were conceived. A devilish cat pulled out McMahon's tongue and sliced it off with a single, sharp claw; a shovel-jawed clown with Xs for eyes sprayed acid from a flower on his lapel and melted McMahon's face; a yellow, spiky-haired kid with an overbite slurped the liquefied flesh with a straw and spit the face fully intact (horrified expression and all) onto the wall.

Reilly planted his back against the wall and froze. Shields took off out the front door and kept going. As he watched McMahon do a spiral dance toward the hallway, Reilly spotted a set of eyes looking back at him from the cracked office door at the other end.

* * *

Hypnotized by the quick edits and the obtrusive colors that screamed at him from the television, the burnout formerly known as Dr. Reigert Everhardt sat in his shabby, one bedroom apartment watching the last fucking thing he ever wanted to watch: cartoons.

The last three years had been rough, ducking in and out of boarding houses and cheap motels. That night at Harrington House was still fresh in his mind, especially when he closed his eyes. He had seen the entire thing. He hid behind the door of his office and watched as the Coloureds (what the cartoons preferred to be called) murdered five nurses, eleven patients, and five cops. Three years and he still couldn't shake the images and the voice that reminded him that it was all his fault. He knew that. Boy, did he know it.

It's all your fault... The words hurt like a sonofabitch.

Could've just as easily have been the Coloureds fucking with him, though. You wouldn't believe the kind of shit they pulled. People have the wrong idea about them based on what they see on television and in movies. That perpetually pleasant shit was just an act.

The Coloureds weren't bound by the same limits as humans. Unless specifically integrated into the personalities of the characters by the "artist," the Coloureds couldn't experience feelings like guilt or remorse. There was no right or wrong. Some had good natures and were willing to play by the rules; however, most of Coloureds were downright scary in person. They could bleed, lose an arm, a leg, even a head, and it didn't mean a thing. The only way that they could be killed was if they were erased.

Now, there were a number of ways to do such a thing, depending on the medium. Fire, turpentine, bleach, or good old-fashioned rubber worked against the Sketches, who were the slum-dwellers of the cartoon world.

The Coloureds will tell you that the art came before the artists. They pointed to the cave paintings to demonstrate that they communicated with early humans. Their numbers were few back then. Through their visual allure, they manipulated inspired especially perceptive humans (eventually known as artists) to fashion images, propagating their species and forming a bond with humans that endures to this day.

It wasn't until 1906, when J. Stuart Blackton made the first animated film, that the Coloureds started to become a force. A minority opinion held that the invention of the phenakistoscope in 1831 predated Mr.

Blackton's invention. Before that, they were relegated to communicating through static images, with the exception of nighttime dreams and the waking reveries of the crazy, the religious, and the stoned. Because of their volatile nature, Coloureds rarely interacted with humans in person. Film and TV were the safest ways. "Only for the purposes of education or entertainment" was what the Interaction Treaty stated, which had been carefully drawn up and deliberated by leaders of both sides long ago. Except at the highest level, direct communication between species was not allowed. The underbelly of Coloured society (Sketches or Rough-Sketches) preferred it this way. They liked to fuck with humans in traditional ways, such as through hallucinogenic drugs. It was the Coloureds behind Swiss chemist, Albert Hofmann's accidental "trip" in 1943.

LSD was known to them as the "master key"; however, mescaline, psilocin and psilocybin, PCP, and ecstasy were popular as well, as were a variety of herbs and preparations from all corners of the globe. Such interactions almost always ended badly, so contact with humans through these means was officially illegal.

Everhardt first stumbled upon the world of the Coloureds in 1953 while working on project MK-ULTRA (conceived by the Clandestine Services Department of the United States government to develop mind-control drugs) for the CIA at Edgewood Arsenal in Maryland. His concoction, TX-260, which was derived from henbane, was hailed as "the real super-hallucinogen" after tests with BZ (quinuclidinyl benzilate) by the Army Chemical Corps tests failed to produce "actionable results."

TX-260 was so potent that it left the user permanently intoxicated and susceptible to all kinds of suggestions and hallucinogenic distortions. "They seem aware of my existence," stated one of the test subjects while under the affects of the drug; other subjects made similar comments.

By the time Everhardt had completed lab and field testing of TX-260, project MK-ULTRA was losing steam.

The CIA pulled the plug on the program after a young woman confessed to reporters about her part in something called Project Midnight Climax. She provided the media with lurid details of sex, drugs, and espionage. Her claim was that she was paid by government agents to seduce men, bring them back to a motel that had been financed and outfitted by the CIA, and slip them LSD while military officials watched through a two-way mirror.

Everhardt never knew what happened to the test subjects as the project ground to a halt. He had a good idea what became of them, and he decided to leave it at that. He didn't want outright murder on his hands or his conscience. Sure, he figured, TX-260 fried their brains, but at least they were alive.

The CIA forbade Everhardt from taking anything when he left: not his research notes; not the remaining TX-260; not even the supplies and personal effects that he brought with him to the lab. Fearing that they might one day talk, the government quietly discredited all the scientists and medical personnel who worked on the project. A few of them just disappeared.

Warner Brothers found Everhardt in the early '70s. By then, TX-260 had made its way to Hollywood via self-destructive rock stars and counterculture celebrities like Timothy Leary and Dennis Hopper.

Warner Brothers was a hotbed of animation in the '60s and '70s. Coloureds who liked to interact with humans would often look to the Hollywood production companies for opportunities, as mixing for the purposes of entertainment was allowed by the Treaty. Disney was the people's choice, but they focused mainly on programming meant for young children, which required the

Coloureds to tone down their language and antics. Mickey and the gang never heard the end of it. The Coloureds who found fame in the human world by obeying the humans, performing "clean" for the kids, and fostering images for themselves that were just as squeaky clean were decried as sellouts by their peers.

It was seen as a little more respectable to work for Warner Brothers. Warners had their rules and censors, but at least they had a knack for infusing adult humor into their animated shorts. It was a formula for success. The Warners got rich—richer—and the Coloureds got their first taste of semi-legitimate fame.

The Coloureds took to their status and power in the human world in the worst ways. They were always difficult to work with, but now, they were impossible. They saw the praise and accommodation lavished upon movie stars and felt that they deserved the same. Soon, rumors of after-hours parties, where Coloureds and humans could be seen brazenly drinking, fighting, and fucking together, hit the gossip columns.

The Coloureds got tired of languishing behind the scenes. Some began to resent the fact that the credit for the success of their films was always going to the human artists. All over town, tensions simmered. Some of the more aggressive Coloureds began to act out. Warner Brothers saw TX-260 as a possible way of controlling them, or at least reining them in. The troublemakers were well aware of the Treaty. If the Coloureds were willing to break them, they were going to have to pay.

The studio hired Everhardt to oversee their new clandestine operation; Project Toon-Out they called it. (Author's note: Clandestine operations were big in the '60s and '70s.)

During its five-year run, Everhardt watched the program spiral out of control. Coloureds were allowed to pass freely through the human world. The studios paid the news media big money to float "drug epidemic" pieces whenever someone reported seeing a "cartoon" walking down the street, or shoplifting, or raping their wife, etc.... If that angle didn't fit, they could always resort to suggesting "paranormal phenomena." The last resort was always an attempt to discredit the interlocutor using propaganda and misinformation in the form of "new developments" or "shocking revelations."

A new trend was emerging. Without a human host, a Coloured could only exist in the human world for up to 72 hours at a time. As a result, Coloureds were making under-the-table deals with ambitious but limited B- and C-list celebrities to share bodies in a state called "coexistence." Coexistence allowed the Coloureds to exist indefinitely, and for humans, it had a way of reinventing a person. Or at least it worked wonders for the complexion. And everyone loves an "animated" personality.

You'd know one if you saw one. They looked bizarre and sometimes horrific, like "after" photographs that were never going to end up hung proudly on some plastic surgeon's wall. Claims of botched plastic surgery were commonly made to cover up the physical marriage of a Coloured and a human.

There was one other way around the 72-hour limit. Some Coloureds took to robbing graveyards or finding worthy human candidates and waiting around for them to die, or in some cases, helping the process along. Afterward, they'd use the deceased human's body as a shell. But this way was even easier to detect as the "artificial" look was undeniable. Everhardt's list of suspects included:

1. Michael, Jermaine, Janet and Latoya Jackson (especially Michael and Latoya)
2. Joan Rivers
3. The Barbie twins
4. Pricilla Presley
5. Melanie Griffith
6. Demi Moore

7. Dolly Parton
8. Lil' Kim

Legitimate coexistence was like living on a perpetual high, which was why so many celebrities turned to drugs and alcohol to try to hit the brakes on what was termed "fast living." Many of those in coexistence burned out or died young.

Everhardt had seen many of them end up as suicides. The program was out of control, and he wanted out. He knew better than to go public with what he knew, so he left the studio one afternoon and simply disappeared, like a ghost, into the population.

Everhardt managed to stay under their radar until that night, three years ago at Harrington House. They had done a good job of making him look bad, thanks to that TV movie. The movie (a Lifetime Channel hack-job starring Bruce Boxleitner as Everhardt) painted him as an out-of-control deviant and drunk.

Everhardt was keen on continuing his experiments with TX-260. He figured that the elderly patients would be gullible and easy to control, so they formed the perfect patient population. He'd deal with the moral ramifications later. Hollywood and the government taught him how to do that.

Everhardt's research yielded some unexpected results. TX-260 was evolving. It no longer needed a host mind to act as a bridge between worlds. It was as if the drug, in its liquid form, was a living doorway, able to stretch and grow and move like a sentient being.

Of course, the Coloureds were to blame. Apparently they had learned to control the liquid. The elderly folks who took the drug saw the Coloureds come to them as angels and demons, as ghosts and imaginary friends. The Coloureds seemed to enjoy the creativity involved in fucking with them.

Everhardt had to put a stop to the experiments. He locked the remaining TX-260 in a freezer and destroyed his notes. But some

of the folks had caught on to what Everhardt was doing and what was bringing on the strange and powerful sensations. It was the clear stuff. The clear stuff brought the visions and made everything alive again. The clear stuff brought friends and comrades. No one was alone when the clear stuff was around. They had become addicted to the companionship. And Everhardt knew. He knew that the clear stuff made everyone happy, and that's why he took it away. A plot to raid the lab to steal the frozen vials made its way around Harrington. Things went back to normal—that is, until that night when the old folks rose up, and Everhardt went back into hiding.

The burnout formerly known as Dr. Reigert Everhardt had taken to watching the new girl across the hall in 203 through the peephole. Lately, it was the high point of his days, gripping him like a mini-addiction, all jubilant highs and terrible lows. It all depended on whether or not she was there when the sound of light footfalls or jingling keys brought him running to the door to look out. Her name was Christie Douglass, and she was married to a nervous-looking fellow named Burt or Burke. So far, that was all he knew.

When he was feeling especially lonely, he liked to think of Christie twisted into compromising positions. But that was only good for five minutes, tops. That was as long as he could last these days, at least with the furious pumping of his hand and a generous glob of petroleum jelly. He'd probably explode at the mere sight of a real, live woman standing naked before him.

But even the thought of that would have to wait until the cartoons were over.

Fucking Coloureds…

Hollywood's latest assassin was a no-talent rapper/R&B crooner called Lil' Zeus. A few days earlier, Everhardt had rushed to the peephole after hearing footsteps, only to see Lil'

Zeus making his way down the hallway, leaning his ear carefully against door after door, listening in. Everhardt recognized him from TV.

Lil' Zeus was one of those guys who belted out what amounted to sexualized nursery rhymes while trying too hard to frown his way into masculine poses. He liked to dance around shirtless trying to pass off his skin-and-bone physique as lean muscle. He kept himself greased up and glistening, glossy lips pursed in pout, Sharpe-rendered beard and sideburns laser-cut to fine edges.

When Lil' Zeus was just outside his door, Everhardt held his breath and shrank away. He shut off the lights and sat there silently watching the sliver of light beneath the front door, hoping to God that Zeus hadn't seen him. A pair of feet appeared, darkening the space. Everhardt could hear breathing through the silence—deep, heavy breaths punctuated by a stuttered exhale, suggesting arousal or maybe drug withdrawal.

It was only a matter of time until Zeus found him. Everhardt had no choice but to ask for help. The Coloureds were the closest thing to friends that he ever had. Friends or not, a favor from a Coloured came at a hefty price. He used to think that watching cartoons 24/7 was worth it. Currently, he was on hour 29. Until the job was done, and Zeus was out of the picture, Everhardt wasn't going anywhere—not for 43 more hours at least.

Everhardt leaned forward and arched his back to work out a cramp when large, beefy hands like damp, ice-cold catchers' mitts clamped around his biceps and pulled him upright in his seat. The goon-thing that stood behind his chair loomed down over him with its smooth face, long, droopy nose, and dot eyes. He called it a goon-thing because it reminded him of those things from the old Popeye cartoons that creeped him out when he was a kid.

The goon-thing made a vibrating hum. Although the words weren't clear, Everhardt could sense a tone of frustration. Pointing at the TV with its big, beefy right hand, the goon-thing palmed the top of Everhardt's head with its left and forced him to watch.

* * *

Running through Clifton Heights in broad daylight probably wasn't such a good idea for a falling star of Lil' Zeus's caliber.

Traffic was backed up for half a mile as cars waited to turn from Springfield Road (where Zeus was) onto busy Baltimore Pike. Eyes snapping out of road hypnosis glazed over the small businesses and slant-roofed houses on either side of the road and the few people on the sidewalks.

"Hey! Aren't you…" a redheaded Asian girl said as Zeus bolted past her like a bat outta hell. He was clutching his right arm in his left hand and holding both close to his body.

She didn't seem to notice the blood on his clothing or that he was missing a hand. Nobody noticed. Or maybe they did notice and simply blew it off as being part of a video or a movie he was shooting. You never knew with celebrities.

"Oh my God! It's Lil' Zeus!!!" a different female voice cried out.

Zeus glanced over his shoulder. A late-model SUV….

Thank God!

He expected to see the car he was running from: an old, black Buick hoopty with tinted windows and two obese white Coloured girls inside. The word on the street was that Zeus liked the white women with the big arses. "Two-toilet-seat big," he liked to say. He denied it in the interviews, fearing a backlash from his target demographic of young black women.

"Pictures don't lie," his detractors would say, referring to the tabloid snapshots of Zeus, in disguise, sneaking into cheap motels to get his freak on with pear-shaped white girls.

"Why not just admit it," his (white) lawyer suggested. "It's 2006, for cryin' out loud. I would think people have moved past that sort of thing. Well… except maybe down south."

"It ain't just the south."

"Okay… the south and… and the midwest, then."

"I don't know what planet you've been livin' on, homes, but I catch muthafuckas screwfacin' me just about everywhere."

"That's probably because you lie about it. People hate liars."

"Whatever, man…"

Even if the girls weren't so big, and sometimes ugly, the fact that they were white was enough to make a lot of the sistas start hatin'. He didn't care so much about what everyone else thought.

Big and ugly was an understatement when it came to the Coloured white girls in the old black hoopty. Arm and shoulder fat squeezed out from the driver's side window like warm bread when the car pulled up to him in the motel parking lot and the tinted glass hummed open. He had just returned from another fruitless search for Dr. Everhardt.

From inside the hoopty, a throbbing beat caused the car to literally expand and contract, its outer skin pulsating and lifting from its frame and settling back in place. The driver flashed little yellow teeth pointing out of receded gums and hair jutting from her nostrils like antennae. It was the most busted smile he'd ever seen. Her skin was a strange shade of Caucasoid: blotchy, with obvious brushstrokes, as if she was painted in haste. He felt her enthusiasm even before he saw her. It was a feeling that he had grown used to, like a celebrity sixth sense.

"Hey, sexy." She leaned out the window and blew him a kiss. Even her voice sounded fat.

Zeus caught a glimpse of the pas-

senger when the driver leaned back. She looked even worse.

Apparently, the disguise (a baseball cap pulled down in front and a bulky jacket) wasn't working. Or the hundred-dollar bills that Zeus used to grease the motel manager and the maid weren't enough for them to keep their fucking mouths shut about his being in town. The rags probably offered them five times that to rat him out. All it took was one sighting, and word was out. Some things never changed.

Zeus was going to ignore them and keep on walking. He thought about his situation. He knew how volatile the Coloureds were. Pissing these chicks off might somehow get back to whoever was in charge and fuck up his deal.

Zeus looked to see if there was anyone else around, took a deep breath, and walked over to the old black hoopty.

"Oh my God, he's coming over here," the driver whimpered.

The passenger shook with excitement. The car rocked.

Zeus squatted and leaned toward the window.

"'Sup, ladies," he said, forcing a smile despite the nervous energy that had him fidgeting like a crackhead. "It's ah… nice to know I have such… beautiful fans like you two"

The driver was panting. The passenger was just staring.

"I just love your music," said the first fatty, flagging herself with her hand. "C-c-can I… Can I touch you?"

Zeus stuck out his hand. She took hold of it and puckered, her big lips folding into a wet meat tulip. Her hand dwarfed his own. Her touch was cold and damp, like wet paint. The fumes caused him to squint. He held his breath to escape the strong odor, looked away, and awaited the warm—or maybe it would be cold—touch of her lips. She was cooing like a fresh-stuck virgin surfing orgasm shockwaves. Coming from the obese

Coloured bitch, it turned his stomach.

An explosion of sensation caused Zeus to yank his arm away from her, or at least try to. The girl had his arm in her mouth, pinched between her teeth. She clamped down when he pulled, teeth grinding and slicing through flesh, muscle, and finally bone. She was growling like a dog as she tore it away.

Zeus stumbled backwards gasping and staring in disbelief at the stump. It was, by no means, a clean break. Flaps of fibrous muscle and sinew drooped from the wound like heavily textured tongues overlapping each other and spitting blackened red saliva.

"I bet he tastes as good as he looks," said the girl in the passenger seat.

"Ummm-hmmm…" replied the driver, her cheeks punching outward. Zeus's severed arm twitched and flexed while she chewed. She finally swallowed enough to speak coherently: "Even better, gurl."

Physically, the pain registered as extreme cold, radiating up from the stump to the rest of his body. Delirium was challenging shock. Zeus fought back the wave of weird euphoria that he knew would only lead to him passing out.

The drainage from the stump slowed when he squeezed it with his hand, so he grabbed it as hard as he could, turned, and ran. His first thoughts concerned how this was going to affect his career and how bad (nappy-headed and ashy) he probably looked. Nappy-headed and ashy was right up there with death to a guy like Zeus.

"Where'ya goin', sexy?" the biter yelled, her voice interrupted by a deep belch that jumped up from her stomach and surprised her. "I thought you said I was beautiful."

Zeus managed to duck into an alley to wrap the stump with a dirty old scarf he found floating in the gutter. It was a bitch to knot using his teeth and his one good hand. It stopped the bleeding but brought back the

pain, which was so intense that he vomited. Suddenly, he saw the hoopty at the far end of the alley and took off running again.

It was chaos when he hit the street. For the first time in his life, Zeus wished that he was anonymous, that he was just plain old Kenny Scruggs.

The blonde woman (wearing an Eminem T-shirt) who called to Zeus from the SUV had started a chain reaction of mostly women who leaned from their windows and stepped out of their cars to see the big star. There were horns blaring, girls and grown women screeching and carrying on as if the mere mention of his name brought them to orgasm. Zeus ran for a block and turned down a side street, then another, until he lost the crowd that was following him.

Why didn't I listen to Odell?

Odell Mitchell was his manager. He was always going on and on about Zeus's safety and preaching to him that all of his fast living was ultimately going to catch up with him, but he wouldn't have believed this shit. Lil' Zeus smacked his stump against the wall behind him over and over, then cradled it against his body, stifling his screams and sucking breath through clenched teeth.

Zeus was crouching in front of a fence that bordered a neighborhood and the back of a low-rent strip mall. He contemplated climbing it. With one good hand, it would be difficult, but he was determined to try once he caught his breath.

Activity from the front painted a picture of busy shoppers getting in each other's way in the parking lot. Hovering somewhere in the back of the noise was a muffled beat. Clifton Heights, like many suburbs of Philly, had lots of cars that spewed out muffled hip-hop or some R&B variant masquerading as hip-hop (the kind of music Zeus produced). Fuzzy speakers and ear-splitting volume usually made all the songs sound alike, but when he heard the chimes, then the church-bell, he knew it was the opening of his latest album. Next came his voice, speaking softly, supposedly into the answering machine of a girl he had cheated on. The un-original closing line of the message set up the following track: "You never know what you've got until it's gone."

Zeus straddled the fence, one leg dangling on either side. On the mall side, his pants snagged a broken link. He panicked and tugged on his leg, which only tore the fabric and got more of it stuck. He laid down flat on his stomach to keep from falling to either side. With one good hand, it was hard to maintain his balance. Getting to the top of the fence was a struggle in itself. His stump was throb-bing.

The sound of his own music ech-oed down the corridor between buildings and back to where Zeus laid atop the fence, arch-ing his ass in the air to keep his scrotum from being crushed under his weight. The music suddenly poured into the open space when the black hoopty bled slowly from the mouth of the corridor and crept to a stop thirty feet from him, its outer shell pulsating.

The sight of the car made Zeus tug faster. He struggled. His leg had been cut by the fence and was bleeding, but he could hardly notice.

The tinted window on the driver's side bucked and began to ooze downward.

"I think I saw him come this way," the blonde SUV-chick squeaked. The pack of rabid fans followed her down the corridor. A few of them were screaming as they ran. One was crying and shaking.

Dead center in the clearing just be-yond the corridor, the black hoopty sat di-agonally with both doors wide open. Zeus's voice continued to pour from the stereo.

The SUV-chick was the first to reach the hoopty, the first to see…

Two animated fat chicks fighting over a man—Zeus. They were huge, maybe seven feet tall, and dressed in ghettofied clothing that looked about three sizes too small.

The driver had the kind of hairstyle that would've looked better on a black girl. She wore a halter top and low-rider jeans that showed the top of her thong in the back. Her fat ass devoured all but the triangular piece at the top, and even that was hard to see. It was so big that it bubbled over the edge of her pants all the way around to her exposed belly and flapped like a dimpled meat-wing when she moved. Her cleavage heaved and jiggled.

The passenger was just plain fat. Her hair was pulled tight into a short, dookie ponytail that curled under at the tip. She was wearing a T-shirt that read "Can't Touch This" in bold letters and a skirt that barely hid the bottom of her droopy ass, which looked like a bag of wet mud. Broken veins and pimples decorated her lumpy thighs. They looked like they could snap a man in two with one squeeze.

"He's MINE!" the driver growled. "I saw him first."

"You just want 'em all to yourself," replied the passenger. "Now gimme!"

They each had Zeus by an arm. The driver had the stump. They held him off the ground between them and tugged on his body like children fighting over a doll.

Zeus was starting to fade. His eyes were rolled up; his mouth hung open. His face barely registered their tugging and twist-ing. The SUV-chick in the front of the pack caught his unfocused eyes and felt instant terror.

"I'm swear ta God I'm gonna hurt you if you don't let go," the driver warned.

"Well, I guess we goin' be fightin', then, 'cause I ain't lettin' go."

As they continued to tug, Zeus mouthed something to the SUV-chick. He re-peated it over and over.

The rest of the group had either scattered upon catching sight of the scene or just stood there in a daze, trying to figure everything out.

The SUV-chick was shaking her

head "No." No to the violence; no to the sight of two giant cartoons; no to Zeus's message, which she couldn't understand; and no to the buckle and fold of his torso as his skeleton broke into pieces underneath his skin.

She cupped her hands over her mouth and cried for him.

"D-d-d-don't l-look at meeee…" Zeus rasped once more before he broke like a wishbone and split open from his left clavicle down to his right thigh.

* * *

The burnout formerly known as Dr. Reigert Everhardt awoke to the sound of his own breathing. He yawned away his sleep induced narcosis and allowed the new day to accept him. As usual, the facts fell into place clumsily, and with little concern for a sequential timeline; the Coloureds, Lil' Zeus. And, as usual, it left him lingering on how much he preferred the sleep-stupor to blunt reality—until he remembered the time.

He looked at the clock on his nightstand. The LCD display flashed 9:47 am. It was over… The Coloureds' 72 hours were up.

Halle-fucking-luiah!

When working with the Coloureds in this capacity, Everhardt generally preferred to be there to send them on their way when the gig was up. That way he could make sure that the deal was honored and, through his own eyes, confirm their departure. Once the 72-hour limit was reached, the Coloureds had no choice, but it reassured him to see it for himself.

Watching them break down (into a clear, gelatinous goo) was an unsettling experience as it was extremely painful for them. Sometimes it came out of the blue. They'd be in the middle of a sentence then, BAM! The next thing he knew they were screaming and thrashing about in a way that made the pain palpable to him. It only lasted a few seconds before their shape lost its hold and sent them splashing to the floor and leaving Everhardt to clean up the wet spot, or spots depending on the level of assistance he requested.

His eyes had taken a beating from 72-hours worth of cartoon-watching. It had been so long since he last required their assistance that Everhardt had forgotten just how hard that part of the deal was. Besides, his eyes weren't what they used to be. He tried to stay awake to see the goon-thing and the fat-white Coloured chicks off, but sleep was more persuasive. As a result, Everhardt harbored a touch of anxiety. Had they done it? Had they taken care of this Lil' Zeus character?

He checked the living room first. He was looking for the wet spot, or possibly even a body. He told them specifically that he didn't want to know what they did to Zeus or how they did it. But the Coloureds were notorious practical jokers.

There was nothing in the living room. He turned on the TV for some passive listening and moved on to the kitchen, and bathroom. He was about to declare both empty when he slipped and feel on his ass just outside the bathroom door. He didn't need to look down at his hands to realize what the sticky substance that oozed through his fingers was.

When he put it together with the living, breathing Coloureds (especially the goon-thing) that he had seen just hours ago, the sticky substance seemed to him like blood, their blood. Looking at it that way gave him the creeps.

Holding his goo-soaked arms away from his body, Everhardt pinched his wet clothes off and hopped in the shower.

The hot water took him to a comfortable place as he stood under the shower-nozzle with his eyes closed. He remained there until the water ran lukewarm. He would've stayed even longer, fumbling with the faucet to savor every last bit of heat, but he suddenly thought of Lil' Zeus and his comfort level dropped considerably.

Everhardt did little things around the apartment to distract his thoughts while he listened for a report on Zeus's death. The news was good for running that kind of shit over more important events.

It suddenly dawned on him that he never checked under his bed. That was where he kept the metal briefcase that contained his remaining vials of TX-260. He had no reason to think that it wouldn't be there, but he felt compelled to check just the same. His stash was his lifeline. The years had earned him a dependency, not on the chemical itself, but the safety that the things that dwelt within it provided. Sure it came at a price, but at least he was alive. At least he was alive….

If it came down to it, he could find more—the ingredients to make it, that is. It wouldn't be easy. First of all, he'd have to leave his apartment for an extended period of time. That was out of the question. The years had earned Everhardt an addiction to solitudel, topped off with a fear of crowds and an aversion to people in general.

Everhardt walked into the bedroom, got down on his knees and lifted the edge of the bedspread off the floor.

The briefcase was gone. And there was something lying in its place; a severed head. It was Lil' Zeus. His eyes were frozen wide open and staring right at him.

Everhardt gasped himself winded and dropped the spread, his heart pounding like elephant footsteps. He waited a few seconds and lifted it again. Still no briefcase.

For a moment, (Oh!) Everhardt tried to cajole (God!) some forgotten memory of moving it to a safer place (No!). But he knew he hadn't.

As grizzly a sight as it was, Zeus's head was secondary to losing his lifeline. In fact, it didn't even faze him… yet. At the moment, Zeus was a non-factor, until he heard the newscaster mention his name.

"THE HEADLESS BODY OF TROUBLED RAPPER, LITTLE ZEUS WAS FOUND EARLIER THIS MORNING IN AN ALLEY BEHIND THE BARCLAY SQUARE SHOPPING CENTER IN UPPER DARBY, PA. A SURVEILLANCE CAMERA MOUNTED ABOVE THE FIRST TRUST BANK CAPTURED FOOTAGE OF THE MAN, WHO ACCORDING TO WITNESSES AT THE SCENE MURDERED THE RAPPER AND DISMEMBERED HIS BODY IN BROAD DAYLIGHT."

Everhardt ran into the living room, his eyes gunning for the screen even before he entered. He got there just in time to see grainy, surveillance footage of himself running from the alley. The version in the footage was slightly different, almost photorealistic, but not quite.

Coloureds!

Everhardt had been set up. But by who? Hollywood, the Coloureds, themselves?

On the screen, the image of a young blond (the SUV-chick) dressed in an Eminem T-shirt.

"THE BODY OF 22 YEAR-OLD JACKIE DERBIN WAS ALSO FOUND AT THE SCENE. DERBIN HAD BEEN SHOT EXECUTIONER STYLE AND STUFFED IN A DUMPSTER."

The image cut to an old photo of Everhardt dressed in the suit he used to wear for special (informal) occasions. He only owned two at the time. The other one was for business.

"PHILADELPHIA POLICE HAVE ISSUED AN ALL POINTS BULLETIN FOR THIS MAN… DR. REIGERT EVERHARDT."

That was all Everhardt needed to hear before the moment became about keeping himself from loosing control. His blood ran cold. He backed away from the television as the old photo cut to a live witness, a man who looked quite suspect to him, like a Coloured living inside a dead human.

"I saw em' with ma own eyes," the artificial-looking man said. "He came running outta the alley all covered in blood like he was gonna…"

There was a knock at the door, a stern, confident knock. It sounded as if the person on the other side had big knuckles that were calloused over.

"Dr. Everhardt. This is the police. Come out with your hands up, or we'll be forced to break down the door."

Everhardt felt the room close around him and begin to spin. He was nauseous from the impact of losing his lifeline. His vision was fuzzy around the edges. The Coloureds had done this to him. To him… After all that he had done to bridge the cultures. After all the time he'd put into it. After everything that had happened to him as a result. He could've been a household name. Instead he was a recluse. Not even a recluse, but a prisoner.

"We know you're in there, doctor. Come out, NOW!"

He pondered opening the door and trying to reason with the officers. What would you tell them, he thought, that the cartoons did it. Yeah… Okay… Good luck with that one. Maybe you should just go out there and let those knuckle draggers put you out of your misery. What have you got to lose at this point?

Everhardt was desperate for the initiative to do… something… anything but stand there perusing the same places over and over hoping that the briefcase might suddenly materialize.

"This is your last chance, doctor. I'm going to give you 'til the count of three, then we're coming in. One…"

Throughout all his mental babbling, Everhardt's mind kept stopping on the bedroom dresser, like it was trying to tell him something…

"Two!" The officer's voice was revving up for something big.

Everhardt could picture the officer locking into his combat visage. Based on the voice he pictured a large man.

"One! Okay. Do it!"

The syringe!!! There was another syringe. Everhardt had left it under a stack of folded pants in his dresser drawer after using it to summon the Coloureds 79 and ½

hours ago.

A bombastic thud shook the door, the frame around it screamed under duress. Everhardt high-tailed it toward the bedroom. Behind him the door flew open and backhanded the wall next to it. The wobbly, brass knob left an indentation.

Two officers entered and immediately began to chase him. The faster of the two men dove for Everhardt's legs, wrapping his arms around them at the ankles and squeezing them together.

Everhardt had made it to the dresser, slid the top drawer open and reached his hand inside before he lost his balance and began to fall. The second officer tackled him at the waist on the way down, winding him.

Everhardt lay motionless, gasping for air beneath the two burly husks. His mind was scrambled by the second blow, the one that momentarily hyper-extended his back.

"His hands… Get 'is hands!" the officer at Everhardt's ankles yelled to the one who lay directly on top of him, palming his face into the dirty carpet.

He grabbed Everhardt's wrists to cuff them together and hesitated.

There was a needle stuck in the meat of Everhardt's thumb. The syringe was broken in half and it was empty.

The officer turned Everhardt's palm up and showed it to his partner.

"Heroine, PCP?" he questioned.

"Just cuff him," the other officer said. "We'll figure it out later."

Everhardt came out of the daze with little knowledge of how he wound up on the floor, handcuffed. The last thing he remembered was the police breaking down the door. There was a burning sensation in his right palm, a funny taste in his mouth, like paint. His hearing was muffled, and filtered through his discombobulated brainscape.

About five feet in front of him, painted hands reached up from a colorful puddle that surrounded one of the officers's feet and slowly pulled him down beneath its surface.

"No!" Everhardt belted realizing that he was looking at the remaining TX-260 from the syringe. "NO! NO! NO! NO! NO!"

The officer fought valiantly, but there were too many arms. Each one was a different size. Some looked as if they belonged to animals or… something.

The other officer had hold of the sinking one's right hand. Dropping his stance and leaning back, he pulled as hard as he could. He kept holding on after his partner was completely submerged. The remaining officer's hand had broken the surface as well.

"Gaskins! Gaskins!" the officer yelled down at the liquid. "Hold on, brother. I'm coming in."

The officer took a deep breath, cheeks puffing out, and plunged his face down into the puddle to try and locate his partner.

Everhardt opened his mouth to warn the officer not to do it, but something literally had hold of his tongue. When his hand brushed against the wall he was propped up against, he felt something sticking out of his palm. He knew right away what it was.

The officer snatched his head from beneath the surface of the puddle and fell backwards. His eyes were as big as golf balls. He looked over at Everhardt as if to relay the horrors that he had just seen when he began to choke. He grabbed his throat, climbed to his feet and stumbled from wall to wall like a pinball.

A painterly hue suddenly overtook him from the feet up until his entire body was tainted with artistic embellishment.

Everhardt cried as he watched, not for the officer's fate, but his own. Using the wall for leverage, his back pressed firmly against it, he slid up to his feet and plucked the needle from his palm using his index and middle fingers.

The officer was tearing at his uniform as if he was still normal underneath it.

Wrong.

He cried out in pain as his shirt began to part. It felt as if his was tearing at his own flesh. Apparently the shirt had fused with his skin.

Everhardt moved stealthily toward the door as the officer dealt with his dilemma.

The officer's bones began to crack and reshape inside of him. He coughed up what he thought was blood, except it was multicolored.

He looked over at the wall where Everhardt was sitting, then whipped around to find him standing just outside the bedroom, his hands still cuffed behind his back.

The officer reached out to him, "Help meeeeeeee…," he whimpered as he began to morph through a rapid-fire, Tex Avery-style shape-shifting montage of characters. His heavily altered features remained intact throughout each guise as if to verify beyond a doubt that it was him (the officer) looking out from each colorful facade.

Everhardt watched the guises come and go as he backed away. He saw:

A little girl in a frilly dress singing "A Trisket a Trasket" as she held a lollipop with a sneering face on it.

A dimwitted hilly-billy in the form of a bipedal dog dressed in overalls and singing "Oh ma Darlin'"

A caricature of a Chinaman speaking jibberish in some a mock-Asian dialect.

A Carmen Miranda-esque woman with big, red lips.

An Al Jolson inspired bulldog in a coat and tails.

The officer's terror shined through in the eyes of each guise. The feeling resonated out to where Everhardt was standing.

Everhardt turned and ran out the front door of his apartment and into the hallway. The walls were stained with smoky soot, scrawled pencil markings and years of neglect. For some reason it stood out more now than it usually did.

The DING of the elevator gave him incentive. He hurried down the hall and peeked around the corner. All clear. He ran up to the elevator and ducked inside just as the heavy doors were closing.

Everhardt fell against the rear wall and watched the descending numbers light up as the elevator glided down.

* * *

There was a reason why everyone called the two blocks between 52nd and 54th Streets, Homeless Row. The streets were narrow, and lined on both sides by the backs of restaurants and designer clothing boutiques. Dumpsters outside of each one served as a stabilizing wall for the cardboard and discarded wood domiciles that decorated the undergrowth of refuse. Rickety fire escapes zig-zagged up the surface of the buildings and appeared to touch the sky. A sweaty-funk mist lay heavy in the air and stung the senses of outsiders. Enough light passed between the buildings and down into the street that impatient folks looking for a short cut felt safe enough passing through. When they did, they pinched their noses shut and walked straight down the middle of the street. The residents of Homeless Row didn't seem to mind. If they weren't caught up in some seemingly one-sided conversation with empty air, or sleep, or passed out drunk, or high, or both, they took it as an opportunity to solicit money—for something to eat, they were fond of saying.

As far as the frazzled young worker bee of a woman who entered at 42nd Street with a little girl in tow could see, there was only one of them up and about—an older man. Aside from his disheveled clothing, he appeared too clean, his features too indicative of some underlying brilliance. There was something dangling from his wrists. It looked like snipped chain links leading up to a steel bracelet. The man was pointing and cursing at the dark crevices all around him. If she

wasn't so late for work, the frazzled woman might have decided against entering.

"Just a second, honey," the woman said to her daughter as she paused to search for the pepper spray that she kept in her purse.

She wrapped her hand around it, kept her arm in her purse and continued.

The little girl wasn't even trying to keep up with her mother, whose hand she held. As a result, her gait was too wide for her short legs, causing her to bounce, her little head flopping.

"Look at that guy," the little girl chuckled at the man with the bracelets who stumbled down the block toward them.

"Now that's not nice, honey," the mother replied.

The man suddenly stopped, clamped his hands over his ears and squeezed his eyes shut.

"I'M NOT LISTENING TO YOU ANYMORE!" he yelled. "YOU'RE ALL WASTING YOUR TIME!"

Until he opened his eyes, Everhardt hadn't noticed the frazzled woman and her daughter. At first he thought they were Coloureds and took on an aggressive stance in reaction. It caused the woman to stop, turn around and hurry back to the opening at 42nd Street with her daughter bobbling in her tightened grasp.

The block lit up with sickening color as soon as the frazzled woman and her daughter were out of sight. Now that Everhardt was himself a gateway, the Coloureds flocked to him from the other side. Until he figured out a solution (which he was determined to do) Everhardt dwelt among the homeless, with whom the Coloureds had a long-standing relationship. This way, he didn't stand out.

VINCENT W. SAKOWSKI

LOCATION:
Saskatoon, SK, Canada

STYLE OF BIZARRO:
Blender Fiction

BOOKS BY SAKOWSKI:

Some Things Are Better Left Unplugged
The Hack Chronicles
Not Quite One of the Boys
Misadventures in a Thumbnail Universe

DESCRIPTION: Vincent writes blender fiction (slipstream with a darker, sharper, jagged edge) that tends to be humorous, satirical, and filled with irony. Often there are dream-like logistics, but everyone's awake and suffering just the same… whether or not they're enjoying their suffering is another matter entirely.

INTERESTS: Music and movies. Art and plays. Trying to avoid a meaningless life and death. Playing guitar, bass, and the mandolin (Vincent used to be in the band *The NPO Conspiracy*). Archaeology. Games. Rappelling, zip-lining, and being held upside-down 100 feet off the ground despite the fact that he suffers from a severe case of acrophobia (Vincent is a big believer in irony and stupidity).

INFLUENCES: Vincent is more inspired by music than books. Then art, such as H.R. Giger and Salvador Dali. Then writers like William S. Burroughs, Philip K. Dick, James Douglas Morrison, and Lou Reed. All those and so much more.

PLAYS PRODUCED: The Progression of the Psychopath (a comedy), History Has Been Cancelled Today, Cain: A Mystery (The Prologue and Interlude), The Exchange, The Arena, The Puzzle In The Box, Where is God?

WEBSITE:
www.myspace.com/vincentsakowski

THE SCREAMING OF THE FISH

I once had a friend who had a fish-bowl for a brain. So needless to say, he had a rather large head. But he carried it well—powerful neck muscles built up over the years—and he carried it with pride.

He changed the water regularly—he liked to keep it fresh. But he also lost a lot of it, since he was an avid jogger. Despite his strength and poise, sometimes that water bounced right out of there. He never worried about it though, or complained about the loss. The water kept him cool inside and out. There wasn't anything he could do about the evaporation, but he always carried a full water bottle just to be safe.

The two goldfish in the bowl didn't seem to be too crazy about him jogging every day—with all of the rocks from the bottom getting stirred up, swishing around and scraping their sides. Way too many scars over the years, but what could they say?

My friend kept them well-fed, and they certainly got their exercise. And even though they were stuck in a small home, they got to see a lot of the sights. Especially since my friend liked to jog a new route everyday if he could. He enjoyed new scenes himself.

Folks thought he was a pretty strange sight, and since he passed some new people each day, word about him traveled fast. So, he was often sought after, and although there was little he could do about video cameras and photographers, he never granted an interview. Neither did he pay any attention to the occasional rude person who would call such lame remarks as:

"I see you have a little water on the brain today, buddy."

And: "You mind if I go fishing with you sometime?"

And: "Do you want me to feed your fish while you're away?"

It didn't matter who was doing the shouting, and it didn't matter what they were shouting out. Or if his two fish could speak and they could tell him all about the unpleasantness of bouncing around in the bowl swimming for their lives and how his knee joints were getting rubbed raw and how he was developing shin splints and if he wasn't careful how—

None of this would matter because he wasn't much of a listener. In fact, he couldn't hear anything at all—no ears. He only felt the pressure of their voices…the pressure of the sounds…and the pressure said enough. And he was quite happy not to know any more than that.

Until the day he died.

My friend died while jogging, of course. He tripped over somebody's Chihuahua, which happened to get off of its leash. So even though the dog was barking, and the owner was trying to call it back and shouting at my friend at the same time—and even I was foolishly trying to warn him—my friend didn't hear a word, he only felt the sudden agonizing pressure from all around. It caught him totally unaware, confusing him. So he tripped over the Chihuahua, and he fell, and man did those fish fly!

Just as the fish-bowl shattered on the sidewalk, the Chihuahua scurried over to the flying fishes and it snapped one right out of the air. The dog quickly chewed that goldfish, likely hoping to get to the other one before it got too dirty on the sidewalk; not that the dog still wouldn't eat it anyway, mind you. The second goldfish laid there flopping around in its own small way, gasping, gills contracting, watching its schoolmate being gobbled up. What else could it do?

Without wasting another moment, I scrambled over to the second goldfish. I popped it in my mouth, hoping that the moisture would keep it alive, until I could squeeze it into my friend's water bottle, or into a glass of water, or a fountain, or—but it was still flopping around in my mouth—so much so that I accidentally (or perhaps instinctively?) swallowed it.

As the goldfish digested, I got a real taste of my friend's memories…his life…particularly before he met me. And although I'm not sure if I understand him any better, I'm just really glad that he kept his fish-bowl so clean.

PEEL AND EAT BUFFET

Suit enters the cell. Black on six sides. With a duplicate door across from him. Illumination of a sort filtering down. Dull yellow glow like cancer consuming a lung. Straight back stainless steel chair before him. In front of the chair: a small raised wooden platform. Also black. Soap box for an audience of one. Otherwise the room is empty. Hollow. Dull.

Door clicks shut behind him. Locks slide and snap into place.

For whose sake? he wonders nonchalantly. Smiles. Lipless. All teeth. Sharp. Glistening. A new shark in these waters. Sits. Molds. Crosses his leg: left over right. Checks the crease.

Perfect. As always. And not a hair or bit of lint to be seen anywhere.

Leans back. Laces his fingers. Waits.

But not for too long.

Lights dim.

Door before him opens.

Silhouette takes the stage, as the door swings shut, and it too is locked.

Fade up.

Eyes meet. Business is pleasure.

Vision holds.

Pleasure is.

Now Suit surveys the rest: soft, full-figure—just curvaceous enough, but well muscled underneath. All natural. Almost shocking in its rarity. Skin as pale as Suit's is tanned. Powder dry as he is slick. But like him: plastic, elastic. Covered in film. Literally. Gray-brown reels wound tightly. Occasional tiny images flash out of focus. Even with his sharp, beady, dead eyes, Suit can't distinguish one frame from the next. Not that he cares too much anyway.

He nods. Once.

To a song that only she can hear, she begins to undulate and slowly turn on the platform—her body in constant motion—but every move deliberate. Sensual. As she turns, her hips gyrating, she begins to pull at the film, working the knots open. Stretching out scenes. Letting them fall. Editing in her own way. There is only the crinkling of the film to be heard as it unwinds and she crushes it underfoot.

Suit remains motionless, but interested. Waiting. Expectant.

Her breasts exposed, she takes one up in both hands, alternately twisting and flicking the nipple with her thumbs. Then bending her head down she takes the nipple in her mouth, sucks on it once. Hard. Baring her teeth, she grips it tightly and bites it off without uttering a sound. Whipping her head up, she spits it at Suit. Blood runs down her chin and squirts out from the hole in her breast.

The bloody nipple bounces off of his chest, and into his open palm. Suit rolls it onto his fingertips, then he holds it before his eyes, admiring it like a fine jewel. He is also acutely aware of the stain on his silk tie, but he will live with it. Almost worth the price of admission. So far. After a moment, he brings the ravaged nipple up to his lips giving it a quick flick of his pointed tongue, then pops it into his mouth. Sucking. Savoring. Chewing it lightly. Playfully. Rolling it on his tongue. But he does not swallow. Yet. And in the meantime, he continues to observe.

Iron is in the air.

Silhouette sways before him, missing a beat or two, probing the bleeding hole in her breast. Meanwhile her other hand wanders down between her legs, and peels away the film. But it is more of the same—until she is naked and standing with a minute's worth stretched out in her hands. Rotating her wrists, she takes an edge and runs it across her soft belly.

Flushing.

Scarring.

Opening.

Bleeding.

A thin under layer of pale yellow fat like cottage cheese.

Swooning.

Bleeding.

Intestines exposed, she stuffs her hands with the film inside herself, and pulls out a length of her entrails. Taking small steps, she continues to try and dance. Twirling her entrails like a key chain one moment. Stumbling. Wrapping them around her like a boa the next. Knees buckling. Running them back and forth in between her legs. She lunges forward into his lap.

Suit catches her, knowing that since his tie is already ruined, the rest will have to go with it anyway. Silhouette holds her intestines out for him, a silent appeal in her eyes. She tries to squirm seductively, grinding into his lap, but she doesn't have much strength left.

Suit holds her as she dies, feeling the anticlimax, and he brushes her lids with his fingers as she draws her last breath—no longer wanting contact with eyes that now match his own. Curious, he reaches into her abdomen for the minute of film. Digs around ignoring the odor and ooze, but it is lost.

Consumed? Suit wonders as he hears the locks being released on the door before him. Fascinated. Raises an eyebrow.

Finally, he swallows the nipple.

What's next? Suit smiles. All teeth. As always. *What's next?*

IT'S BEGINNING TO LOOK A LOT LIKE RAGNAROK

A TASTE FOR THUMBNAILS

Image: bathroom. Modern. Tiles shining. Porcelain glowing. Fans humming. Fluffy towels that look and feel great, but absorb water about as well as a sheet of steel. Would make a great set-up for a commercial. There's a couple included, and they're real. Well, sort of: GQ and Vogue, late twenties, slick and pointy, ripped abs, dyed hair, fake bake, and all.

The time: morning. Even though there are no windows. No clear, bright sunshine. No fresh air. Even if there were windows, the bright sunshine and the fresh air wouldn't be there. Not invited. Not missed.

Not a situation comedy? Hardly. Or does that remain to be seen? Depends on one's sense of humor, of course.

Rather simple actually. Morning ritual before they part ways for the remainder of the day. Both naked, showered, squeaky, but absolutely unaroused—never time for that. Such a spontaneous action could kill one or the both of them.

Vogue has just finished waxing her underarms and legs and is disposing of the unsightly strips. They're reusable, of course, but she always buys new ones. She can't conceive of going through all the trouble of washing them, or even worse is the thought of ever having to touch them again. Their mere presence makes her empty, stapled stomach heave.

GQ ignores the flash of her grimace and speaks to her for the first time today: "Pass me my electric razor would you, my dear."

"Only if you pass me the nail clippers first."

They smile smugly in unison. Nothing like a bit of humor to start their day right.

They exchange the desired items, careful not to make any fleshly contact. No need to tempt Fate and be scratched or bruised through some carelessness. Their Teflon coating can only take so much abuse.

Razor on. Buzzing. Fistful of angry bees. Second snap. Clippers chattering in their place. Raised high. Jaw locked. Fingertips on his face. Skin pulled tight.

"You're not serious. You've had that beard for years. You finally have it trimmed just right: manicured to perfection. It doesn't even irritate me any more. And despite—"

"I feel the need for change… something in the air, perhaps? So, keep your concern. I may need it later. Don't mind me. You have your nails to trim, and the clock *is* ticking, my dear. So focus."

Hairs fall. Nails fly. Transformation all around. Just see the results.

Aftershave. Expletives: but barely evoked in his mind, never uttered aloud. Still: pain. Sharp. Electric. Burning. Looking for something…some release. Glances in the nearby garbage pail. Pauses. Frowns. Picks it up. Holds it out to her.

"I think you've lost a nail. I've counted, and there are only nineteen crescents, not twenty."

"Really now. It's not the end of the world."

"Listen, *dear*. After you fell asleep last night, I saw the Norse God Loki building a long ship from people's discarded hair and nails. When he finally had enough and the ship was completed, Ragnarok began. And Ragnarok is the battle at the end of the world. Granted, this was only a re-enactment on television, but it seemed quite plausible to me.

So don't tell me that the world isn't going to end because you lost this nail. *Find it!*"

He pauses; breathes, but with little depth. "Now, I have to go or I'll be late." Hands the pail with his clippings, then crosses over to his clothes. "Take great care with those, and yours, after you have them all, of course."

"But if I don't have them all and the world is going to end, then what does it matter if you're late? There won't be anything to be *late* for."

"Just find it."

"And if the world is going to end, do you really want to die wearing those socks with that suit? *And those shoes?* What's come over you this morning?"

"I have no time for this." And he is gone.

Search: an exercise in futility, but she continues nonetheless.

Sighs. "Now I'm going to be late, too."

In haste. Abandonment. But a reminder: Garbage Day. Rushing. Rubber gloves. Disinfectant spray. Bags from each room. Takes them to the foyer. Back upstairs, her own layers are applied. Quickly. Methodically. Machine-like in her efficiency. Finally, out the door. Security system armed and quadruple locks in place. Then, by the garage: lid up. Bags dropped. Lid down. Wheels the bin to the sidewalk.

"I can't believe I'm doing this."

But being privileged only means so much sometimes.

Turns back to the garage. Feels a presence: *Derelict*. Suddenly, in her face. Silent. Sultan of Scatology. Smoldering, yet smiling. Teeth: rotting. Breath: reeking. Eyes: deep, dark, indecipherable. Long, greasy, stringy salt and pepper hair and beard. Bursting burlap sack over his left shoulder. Hairs and nails poking through its entire surface.

"Good morning, my dear. I was wondering if you could spare some—"

"Is your name Loki?"

"Do I look like a Norse God to you?"

"I don't watch that much television. I have no idea how a Norse God is supposed to look, but I couldn't help noticing that sack of hair and nails. Are you building a long ship with them?"

"This is the suburbs, my dear. No open water for tens of miles…will you be my friend?"

"Is that really necessary?"

"It would be nice." The derelict flashes a brown, hourglass toothed smile.

Vogue steps back, grimacing. "Let me think about it."

"Uh huh…bad day, my dear?"

"I've just discovered that my husband's an asshole."

"Only this morning? You have my sympathies."

"Thank you."

"But not to worry—"

"Yes, yes, I know. The end is near, and if I can be of any help—"

"Why, that's very gracious of you."

"Think nothing of it." Vogue lifts the lid of the garbage bin. "Top bag on the left. Knock yourself out. And here—" She digs in her small purse and holds out a fistful of change, just in case. He snatches it away and pockets it before she even realizes it's gone. "But I must be going."

"To work?"

"How much time do I have?"

Hefts the sack. "Not too long."

"Then definitely not…today is just full of epiphanies, isn't it?"

"And so much more."

"Well, good morning then."

"I will remember you; this day."

"I'm counting on it."

And with that, she strides away and gets in her car. Vogue is gone. For good.

"That is one strange broad…it won't be long…what a laugh…but then again, let me take a look at what she's left for me…it might just be…

THE DANGERS OF BLACK SOCKS

But, first, see the man: GQ, late twenties, slick and pointy, with his ripped abs under his two-thousand-dollar suit and his hundred-dollar shirt. Abs like those shouldn't be covered, but he is on his way to work, after all. Plenty of time to admire them later in his mirror at the office, perhaps while his male secretary is blowing him. (Hey, when you close your eyes, a blowjob is a blowjob. And when your eyes are open, and you don't mind what you see—well, perhaps you need to have a talk with your wife.)

If he ever gets there, that is.

The idea persists—dominates his thoughts while his car remains gridlocked on the "freeway"—but not about his abs, or the office, or his secretary. Rather, this is something worthy of a good water-cooler discussion: he just can't shake the idea of the end of the world—although, in a Ragnarok kind of way.

He slams his fist on the dash. "Damn you Public Television for planting that evil seed of knowledge in me last night!"

However, in consolation, while the seed is planted, growing, he is still aware that his day planner is completely filled. Too many commitments. Besides, he could easily be mistaken of course, so why cancel all of his appointments, until he has some more solid proof?

Nonetheless, it doesn't help that his wife lost one of her fingernail clippings this morning: only mere hours after he sees the Norse God Loki completing the construction of his long ship from discarded human hair and nails. And then, after the last plea for donations, Ragnarok followed. Naturally.

"Why did you have to do that, woman? And then to top it off—those cracks about my wardrobe? This hasn't been a good morning."

Still gridlocked. Then, in the mirror: brown blur barreling along from behind. Shock. Focus. Definitely a man approaching.

Is traffic moving that slow, or is that

guy moving so fast? GQ wonders.

Passing by: *Derelict.* Singing. Slumming along. Long coat whipping out behind. Bursting burlap sack over his shoulder—hairs and nails poking through its entire surface.

"Hey!"

Eyes over the shoulder. Briefly. But he keeps on going.

"Hey!"

Opens the door. Starts to get out.

The derelict stops. "I'd put on the emergency brake if I were you."

Car rolls forward. Stalling in the process.

GQ sits back down in time and stomps the brakes before he hits the car in front of him. Pulls up the emergency brake. Meanwhile, the derelict continues to cruise.

"Wait! Loki, is that you?"

The derelict stops once again. Spins around as GQ runs up. Agitated. Severely. "Do I look like a Norse God to you?"

"I'm not sure. The guy playing Loki last night looked different, *a lot different*, but I know he was just an actor."

"Wow. I applaud your wisdom."

GQ points at the sack. "Are you building a long ship with that?"

"That's really wacky, my boy. You sound as weird as your wife."

"*My wife?* You spoke to my wife?"

"Just a little bit ago. She was going on about the same thing. I tried to explain to her—"

"Yes! Yes! Yes! I told her all about that stuff. I saw it all!"

"In a vision? Wow. I wouldn't have expected that from—"

"No. No. No. Like I was trying to say before: I saw it all on television."

"Oh, yeah, right. Well, that's not so remarkable then, now is it?"

"But it was on Public Broadcasting!"

"Point taken. But I really must be going." Steps away. Then, turns back. "Oh, and by the way, thanks for the beard."

Grabs at his chin. Awakening. "Oh my! Wait! How much time do I have?"

"You and your wife are like a couple of broken records...you *do know* what a record is, don't—"

How much time?"

Scowls. Hefts the sack. Then smiles. "Oh, I'm sure you'll be fine for awhile. Why don't you just go to work."

"Ragnarok's approaching, and I should just go to work?"

"That's just all the horns blaring around you because your car is holding up traffic, my boy."

In desperation: "Can't I give you a lift or something?"

"In this gridlock? It's faster walking. See you around. Oh, and by the way, nice socks." Winks. And with that, the derelict is gone.

Hell's orchestra honks around him. Finally, with his head down, GQ returns to his car and moves forward the five feet that opened up for him. Uncertain and afraid, but also aware that he is late for work. *Very late.*

"Is that a coincidence or what?" He pauses. Thinks. *He said it was okay to go to work, and, if he* was *Loki, then I should be fine. Who am I to argue? Or, if he* was *just a derelict, then I really have nothing to worry about...except maybe my sanity...work it is then.*

Now: almost lunchtime. Arrival. Everywhere: eyes. Peering. Probing. Senior Partner approaching. But GQ makes a few quick moves. Deftly creates a diversion with two secretaries, and makes it to his office relatively unscathed.

"See me in my office." Barks at his secretary, who obediently follows, pen and pad in his hand.

"Lock the door."

The secretary, well aware of his duties, does so, then crosses over to the full-length mirror and discards his stationary. On his knees, he adjusts himself so that his boss will have the perfect angle to admire all.

The things a person has to do to

get ahead in this world. The secretary sighs. Unbuckles and unzips his boss's pants. Lowers them and his boxers. Makes a few final adjustments, before swallowing GQ whole. While maneuvering, he notices his boss's socks. He grunts, laughing.

"Watch the teeth, buddy. I've had a hard morning."

"Show I shee." And he continues.

Meanwhile, GQ pulls up his shirt and admires his waistline. Some consolation. *If it is the end of the world, at least I'll meet my maker with perfect abs.* That *has to say something.*

Ridiculous, the secretary thinks. *Sometimes I just can't believe he's my boss. I could never dream of doing something so shocking, so…*

Laughing. Choking, while GQ is ejaculating.

Choking.

Laughing. Hands on his throat.

Choking.

Dying.

Dying?

Truly.

I can't believe this is happening. Their thoughts echo.

GQ in panic. *Mouth to mouth? With that much semen on his lips? Guess again…Heim…lime…or something. Just like on television. Yeah!*

Ribs crunch, implode, but he is unsuccessful.

Starts to run, but he is caught in the doorway to his office. Pants around his ankles, GQ stumbles into the foyer. Changes his mind. No need to be charged with fleeing the scene of a crime. But *what* crime? Death by lethal sperm injection?

"Help me! A doctor? Someone? *Anyone?*"

Everyone thinks he's joking, but nobody's laughing. Blasé. Totally.

In consensus: *how rude and inappropriate. What is this, a sitcom?*

But, after he pathetically and desperately goes about the foyer with his pants still around his ankles, they conclude he is insane. Most leave before he takes hostages and starts knocking them off.

Finally, the Senior Partner appears and takes control. Leads the remaining few, including GQ—after he pulls up his boxers and pants—back to "The Scene of the Crime." Too late, it seems.

"Something either severely surprised or frightened him, and instead of swallowing properly he choked and ended up with a lung full of semen." The Senior Partner concludes with a slow shake of his head.

Army of eyes on GQ. Accusing. Assaulting.

A voice from behind: "Now that's what I call a cumshot!"

Silence.

Titters.

Laughter.

Scowling, the Senior Partner doesn't bother to quiet the crowd. He makes a couple of quick nods and gestures, getting his key people in motion to take care of this situation.

"Come with me." He walks away without looking at GQ, but GQ knows to follow. Eyes forward, he gets into step behind the Senior Partner. Avoiding all eye contact, he tries to shut out the disgusted glares and whispered rebukes. He still can't believe this is happening to him, but there is no escape…not unless Ragnarok is going to happen any time soon.

They enter his spacious office, and the Senior Partner sits behind his desk, reclining. GQ stands opposite. Afraid to do anything more. Police and ambulance on the way.

"Don't worry, I know who made that cumshot crack. He's packing his things as we speak. We simply cannot tolerate these kind of outbursts…from him or from you—"

"From me? *Me?*"

"Now don't get me wrong, this is not sexual discrimination. I'm all for gay rights—big business—*good business* for us right now, in fact. In any case, an asshole is an asshole and a blowjob is a blowjob, correct? Especially if your eyes are closed. Were they?" Throws his feet up on his desk. "Maybe don't answer that…let me get straight to the point."

"You're worried about a scandal?"

"Hell no. We've covered up worse messes than this; although, word will leak out, I'm afraid. No real open scandal, but rumor and innuendo, which is even worse in some ways. In any case, I'm not especially concerned about that. Your sexual escapade is not really at issue. Well, not the main issue. Taken on its own, I couldn't give a rat's ass, or even two or three. Hell, throw in some squirrel nuts, but—anyway, the real point is, this last incident was simply the frosting on the cake—that extra green on the convenience-store wiener. Until today, I was willing to let things slide for a bit, allow you time to adjust in your new position with us, but then this morning—or, I should say, it was almost noon, I caught a glimpse of—"

"I can explain!"

"Not just your tardiness, but we have a certain image to maintain, and we can't allow for such…*indulgences*, particularly when they are so, so…" Feet drop. Leans in. "I mean, my God man! What were you thinking about when you were getting dressed this morning?"

"I—"

"Don't answer that. There's nothing you can say. I'm so disappointed in you. I thought you had a better sense of fashion than this. Black socks with *that* suit? *And those shoes?* Where was your wife when you were getting dressed? Didn't she see what a mistake you—"

"She—"

"I don't want to hear it!"

"So I'm being let go?"

"Yes. And you can go now—the back way. You are familiar with the back door, aren't you?"

"…This is it?"

"Your things will be sent. Now please go…and you may want to consider getting some help, or switching to someone else—with your wardrobe *and* your psyche—because whoever you may be with doesn't seem to be doing much good for you."

GQ leaves. In silence. Help still on the way. Told not to worry about "the incident," *for now*, anyway. It'll be taken care of—part of his severance package.

Behind the wheel. Eyes dead. Eventual resurrection.

"But Loki said…*that bastard! He tricked me!* I should have known better. Lots of time to go to work, *my ass!* He set me up! I wonder if my wife is in on this? I'll find out…if it takes my whole life and fortune, well…most of…uh, some of…in any case, I will find you, Loki, and you too, my dear wife, and I will make you both pay before Ragnarok begins. It's going to be the end of the world alright! Yes indeed. We shall definitely see…

THE BED BUGS BITE

In this hotel suite: shadows and silence reign. Curtains drawn tight. A/C off. Everything on autopilot. Waiting for the next guest to arrive and bring life.

No.

Hold on.

Life does exist here, but for now it is asleep. In hibernation. Just barely.

Waiting.

Then: footsteps.

Arrival.

Presence.

Well, sort of.

Vogue manages to get the door open with her arms overloaded. Quite the feat, but she's done it before. Never dreams of hugging anyone, but she can wrap her arms enough packages doubling her body weight and still be able to sign on the dotted line at the same time.

Illumination is lacking, so she reaches for the light switch. There is a slip, but in a phenomenal display of speed and dexterity she hits the switch and saves the bag of breakable bobbles before it meets its untimely demise. Sighing in relief, she slides past the door and steps over to the bed. As the door snaps shut behind her, Vogue lowers her bundles of joy onto the quilted surface with practiced ease.

She spins, kicking off her stilettos, slapping them against the wall. Then, underhands her massive carrying bag into a chair across the suite. Again she sighs. Again she spins. Several times. Smiling. Laughing. A little maniacally? Perhaps. Perhaps insanity has settled in her lobes. But she's enjoying herself, so who's to criticize? Who's to know or care that she's maxed out most of her credit cards in just one morning? (Well, possibly her husband for one, but he hasn't found out just yet, nor does he count in her books anymore, anyway.) Besides, she's got mondo overdraft to boot, so it's cat's-ass-living-the-sweet-life until Ragnarok approaches.

Then she could be screwed, of course. But she's not worried. Not about her credit, in any case. About Ragnarok itself? Well, Vogue figures she's gotten in good with Loki so far, but she doesn't know if that in itself is such a good idea. From what she's gathered, Loki's the "Bad Guy," and the bad guys *usually* lose in the end—on TV and film, anyway. And she doesn't know much beyond that. Normally, she would embrace her ignorance—actually, she's usually unaware of her ignorance—but Ragnarok seems like a pretty big deal. So, she's even put some of her non-existent funds to good use and bought a couple of books on the subject. Vogue would have preferred the videotape versions, but they would have taken too long to arrive on special order "for preferred clients only." And she's not sure if she has the time to waste learning to read once more. But again, is it the only way to escape the inevitable? It's a possibility, especially with so many outside forces at work beyond her understanding.

Vogue picks up one of the books and scans the cover, then flips through the pages looking at the picture for any clues. Pictures are good, as long as they are not too abstract, because using one's imagination can be difficult, and *difficult is not good*. And using one's imagination can be pretty scary, and too much like work, and *work is not good*, either. Not *that* kind of work, anyway.

Fortunately for her, the illustrations are fairly straightforward. Depicting Vikings. Doing what Vikings do. Trading. Killing. Conquering. Lying with their women. Telling stories to each other about trading, killing, conquering, and lying with their women. And yes, there are images of their gods: trading, killing, conquering, lying with their women, and doing all those other things that gods do in a Viking kind of way.

She drifts. Lying back, book in hand, she soon falls asleep. Exhausted. There's only so much shopping a woman can enjoy in a morning. Actually, there is no known limit, except for what time provides.

She dreams: of herself. Of her husband. Of Ragnarok. Of more. But she understands little of what she sees and experiences. Flashes of their future? Could it be? So much darkness…but they're just *dreams*. Never taken stock in them before, but then again, they've never been so vivid before. So detailed. So realistic. All around her: sights, sounds, smells, pressing in against her. Seizing. Squeezing. Nibbling. Gnawing on her mind—her whole being.

She wakes. Bound to the bed. Wrists and ankles wrapped around by the sheets. Somehow secured. She struggles for a minute to no avail, then tries to scream. Before a sound escapes her lips, however, the pillow beside her flips over her face, smothering her. Panicking, she struggles harder, but, surprisingly, she soon learns her mistake and lies still. The pillow presses down for a moment longer, but then it flips back beside her.

Her purse lies open. Beckoning. Something that enormous must have something useful inside in it—in theory, anyway. The previous lesson already forgotten, Vogue tries to ease her hand towards it. The purse appears to open wider for her and draw nearer—almost within her reach—a nail file glimmers, shimmers.

Closer.

Laughing.

Laughing?

Not her laughing.

Laughing at her.

Around her, the room echoes with guffaws. She stops her straining and struggling. Listens. Her eyes dart all around the suite, but she sees no one. Yet everything has changed. Or has it? Vogue can't remember if she ordered a theme room or not. A little too realistic for her liking in any case: tapestries of ancient battles cover the walls; spears, swords, and shields line the perimeter. Across from her a fire blazes. Before it lie an empty plate and a long knife on the dirt floor.

Dirt floor?

I didn't pay all that money for a dirt floor, did I? Whimpering, she continues to look and listen, trying to pinpoint the laughter.

It's coming from the bed. Reduces to soft snickers, and, in its own way, does some "listening" of its own. Waiting to see what her next move will be. The bed doesn't have to wait too much longer.

"Who's there?"

Vibrating, the bed answers. "Just the two of us."

"And who's that?"

The bed shifts beneath her. "Who's that where?"

Exasperated, she cries: *"Who's that under my bed?"*

"No one is under the bed, Mama Bear, and the bed is not *yours* to begin with."

"Is that you again, Loki?"

The bed sighs and the woman sinks. "You really have no clue what a Norse God looks like, do you?"

Lower, the bed enfolds her.

"Will you stop playing tricks on me? I helped you out, remember?"

The bed pauses. Hardens.

"Don't you know that Loki is the Ultimate Trickster, Baby Bear—it's what he does—well, when he's not killing, conquering, laying with women, doing what Vikings do, or, well, whatever. And I must point out that you have never helped me at all. *Ever.*"

"Stop this already, Loki, and just tell me what you want."

"First of all—stop calling me Loki."

"What do you want me to call you then?"

"You're talking to a bed, Goldilocks, what do you think?"

"I'm not thinking much at all. For all I know, I'm still sleeping and dreaming...*and I didn't want a dirt floor!* So give me a break already. Let me wake up, or let me go. I'm not going run away."

"Hmmm...so much to consider..." The bed inflates, but the sheets do not loosen.

A voice erupts from across the suite. "Enough of this idle bantering, Veikur Rum!"

Vogue turns her head to see a beautiful, buxom, naked woman with long blond braided hair reaching down to her waist. Lying there, Vogue is both deeply envious and strangely aroused, admiring the perfection in her form, searching for some flaw. Finding it fast. As she glances below the waist once again, her envy and anticipation are turned into gloating and revulsion. So much for perfection. The beauty stops at the meridian. From the waist down, her figure is rotting and putrid. Dead flesh hangs in sinewy strips. Every movement brings a watery, squishing sound and an escape of septic gases. Slowly, purposefully, she moves towards Vogue, leaving a trail behind her like a massive slug.

She cries out as the Valkyrian female draws nearer. Her body trembling, tickling, then burning and bruising as her body is bitten—her clothes being eaten away.

Weeping. "Who are you?"

"Hel, his daughter."

"You mean Loki's daughter, right? What's your name?"

"I just said, *Hel.*"

"You mean your name is Hell?"

"Not *H-E-L-L!...H-E-L!* Why do I *always* have to go through this with everybody? Aren't you listening—"

"Okay! Okay, already! What does Loki want with me now?"

Sitting on the bed, squishing and farting, Hel coldly caresses Vogue's cheek. Somehow soothing and scaring her at the same time. She trails her frigid fingers down her neck. Feels Vogue's pulse quicken.

"He wants you and your husband to be the last two people in Midgard to restart humanity after the end of the world."

"And where exactly is Midgard? Do I need my passport or any shots first? And...did you just say that only the two of us are to survive?"

"Yes."

"...And it *has to be* with my husband?"

"Yes."

"But Loki knows what an asshole my husband is."

"Yes. Everything has its price."

"So it seems...can't we negotiate?"

"No. You're to join with him shortly."

"What exactly do you mean by *join*?"

"Just meet with him."

"And then?"

"And then you go into hiding until Ragnarok is over."

"That's it?"

"That's all."

"And you needed to tie me, and...and all of—well, just to tell me this?"

"Not at all. He only wanted me to pass on the message to you. The rest was all my idea."

"Don't forget about me! I helped, too." Veikur Rum chimes in, but Hel ignores it. She leans back and reaches across Vogue for her bags.

"Now let's take a look at what you've bought to help you make it through Ragnarok."

"And have ourselves a little fun in the bargain." Veikur Rum adds, and Vogue's bindings tighten once again.

"Isn't Loki expecting me? Shouldn't I be on my way? Won't he be upset that you've kept me as it is?"

They hesitate. Retreat. Regroup. Reconsider. Hel settles in her seat. Minor eruption underneath.

"Perhaps..."

"We're dead anyway, soon enough." Veikur Rum rumbles and starts to nip at Vogue again.

"Just for tying me up—that's harsh." Vogue doesn't really sympathize, being totally unfamiliar with the experience of being sympathetic. However, she is starting to think on her feet, so to speak. And she wants to get away relatively unscathed.

Hel explains: "No. No. Almost all of us are to die—it's our Fate. After Ragnarok, very few will remain alive." She nods, contemplating. "Yes, we must satisfy honor. Fate is calling us."

Remembering her dreams, realizing there may be some truth to them, Vogue changes her mind and decides to stall.

"Well don't you have call display or message manager? Don't answer. Just ignore it. That's what I do. I don't think I'm ready for this yet. Let's put Fate on hold for awhile."

"Loosen her bonds, Veikur Rum. It's time for her to be on her way."

Whimpering and groaning, Veikur Rum complies.

Vogue sits up and rubs her wrists and ankles. Still desperate, she asks: "But what about Free Will?"

"Do we look Catholic?"

"...uhhhh..."

"Don't answer. Just get dressed." Hel stands and shifts away, her lower body burping and oozing.

"But Vayker Room here ate my clothes."

"Sorry." Veikur Rum rumbles, but not too apologetically, still enjoying the feel and the view.

Hel gestures, dismissing her. "I'm sure you have something in your bags."

"I suppose," Vogue pouts, "but I really think you owe me."

"Perhaps," Hel smiles darkly, "we shall see what you deserve in—

SHAVING THE WEASEL

Slowly, carefully, the derelict lowers his bursting burlap sack on to the beach. He's spent too much time collecting discarded human hair and nails to have them spill all over the sand now. Satisfied that his bag is safe, he sits down beside it on a nearby log and watches the waves lap up against the shore.

Waiting.

Knowing he won't be alone for long.

Soon, he hears their approach from opposite directions. Man and woman. GQ and Vogue. Slim and stylish...well *usually* anyway, but not today. Sure, they're still slim and Teflon coated, possessing abs of envy and buns of stainless steel. But they are also haggard—dirty and sweaty from running around store to store, trying to find the right things to get them through Ragnarok. But they've never had this kind of experience before, so, mostly, they've bought a lot of crap. During their sprees, knowing the clock is ticking, neither made their usual pit stops to check the hair, the makeup, the dandruff flakes, the creased clothes, and the runs in the nylons. Or to change those cursed black socks. In any case, Teflon may be a breeze to clean, but it gets filthy just as easily given the opportunity. So for many reasons—including the awareness of their lack of cleanliness—they are also angry.

At themselves.

At each other.

At *him*. They both yell, "There you are—I've been looking all over for you!" Then they run, shopping bags slapping their thighs, converging on him.

He sighs. "I figured you folks would

be by sooner or later." And he doesn't bother to look up at them. Scratches at some mud caked on his pants. Flicks away the dust.

Scratches.

Flicks.

Not expecting to be so blatantly disregarded, the two stand above him, chests heaving, eyes darting around dubiously. Searching.

Finding...*nothing*. Certainly not what they were expecting. Well, they were expecting Loki, here, at the only nearby body of water: a shallow river in a park at the edge of the city. And they figured that by finding Loki, they would also find each other, but something is missing.

"Where's your long ship?" Vogue asks. "I thought you'd be almost finished by now. Isn't that your last sack? What about Ragnarok?"

Attacking from another angle, her husband shouts: "You said I had *lots of time!* You set me up! I lost my job! My only wish was to see you pay before Ragnarok begins—but now it seems Ragnarok is nowhere in sight and I'm unemployed! What am I supposed to do now? I'm hungry. Thirsty. Filthy. My teeth feel like they're coated with—"

"You would go and lose your job, wouldn't you? Well, if there's no Ragnarok, at least I won't have to be stuck with you to rebuild humanity." Vogue glares at her husband. "I want a divorce."

"What are you talking about?"

"You know what a divorce is—almost all of our friends and family have—"

"No. Not that. The being stuck together part and rebuilding humanity. How are we supposed to do that when we've both been snipped?"

"Well, it's a long story, but this morning I went on a bit of a shopping spree—"

"Shopping spree?"

"—and I got a hotel suite—"

"A suite? For one person?"

"—and I was laying down reading about the Vikings, and I fell asleep. I had all these dreams about you and me and

Ragnarok—"

"Whose credit cards did you use?"

"—and then I woke, or I thought I woke, and Loki's daughter, Hel—"

"His daughter's name is *Hell*? Man, who are we dealing with?"

"Not *Hell*, you idiot, *H-E-L*! I understand why she complained so much now. Anyway, she explained everything to me—"

"Did you get a refund for the room since you left after staying for only a couple of hours?"

"Don't you want to hear about what Hel had to say, or about my dreams? I think they were prophetic, you know like on that mini-series that was on last weekend—"

"You kept your receipts, I hope."

The derelict clears his throat. "Why don't you two stop arguing, sit down, and relax." He pats the log on both sides. They hesitate. Both about to speak. Then they drop their eyes and their seats soon follow, with their bags still held before them. "Did *I* say Ragnarok *wasn't* approaching?"

"…no…" They glumly answer in unison.

"Just because you don't see a long ship moored here, it doesn't mean that it isn't somewhere else, now does it?"

Again, they reply: "…no…"

"Well then, you two have a date with Destiny, don't you? Humanity is in your hands, or perhaps more appropriately, it is in your loins, and I don't need you two bickering over such trivialities. Right?"

"…right…"

"That's better. Now do you two want to go to that cave in the hill over there?"

"*A cave?* Do we have a choice?" Vogue pouts.

The derelict only answers with a smile.

GQ whines. "We have to spend Ragnarok in a cave? For how long?"

"Until it's over."

"You're still being vague."

"You think I don't know that?" He flashes a brown, hourglass grin, which nei-

ther returns. "Now take your things and get going. I'll have to seal you in pretty soon."

"Seal us in?"

"It's for your own protection. Besides, what else did you expect?"

"You're going to seal us in a cave? How do we know when Ragnarok is over? How do we get back out? How are we to survive? More importantly, how do we even know this isn't just some trick on your part?"

Vogue cuts in: "I really think I should tell you about my—"

But the derelict ignores her interruption and speaks over her.

"Everything you need is in the cave. Go ahead. Take a look for yourselves. But if you two want to stay out here instead while Ragnarok is running amok, then be my guests and you can die with everyone else. Let me know right now though, because if you want to stay out here then I have to find another couple to rebuild humanity…*fast*…so what'll it be?"

"…the cave…" The couple agrees, albeit reluctantly for a number of reasons, but neither wants to die so soon—not when they have so much to live for.

Getting up together, the trio walks away from the water towards the cave's entrance; husband and wife each holding on tightly to their purchases. A mass of huge boulders is suspended above the opening, ready to block it at the pull of a rope. The derelict stops.

"I forgot my sack. Go on ahead. I don't want it to get wet." He pats them both on their shoulders. Simultaneously they cringe but remain silent. "Oh, and thanks again for your contribution, I couldn't have gotten this far without you."

"How stupid do you think we are?" GQ scowls.

"Is that a rhetorical question?"

"What does 'rhetorical' mean?"

"Just get going, I'll be right behind you. Besides, you know I'm going to be sealing you anyway, soon enough."

Slowly complying, knowing that this

is where their Fate lies, the couple enters the mouth of the cave. Nearby, there is a gas lantern—which fills them with hope and despair: hope in that it appears Loki did leave provisions for them, but despair because neither of them has ever operated a lantern before. Sure, they can ask him when he comes back, but what about *after* they are alone together? What other complex mechanisms may they be forced to learn how to use? They can only continue to hope that Loki provided something a little simpler for them to operate. GQ takes hold of the lantern. Continues into the darkness. Eyes open for a flashlight. His wife is at his side but neither reaches out for the other.

The derelict returns. Sack over his shoulder, he pauses at the entrance and takes hold of the rope.

"I really should go in and make sure they're alright first, but—" He shrugs indifferently and pulls the rope. The massive boulders come crashing down, covering the cave's entrance. As the rocks and dust settle he steps away and shakes his head: "That is one gullible couple. Oh well, I suppose there is no other way."

Inside the cave, they hear the rocks tumbling behind them. Both know they are here to stay for quite some time. Rather than trying to find their way back to the entrance, they feel their way around the cave. Soon they find a wooden table with a large flashlight on it, among other items. After dropping their bags, GQ wrestles the flashlight away from his wife and thumbs the switch.

On the table there is a brief note, which reads:

Hey folks:
　　Perhaps we'll meet again　in Valhalla (ha ha). You should have enough to get by, but take it easy. Batteries -- like most things in life, and in this cave -- don't

last forever. Let's see how long you two last together.
　Score one for Midgard.
　　Cheers,
　　　Loki

Sighing. Shining the flashlight in his wife's frowning face, GQ takes a step back.

"Boy, have we been screwed."

"You think so?" Vogue snaps. "Now will you get that light out of my eyes?"

He turns off the flashlight. Both are happy not to see the other. They remain standing, eyes adjusting somewhat to the utter darkness.

"Well Ragnarok or no Ragnarok we've got a long haul ahead of us. I wonder if Loki left us anything to dig ourselves out?"

"How long do we wait though? Shouldn't we be certain Ragnarok has come and gone—if it's going to come at all? Although, from what Hel was telling me—and why didn't you listen to me in the first place about my dreams?"

"You have plenty of time to tell me now, don't you?"

"If they even matter anymore...how did we get in this mess in the first place? You and your wanting to get some culture...damn you and Public Broadcasting straight to Valhalla!"

"It doesn't matter anymore. What matters is how we make it through—

SUCKING ON THE MARROW OF LIFE

Spitting out the small bones, GQ reaches for another rack of rat heating over the gas lantern in the middle of the cave floor. Charred on the outside, raw on the inside. Even after all this time, he still hasn't got the hang of barbecuing. Too blue collar for him, and Vogue has never been a cook. (Why get your hands dirty and cook when you can dine out or have it prepared and delivered?) Besides, being in the cave all this time, it's not like Loki left them any spices besides a red-and-yellow plastic salt-and-pepper set, or anything other than the lantern to cook with. They almost starved before they finally relented to eating their first rat, oh, so long ago. So now, they eat what they can, when they can.

Across from him, Vogue sits with her legs crossed, avoiding his gaze in the shadows.

"Did you know a rat only needs a hole a quarter inch wide to fit through?"

"Kinda like something else, hmmm?" Vogue picks at the meat on her stick.

"No need to be snippy." He blows on the rat. "It's not like size matters anyway, when you're not getting any to begin with."

"What's the point—with your vasectomy and my tubes tied? No children to repopulate Midgard."

"I asked, but you never said anything back then either. Besides, I assumed Loki took care of those things—"

"Nice assumption—"

"Just like he took care of this..." Pulling the skinned rat off the skewer, GQ stabs her in the heart, until the stick pokes out the back of her blouse.

"*Owwww!* Would you stop doing that already?" Vogue pulls the skewer out and throws it on the stone floor. The wounds close over before much blood is spilled. Still: "You've just ruined another blouse. It's not like I have that many to chose from."

"You're still alive, aren't you?"

"Yes. Just like all the other times you've tried to stab me, choke me, smother me, bash my brains out."

"And don't forget about trying to kill me too."

"How can I forget when you're sitting here nagging me all the time? Just quit it already, I'm so *bored* with all of this: living in the dark, sleeping on a stone floor, the stench, your endless bits of trivia, eating rats, bugs—"

"But we're immortal..."

"Big deal. We've known that for decades, and what good has it done us? We still get hungry. Still feel pain. Still can't get out of here."

"Well, why don't you open up already, and we'll find out what Fate has in store for us?"

"Despite what I saw in my dreams in that suite all those years ago, I still can't bear the thought of having sex with you anymore."

"But that's *exactly* what we're supposed to be doing. What about our Fate? Did it ever occur to you that maybe if we started having children, Loki would come back for us, and set us free?"

"Of course not! If Ragnarok is over, he's dead. We have to find our own way out...*somehow*...or maybe there will be someone—"

"You *know* there is no way out. The only entrance is blocked with stones too large for us to move, and we have nothing to break them down with. 'Everything you need is in the cave'—*my ass!*"

"Stop whining already...maybe Ragnarok isn't over yet anyway. Who knows how long it's supposed to last?"

"I still think we need to have sex."

"I didn't want to thirty years ago, when you still looked half decent, and when you didn't smell so...so..."

"You think you stink any less than I do? We've been out of soap, cologne, and toothpaste for more than twenty years. It's not going to get any better..."

And so the two argue and argue, still try to murder each other on occasion, and slowly go insane until...

MISADVENTURES IN A THUMBNAIL UNIVERSE

Watching the sun set, Loki and Hel sit on a log on the sand a short distance from the cave that holds GQ and Vogue. A low fire at their feet. Loki pokes at it with a length of driftwood, while Hel scruffs her brother Fenrir behind the ears—the massive wolf's head in her lap. His eyes closed, he growls lowly, contented. Loki is still dressed as the derelict, with the bursting burlap sack of hair and nails beside him. He has a *long* way to go yet before he has enough to build the long ship, but he's in no hurry, especially since he knows that he will be killed at Ragnarok.

"How long are you planning on keeping them in there?"

"I don't see any reason to release them, especially since they're not living up to their end of the deal. So, I'll just keep sending a rat or two their way to keep them going, driving each other crazy."

"But what about their children—if they *ever* have any? You did take care of them, too, didn't you?"

"Of course. I made them fully functional just before they entered the cave."

Hel shakes her head. "They're about the worst possible parents I can imagine."

"Considering you're the goddess of the underworld, that's saying a lot."

"It is, isn't it? Still, that's been your plan all along, hasn't it? No children, they go insane together in a cave for eternity, their own special room in Niflheim, so to speak. And if they do have any children, Midgard will be reborn with the worst possible offspring."

"Pretty funny, don't you think?"

"Always like having the last laugh, don't you, Father?"

Loki grins, makes no reply, and stabs the smoldering driftwood into the sand. He pulls out a chipped and rusted Swiss Army knife—with only eleven tools, including the main blade—so nothing too fancy. He digs his thumbnail in the groove of a smaller blade and snaps it open. Holds up his thumb. Inspects the scratched and broken cuticle; the dry and cracked skin; the caked dirt underneath the yellow half-moon of the nail. Raises the small blade and sets in to scrape the dirt

away. Maintaining a disguise or not, he can only stand so much grime after all.

Hel nudges him, and he almost stabs his hand. Somewhat irritated, he turns his head.

"What was that for?"

Hel points at his still-raised thumb.

"I thought you knew better than that?"

"What're you talking about?"

"What? Don't you know? Haven't you ever watched Public Broadcasting with all those science programs?"

"Yes. It's funny. That's kind of what got GQ into trouble in the first place. So…?"

"So…see that dirt under your thumbnail?"

"Of course. That's what I was going to scrape away until you shoved your elbow in my side."

Hel raises an eyebrow. "Well, think of all the millions and billions of people I probably saved…?"

"Start making sense, or it's going to be more than my nails I'll be cleaning out." But there isn't much of a threat in his voice, or in any other part of his body.

"That dirt is made up of molecules, and those molecules are made up of atoms. Perhaps every one of those atoms is a whole universe, filled with planets and stars and people. Perhaps we are—our whole universe—just one of those atoms that make up the molecules in some other 'old man's' thumbnail sitting on a log on a beach somewhere else…ever consider that?"

Hel holds a superior smile, but she is also happy to pass on this "knowledge."

Loki considers her words for a moment and answers: "No. Can't say that I have. Nice story…although I wouldn't be telling that to anyone else in Niflheim or Asgard if I were you. Not a very Norse idea." Holds up his thumb again, and places the blade under the nail. "And maybe you're right, but it's still just dirt to me." And he draws the blade across, creating a tiny shower on the ground before him. "Besides, if their universes are anything like ours, they aren't really worth keeping anyway." Blows the bits of dust. "Now I've got nine more nails to do, not counting my toes if I feel like doing that much today. So why don't you just sit back, relax, and enjoy the sunset, rather than worry about any other possible universes, or that couple, or...

RAGNAROK

STEVE BEARD

LOCATION:
Brighton on the south coast of England

STYLE OF BIZARRO:
Metrosexual

BOOKS BY BEARD:

Meat Puppet Cabaret
Digital Leatherette
Aftershocks
Logic Bomb
Perfumed Head

DESCRIPTION:

"Steve Beard is a thorny weed in the parking lot of postmodernity."
    - Bruce Sterling

INTERESTS: abject objects, absolutism, acid house, aerosol art, aesthetic recommodification, Afrocentrism, alchemy, alien invasion movies, ambient music, anarcho-mysticism, archons, assassination, astro-physics, avant bardism… and that's just the things beginning with 'a' (list taken from his book *Aftershocks*).

INFLUENCES: Charles Babbage, J G Ballard, Lester Bangs, Barbie, Georges Bataille, Jean Baudrillard, Sleeping Beauty, Beavis, Walter Benjamin, Hakim Bey, William Blake, Bugs Bunny, William Burroughs, Tim Burton, Butt-head… and that's just the folks beginning with 'B' (list taken from his book *Logic Bomb*).

WEBSITE:

www.mappalujo.com

Survivor's Dream

(1) Transplantation

You are being choppered into hospital. You are flying through the air over East London. You were picked up at Mile End. That's where you used to live. But now you are going to the big hospital in Whitechapel. You are going to land on the roof. You are inside a helicopter. It's the colour of blood. You've seen it whirling high above you like a tireless metal insect. But that was back when you were safe on the ground. Now there is blood in your throat. Someone is shouting beneath the noise of the blades. You close your eyes. They want to know your name. Someone wants to know your name. You are bleeding. You don't know your name.

What is your name? You don't know. You've forgotten your own name. Let it go. You let it go. You are losing it. Losing your own life. Let it go. You drift into a cold dark space. You are no longer yourself. You dream you are this dead girl. You dream you are no longer alive. What is your name? You don't have a name. You are Dead Girl.

>>

Dead Girl was calling out to someone. She didn't have any clothes on. All she had on was this fanny-pack around her waist and she was calling out to her Fairy Sugadaddy. But he wasn't there.

It didn't matter. She could always look at all the stars rushing past in the darkness. They were pretty and she tried to catch them. But she was going too fast. She was falling. She was hurtling through outer space down towards Planet Earth.

It was cold.

<<

Dead Girl was travelling. She was crossing the Atlantic Ocean. She was going from a place in London Town to an island in the Caribbean Sea. She was hiding inside this ship. She had been put there.

It was cold. There was a massive amount of heat coming out of these engines. They were huge engines. They were big and fat and the colour of silver. There was this intense heat radiating out from the engines into a very cold space.

Dead Girl had her own little bed throughout the voyage. It had a little cabinet next to it. But she never used it. She didn't have the key.

The only thing that Dead Girl owned was her fanny-pack. It was a little purse on a belt made out of what they call mock crocodile skin. She always wore it round her waist with the purse at the front. She liked to unzip the purse to check her photo was still inside. It was a black and white photo. She kept it in one of the pockets so that its torn white border was always visible. It was the only thing inside her fanny-pack and she always wore her fanny-pack. That way she knew her photo was always there close to her. She found that very comforting.

Dead Girl wore her fanny-pack underneath this white hospital gown that tied up at the back. She didn't have any shoes or socks on. She wasn't wearing any knickers.

She had these sticking plasters on her arms. That must have been because she'd been cutting herself. They called it self-harming back at the children's home. But it wasn't that. It was because she couldn't stand it. That's why she'd run away. She'd run away from the Silver Birches because she couldn't stand it.

She was going to Paradise.

>>

Dead Girl was falling through the atmosphere. She was rushing like a meteorite towards London Town.

She didn't have any clothes on. She

didn't have a home. She wanted to hear the voice of Fairy Sugadaddy. She wanted some comfort. But all she had was her fanny-pack.

Dead Girl screamed. She was burning up.

<<

Dead Girl arrived at this island in the Caribbean Sea. It was Paradise. She saw its name on a postcard when she got off the ship. The postcard showed these empty white beaches and shady golf-courses. It had a picture of the big honey-coloured casino where all the glamorous people went. The casino was called Atlantis.

Dead Girl stood on this red carpet inside Atlantis. It ran past rows and rows of slot machines lit up like television screens. There were all these empty chairs in front of the slot machines. They had these plush blue seats.

Dead Girl was wearing her white hospital gown and her fanny-pack. She was the only one in the casino. She walked down the red carpet in the warm silence. She called out but nobody answered. Even the slot machines were silent.

There was this bandstand in the middle of the casino. It had a domed roof held up by these thick white pillars. Running round the top edge of the bandstand were these pictures of dogs and birds and naked stick people. There was a red velvet rope surrounding the bandstand. Inside the bandstand there was this glass aquarium which went from the floor to the ceiling. It was all blue inside with little pieces of coral and shoals of fish that flashed from side to side. It was a very important place. The sign outside said it was a Beautiful Person Lounge.

Dead Girl touched the rope. Her hand was all sweaty. She could see how the rope was attached to the nearest pillar with a brass hook. She wanted to unhook the rope. She felt like she wasn't supposed to do it. But she wanted to go inside and get closer to the aquarium. She wanted to be a Beautiful Person. But she was dirty and smelly and her hair was a mess.

Suddenly she wasn't wearing her hospital gown anymore. The only thing she had on was her fanny-pack.

Dead Girl unzipped her purse and took out the photo. It had a torn edge. She only took out the photo when she was feeling very low. She didn't do it very often. She only did it now and again.

The photo was all dirty and creased. It was a black and white photo of a little baby wrapped in tissue paper. The baby was lying in a shoe-box.

Dead Girl stroked the image on the photo and then turned it over. On the back there was this logo showing two little animals standing up on their hind legs. It was what they call a Royal Crest.

>>

Dead Girl was falling naked through the air. Old River Thames was looping across London Town far down below.

Dead Girl was caught in a hail-storm or something. She kept twisting and turning, but it did no good. She kept getting jabbed and bombarded on all sides. She kept getting hurt.

She felt that she was splitting apart. She felt that there were pieces of her that were just shearing away. She was coming apart as she fell through the air.

What had happened to her Fairy Sugadaddy? She didn't know.

Dead Girl saw her arms and her legs and other pieces of herself raining down through the sky. She saw her head falling down with its eyes closed. They span away from her and disappeared.

Dead Girl was just this lump of flesh left over from herself. She was what they call a torso. She still had her fanny-pack. She was falling.

All this brown water came up to meet her. Dead Girl splashed down in Old River Thames.

<<

Dead Girl was inside the Beautiful Person Lounge. She was lying on this bed made out of coral and there were these Silly Bitches fussing over her. They were dressed in short white skirts and looked like nurses. They had mean little eyes and long rows of sharp white teeth.

Dead Girl was nervous. She held tightly on to her fanny-pack under the white linen sheet that covered her body. There was a light shining down on her. It was a light like the ones they have in operating theatres. It had all these bulbs arranged in a circle under an umbrella of mirrored glass. Dead Girl felt very hot.

One of the Silly Bitches smiled at her and said something about how she was going to be made into a Beautiful Person. She was going to get what they call a makeover. Witch Doctor was coming to treat her himself. Didn't she know how lucky she was? That was why she was here.

Witch Doctor. Who was that? Dead Girl became excited. She felt embarrassed and looked down at the carpet. It was handwoven and showed the Atlantic Ocean floating in a cosmos with little stars and a big sun and a moon on either side. The sun and the moon had these smiling faces.

The walls of the Beautiful Person Lounge were dark and made of glass. There were these lovely drapes hanging down on one side. They were made of velvet and they were the colour of champagne.

One of the Silly Bitches said Dead Girl had to put her feet in the stirrups hanging either side of her. She told her to be a good girl. Dead Girl lifted up her legs so that the sheet was in her face and her bare bottom was exposed. She was cold now. She could feel the cold air on her bottom.

One of the Silly Bitches she couldn't see made a joke and all the others laughed. Dead Girl looked out to see the reflections of the Silly Bitches in the glass walls. They were like ghosts. They were busy tending to all this glinting machinery. One of them put a cassette tape into a machine and all this soothing ambient music came out. Another one inspected a glass box full of flying blue sparks.

Dead Girl looked closer. She saw that the glass box had a long twisted flex coming out of it that connected it up to a glass wand. The wand was as long as a sword and hollow like the barrel of a gun. It had a hand-guard at one end and at the other it twisted round and round on itself in a spiral until it tapered to an open nozzle. It lay on a trolley next to a box of tissues.

Dead Girl saw the drapes twitch. She tensed.

The Silly Bitches came back to Dead Girl. One of them pulled the sheet away from her face and gave her a round plastic box with two little brown seeds inside. She was told to take them to make her feel better. She was given a glass of water and she drank them down. It was like taking headache tablets or something.

Dead Girl looked at the drapes from the corner of her eye. She saw first one foot and then another move out from under the drapes. They were bare and dirty with very long toe-nails. There was somebody standing behind the drapes.

One of the Silly Bitches was busy with a big magnifying glass. She swivelled it over Dead Girl's bottom. She was looking down at Dead Girl's thing. She was looking at what they call a vagina.

Dead Girl looked at the drapes again. There was nobody there.

Another one of the Silly Bitches was smearing something cold on the fleshy lips around Dead Girl's vagina. She was getting it from this tub of ointment and smearing it on with her fingers. She said something about a Magic Wand. She said it was so the Magic Wand wouldn't slip.

Dead Girl wanted to get up and leave but she found she couldn't move. She couldn't control her arms or legs. It was like they were stuck.

The Silly Bitches backed away from

her. They started giggling and curtseying. Someone was coming. There was someone moving into the light. It was this thin old man. He had these grey whiskers tufting out of his ears. His pink lips were very thin like a slit in his face. He had all this wild hair like white candyfloss. His clear blue eyes had this blank expression. It was like they weren't taking anything in.

Dead Girl couldn't stop looking at him. The Silly Bitches called him Witch Doctor. He began to caper in his long black coat. He jabbered and sang snatches of a Gary Glitter song. The Silly Bitches gave him tweezers and scissors and scalpels and he dropped them all over the floor. He was making these deep barking noises.

Dead Girl was hypnotised. It was madness. She wanted to kiss Witch Doctor all over. She wanted to stroke his lovely hair. But she couldn't move. She could only watch. It was so sensual. Her eyes caressed Witch Doctor. It was like eating chocolate.

Witch Doctor picked up the Magic Wand in his right hand. He began to feint and parry with it in the air. One of the Silly Bitches pressed a switch on the side of the glass box. The blue sparks inside the box started to move faster. Witch Doctor said something Dead Girl couldn't hear and the Silly Bitches all laughed in one go.

Now there were blue sparks moving through the spiralling glass barrel of the Magic Wand. They surged towards the open nozzle and sprang out in a shower. Witch Doctor giggled and waved the Magic Wand in the air. He began to form patterns with the blue sparks. The Silly Bitches gasped and clapped.

Dead Girl broke out into a sweat. The sweat poured off her. First it was hot and then it was cold. It soaked through this bit of paper between her and the bed of coral. The bit of paper was dripping wet.

Witch Doctor was there between her legs. His eyes were wild. He told her it wouldn't hurt and she believed him. The Silly Bitches were still talking about a makeover.

The moment Witch Doctor touched her with the wand she started laughing hysterically because of the shock. She was crying with laughter. There were these tears running down her face.

Dead Girl turned her head to shield her bright red face from Witch Doctor. She was shaking.

Witch Doctor was shoving his Magic Wand in and out of her vagina. He kept on doing it. He did it for about an hour until he got tired. Dead Girl was so wet with sweat that eventually the nozzle slipped and touched her skin where the ointment was. Dead Girl screamed when that happened. She screamed and leapt up into the air. Witch Doctor had burned her with his Magic Wand. She wanted to push him away but banged her head against a tray of tweezers and scissors and scalpels held by one of the Silly Bitches. The Silly Bitch cried out in alarm. Dead Girl collapsed back on the bed. She leaned over and was sick on the floor.

She was ashamed. There were the two little brown seeds in the middle of all the vomit. One of the Silly Bitches immediately rushed over to clean up the mess. She knelt down with a tissue. She didn't notice the seeds.

Dead Girl was still leaning over the side of the bed. She had her head upside down. She could see what was happening through the gap under the bed. The Silly Bitches were turning off all the equipment and putting it away. They were moving around on their long white legs. Witch Doctor stood alone in his long black coat. He was panting. She could see only the lower half of his body. He didn't have any shoes on. She stared at his feet. They were covered in mud and his toe-nails were all long and twisted.

>>

Dead Girl was floating in the Old River Thames. She was very badly cut up. It felt like there were pieces of her missing. She didn't know where they were.

Dead Girl was aching all over. She

hurt on the inside. She was just this torso now. How did she know that? It was a philosophical question.

She drifted in the water. She felt she had to find the missing pieces of herself. But she didn't know how. All she had was this old fanny-pack. It was strapped round her waist. It was the only thing she owned.

Then she remembered what Fairy Sugadaddy had said. He had told her she had got this blue light deep inside of her. She could take control of it. She could use it to make these images and project them on her skin. He said that she had got these Extra Special Powers. Could it really be true?

Dead Girl reached deep inside of herself and found the blue light. It was warm and wet and faint like quicksilver. It was hard to catch. Dead Girl knew what she wanted. She needed something to keep her going for the time being. She grew some spare body parts from the blue light deep inside her. It was like creating something in a hot blue forge. She had these new arms and legs. She made herself a new replica head. They glowed like holograms as she put them on. So now it was just her torso that was made out of flesh and blood and bone and marrow. The rest of her was made out of the blue light.

Dead Girl blinked and checked how her new eyes worked. She gazed at the stars high above her in the night sky. It was like seeing the world through a blue filter.

She drifted some more. She let herself be carried along by Old River Thames.

<<

It was not until Fairy Sugadaddy contacted her some time later that Dead Girl understood what had happened to her in the Beautiful Person Lounge.

Witch Doctor had injected these blue sparks into her belly and they had grown into a ball of blue light. She could use the blue light to make creatures and project them outside her skin. That was one part of her Extra Special Powers. The other part was that she could make herself look like whatever

secret guilty things other people wanted her to be. She could change shape just like that.

Except the one thing she could never change was the place where Witch Doctor had burned her. His Magic Wand had left a big red lump on the outer lip of her vagina. It was incredibly painful and swollen for a day and a half after her makeover. It left a scar that never went away.

(2) Trepanation

>>

Dead Girl was floating. She was floating in Old River Thames. She was crying out for her Fairy Sugadaddy. Where was he? He must have gone away.

The water was very cold. Dead Girl shivered. She had all these goose-bumps on her skin. But the only place she had skin was on her torso. The rest of her was made from blue light.

There was this rash on her belly from her fanny-pack. It was chafing her. Maybe it was strapped on too tight.

<<

Dead Girl was on this Old Royal Spaceship in orbit high above Planet Earth. She was trapped inside. She had been taken there from Atlantis to work on a farm but it had all gone wrong after she had done something bad at the Royal Harvest Festival or whatever it was. Her memory was all fuzzy.

Dead Girl had used her Extra Special Powers on the Old King. That was the thing. It was the very first time she had used her Extra Special Powers. She didn't even know what they were at that point. She was just playing. She surprised herself. Dead Girl had used the blue light inside her and made herself into the Old King's guilty love. She had pretended to be his Lost Princess. But he hadn't got it. He hadn't got it at all. He was angry. He shouted at her but she only laughed at him in contempt. So they took her away.

So now she was being taken to

where they threw away all the waste and the dead bodies on the Old Royal Spaceship. She was strapped down on this trolley with a sheet thrown over her. They had let her keep her fanny-pack. She kept touching it as the trolley was pushed down a long corridor.

The corridor was made of glass on all sides. Dead Girl could see the green and blue swirl of Planet Earth outside. She could see her own reflection. The steel columns set in the walls supported this railway running directly above. Dead Girl could hear the rumble of the tube trains as they went backwards and forwards. She could feel the air whoosh as they passed.

She got pushed down the corridor for a long time. There was this old blue carpet which seemed to go on for miles. Dead Girl was drowsy. She closed her eyes. She dreamt of the trains. She saw all these young girls sitting inside. They had bashed-in faces and missing limbs. They didn't look very well. They looked like broken dollies. That made Dead Girl sad.

She woke up when the trolley got pushed through these double doors. They swung open and swung back closed behind her. One door said GARBAGE and the other said DISPOSAL. So that's how she knew where she was. She was inside Garbage Disposal. She was alone.

The place was deep underneath this train station. Dead Girl could hear the trains pulling in overhead. The metal struts in the ceiling shook from all the busy movement. But down below with her it was dark and empty.

There was a curved window at the edge of Garbage Disposal. The glass was scored by these thin steel beams. The stars outside were cold and blank. They made it like twilight inside Garbage Disposal. The floor was paved with black and white ceramic tiles. The tiles were an oblong shape. There was water on the sloping floor. It ran off into a gutter which followed the curve of the window.

Dead Girl could hear her own breathing in the intervals between the trains pulling in and out overhead. She couldn't get off the trolley. She couldn't move.

At the centre of Garbage Disposal was this tall round building. It rose all the way up to the top of the ceiling. Dead Girl guessed it extended to the train station above. So that meant she was looking at just the underground part of the building.

The building was lined with thick white marble streaked with heavy blue veins. It looked like it was made of Italian ice-cream. There was this riveted metal door in the middle. It had these yellow and black chevrons around the side.

At the edge of Garbage Disposal next to the gutter was an old white ceramic bath with all this electrical equipment. The bath rested on these iron feet made to look like lion's paws. They were flaking with gold paint. The bath was very big and must have been quite nice once. But now it was stained with deep brown marks. There was a wooden board over the top of the bath. Dead Girl could hear this water slopping around underneath.

There were cigarette stubs and what looked like pieces of old orange peel blocking the drain under the bath. Dead Girl squirmed on the trolley and it moved towards the bath. It bumped against it and disturbed the lid. Dead Girl was hit by this vile smell of dung and chlorine all mixed together. She felt sick but couldn't move.

This shadow fell across her. Dead Girl tensed up. She could hear someone moving across the wet floor tiles behind her. Someone else had come into Garbage Disposal.

>>

Dead Girl was being nudged by the tide. She was getting washed up on the shore of Old River Thames.

There were all these pieces of brilliant rubbish in the shallow water. There was an empty glass bottle of perfume, a winding stretch of red cloth stitched with oblong glass slides and also a six foot long ostrich feather. These things were there bobbing in the water next to her. They kept touching her stumps.

Dead Girl was glad she had the blue light growing out of her. She checked her fanny-pack with glowing blue fingers. It was still tied to her waist. She didn't have to worry.

She let herself get washed up on the shore.

<<

Dead Girl was in this place called Garbage Disposal on the Old Royal Spaceship. She wasn't on the trolley anymore. She had been moved. Now she was lying on the board over the bath.

Someone had taken the sheet away. Dead Girl didn't have any clothes on. But she still had her fanny-pack. She fiddled with it. She kept moving the zip up and down. She felt bad. She wanted to get up and leave. Nothing stopped her. She wasn't tied down anymore. But maybe if she got up she would only make things worse. Maybe it was better to stay where she was. She stayed where she was.

Someone was behind her. Dead Girl could hear them moving in between the noise of the trains rumbling overhead. They were talking to themselves. They were making these humming noises. Dead Girl hoped that everything was going to be all right.

There was this little black and white CCTV screen on a jointed arm right next to her. Dead Girl could see everything that was happening to her. She had an overhead view. She could see everything on the little screen.

There she was lying on top of the bath looking very small and frightened and there was this Crazy Lady standing over her. It was the Crazy Lady who was making the humming noises. Her head was covered by this white swimming cap and she had this white coat on with brown stains all over it. Her legs were bare and she was wearing these green Wellington boots.

Crazy Lady snapped on these white surgical gloves. She started to talk into this

microphone next to her lips. She had this guttural tone. Dead Girl thought she must be from Central Europe or somewhere. When Crazy Lady looked up into the CCTV camera that was in the roof Dead Girl could see how old she really was. Her face was all pulled back and taut and her eyes were covered in a little pair of blue goggles. She was wearing this blue one-piece swimming costume under her white coat.

Crazy Lady began to brush Dead Girl's hair. She brushed it with a gold plated brush. Dead Girl's hair was made of lots of different colours and thick as fuse wire. Crazy Lady talked as she brushed. She talked about how she was a Professor who knew about strange drugs and hidden space aliens and lots of other secret stuff. Dead Girl didn't understand it at all. But it didn't matter. Crazy Lady brushed her hair so it shined.

Crazy Lady ran her fingers through Dead Girl's hair. She massaged the scalp. Dead Girl allowed herself to feel safe. She shivered with pleasure.

The Crazy Lady was interested in the bit of Dead Girl's head at the front just above the hairline. She dabbed at it with shaving foam and scraped off the hair with this cut-throat razor. Soon Dead Girl had a bald patch high up in the middle of her forehead. She didn't cry or anything. Even when the Crazy Lady jabbed her with a hypodermic needle and her skin went all cold.

Then the Crazy Lady picked up this scalpel and cut the skin on Dead Girl's forehead. She pressed into the flesh and this blood came out. It didn't hurt. The Crazy Lady made lots of little cuts and none of them hurt. They intersected to form a sign like a cross.

The Crazy Lady wiped the scalpel clean and picked up this weird instrument made of rusted metal. It was very old, like it had just been dug out of the earth somewhere. It was shaped a bit like a corkscrew with a wooden bar across the top. There was a spike at the end which the Crazy Lady drove into Dead Girl's skull by pressing a button in the handle.

Dead Girl felt the jolt even through the anaesthetic. She gritted her teeth as this blood started to trickle down over her ears. Now she could feel this headache from very far away. There was this barrel round the shaft of the corkscrew thing which had sharp saw teeth set in a ring at the bottom. She watched as the Crazy Lady twisted the handle and the revolving saw started to cut into her forehead.

Dead Girl stopped looking at the TV monitor after that. She looked at the stars outside the window instead.

She guessed the operation went on for half an hour. There was all this white dust flying around. Dead Girl got it between her teeth and it was gritty. After a while she realised it was powdered bits of her own bone.

At one point she used her Extra Special Powers on the Crazy Lady. She didn't really know what she was doing. She was just trying to escape from the situation. That was why she pretended to be what the Crazy Lady wanted deep down inside. She pretended to be a Space Alien. But it didn't do any good. It was obviously a feeble imitation. Crazy Lady laughed and kept calling her this name that Dead Girl didn't recognise. She must have looked stupid. Crazy Lady could see right through her act. It wasn't like with the Old King. The Crazy Lady wasn't fooled. She knew what was going on.

When Dead Girl felt this cold air inside her head and had all this blood in her eyes, she wanted to scream. She couldn't use her Extra Special Powers on the Crazy Lady any more. She couldn't do much of anything. She opened her mouth and closed her eyes and she tried to yell at the top of her voice. But no sounds came out. All she could hear was this slurping noise from the blood that was spilling out of her head.

She opened her eyes again and looked back at the TV screen. The Crazy Lady had pulled the corkscrew thing out of her forehead and there was a solid chunk of bone inside the barrel at the end. It was at least an inch thick. The Crazy Lady was chuckling now as she dabbed at the edges of the hole in Dead Girls' forehead.

>>

Dead Girl was beached on the shore of Old River Thames. There were these cosmetic jewels lying on the tide-line. They were made of cut glass. She felt them digging into her side just below where she had the strap of her fanny-pack. Dead Girl was what they call a torso. Except now she had this head and these limbs made out of blue light. She had this faint glow.

The strand was covered in all this fine sand and silver glitter. The bank of the river was lined with a red-brick wall. On the strand between the river and the wall was this open square tent. Its frame was made of red painted wood and it had these open sides with long white gauze curtains pulled in at the four corners. Fluttering from the top of the pitched roof was this triangular flag with an emblem on it. The emblem had these little animals standing up on their hind legs. It was what they call a Royal Crest.

Next to the tent was this wrought iron spiral staircase. It led up from the strand to the top of the river bank. The lower steps were covered in green sludge.

Dead Girl saw something coming down the steps. It was moving fast. It was leaping down the steps. It was a bundle of rushing black energy.

<<

Dead Girl was in Garbage Disposal on the Old Royal Spaceship high above Planet Earth. She was inside the bath now. The wooden board had been slotted into place on top of her. It was like she was in a coffin. It was dark and she was lying in two inches of cold smelly water.

Crazy Lady had tried to be gentle. She had dried the blood from her ears with a rough towel and brushed the pieces of bone from her fanny-pack. She had wrapped a bandage round her head to cover the wound.

She had done all this before she had put her in the bath.

Dead Girl tried to push the lid off but it was no good. It was locked down tight. She felt this panic in the back of her throat. Her head hurt from where Crazy Lady had drilled this hole in her forehead. She didn't know what to do.

That was when Fairy Sugadaddy first spoke to her. He spoke to her inside her head. He had a lovely musical voice that faded in and out. It was difficult to catch. It was like listening to something off the radio late at night. It was full of these clicks and whistles. Dead Girl guessed the voice must be coming through the hole in her head. She guessed it was coming from very far away. She thought Fairy Sugadaddy must live on a distant star.

Dead Girl closed her eyes. Fairy Sugadaddy said he would grant Dead Girl a wish. Dead Girl's fear ebbed away. She was calm. She listened to Fairy Sugadaddy. He said he would make her wish come true. But she had to do one thing. Would she do this one thing? Dead Girl nodded. She would have to find Witch Doctor and point him out to Fairy Sugadaddy.

Dead Girl understood. Fairy Sugadaddy wanted Witch Doctor but he was hiding. She had been given a very important job. Fairy Sugadaddy said he believed she could find Witch Doctor. That's when he told her about her Extra Special Powers. They would help her. All she had to do was reach inside for the blue light. It was like her own special power supply.

Dead Girl nodded again. Fairy Sugadaddy flashed this picture up inside her mind's eye. It was like something off an old videotape. It had these bright colour bands floating away from the outlines and it was all fuzzy and grey at the edges. It was a surveillance image of Witch Doctor leaving this building late at night. Dead Girl recognised him by his white candyfloss hair and his bare feet all covered in leaves and dirt. He was coming out of a door which was all painted black and he was stepping down into the street. The door had a bell with broken wires sticking out of it. The street was silent and empty.

Dead Girl thought Fairy Sugadaddy must be showing her quite an old picture of Witch Doctor because he didn't look mad or confused. His eyes were like shining blue sparks in the night. But they were taking everything in. They were alert and focussed. Witch Doctor was wearing his black coat with the collar turned up around his neck. He was looking good. He stood on the street and lit a cigarette. He smiled a secret smile.

Dead Girl tried to hold on to the image of Witch Doctor as it faded in her mind's eye. She tried to pull it back. She was excited. She wanted to grab Witch Doctor and take him deep down inside her. She wanted him. He had burned her with his Magic Wand. She was angry with him. He didn't even know what he had done to her. She would show him. She would track him down and point him out to Fairy Sugadaddy. She would get a wish come true.

Dead Girl was sinking. She opened her eyes. It was cold and dark but she wasn't in the bath anymore. She was falling through space.

The Old Royal Spaceship got smaller and smaller above her. She had been dumped out of Garbage Disposal. The Old Royal Spaceship was a shadow in the sun.

(3) Assault

>>

Dead Girl was all alone on the Heath of London. She was wandering through the forest. The earth was parched and the grass was dry and yellow.

Dead Girl was sweating. The sun was high in the sky and it was hot. She had her white hospital gown back on. She kept checking her fanny-pack was still there underneath it. Her hands were not made of blue light any more. They contained veins and nerves. They were made of flesh.

Dead Girl could feel this cool breeze on her face. She had all this lovely new skin. She touched herself all over. The only parts of her that were still made out of the blue light were her legs. She still didn't have her real legs.

She was carrying this Magic Wand in her hand. She looked at it. It was a long spiralling tube made of glass.

Dead Girl had found Witch Doctor. She knew where he was hiding. She smiled to herself. She had stolen his Magic Wand.

<<

Dead Girl was lying on the strand of Old River Thames. There were all these cut glass stones next to her. There was this empty bottle of perfume. She could smell the Chanel Gardenia.

Dead Girl was this grey slab of meat in a rotting fanny-pack. The rest of her outside her torso was just this flickering blue light. She had a ghost head. That was what it was. She had a ghost head and she had these ghost arms and legs.

Dead Girl itched all over. She wanted to scratch herself but she couldn't move. She wanted to put herself back together but she didn't know how. She wanted to howl.

There was something rushing towards her. It was moving fast. It had raced down this spiral staircase on to the strand. It was big and black and angry. It had all this matted fur and its breath smelt of urine. It was a Black Dog.

Black Dog skidded to a halt before her and cocked his head. He was looking down at her with these red eyes that were ever so intelligent. It looked like he was grinning but it was just that he had all these sharp yellow teeth crowded into his lower jaw. The saliva kept dropping down from his gums.

Black Dog's nose was all wet and black and wrinkled. He was sniffing her from close up. He was investigating her scent. Dead Girl tried to shrink back but she couldn't move. Black Dog finally touched Dead Girl.

He nosed her shoulder gently and backed away. Then he came in again and started to lick her neck. He was very hairy. He had this long matted hair down his back and he had these fine little hairs on his belly. His paws were all dirty and his claws were sharp.

Black Dog was all over her. He was licking her bruised skin and biting her sore nipples. He was slavering over her. She used her Extra Special Powers on him but it was no good. He ignored the blue ghostly parts of her. He wasn't interested in them. It looked like a human torso was already exactly what he wanted. Black Dog simply kept going and she went along with it. There was nothing else she could do.

Black Dog had this stiff black penis. It was growing out of this dirty bush of hair between his hind legs and it had all these veins on it. The glans of it was pink and glistening. Black Dog kept rubbing it against her and whimpering. He has his eyes closed.

He kept putting his penis inside the cuts and holes in her flesh. He was opening up the old wounds. They were starting to leak all over the place. He bit her neck until the old scabs came away and he found the soft wet channel of her open throat. He shifted his weight back on his haunches and moved his penis in and out of this newly discovered hole.

Black Dog was panting. He was building up a rhythm. Dead Girl could feel him moving in and out of her. She could feel his tiny sharp claws digging into her belly. There was fresh blood on his gums. He opened his fiery red eyes so they were just these narrow slits. He went into this spasm and whimpered.

Black Dog was squirting all this semen inside her open bloodied neck. He was leaning over her and his legs were shaking and wobbling. It was like he could hardly stand. There was all this spit bubbling out of his jaws and dropping down on top of her. She was all sticky and wet on her shoulders. She didn't like it. She wanted him to stop.

There was this whistling sound from

the top of the river bank. There was this clapping sound and the shouting of a name. Black Dog cocked his ears. He looked up to the top of the spiral staircase. He backed off from Dead Girl. He turned round and raced back over the sand.

Someone was coming down the spiral staircase. Dead Girl couldn't quite see who it was. They were breathing hard and moving very slowly. They were coming down one step at a time. They were bumping themselves down on their arse.

Black Dog stopped when he got to the tent. He slumped down with his head on his paws.

>>

Dead Girl was wandering on the Heath of London with the sun going down. She came to this old silver birch tree growing by a lake. The lake was covered with the green flat leaves of all these water lilies.

Dead Girl sat down under the tree. Her legs were made of this blue light. They fizzled and glowed under her waist. It was like she was propped up. She was tired. She just didn't care.

The branches of the tree stretched out over the water. One of them had these chrome rings attached to it next to the leaves. They were clinking in the breeze.

Dead Girl adjusted her fanny-pack under her hospital gown to get comfortable. She still had the Magic Wand. She ran her fingers along the smooth spiralling surface of the blown glass.

<<

Dead Girl was lying on a soft bed of sand next to the Old River Thames. She was just this torso with fuzzy blue extensions. All she had was her fanny-pack. She was surrounded by glitter and shiny beads of glass.

There was this tent on the strand with a crisp red and white pennant fluttering in the breeze. It was guarded by this sullen Black Dog. He was lying on the sand licking the blood from his paws.

Someone was coming towards her. It was this Freak Boy. He was crawling along the ground. He was dragging himself along on his knuckles. Dead Girl could see from the way his Joe Bloggs jeans trailed flat along the ground that he had these withered legs. Freak Boy was breathing hard. He had this barrel chest and these big powerful shoulders. He was wearing this hooded grey top that partly covered his face.

Freak Boy loomed over her. He had this gaunt face with pink little eyes. He had all these pimples on his cheeks and fluffy white hairs on his chin.

Dead Girl dug deep inside and found the blue light. It was growing there where she hurt the most. It grew out of her shame at even being alive. She wasn't going to let Freak Boy do anything to her. She didn't care that her Extra Special Powers hadn't worked on Black Dog. He was just an animal. Freak Boy was human. Things would be different.

Freak Boy reached out to touch her fanny-pack. Dead Girl sparkled with a furious blue light.

>>

Dead Girl was sitting next to this lake on the Heath of London with her back against an old silver birch tree. She was wearing her old white hospital gown with her fanny-pack on underneath. Her thin little legs glowed blue.

It was a cool night. The stars were laid out on the purple sky above her. The moon shone down on the lake.

The flowers of the water lilies were opening. Their petals were big and white and square. They opened right up under the moon.

Dead Girl brought the end of the Magic Wand up to her lips. She blew down the open glass nozzle. The musical sound of her breath reverberated over the Heath of London.

It was time for her to tell Fairy Sugadaddy she had found Witch Doctor. She knew where he was hiding. It was time for

Witch Doctor to pay for what he had done.

(4) Abortion

>>

Dead Girl sat on the edge of the lake on the Heath of London next to the old silver birch tree. She was wearing her white hospital gown and she had her fanny-pack on underneath. Her legs were made of blue light that shone over the water.

The water lilies were opening under the light of the moon. They opened right up. There were these beetles flying out of the flowers of the water lilies. The big white petals of the flowers turned pink and fell into the water. There was pollen in the night air.

Dead Girl clutched the Magic Wand. Its glass was cool under her hand. She had told Fairy Sugadaddy where Witch Doctor was hiding. She had sent him a message.

She tried to think of a wish to have come true.

<<

Dead Girl was this little ghost made of blue light. She was flickering at the edges like a naked candle flame. Only the middle bit of her was made out of flesh and blood. Only her torso was real.

Dead Girl was drifting through the Heath of London. She was in the woods with trees all around and branches covering the sky. She was looking for Witch Doctor. She was lost.

The ground was all parched and dry and cracked. There was no breeze. She was hot. The only thing she had on was her fanny-pack. Dead Girl had a sudden thought. She stopped and unzipped the pocket of her fanny-pack. It was empty. There was nothing inside.

Dead Girl panicked. She wanted to go back. She wanted her little black and white photo, the one with the torn edge. She wanted to touch it. She wanted to stroke the picture of the little baby. But she couldn't. It was gone.

Freak Boy must have taken the photo when she wasn't looking. It must have been when she used her Extra Special Powers on him. Dead Girl started to cry. Her tears were made of blue light.

She tried to remember what had happened. Freak Boy had reached her when she was lying on the strand of the Old River Thames. He had reached out for her fanny-pack. But she had used her Extra Special Powers on him. She had changed herself into what he secretly wanted. She became his Fish Girl and laughed at the desire in his eyes. Freak Boy had whimpered and gazed at her in fear. He had been transfixed.

That was when Dead Girl had found something at the back of his mind. It was deeper than his secret desire for Fish Girl. He didn't even know it was there. It was this radio connection. Dead Girl found the trace of an old signal. She decided to follow its trail back through the atmosphere. She wanted to see how far her Extra Special Powers would take her.

So while Freak Boy was distracted by her Fish Girl act she had pulled in the source of the signal. She had pulled it across the open skies of London Town until she could see it inside the mind's eye of Freak Boy. She was thrilled when she saw the vision of Witch Doctor. His white candyfloss hair floated above him like a vapour cloud and his eyes glowed a deep blue. It was a live image. She had to be careful. But she was so excited to find out where he lived.

Witch Doctor was crouching on the ground. He was in a damp place surrounded by patches of earth and swaying green leaves. He was wrapped in his big black coat but underneath he was naked. Dead Girl could see his loins beneath the tuft of hair on his belly. She could see the claws in his toes. He was moving around on his hands and knees. He was muttering something to himself.

Dead Girl could see that he had his Magic Wand. It was made of glass and spiralled round on itself like a snake. He took it and used the nozzle to draw some lines in the earth at his feet. He drew this circuit diagram and Dead Girl felt that it spelt out her name. She was frightened but kept on looking at the vision.

Witch Doctor put the Magic Wand on the ground and pulled a little black bag from his pocket. It was a drawstring bag made of black leather. Witch Doctor opened the bag and scattered its contents over the diagram at his feet. All these precious stones tumbled on to the earth. Dead Girl gasped. There were flashing green emeralds and deep red rubies and little white diamonds. She wanted them. There were eleven in total. She felt they belonged to her.

Witch Doctor began moving the precious stones around the circuit diagram. He moved them into a funny pattern, sat back to look at them and then leaned in to rearrange them once again. He was chanting now but Dead Girl didn't understand the words. She was hurting too much. Her stumps were enflamed. She was aching inside.

She began to pull back from the image of Witch Doctor. It was too painful to carry on looking. He was doing something to her. Somehow he was affecting her thoughts and feelings. She pushed the image away. Witch Doctor looked up and smiled. He smiled right at her. She was ashamed. She saw where he was hiding. It was in this little cave under a hill shaped like a big pregnant belly. The stars shone down on the hill. It was covered in grass. She identified the coordinates of the place in her mind. It was on the Heath of London.

Dead Girl had got rid of Freak Boy and come to the Heath of London. But he must have taken her photo out of her fanny-pack while she was inside his mind. So now she was lost in the woods with nothing to console her.

Dead Girl dried her eyes. She decided to go on. She wanted to check that the vision she'd had of Witch Doctor was true. She wanted to find out if he really lived under a hill. Then she could get back to Fairy Sugadaddy and tell him her wish.

>>

Dead Girl sat by a silver birch tree next to a lake on the Heath of London. She was wearing this white hospital gown. It was cold. The night was coming to an end.

Dead Girl kept unzipping the empty pocket of her fanny-pack. She tried to count the stars. She used the glass nozzle of the Magic Wand to scrape some bark from off the tree.

Fairy Sugadaddy had still not got back to her.

This breeze came up and dislodged some of the leaves of the birch. The chrome rings in the branches made a clinking sound. The green and golden leaves dropped on to the surface of the lake.

Dead Girl shivered and got into the water. Her legs glowed blue under the stars.

It didn't matter. She couldn't think of a wish to have come true anyway.

<<

Dead Girl was fighting her way through all these brambles and sharp twigs on the Heath of London. She was battling through the undergrowth. The only thing she had on was her little fanny-pack.

It was dark. There were grey clouds sliding over the moon. Dead Girl was just this torso. The rest of her was made out of blue light.

She came to this clearing and saw the dark mass of a hill up ahead. It was in the shape of a woman's pregnant belly. The clouds parted. It was outlined against the moon.

Dead Girl saw there was a light shining at the bottom of the hill. It was a yellow light tinged at the edges with shades of green and red. She moved closer and saw an electric light shining out of an open window. The window was set into the side of the hill behind the leaves of this bush. Dead Girl crept up and moved the leaves aside. The window was oval-shaped and hinged into the earth at the sides. It was pushed half-open like a port hole. Dead Girl could see that the pane of glass was decorated. On the side facing her it was lined with a thick black paint. But on the side facing inwards it was beaded and lined with a trace-work of lead.

Dead Girl tugged at the window with both hands so that it swivelled open to its full extent. The yellow light spilled out from under the hill. Dead Girl poked her head through the gap. She saw an ornately decorated bedroom lined with arched doorways leading further back into the hill.

The room was empty. Suspended from the high vaulted earthen ceiling by a metal chain was a chandelier of shaded electric lights. Each bulb was screwed into a perforated silver clasp and ringed with a drop curtain of coloured glass beads. The shadows cast on the walls were tinged with yellow and green and red.

Dead Girl touched her fanny-pack. She didn't even think about how scared she was. Instead she climbed through the open window and shut it after her.

Dead Girl found herself crouched on the lid of a square-shaped box directly beneath the window. The wooden box was edged in brass and painted with geometric patterns of white and pink flowers. Next to it in the corner of the room was a brass four-poster bed. On top of its snow white quilt were these white pillows spattered with red dye at their tips.

The walls were made of dark earth and the floor was set with a mosaic of midnight blue tiles cut with swirling yellow star-shaped motifs.

One archway to the left of Dead Girl opposite the foot of the bed was set with a half-open slatted wooden door. Beyond was silence and darkness. The other archway in the far right-hand corner of the room opened into a shadowy corridor. Dead Girl thought it must be a walk-in closet or something.

The sunken chamber was warm and still. Dead Girl thought this must be the place where Witch Doctor lived. But how could she be sure? She remembered the precious stones she had seen in her vision. They had flashed with a hidden fire. They had seemed to wink at her. Where could they be kept?

Dead Girl looked under the bed but there was nothing there. She could feel her heart beating wildly. She felt under the mattress but there was nothing there either. Her breathing sounded very loud. Dead Girl pulled up the lid of the box and gasped when she saw Witch Doctor's Magic Wand inside. It was all made of glass and twisted around on itself just like she remembered it. It was lying at the bottom of the chest next to this black bag.

Dead Girl looked closely at the bag. It was made of leather and it had a brass clasp. It was much bigger than the little bag she had seen in her vision. She wanted to check what was inside the bag. But what if Witch Doctor came into the room? She thought about it and realised she didn't care. She released the clasp on the bag and opened it up. She was still half expecting to see all these sparkling gems inside just like in her vision. But instead she saw these hunks of dead meat.

Dead Girl felt sick. She nearly passed out. She recognised what was inside the bag. The grey flesh with the coarse black hairs? That was her skin. And all the red meat around the cut white bone? That was her flesh.

Dead Girl was very angry. She hauled the bag out of the chest and tipped its contents on to the bed. All these body parts spilled out on to the white quilt. Suddenly there was real blood on the pillows. Dead Girl saw her arms and her hands and her fingers. She saw her lips and her teeth. Her own sightless green eyes stared up at her.

Dead Girl picked up her head. It was cold and heavy and covered in all this long black hair. There was a hole in its forehead. She screwed the head back on. The blue light acted as a kind of solvent. It made sure that her head stayed stuck to her neck. She rolled her tongue over her teeth. She sniffed the damp air. She shook her hair all over the place. The head stayed firmly in place.

Dead Girl was ecstatic. She put her arms back on. The blue light showed up at the seams in the shoulder joints. She swung her arms and flicked her wrists. She clenched and unclenched her fists. Everything seemed to work fine.

Dead Girl had nearly put herself back together again. She had found all the parts of her that had gone missing except for her legs. The legs on her body were still made out of the blue light. They looked even more forlorn now she had got the rest of herself back. They were shivering and flickering like a bad television picture. Dead Girl climbed up on the bed and looked everywhere for her missing legs. She looked under the pillows and felt under the quilt. But she just couldn't find them.

That was when Witch Doctor appeared. He came out of the shadows at the back of the archway leading into the closet. His hair floated above his head in thin white cotton-candy wisps and his eyes glowed with a hypnotic blue light. He was wearing his long black coat and it was covered in these beautiful pink petals. Dead Girl thought he looked like a bride-groom. She was still kneeling on the bed in the corner of the room. She was transfixed by the sudden appearance of Witch Doctor. He was all naked and dirty under his coat. He smelt of dung. He had these long sharp nails on his fingers and toes.

He came up to the bed and he rolled up his sleeves. He was looking down at her. She shrank from him until she was lying on her back. What was he going to do? She wanted to disappear but she couldn't. She tried to get away from Witch Doctor but it was like she was pinned to the bed and couldn't move. There was only one thing to do. She would have to put him off with her Extra Special Powers. She would have to do a number on him and hope that it worked.

Witch Doctor looked her up and down like she was a slab of meat or something.

Dead girl shivered. She felt ashamed of the blue light which showed through at the seams all over her body. She wanted to cover her pathetic weakly glowing legs.

Witch Doctor's eyes were cold. Dead Girl had the sudden chilling conviction that he had expected to find her here. He had let her go and now he had brought her back. Wasn't that it? There was something inside her he wanted. Dead Girl thought that he knew all about her Extra Special Powers and that was what he had come for. He was expecting the blue sparks he had injected into her belly in the Beautiful Person Lounge to have grown into this Little Thing. That was what he was expecting. Dead Girl instantly became very calm. She knew what Witch Doctor wanted. That was enough. She was going to have to be very clever to trick him. But she was sure it could be done.

>>

Dead Girl was floating among the water lilies in the lake on the Heath of London. Her white hospital gown billowed out on the water. She held the Magic Wand over her chest. These dead leaves were blowing all around her.

She closed her eyes. She moved her legs against the coarse stems of the water lilies where they were underwater. Her legs were only made of blue light. She kicked and went under.

Fairy Sugadaddy didn't care about her.

Her head felt like it was bursting with emptiness. She breathed out and drifted down through the murk. Her fanny-pack felt loose. She let herself go all the way down towards the bottom of the lake.

<<

Dead Girl was lying on this beautiful white bed that was all covered with her own blood. Her joints ached. She was spilling all this blue light at the seams from where she had put herself back together. Her legs were still made of blue light and she had tucked them underneath her. She couldn't move.

Witch Doctor was standing over her in his long black coat. He was looking at her with his head tilted to one side. There was a grin on his white face. His long toe nails made a clicking sound on the floor tiles as he moved closer. He was panting. The nails on his fingers were long and hard and sharp.

Dead Girl was using her Extra Special Powers on him. She was concentrating hard. She was trying to pretend to be the one thing he loved so much he kept it hidden from all the world. He jumped back when Tattooed Lady suddenly pulsed out of her like a solid hologram. He gave a little yelp. But all she could do was laugh.

Witch Doctor stood there in shock. Something was happening to his mind but he refused to accept what it was. He could not speak the name of his secret desire like Crazy Lady had done.

Dead Girl lay on the bed doing her Tattooed Lady act. She was naked except for her fanny-pack, which was pushed up against her breasts. Her belly was all fat and lumpy. It was big and swollen. It felt really heavy and was pressing down on her. It was like there was something coiled inside. The strange thing was that her belly skin was all brown and hard. It was bristling with these soft spines which looked like big hairs. It was like she had this big hairy belly.

Witch Doctor was very agitated. Dead Girl kept pretending to be Tattooed Lady as he leaned in close to her grotesque belly. She could see there was this old wound in her belly. It was a cut. The two halves of the skin either side of the cut had been stitched back together with thick black thread. The stitches ran in a jagged line from the top to the bottom of her belly.

Witch Doctor leaned in close. His breath smelt of alcohol. The blue fire in his eyes was deep inside. He was a shadow now obscuring the light from the ceiling. He flexed his fingers and his glittering nails made a skittering sound. Then he sliced through all the stitches just like that. It was very quick. It was painless. Witch Doctor's finger nails were very sharp. All this water and seaweed and stuff gushed out of her. It soaked the bed. She stank of old fish. Witch Doctor didn't care. He was delving around inside her belly with both hands. He was hurting her. Dead Girl gritted her teeth. She could feel him pushing and pulling deep inside.

That's when Dead Girl really let him have it. She still had her little ghost legs tucked up beneath her. They were made of blue light. She concentrated on the light and pushed it up into her belly. Now she made the light into the thing that Witch Doctor wanted most of all.

Witch Doctor pulled this weird Little Thing out of her belly. It was made out of blue light but he didn't notice. He had found what he was looking for. He held it in both hands. The Little Thing was an old man the size of a baby with all this long white hair. It had wrinkled skin on its face and its eyes were half-closed. Its mouth was this bubble of wet flesh. It was squawking and giggling.

Witch Doctor looked very serious. He was taking deep breaths. It was like he was in shock.

Dead Girl sat up on the bed. She did this thing with her mind where she cut the cord of blue light that still connected her to the Little Thing in Witch Doctor's hands. It was easy. She didn't know why she had never done it before. She had made this spectre and now she was cutting it loose. She took down great lungfuls of air.

Witch Doctor was moving away from her back through the archway to his closet. He was carrying the Little Thing as if it were a prize. The lights in the ceiling were shaded with glass beads. They looked like veils. She thought the lights must be weeping. She slid off the bed and crawled after Witch Doctor. She wanted to know his secret.

Witch Doctor's closet was at the end of this snaking tunnel. The closet was a narrow space with a high ceiling made of stained glass. The glass was all in the shape of hundreds of flowers. They were of varying shapes and sizes and colours. Some had big blue ridged petals. Others had delicate little red petals. The glass flowers were lit from within. It looked like they were growing from the ceiling.

Dead Girl marvelled at how beautiful it all was. The last of the blue light which made up her legs looked very weak and feeble now. She felt faint and found it hard to breathe.

Dominating the closet was this open-framework four-storey tower made of wrought iron and laminated glass. It stretched from the floor to the ceiling. The core of the tower consisted of a four-sided column of open square-shaped shelves. Each of the shelves contained a rack of glass specimen jars. The jars were all filled with this thick red liquid and covered with a muslin cloth.

Witch Doctor had strapped himself into a leather harness and was rising up the outside of the tower. The noise was like one of those old lifts. There was this hydraulic pulley system next to all the glass flowers in the ceiling and it was pulling him up by these metal cables. He was still carrying the weird Little Thing and his black coat flapped in the air.

The noise of the pulley stopped when he got to the top storey. He swayed in the air as he reached out and selected a jar from one of the shelves. He pulled back the cloth lid and plopped the Little Thing inside. It dropped into the red liquid and Dead Girl saw its horrible grinning little face magnified by the glass. There was this brief smell of ammonia mixed with bananas. Witch Doctor covered the glass again and sealed the cloth tight round the rim with an elastic band. Then he began to write out a label.

Dead Girl looked at all the jars of red liquid stacked in the tower. They all seemed to have these little wizened creatures preserved inside. The creatures looked like the Little Thing she had projected except they were made out of real flesh and blood. It was like Witch Doctor was collecting them. There must be hundreds and hundreds of them. She

squinted to read the label Witch Doctor had stuck on the jar. It said 'Horus 1000'.

Witch Doctor pressed a button on his harness and the hydraulics started up again. He started to come down. He was relaxed now. He was laughing to himself. Dead Girl didn't move. She was still looking at the Little Thing trapped in the glass jar. It was made out of blue light but Witch Doctor hadn't noticed. He obviously thought it was something that was made out of nerves and skin and blood. Dead Girl saw the spectre open its mouth wide. It was shrieking from inside the red liquid but nobody could hear. It didn't matter. The Little Thing inside the jar popped like a soap bubble and was gone.

Witch Doctor had got caught up in the cables. The hydraulics had jammed. That was when he saw Dead Girl down below. She was no longer doing the Tattooed Lady routine. He shouted at her but she ignored him. He thought he had taken her Extra Special Powers away from her to add to his collection. But he hadn't. She had used her Extra Special Powers to trick him. He dangled helplessly above her. He didn't realise there was nothing inside that last jar.

Dead Girl ran back to the bedroom but now it was all different. It was just this dingy cave hacked out of the ground. There was a naked ten watt bulb hanging from this low ceiling by a twisted length of flex and in the corner was a stained yellow mattress and a screwed up plastic bag. The ground was sticky. It was covered in all these crushed brown seed-pods. They were in these layers. The ones on top were all bristly and springy and the ones underneath were all slimy and rotting. Dead Girl walked carefully over to the window. It was just this sheet of polythene tacked over a hole in the wall.

Everything was changed. She gave the room one last glance. Opposite the mattress was this open door leading into a dark passage-way. It smelt of damp. On the other side of the room where the walk-in closet had been there was just this pathetic wooden cupboard. The door had a full-length mirror on the front. It had swung wide open to reveal Witch Doctor's black coat hanging from a rail. Piled on the floor of the cupboard were all these old papers. There were Court circulars, kiddie porn magazines, death certificates and skull X-rays.

Dead Girl reached for her fanny-pack. It was underneath her white hospital gown. Suddenly she had got her old clothes back again. That was when Dead Girl realised she had done what Fairy Sugadaddy wanted. She had found where Witch Doctor was hiding. The polythene window fluttered in its earthen frame and this cool breeze wafted into the damp room. It was time to leave.

Underneath the window was this old cardboard box. The Magic Wand lay inside. It hadn't changed. It was still made of this twisted and braided glass. It looked like these two snakes made of crystal that were curled up around each other. It shone in the light.

Dead Girl hitched her hospital gown up around her hips. Her ghost legs were still giving off this soft blue glow. She climbed back out through the window on to the Heath of London. It was early morning. She had spent the whole night underneath the hill.

Dead Girl walked away from the hill. She ached on the inside. The sun was peeping through the green leaves overhead. She was carrying this twisted glass rod. It was hollow with a nozzle at one end. She knew it was really a Magic Wand.

>>

Dead Girl was falling down through the water in this lake on the Heath of London. It was a deep lake. She was wearing this white hospital gown over her fanny-pack. Her legs were made of this thin blue light. It was dark all around.

Dead Girl had this Magic Wand made of twisted glass. She was holding on to it ever so tight.

Every so often she would bump into the thick stems of all these water lilies. She would kick against them to make sure she kept on going down through the deep water.

Eventually she landed on this mud-shelf. This was where the water lilies were rooted. There were big fat seedpods all around. They were brown and bristly and ready to burst.

Over the edge of the mud-shelf the ground gave way to become a sheer drop. There was this chasm. Dead Girl peered into it. She had never seen anything so deep. Far away at the bottom of the watery chasm it was very dark. She could see this dark light.

Dead Girl wished she could go to the dark light. That was her wish. She wanted to disappear and start all over again.

That was when Fairy Sugadaddy came back. He spoke to her inside her head. His voice was like an amplified echo. It was much clearer than before.

Fairy Sugadaddy soothed her. He said that she had landed on the lip of a Silly Black Hole and that the dark light at the bottom of the chasm was what they call a Singularity. He said he would take her there. But first she had to go to a place called the Temple of Osiris.

(5) Crash

>>

Dead Girl had been through the Singularity at the bottom of the lake on the Heath of London and was trying to get out of this Silly Black Hole. She was being carried along by this torrent of boiling water. She couldn't get a grip. Everything was soft and slippery.

Her hospital gown was in tatters. She had lost the Magic Wand. Even her fanny-pack was gone.

The water surged over Dead Girl's head. She was tumbling through all this loose mud. There was a silence in her head where Fairy Sugadaddy used to be. He was gone now and he wasn't coming back. She knew that much. The skin had grown over the hole in her head.

Dead Girl wanted to slow down. She wanted to get back to her life.

<<

Dead Girl was falling down through the dark water in this lake on the Heath of London. She was wearing her hospital gown with her fanny-pack on underneath and she was holding this Magic Wand made of glass.

Fairy Sugadaddy was guiding her. He was whispering soft words at the back of her head.

Dead Girl landed on this mud-shelf with these big fat seed-pods all around. The jolt went through her legs. Fairy Sugadaddy said this was the opening into a Black Hole. She massaged the pain in her knees as she looked down over the mud-shelf into this watery chasm. That was when she realised she had got her legs back. They were thick and strong and hairy.

She tried to remember how she had got her legs back. She couldn't think. The memory was dim. Fairy Sugadaddy had taken her to this place called the Temple of Osiris. It was like a big cave full of rubbish. Her legs were lying on the ground.

She crept towards the edge of the mud-shelf and peered over it. Far away at the bottom of the chasm was this dark light. Fairy Sugadaddy said it was called a Singularity. It was where she wanted to go. But there was just one problem. Witch Doctor wanted to go there as well.

Fairy Sugadaddy said she would have to leave part of herself in the water at the mud-shelf to guard against Witch Doctor. She would have to split up. So that's what she did. She used her Extra Special Powers and pretended to be Tattooed Lady again because she knew that would confuse Witch Doctor the most. She made Tattooed Lady out of the blue light she still had deep inside and cut her loose just like she had with the Little Thing.

Tattooed Lady crouched down on the mud-shelf with her eyes wide open. Dead Girl gave her the Magic Wand to hold. She thought she might need it to frighten Witch Doctor and ward him off. Tattooed Lady grinned through the water.

Fairy Sugadaddy said it was time for Dead Girl to go. So she jumped off the mud-shelf into the Silly Black Hole. The muddy water slid past her. She was going very fast. She was aiming for the dark light there at the bottom of the lake. She could see that it was very far away.

>>

Dead Girl was caught in a Silly Black Hole at the bottom of this lake on the Heath of London. She was trying to find a way out but the muddy water was battering her from all sides. She no longer knew which way was up or down. Her white hospital gown was in shreds.

She closed her eyes. She tried to remember what Fairy Sugadaddy had said. He had taken her to the Temple of Osiris and something had happened. She had lost nearly all of her Extra Special Powers. The blue light had started fading away inside of her from that moment on. Now she could only use it to make the spectres she remembered from the past. She couldn't pretend to be new people anymore. That's what Fairy Sugadaddy had said.

Dead Girl's ears were bleeding. She was grinding the enamel from her teeth. There were these painful little rashes flaring up all over her skin.

What else had happened at the Temple of Osiris? She couldn't remember. Someone else had been there. Hadn't he been dangerous or something? She had reached for the blue light one last time. She had used her Extra Special Powers to frighten him off. She had laughed at him. Wasn't that it? She had pretended to be one last person. She had become this big person clad head to toe in rubber. Who exactly was that?

Something tough and hard brushed against Dead Girl's fingers. It was this gnarly root growing out of the mud.

Some last part of Dead Girl hidden deep inside took over and made her grab the root. The big person she had become in the Temple of Osiris was in charge now. Dead

Girl sighed with relief and let go. Her Extra Special Powers faded away to nothing. She was all that was left of the blue light now.

She thought she must be a Dreaming Girl.

<<

Dead Girl was sliding towards this Singularity at the bottom of a Silly Black Hole. She was moving very fast. She was sat in the back-seat of this big car in just her white hospital gown and her fanny-pack. The car was painted black. It had smoked glass windows and lots of armour. It was what they call a Merc and it was out of control.

Dead Girl couldn't see who was driving. It was very shadowy inside the car and all she could see out the window was this long thread of water flashing past. Fairy Sugadaddy said it was the Old River Seine in the City of Paris. He was guiding her now.

Then everything went dark as the Merc shot into the mouth of this tunnel. Time slowed down as the car got faster. Dead Girl gripped the edge of her seat and pressed her feet against the floor. She was bracing herself for a crash when this brilliant white light went off in front of the car from the end of the tunnel. It flooded the windscreen so she couldn't see what was going on. She closed her eyes and felt the wheels of the car go into this skid.

Fairy Sugadaddy was whispering in the back of her head. He said that the Singularity was not far away and she had to get through it. She felt exhausted. Her metabolism had seized up. She was very sluggish. The light faded away and she opened her eyes to see this pillar in the central reservation of the roadway coming to meet the car. Her bowels refused to work. She was full of shit. She felt very very heavy. She felt like she was gaining weight. She couldn't move.

The pillar hit the Merc between the front headlights and the car buckled. Dead Girl was thrown forward into the seat in front as the windscreen shattered and all these little pieces of glass showered over her like confetti. The force of the impact went into her chest. Then she was thrown back as the car rebounded from the pillar and sailed through the air. It was like she was in this funfair waltzer as the car span round and she felt sick. Then there was this jolt which came up through her spine as the Merc landed back on the roadway facing the way it had come.

She shat herself. It was all warm and sticky inside the hospital gown she was wearing. She was in a state of shock. The Merc was a wreck. Its horn was blaring too late and there was all this steam coming out of its busted radiator. But all she could think was that it was a good job she still had her fanny-pack on.

She looked out of the crumpled door to see this surveillance camera mounted on the roof of the tunnel. It had these tiny gripping feet and it was moving round to track her. She squinted up at the lens of the camera. It was round and dark. She thought the Old King must be watching her on closed circuit television somewhere to check she really was dead. She imagined him sitting at a leather desk in his dressing gown with the Royal Crest or whatever stitched on his pocket. He was looking very furtive. There was the ghost of a smile on his lips.

Dead Girl thought about using her Extra Special Powers. She found some more of the blue light from somewhere inside herself and she pretended to be the Lost Princess. That would show the Old King. That would teach him to laugh at her. That's what she thought. She rested her eyes. She imagined how shocked the Old King would be to see his Lost Princess lying in the tunnel. She saw him crying and whining. She laughed as she coughed up some blood…

What is your name again? Someone wants to know. It's important. What is your name? You don't know your name. You don't have a name. You are dreaming you are no longer alive. You are this Dreaming Girl who thought she was a Dead Girl. That's how it is.

> *You are bleeding. There is the taste of blood in your throat...*

>>

Dreaming Girl was coming out of this Silly Black Hole at the bottom of a lake on the Heath of London. She was using this tough old root to climb up through all this loose mud. She pulled herself up hand over hand and kept helping herself along with big powerful kicks of her legs. She was tired.

Dreaming Girl was rising through the thick muddy water. She was covered in this protective gear from head to toe. It was a white rubber body suit with a hood a bit like a deep-sea diver's outfit. The suit was partially inflated with air and it was cinched in at the waist by this green leather strap thing. The strap thing was buckled up really tight. It was what they call a dildo harness.

Dreaming Girl had this little metal pipe coming out of the hood at the mouth. It was like so she could breathe. She unzipped her eye-slots. There was sun-light coming down through the water from above. Below her was this dark light at the bottom of a chasm.

Dreaming Girl saw that the root she was holding on to was connected to all these other roots. There was this network of stems in the mud and water. Climbing was easier now. She found foot-holds and hand-holds. Soon she poked her head through a crack in this sloping mud-shelf. There were all these rotting seed-pods in the water and brown leaves and dead water lilies all around the place.

Dreaming Girl hauled herself out on to the mud-shelf where the water lilies were growing. There was no sign of Tattooed Lady or the Magic Wand. She looked back down through the crack in the ground. The roots of the water lilies went down through the mud and the water. Far away down below caught in some of the stems was this Dead Girl. She was wearing a ragged white hospital gown that billowed in the water. Her skin was glowing with this shimmering blue light.

Dreaming Girl stopped looking. She didn't want to think about the Dead Girl. She didn't want to think about what had happened at the Temple of Osiris. She remembered that Freak Boy had come back. Only this time he had been wielding a knife. Dead Girl had been in danger. That was why Dreaming Girl had been called up. She had frightened Freak Boy off Dead Girl. It was Dreaming Girl who had been this spectre made out of blue light.

But now Dead Girl was made out of the blue light and Dreaming Girl was real. Wasn't that it?

Dreaming Girl closed her eyes and swam back up to the surface of the lake.

<<

Dead Girl was lying in the middle of this Singularity at the bottom of a Silly Black Hole. She was alone in the back of this stupid Merc which was all smashed up. All she had on was her fanny-pack and her white hospital gown. There was a deep pain in her chest and she could hardly breathe.

Dead Girl did this thing where she separated from Lost Princess and got out of the car. She looked down at Lost Princess. She was just this hologram made out of blue light. Dead Girl felt lighter. Fairy Sugadaddy was still saying things to her in the back of her head. His voice was very calm. He said she had to get into the Antigravity Universe which was behind the crash scene at the Singularity. So she left Lost Princess flickering on the back seat of the wrecked Merc and drifted across the empty roadway towards the central reservation. There were these orange sodium lamps set in the walls of the tunnel. They were flashing and buzzing. She was looking for the pillar which the car had crashed into. She used her sense of touch to find it. It was like she didn't trust her eyesight or something.

There was this vehicle coming towards her from the mouth of the tunnel. It was like it was following her. She could see the twin pools of its headlights and hear its engine. It was a big white vehicle and it was moving very fast.

Her hands closed on this door handle that was set in the pillar. She worked it and the door in the pillar opened. She stepped through into the space beyond and the door sprang shut behind her.

Dead Girl found herself on this old stairwell like something out of a multi-storey car park except it stretched to infinity up and down in both directions. Fairy Sugadaddy said it was the Antigravity Universe. The square walls were made of red brick and the stairs were made of concrete. There were cigarette butts and old plastic bags on the landing.

She moved up to the next landing and opened the door a crack. It looked out of the central reservation pillar on to the crashed Merc with the Lost Princess lying in the back with her legs like a broken doll made of blue light. There was all this glass rubble on the road but this time it was quiet. The car horn was not making any kind of a sound. Fairy Sugadaddy said she was looking out on to a parallel universe which was only a bit different from the one she had just left. She let the door close and moved on.

Dead Girl checked the view from lots of different doors as she raced up and down the stairwell. One thing at the Singularity always stayed the same. The Lost Princess was always lying in the back of the crashed Merc. But little things would change. Sometimes she was on the left seat rather than the right seat. Other times the Merc was facing in the direction it was originally going in rather than back the way it had come. One time the Merc was on fire and there was all this thick black smoke in the tunnel.

Another thing that also stayed the same was the other vehicle racing up to the scene. Dead Girl could see after a few times that is was an ambulance. It had a red cross painted on its white side and its windows were all blacked out. It usually turned up at the crash scene and stopped next to the Merc

with its engine running. For a while nothing happened. There was just this electric light leaking from the gaps in its blacked-out windows.

Fairy Sugadaddy told Dead Girl that Witch Doctor was in the back of the ambulance with Tattooed Lady and she was stopping him from getting past the Singularity. She was giving him what he deserved with his own Magic Wand. It was the same in every parallel universe Dead Girl looked at. Witch Doctor could not follow Dead Girl into the Antigravity Universe. He was trapped.

Dead Girl was unbelievably happy. She thought she would faint with euphoria. She sat down on one of the concrete steps in the Antigravity Universe and took these deep breaths. Fairy Sugadaddy said she could go back to any parallel universe she wanted now. He had granted her wish and taken her this far. The rest was up to her. He started to croon an old song deep inside her head. It was like a lullaby. But she couldn't catch the words. It was like there was all this static on the line. Fairy Sugadaddy was fading out.

Dead Girl lifted her fingers to her forehead to feel the hole in her head. But there was just this knotted lump there now. The skin must have knitted back together.

It was time to go. Dead Girl lifted up her white hospital gown and undid her fanny-pack. She ran the belt through her fingers until she got to the little purse. She unzipped it one last time. It was still empty. It was made out of mock crocodile skin. Dead Girl left it on the step. She didn't need it anymore. She got up and opened the nearest door.

Dreaming Girl walked out of the pillar in the central reservation. The emergency lights from the ambulance cast red and blue shadows against the roof and the sides of the tunnel. Lost Princess was lying in the back of the crashed Merc. Her skin was glowing with this blue light. There was blood coming out of her ear and she was shivering. She had these cuts and bruises on her face.

Sitting next to the wreck was the ambulance with the blacked-out windows. Its engine was still running. It was emitting this low throbbing noise.

Dead Girl moved away from the crash scene. There was the sound of rushing water coming from the end of the tunnel. She began to walk towards it. The road surface was wet under her feet. There was water dripping down the sides of the tunnel. The lights were fizzing out one by one. It was becoming dark.

Dead Girl slowed down. There was mud on the ground. She crept along. Before she knew what had happened she was swept off her feet by this torrent of water. It boiled and coursed all around her. It completely carried her off.

>>

Dreaming Girl was swimming in this lake on the Heath of London. She was dressed in a white rubber body-suit with this hood covering her head and a dildo harness round her waist. She was moving with powerful strokes towards the bank.

The stars were out in the sky. Dreaming Girl got out by this bare silver birch tree. It had these gnarled branches that stretched out over the calm water.

Dreaming Girl pulled the metal pipe from her mouth and spat this green slimy water on to the ground. The air was cool on the back of her throat. She remembered what had happened in the Temple of Osiris. Freak Boy had attacked her with a knife. He had stabbed her in the throat. The blood had come up unbidden. It had been hot and thick and urgent. But she had fought him off.

She took off her hood and shook out her hair. It sprang out around her head. It was thick glossy hair composed of very many different coloured strands. There were blonde strands, grey strands and black strands. There were strands of brown, auburn, red and every colour in between.

There was this clinking sound coming from the tree. Dreaming Girl could see the chrome rings fitted to one of the branches. She moved closer. Some of the silver bark had been scraped off the bole of the tree.

Dreaming Girl took off her gloves. The sensation had returned to her fingertips. She traced the edges of the dark wood that had been revealed by the missing strips of bark. There were these letters that had been etched into the tree. Together they spelled out a name…

You are Dreaming Girl. You are dreaming you have come back from the dead. You are bleeding. What is your name? Somebody wants to know. You are flying through the air over Whitechapel. You are going to land on the roof of this big hospital. It is coming up fast. What is it? Somebody wants to know your name. You are inside this emergency helicopter. You remember your name.

Someone is leaning in close beneath the whirring blades. They have their ear to your lips. You say it. You give them your name.

Ada 'Babyface' Wilson. That is your name.

JOHN EDWARD LAWSON

LOCATION:
Hyattsville, MD

STYLE OF BIZARRO:
The Horrible

BOOKS BY LAWSON:

Pocket Full of Loose Razorblades
Last Burn in Hell
Sin Conductor (forthcoming)
The Troublesome Amputee
The Horrible
Psych Noir
The Scars are Complimentary
Tempting Disaster (as editor)
Sick: An Anthology of Illness (as editor)
Of Flesh and Hunger: Tales of the Ultimate Taboo (as editor)

DESCRIPTION: John Edward Lawson writes slithering wet things that compliment your complexion. His focus on hyper-absurdity, moral ineptitude, and profound violence stems from the observation that "life is beautiful." The grimy postindustrial storyscapes his characters are trapped in have nothing to do with real life, because "reality is for people who can't handle fiction."

INTERESTS: Serial killers, pathology, political nonfiction, games, film, exercise, marketing, hiking, travel, cathartic hellmongering, mental illness, massage, meditation, yoga, chin na joint breaking techniques, porn, watching people bicker.

INFLUENCES: Chuck Palahniuk, Skinny Puppy, Guy Maddin, Kurt Vonnegut, Shinya Tsukamoto, Dissecting Table, Clive Barker, David Lynch, The Jesus and Mary Chain, John Waters, William Burroughs, Godflesh, David Cronenberg, Allen Ginsberg, 1980's synth pop, David Fincher, Bret Easton Ellis, Oneiroid Psychosis.

WEBSITE:
www.johnlawson.org

Truth in Ruins

One concealed by many
Unable to understand
With no ideas of yesterday
There's only forever today
A hall of broken mirrors
And masks behind masks
Without the darkness
There is no revelation
—Leif Hansen, *Mysterium Tremendum*

CHAPTER ONE

Overhead, the oil spill stretching from horizon to horizon allows no light through, not directly. The foul vapors deforming the sky are backlit by what could be stars, moon, or sun. It doesn't matter any longer because nobody can remember what those things look like, or how they could possibly affect life on Earth's surface.

Humid air sweeps over ruined buildings in persistent cough-gusts. The weather today is the same as it is every day: too indecisive to rain completely. Instead, a thin arterial spray of dark liquid hangs in the air, gently drizzling, saturating everything with its chemical odor.

Somewhere in the distance a lone vehicle can be heard splashing through puddles. Burned Church Road doesn't get much use these days. The sign simply reads "Burned Church" with "rOAd" added on by hand. Debris is strewn across the pavement.

Humanzees perch on tree limbs, assembled in curmudgeon cloisters, their tiny chimp faces disapproving, their bald lips pursed to support cigars, their hairy little hands giving people the middle finger. The only two people here to receive an eyeful of said finger have their attention elsewhere.

Chosen and Quon have been working on their truck for hours since it broke down. They're covered in so much grease and grime that their ethnicities are indistinguishable. Their age and economic status are hints that they belong to the Iron People, the younger generation burdened with rebuilding the United States after the war.

Chosen breaks the terse silence. "Can't you hand me the ratchet?"

After a tense beat Quon replies. "Hand you the rat shit? That's just plain sick!"

As they stare at each other it is clear that they are about to lose it, which is natural given that they are both serial killers. A sudden, shrill sound halts their escalating emotions, something animal in nature. It is the vocalization of pain. That only excites them, of course, and the men split up to seek out its source. Hopefully it will be a fallen Humanzee or, better yet, a woman. Women have been far too intimidating to approach ever since the latest bestseller was published…Chosen and Quon both shudder and try not to think about it.

In the underbrush they locate what was supposed to be a baby but is, instead, a malformed waste of oxygen. Apparently its parents recognized it as such and cast it away, the men are thinking, for surely not even the Humanzees would stoop to stealing such a child from an open window or stopped vehicle.

Chosen wipes sweat and food from his lip. "Got a phone?"

After another twenty minutes of the baby's wailing, the duo decide to wait for the police a little further down Burned Church Road. Forty minutes later, when Detective Pittman finally arrives, the men are on their second pack of cancerettes and third bag of cedar chips. They watch Pittman exit the patrol car, fifty years of virgin sacrifices stuffed under a suit and tie. His hair and eyes are as black as his heart, his complexion and accent betraying Slavic roots. He's clearly older and better off financially, a member of the Darkness People—those who lived through the war and destroyed the USA.

"Short and sweet. Where?" He steals the cancerette from Quon's mouth and stares hard at the men. It occurs to them that while serial killers are barred from hospital work, teaching, and the like, they are allowed on the police force. Bearing that in mind they curb their instincts and lead the detective to the shrieking infant.

"It's a baby all right." Pittman turns to leave.

"How come we didn't hear it before," Quon quivers. "Think the Humanzees left it here?"

Pittman expels a bloody bundle of mucous. "Fuckers. They're gonna take over one day." The men look at him; he scowls in return. To silence the baby he lifts it in one arm, cursing quietly when its soggy wrappings douse him with unmentionables.

The two men stare at Pittman again, for a different reason this time. The baby has finally gone silent.

CHAPTER TWO

The haste of the hospital's decay is only matched by that of its occupants. They flop and flail, fail and die. It's a busy place these days. The west wing, however, was abandoned some time ago, left to crumble in solitude. The walls there are coated with filth, moss grows on the floor, and the ceiling tiles are crumbling. The rooms are in semidarkness, lit only by the dim smog-light bleeding in through cracked windows.

In one of the rooms a pale woman lays on a cot, staring listlessly at the ceiling. This is Javier. She is in her twenties and doesn't care. Her clothes are made of PVC. Javier's parents had planned on a boy and were too stubborn to adapt to her gender. She has it better than her sister, considering that her sister was named Jorgita after failing

to pop out as a Jorge.

Next to her is a pile of books, all with the same title: *Rape is a Girl's Best Friend* by Javier Jitlé. It's a bestseller, despite the fact that men everywhere are up in arms. It puts too much pressure on them, they argue. Most men don't want to do such things to their female counterparts, and those who do go limp at the thought of it being a boon to women. Javier wonders at the lack of perception in the world. Hasn't anyone ever heard of satire, ever considered the scope of rape to go beyond just women as the victims?

Somewhere a phone begins to ring. Her eyes move to the doorway, although she doesn't. Eventually Javier creeps toward the sound, clutching a copy of her book to her chest. Loose linoleum tiles crack underfoot.

A man emerges from a shadowy doorway next to Javier. This is Reid. He is large, armed, and enraged, his business-casual clothes somehow all wrong.

"Well?" she asks the darkness.

Reid hesitates, then states, "You're the one who wrote the book."

"You came here to try it out on me."

"Bitch, I came here to kill you!"

She clucks her tongue, smirks. "I've got to answer the phone first."

Javier continues on her way. Reid, stunned, tries to formulate words. He remembers something and unsheathes a huge knife. Although he brandishes it menacingly she doesn't see the display.

Running after her he shouts, "Hey, wait!" The thud of his heavy footfalls echoes mercilessly, disturbing dust and vermin. He catches up to Javier in a nurses' station, used more recently for storage and cheap sex.

She picks up the receiver. "Defective Canteen."

A raspy voice in the phone gushes, "Up your mother, you crotched-up cock blocker!" Javier considers the phone's pitted plastic surface as the tirade continues, then hangs up.

Reid turns on the television; the screen presents a debonair man who growls, "Smoke my tumor, baby!" The cancerettes advertisement ends with a woman's lips stretching over twelve inches of bulbous meat.

Javier turns it off and glares at Reid.

"Who was it on the phone?" he asks.

"Same person it always is: a jackhole. Like you."

CHAPTER THREE

"This is it, huh? I've seen jowlitoriums more lickable than this!" Pittman snorts and hawks up a chemical-laced lugie.

Javier observes him—he is typical of the United States after the destruction wrought by World War 3: This Time It's Holy. "This is the Defective Canteen, not The Savoy."

"What's that in your voice, some sort of South Americanism?"

"I was raised in Argentina." She leads Pittman through semi-functional hallways. Sobs, giggles, and all manner of wet noises leak from the various doorways. "You want to leave the boy with us it'll cost a thousand per year. As you can see, we're running out of space so there's a premium on the beds."

"You're one abscondful fascist mofo, you know that?" The baby-thing in his arms gurgles, leaving a trail of drool behind them. "No, I mean it. Argentina? Jitlé? I'm not some kind of idiot."

She wheels on him, a finger jabbing his chest while his eyes focus on her pale cleavage. "So my great-grandfather was Adolph Hitler! Like nobody knew that already. You're a crotching brilliant detective. They must pay you well."

A toddler with both legs fused together into one hideously long and mis-shapen appendage looks out at them, waves a webbed hand. They move on. Looking at the patients, mostly under the age of four, Pittman feels he'll be able to pick his nose with confidence after this move. A thousand CCs of cancer is a stretch even for a corrupt cop like him. Currency such as cancer is fluid, so to speak, making it perfect for unstable times like these. Cancer is the one replenishable thing everyone has in abundance.

After agreeing to the Canteen's terms Pittman hands over the baby, and it immediately starts screaming. An assistant scuttles away with the squealing thing as it works to deafen all within hearing range.

"Reid! Reid, you nipple twister…stop it with the hide-and-seek!"

Reid, more forlorn than angry today, shuffles out from behind a door. Although he towers over the other two he shies away from Pittman.

"Why aren't you down at the station doing the files? You *know* what kind of caseload we've got."

Reid starts to reply, then eying Javier stops and leans in to whisper. "There kept being, uh, prostitutes under my desk. Every time I got rid of one another appeared."

"Of course!" Pittman smacks Reid's head, explaining that he's trained the prostitutes to stay in position under his desk for a certain amount of time every day. "Not for, you know, things of a fucking nature. Just in case is all."

"Just in case?"

"I like to know that I could have it if I wanted it. You'll get to understand and appreciate the feeling."

Javier shakes her head, starts to walk away. "It figures you two would know each other.

"Not so fast, Nazi!" Pittman grabs her arm, slams her against the wall a couple times. "You're the one who wrote that book! Right?"

She glares at Reid. "Didn't we go over this already?"

"Don't worry about that rookie, bitch, worry about me!"

"Don't call me that." She knees him savagely in the groin.

On seeing this Reid massages his own groin, remembering the same thing happening to him after he first confronted Javier.

"You're...a profiler..." Pittman gasps, dust from the floor clinging to his lips.

Somebody has the mutants attempting aerobics in the physical therapy center; their awkward, off-time counting resonates down the halls. And still the horrible discovery Pittman turned over to them shrieks and wails in some unseen room.

Javier plays with the hair in her right armpit. "I'm a foreign national. The profiler/serial killer designations aren't forced on us, at least not until we become citizens of your fine nation."

"Everyone's a serial...killer or a profiler...it's a scientific fact!" Pittman curses, his fingers attempting to drive the pain from his genitals. "But it takes a special...a special pathology to be...*fuck!*...to be a profiler-serial killer."

"You're talking crockery, detective, worse still you speak of 'scientific fact' as if the two have anything to do with each other." Javier eyes Pittman, then decides she'd rather eye Reid, idiotic though he is. "There's no such thing."

After World War III: This Time It's Holy, the United States finally acknowledged that its citizens were either serial killers or profilers. Given that natural balance is achieved by pairing the two, the only form of intimate relationship allowable by law is a serial killer/profiler match-up. The confusion about gender in the marriage vows—and the silly argument that "I will love and cherish in sickness and in health" meant instead "we will have children"—has been replaced with "I promise to ritualistically murder your body" and "I promise to clinically dissect your mind."

"Forget biology," Reid blurts, seeing his superior failing to get anywhere.

"We're talking about reality!"

"We're talkin' about a one in a billion type of personality here, bit—uh, babe," Pittman continues, still rolling back and forth in the dirt. "How many great-grandchildren of Hitler recently relocated to the USA advocating rape while surrounding themselves with retards and deformos?" He fumbles with his gun, attempting to point it at Javier.

While Pittman struggles to get up the Canteen assistant returns, ears dripping blood, and thrusts the wailing baby-thing into Javier's arms.

Reid helps Pittman to his knees. "I've got the devil on a short leash, babe."

Javier runs her hand over the baby's head, smiling. "Looks like I owe you a refund."

CHAPTER FOUR

Javier squints as she looks through the tainted windows of the police station. Gunmen in the sniper towers occasionally fire a shot or two, keeping the hordes of scavengers at bay under the unbound darkness. Seeing it all, she wonders what point of the the Crusades/Jihads was. Surely, the deities of both sides were powerful enough that they didn't need animals like homo sapiens defending them, nor would they want said homo sapiens destroying their creation. Stranger still was the conclusion of World War Three: This Time It's Holy; each side recognized the other's destructive prowess and they joined to become the Allahryans.

And why not? The Arabs are Caucasian, scientifically, although they don't possess the profound lack of pigment found in the Westernmost reaches of Eurasia. Javier knows she is the logical choice to lead the Allahryans, given that her family started up the whole Aryan thing to begin with. Not only is she uninterested but the group seems to be doing just fine without her. According to the news Allahryans have bombed all the cloning centers. That means no more clones of profiler spouses for serial killer spouses to murder. Which, in turn, means no way to keep the serial killers in line. Fires are visible on the horizon.

Javier sighs, leans back in her chair. "I operate a sperm bank out of the Defective Canteen. You two wanna make some extra money?"

A model posing as a news anchor sobs while recounting details of the latest Allahryan attack. Pittman turns off the television with such violence that it is rendered inoperable. The baby seethes in the angry cocoon that is Pittman's embrace. Reid eyes its quivering, wet flesh with suspicion.

"Why don't you tell us about the first killing, babe?"

Javier leans back further, sucking on a cancerette, taking in the brutal landscape outside.

"The one where Miladah Allard was found bludgeoned to death in her hot tub. She was a profiler, just like you."

"I never said I was a profiler." To show her disdain Javier leans back just a little further in her chair.

A woman passes the open doorway, pausing to giggle and say, "Hey 9/11."

Reid nods, his chest puffed out a bit. "Now look here, you best keep your answers kosher Jitlé. None of that Third Reich occultism crockery."

"9/11?"

"Because I'm a raging inferno between the sheets, baby!"

Pittman shakes his head. Not even the sickly baby is dumb enough to believe Reid's tripe. "'Thou thyself art in continuous mutation and in a manner in continuous destruction.' That was found at the scene. Mean anything to you?"

"Sounds like an apologist for the current government."

"What the fuck is that supposed to mean? If you don't like the USA then why don't you leave!"

The Zero-Degree War continues outside, young and old at each others throats, the Iron People no longer content with rebuilding the mistakes of the Darkness People.

Javier leans back too far and her chair topples. She springs to her feet as though nothing happened, wiping mud and broken bits from her clothes. Ignoring the detectives' giggles, she watches a dozen suspects being lined up and shot next to a trash pit. "The greatest good for the greatest number, right?"

Pittman aggressively thrusts the baby at her. "Without our system there would be chaos out there. You have to admit that much at least!" The baby warbles in tune with him.

Javier laughs and laughs.

CHAPTER FIVE

The police vehicle's eight wheels jump and thump, bouncing over carcasses and chunks of asphalt or masonry. The thick plastic armor coating the vehicle deflects sniper fire from rampant Iron People. Inside, the occupants pretend they're capable of ignoring each others' stale sweat. Reid and Pittman take turns poking the deformed baby in its eyes, while Javier picks her nose. Five other police are squished in the cramped space, wondering if the seat cushions are moist from the perpetual precipitation or the urine of past riders. They attempt to distract themselves by sharing a bag of cedar chips.

Javier snorts. "We going on a picnic?"

"It's called confronting the perp with the horror of their own crimes." After it becomes clear she doesn't understand Pittman adds, "We're going to the latest profiler-serial killer crime scene."

"What's that going to prove?"

"That we've got an ace up your hole this time, so watch out." Pittman gestures to the rear, where a woman reclines across several seats, her mud-colored hair disheveled, worry-lines trickling like stress fractures across her multiracial features. The gray suit she wears to convince others she's a professional hasn't been changed in several days. A very strong sex addict vibe radiates from her. "Meet Beulah Faye Nieran. She's the best profiler we've got."

"Looks like she's asleep to me."

"Don't let that fool you. She's sharper than the knife you used on your last victim."

"Maybe you're thinking about yourself," Javier replies. "Serial killer."

"Takes one to know one, babe."

"Then what's your opinion of this?" She hands him the latest newspaper, hot off the press and already mildewed. The lead story is about a serial killer-serial killer. "Not only do you have a profiler who kills only profilers, but now you've got a serial killer who only does other serial killers."

"Bullshit!" Pittman throws open a window and tosses the paper out; the officer next to Reid is hit in the throat by incoming fire. Pittman hastily closes the window, joining the other police in looting their fallen comrade.

The wounded officer gurgles, "Not...fucked up...yet!"

Beulah is the only one not digging in bloody pockets, hacking loose tumors, prying loose authentic aluminum fillings. She flips through NC-17 crime scene photos, oblivious to the antics of the others. Even this proves boring, and soon she is stiching together doll arms and legs, torsos and heads, fidgeting with tiny clothes and eyeballs.

"What's up with that?" Javier takes a seat next to Beulah.

"You believe in Voodun? The power of Obia? The might of Chango?"

Javier considers the question, picking her nose. She wipes her finger on Beulah's back when she's not looking. "So you make voodoo dollies. You know, I always wondered if there were voodoo dollhouses." When that

doesn't get a response she leans in and whispers, "Hey...why do they really call Reid '9/11?'"

Beulah's eyes flick in Javier's direction, oozing eight flavors of scorn. She merely shakes her head and goes back to what she was doing.

Something up in the charcoal sky rumbles, followed shortly by God's Dander: dirty-gray snow carried on the bleeding breeze, crystallized chemical flakes that will soon melt and merge with the poison already saturating the ground.

Pittman opens his window: "P.S.— fuck you all!" After firing a few random shots he closes it again.

"The point?" Javier asks.

Pittman jabs a finger at the baby, laughing. The explosive discharge of the gun has caused the baby's various deformities to quake with fright.

Beulah adjusts her bra and rolls over to face the vehicle's rusty inner wall. "Hell licker."

CHAPTER SIX

The murder victim awaits them in a penthouse hovel, once a fine chunk of real estate worn down to tenement status in the years after the war. Oil paintings hang askew on the walls and ceiling, mutilated canvasses left to dangle like the amputee limbs strewn throughout the trees in the courtyard.

The corpse is female, dark-skinned with spiky blue hair. Five holes have been burned deep into her torso; there is no blood around the wounds. Her feet and hands have been severed, and it is from these wounds that she bled to death. A golden retriever licks at the puddles.

On the wall a phrase is scrawled in detergent: *It is thy duty to leave another man's wrongful act there where it is.*

Beulah picks at a scab, Reid fixates

on the victim's week-old bruises, Javier works on lyrics for a song she is considering writing, and Pittman points an accusatory finger at her. "You're not a man," he bellows, "but this is sure as hell your wrongful act and I'm not gonna just leave it lying there where it is." He motions to some men, but Beulah throws herself onto the corpse before it can be moved. Afterwards she sprawls out next to the body, attempting to see what it sees, trying to feel what it feels.

Reid jabs at the detergent lettering with a pen, then sniffs the residue. When he thinks it's safe he sneaks a few snorts of the stuff, bringing on mild convulsions followed by Pacific-breeze calm and bloody gums.

"So, this pretty much rules out the Humanzees, eh?" Pittman grumbles, with no response. "Fuckers are gonna take over one day,"

Beulah eyes him wearily, silent even though she agrees.

Javier shifts uncomfortably, trying to squash the insect loose in her left boot. "Anybody bother to run a check on these quotes yet?"

The baby looks at Pittman, slime trailing from its eyes. Pittman looks at Reid. Reid looks at the others wishing he had a desk at the ready with a prostitute huddled under it. Nobody seems to know anything.

Being the senior officer, Pittman clears his throat in the attempt to appear on top of things. "What's this blar-hah from, anyway? The Bible?"

"Marcus Aurelius," Beulah drones. She rolls over on top of the victim, grinding its bleeding parts against her. "The quotes come from a series of philosophy books he cranked out centuries ago."

Javier kneels beside her, eyes narrowing. "You have a very interesting method, detective."

"Marcus *who*?" The baby urinates on Pittman's leg.

Blood dripping from her lips Beulah replies, "Ancient Roman dude."

The rest of the officers investigate the victim's dresser, desk, refrigerator, and cabinets to see if there's anything worth taking.

Pittman rushes to a window, throws it open to let the darkness in, and bellows: "*Marcus Aurelius—get stuffed!*" The baby passes particularly wet bursts of gas.

The Humanzees lining the roof's edge all shriek and bare their fangs, scattering to distant hidey-holes.

"You ask me," Javier says, dragging Beulah off the corpse, "we should have this case solved *very* soon." Beulah is already snoring in her arms.

CHAPTER SEVEN

Back at the Defective Canteen things are calm. The staff is asleep for the night, tucked in with moldering sheets and dead dreams while the patients fester in a separate gloom.

Javier slips in with the stealth of a night incendiary. This is the final step of her daily routine. There is a room kept in the west wing, far away from the others. Her prize possession lives within, a prisoner in his own broken body. Nameless fluids seep from numerous sores on his body, coagulating on the sheets bunched up around him. As far as she can guess this one is roughly twenty years old, older than the rest even though he should be dead. Layers of blubber crush his frail body down into the bed, cruel springs straining against his flesh. Patches of coarse hair sprout where there should be none, while other areas that traditionally harbor hair are devoid of follicles. His skin is rotten cheesecloth draped over atrophied limbs.

His eyes come alive as Javier slinks in, her PVC outfit glimmering like pools of dark blood in the sickly smog-light. His lips smack wetly, and his long, gnarled fingernails click together, sounding like a chorus line of epileptic cockroaches. A bulge forms between legs that will never carry him away from this dank pain.

"Hiiiiii Langston. How's my favorite guy today?"

"Uh...uh...uhhhh!"

Mutant bats, snared by bands of Humanzees on the hunt, screech outside. Heavy rain whips against the windows suddenly, then dies down.

Javier smiles, licks her lips, leans over the bed to taunt Langston with her cleavage. "I came to say goodnight." She removes a collection tube from a nearby cabinet.

"Uh...uh...uuuuuuuuhhhhhhhh!"

If she doesn't hurry he's going to finish before she's in place. A box of surgical gloves is in the drawer as well, but she decided long ago she prefers skin-on-skin contact. "Have you been a good boy today?" He quivers and squeaks affirmations as she pulls back his sheet. Gingerly placing the tube under a premature opening in his urethra, Javier begins to lovingly caress the thing that passes for Langston's penis. It is a work of evolution that could only be conceived through a collaboration between M.C. Escher and H.R. Giger. While it could never possibly be put to practical use on a woman's body, he is the father of hundreds—if not thousands—of offspring.

Javier was sincere earlier when she mentioned the sperm donor money to Reid and Pittman. It is the major source of income for her, given that pollutants have caused male infertility to rocket. And sure, Langston's congenital deformities will be passed on to the children of all those desperate women who pay her for artificial insemination, but nothing can be proven in court. As far as the world is concerned Langston died of respiratory failure five years ago. He lives in the hospital's abandoned wing with Javier, in secrecy, his mind long gone. She isn't sure what exactly keeps him alive, but these late-night visits must help.

She sees his children pouring in every day, slowly filling the dilapidated hospital. Soon the Defective Canteen will spread through the entire structure, and this abandoned west wing will be alive with hustle and bustle, despair and pleas for a merciful death.

Her hand works furiously, then rests. It is done. With their nightly ritual complete Langston drifts away from this world, finally allowing sleep to embrace him. Javier caps the collection tube and puts it in cold storage. Soon she'll have more cancer than she'll know what to do with...

CHAPTER EIGHT

The police are dragging Javier in once again. The police station's hallways are morose, unhealthy, saturated with years of contempt and violence. Reid leads the group with a bodice-ripping strut, hoping there will be females to impress on the way to Pittman's office. Pittman, for his part, is doing all he can to simply keep his malformed baby in line. His left arm is perpetually stuck in the same football-clutching position from carrying the defective thing around so much. If his hands lose contact with it the baby goes into Chernobyl mode in zero seconds flat. Beulah, the profiler's profiler, sluggishly marches behind Javier, continually attempting to massage her pale German-Argentinian neck and shoulders. Javier bats the intrusive hands away, annoyed, until she feels the barrel of a gun against her back.

"Fine, have your way, you subby bitch!" The men ignore Javier's outburst.

Passing the entrance to the Sex Crimes Division Javier can't help but notice all the empty desks. Papers and folders and disks and crime scene photos are scattered everywhere. A lone detective sobs quietly at her desk. The feet of her colleagues dangle in midair, their bodies affixed to the deteriorating ceiling with improvised nooses. *Rape is a Girl's Best Friend* has been nailed to the wall. A large red X has been painted over it.

"Hey doll," Pittman hollers. "This

is the one right here. The one that wrote the book."

The detective looks up from her desk. Snot bubbles out of her right nostril, reaching Bubbalicious proportions before bursting with a wet pop. "What?" she wheezes.

"*That* book. Her," he says, using the baby to gesture at Javier.

The sex crimes detective rushes out with a godless howl, but Javier's fist leaves her horizontal. Beulah whispers in her ear, "Everybody needs work. You took that away from them."

"So," Reid exclaims, "we finally see the killer at work! Her method is intriguing."

Javier considers her fist, then puts it away for later use. They make it back to Pittman's office and hunker down for a while, staring at the crime scene messages left thus far:

1) "It is thy duty to leave another man's wrongful act there where it is."

2) "Thou thyself art in continuous mutation and in a manner in continuous destruction."

3) "Penetrate inwards into men's leading principals, and thou wilt see what judges thou art afraid of, and what kind of judges they are of themselves."

4) "The destruction of the understanding is a pestilence."

A watery voice in the doorway says, "Um…excuse me…" Everyone looks to the source: a portly young woman clutching a satchel to her chest, clothes badly torn, tear-streaked mascara drying on her cheeks. Her name is Sylvia. It turns out Sylvia was directed here by the police downstairs. She was abducted by a gang of young boys, roughly twelve years old, then alternately beaten and lashed with a belt for about an hour before the boys lost interest.

Reid is angry at this waste of valuable time. "So, it was 'torture fatty' day, just like always."

Sylvia looks at them, lower lip trembling. Screams can be heard somewhere out in the vast darkness offered by the window.

Glimmering ropes of snot dangle from her chin. "Pu-pu-please…"

Disgusted by this scene the prostitute crawls out from under Pittman's desk and storms out.

"So how about it…wanna take her place?" Pittman laughs as she eyes the desk. "You couldn't even fit down there! Now take ten steps backwards."

"Wu-wu-what?"

Pittman draws his gun, raises it. "I said take ten steps back, ya bombdaclot."

Javier and Beulah share a look. The baby sucks at an imaginary teat while looking at recently-acquired close-ups of the serial killer-serial killer's messy work.

Silvia starts to look back over her shoulder, but an angry sound from Pittman stops her. Her breath now under control, she does as he commands. Pittman counts her steps aloud. On her fifth step the baby leaves a smattering of milky blood on the floor. On Sylvia's eighth step her heel finds no support, and her arms cartwheel in the air absurdly, her face contorted by panic. She tumbles down the stairwell, many loud thumps and screams topped off by a wet thud, then silence.

Reid and Pittman crack up, high-fiving each other. "That shit never gets old!"

Javier walks over to the stairwell and stops, overwhelmingly aroused by the wall of stench emanating from its depths. The lower two levels of the stairwell are filled with obese corpses, bloated by the humid conditions. So far the Humanzees haven't been able to sneak in and get at them.

Javier's gaze slowly focuses on the police once more. "Is it just me, or was that somewhat crotched?"

Pittman snorts. "Hey, everyone fucks up sooner or later." He holds the glistening baby high. "I woulda made her go down on this thing, but a big time freak like her woulda probably enjoyed it too much. Know what I mean?"

"No doubt," Reid grunts, checking under all the desks, chairs, and piles of trash.

He adjusts his crotch, shaking his head in disappointment.

CHAPTER NINE

Reid and Pittman are taking turns doing lines on the dashboard as the police vehicle prowls the streets. Occasionally they stop to rub some of the fine white powder on the baby's gums; somehow it seems less grotesque when it's high.

Javier's armpit hair is itching like mad. "Where are we going?"

"Where do you think? We need some more office supplies."

Young women in scant clothing, boys in torn clothing, men in leather, girls made up to look like women, they all stalk the damp night in search of victimization. One needn't have full-blown tumor sacks—for just a skin carcinoma you can have your way with these wretches. Some people are able to scam them with just a harmless freckle. Those are invariably the Iron People, and the prostitutes are bound to be Iron People as well. The middle-aged or older crowd, having been alive when the war's toxins flowed full steam, have more than enough cancer to get by without such antics.

The Zero Degree war doesn't reach these parts, though. Class struggles are confined to the designated Zero Degree zones…zero degrees of tolerance, mercy, common sense. These here are the so-called A-Bomb Slums, hodgepodge abodes and businesses scraped together from the remnants of a forgotten civilization, untouched by repairs, by progress. Not even the Allahryans would bother striking here. Ironically, the Iron People are forced to live here even as they rebuild areas for the Darkness People to prosper in.

While the men up front peruse the flesh menu, the women languish in the back. Javier can't stand the silence. "Did you hear the serial killer-serial killer struck again?"

Beulah finally perks up, a sharp intake of breath followed by her eyes opening—bright, focused. "Not only that, but our profiler-serial killer has taken herself a hiatus. Do you think that means serial killers are more driven than profilers, so far as killing is concerned?"

"That's just the thing," Reid replies. "Profilers *aren't* driven to kill. And who says it's a she? I think it's pretty clear that a man is behind the profiler murders at least."

Javier eyes Beulah, memories of the massage forced on her sending a chill along the nape of her neck. "You're in for a bit of a surprise then Reid, you hell gator."

Beulah leans in close, scrutinizing Javier. "You're convinced I'm right, that this is a woman we're after. What is it you think you know, hmm?" She pokes Javier forcefully in the chest, tidies her hair, picks the remnants of diseased spinach from between her teeth. "I always found World War II footage emotionally catastrophic."

"Catastrophic?"

"To the point of being arousing. How about you and me go back to my place and create our own private Auschwitz?"

"I'm not into that. Don't mention it to me again." The vehicle has stopped, the men peering back intently in the hopes of witnessing some fem-fem action. "Oh please, you crotching fascist bully boys!"

Pittman shrugs. "At least you and me agree the profiler-serial killer is a female."

Headlines flash on the billboards lying askew among the rubble. If the news is to be believed, hardcore violent Zionists have thrown in with the Allahryans, and now the organization is know as the Kaballahryans. The Holy Trinity's schizophrenia has ended; all three sides of the same God are finally in alignment, with sights set on everyone else in the world, a heavy celestial finger on the trigger.

Reid unleashes a shout, draws his weapon and rushes out into the street. As he wrangles some flesh the baby thrashes, arches its back. "That's right," Pittman coos. "We have ourselves a winner."

CHAPTER TEN

Thadiana is unreasonably cheerful as the police vehicle carries the group through burning slums. She is well over six feet tall, dressed in a purple velvet bikini with synthetic white go-go boots reaching almost to her hips. Her face and body have fallen victim to the cosmetic surgeries expected in the sex trade, leaving something vaguely amphibian in her features. Her noncommittal ethnicity is similar to that of Beulah. Dirty-gold cornrows are gathered high on her head that dribble down in two horn-like pigtails. Currently she is the only one enthusiastic about the murders. "So, cool! You're after the profiler-serial killer?! That's, like, so *very*."

"*Very?*" Reid grumbles, already sorry they chose her from the teaming masses.

"I'll tell ya what's *very*, ya bloodclot!" Pittman shakes his mutant baby at her in the darkness, giving it whiplash. "We've got the perp right here!"

"That's the tiniest serial killer I ever saw!"

"No!" Pittman spits, shoving the baby under his suit jacket. "I'm talkin' about that pale freak sitting next to you!"

"You're a freak?!" Thadiana exclaims, scrutinizing Javier. "Wow! What a freak! You're the, like, first profiler-serial killer ever!"

Javier's eyes roll from her to Pittman and back again. "You have *got* to be jacking me."

"And guess what," Thadiana continues, her cornrows slithering to and fro. "Guess it, guess it, guess!" Then, before anybody can guess: "I'm a serial profiler!"

Reid scans the scrunched-up faces of his compatriots. "There's no such thing."

"Uh-huh, uh-huh, uh-huh!"

Javier grabs Thadiana's jaw, draws her in face to face. "You're one tweaked-out nipple twister, I don't mind telling you."

Beulah stops working on her latest voodoo doll to whack Pittman's head. "Pull over. I need to fuck the world."

The vehicle comes to a stop near the scorched remains of a forest, its charred, denuded trees imitating tortured spirits lined up before Satan's scythe. Lightning streaks in green and orange across the roiling clouds, never bothering to touch down on the befouled Earth, just racing back and forth. This extra illumination forces Beulah to penetrate even deeper into the forest for a secluded spot to relieve herself. A couple minutes later the group is summoned from the vehicle by her cries.

They lackadaisically converge on the scene to discover a Humanzee bound to a tree trunk, its hands and feet cut off. Next to the dead beast are the words "It would be a man's happiest lot in life to depart from mankind without having had any taste of lying and hypocrisy and luxury and pride." Beulah is busy doing her makeup.

Thadiana is the first to summon a comment. "Hoo-wee, that's what I call 'value added!'"

Javier steps forward to examine the dead Humanzee, making sure to squash a family of slugs underfoot. She takes a whiff— these new words from Marcus Aurelius were painted in nail polish.

"That your shade of nail polish?" Pittman juggles the baby with glee, causing it to scream. "Looks like you've struck again, eh Hitler?"

"I haven't left your sight for what…eight hours? More? It's still wet."

Pittman lines his eyes up with her crotch. "What's still wet?"

"The words are!" Her knee explores his eye socket, leaving him in the dirt with the other slugs.

"Could be the humidity," Reid ventures. "Keeping it wet, you know?"

"Hey," Thadiana giggles, "is that live or is it Memorex?"

The others stop to listen—something is moving in the woods nearby. A small band of Humanzees smashes through charcoal underbrush and bombs them with fecal matter, immediately scampering away before retaliation can occur.

Beulah draws her gun, and Reid and Pittman do likewise.

CHAPTER ELEVEN

The Humanzees are tracked to an underground entrance. It is not crude, however—clearly this was constructed by homo sapiens. The further Pittman explores, the clearer it becomes this was once a military installation.

"Hey," he calls back to his companions. "You gonna come with or what?"

Javier ventures forward a bit, fingers trailing over creeper vines and mutant blossoms. Pre-World War III: This Time It's Holy buildings often collapse when entered. "I'm not so sure about this. Humanzees or not, this place is on its last legs."

"And dangerous," Reid adds, adjusting his crotch.

"Yeah!" Beulah is a little too excited by the prospect. To Javier she says, "The offer still stands."

"What...here? Now? How romantic."

The baby slaps itself, much to Thadiana's amusement.

They travel for minutes in darkness. Corrupted water oozes from old light fixtures like blood from empty eye sockets. Further in there are makeshift torches to light the way. Just when they are ready to give up the chase a grand chamber opens up before them, riddled with tiny burrowed passageways leading to Humanzee-knows-where. This, too, is lit by torches. Once a multilevel command center of sorts, all the computers have been removed and cables dangle from the ceiling, the walls, sprout from the floor, rusted tentacles blindly groping for purchase. Several hallways lead away from this room, but only one has not collapsed yet. It offers the glow of artificial light and the faint sound of music.

Pittman gestures to the doorway, which is situated across the chamber. Reid hesitates and Pittman swings the baby by its ankle as if he plans to thrash his subordinate with it. After this display the others hasten into the underground lair. Afraid to make the slightest sound the group moves forward on tip-toe. Regardless, displeased Humanzees begin to appear at the entranceways to the myriad tunnels.

Pittman puts the baby down to prepare for battle. It unleashes a horrid cry that serves as a clarion call summoning hundreds, possibly thousands, of Humanzees to converge on the lair. Too late Pittman realizes his error and scoops up the baby.

Thadiana turns on him. "Smooth move, Ex Lax!"

The Humanzees gather in an organized defense core, replete with heavy-duty denim diapers and sharpened bones. A thunderous unified roar wells up from deep in their diminutive potbellies and they charge.

Thadiana yanks down her velvet bikini top, massive breasts furiously stabbing out at the oncoming horde with no effect. "I saw this on a wrestling show! Why won't it work?!" She heaves her breasts around violently in a continued demonstration of futility. It would seem only human males stop in mid-attack, struck dumb when presented with an infant's food supply.

After emptying her gun into the hairy mass, Beulah is fearless, diving in with a double clothesline. Apparently Thadiana wasn't the only one viewing wrestling shows. Javier, being from south of the border, attacks in a Luchador stylee, using a flying head-scissors to send the nearest Humanzee rocketing into the rest like a bowling ball.

Back to back, each in a wide firing stance, Pittman and Reid unload clip after clip, leaving hairy limbs and soiled diapers floating in a thick viscous soup of muscle tissue and blood. They pause momentarily to observe the frenzied defense orchestrated by the women. "What the bloody blar-hah are they up to?!"

The heel of Thadiana's go-go boot connects with a Humanzee skull cracking it directly into the skull of one behind it. She bellows, "Buy one, get one free—cock blocker!"

In all the chaos Javier realizes her cell phone is going off. Exasperated, she answers with several colorful expletives.

A familiar "Uh…uhh…uuuuhhh!" makes its way to her ears.

"You have *got* to be *crotching* me!" Javier German-suplexes a Humanzee, popping its skull against the stone floor like a ripe boil.

"Uh…uhh…uuuuuuuhhhhhhhh!"

"I'm not coming home tonight, so keep it in your pants, Langston! Here, somebody wants to talk to you." She throws her phone at the advancing Humanzee horde. The closest one catches it, putting the device to its ear in imitation of her. She turns to flee but hesitates, startled by the fact the animal seems to be communicating back and forth with Langston, a bulge growing at the front of its diaper. It strikes her that she could put the mongoloids and misfits housed by the Defective Canteen to work in an Humanzee phone sex operation. The only problem is that Humanzees don't seem to have much in the way of cancer.

Her reverie is ended by Thadiana's tug at her shoulder. Reid, shrilling like a nursing home reject, leads the retreat into the last functioning hallway. Bullets and curses fly as Thadiana drags the other two women behind her.

"What's the big idea," she yells. "You almost left us behind!"

Pittman smirks as they run toward the light. "A man can dream, can't he?"

CHAPTER TWELVE

Digital computers hum, the tapes of analog computers whirl, the humans gasp and wheeze from their various positions on the mildewed carpet. Everyone has cuts, torn clothes, and fecal stains from their encounter with the Humanzees. Beulah, dozed off against a filing cabinet, makes a good shield for Reid to hide behind. Thadiana, face to the floor, heaves until regaining her breath—then she snaps off her boot heels to facilitate smoother fleeing in the future. Javier lies on her back wondering why the electricity works here.

Pittman, for his part, is at the airlock taunting frustrated Humanzees through a small window in the door. They are throwing fistfuls of their seedy shit at the door to no avail. He laughs, alternately giving them the finger and making a masturbatory gesture with his hand. The Humanzees become even more relentless in their bombardment of the door. Soon the window is coated with green and brown turds, spoiling Pittman's fun.

"So," he says, turning to the rest. "What now?"

But the eyes of his comrades are not on him. There is another person here, one who didn't run in screaming while waving weapons around. He is dressed in badly stained Army fatigues, clipboard and calculator at the ready, the accumulation of stubble twitchy on his nervous face. When confronted by jittery eyes and trigger fingers he explains that he works here.

"Here? What is 'here,' bloodclot?!"

"We, um…" The man sighs, adjusts his glasses, stares at the women's chests. "We make life. New life. *Evolved* life." Hoping to impress his first visitors of the year he launches into rambling stories about Stalin's program to develop superhuman warriors by breeding humans and apes. The methods used were primitive at best, if not outright kinky, and the scientists involved ended up biting pillows at Camp Siberia. The scientist holds up a tube of blue fluid and an electroshock collar as though they are the keys to the kingdom. "We're much more advanced now. Just look at what modern technology can accomplish! You can train any lifeform with the proper tools…and electrical current. My name's Simon," he adds with a shy chuckle.

Hearing about her great-grandfather's nemesis makes Javier's nipples stand at full attention. "So you're saying you've completed Stalin's great plan? And all you got out of it was Humanzees?"

Simon is unsure how to respond. He decides to rearrange his desk. Reid looks—there aren't any prostitutes under it.

"So what is this, then…some kind of giant Nerd House?"

"No, this is—was—military all the way."

Pittman and Reid both graduated from Military Nerd Houses with degrees and good careers lined up for them. Reid states, "The two are not mutually exclusive."

It dawns on Beulah there isn't any way out of the room. After a quick scan she locates an emergency exit hatch in the high ceiling.

Pittman is tired of surprises. "Listen," he growls, reloading his gun. "Nobody cares what this place was. All that matters is that you and your pals made those freaky things, and now they're after us."

"Well, I'm guessing you violated the boundaries of their lair…"

The lights start to flicker and the monitors pulse drunkenly.

"You're about to fuck up," Pittman says, trigger finger slowly squeezing, squeezing… "You have any last words?"

"Yes," Simon starts, a finger raised. "I—"

He is cut short by a hail of bullets. "Like we wanna hear that shit." Pittman high fives the terrified baby, then French kisses its wet face-hole.

The door blows open, sent hurtling into the room by an explosive device. Smoke fills the air, as does a howl of Humanzee rage.

"Up the escape hatch!" Beulah says, pulling down the ladder. Thadiana and Pittman have to drag Reid to his feet. Once the escape apparatus is in place Reid charges forward, knocking the rest out of his way. Pittman and Javier are busy bludgeoning the few Humanzees that brave the smoke and flames. The ladder leading to salvation is shaky at best, yet it manages to support their combined weight. The escape hatch itself is another story. It proves to be almost completely rusted shut. Reid's hours working out finally come in handy and, choking on the steadily increasing smoke, he forces the hatch open.

As the group lies moaning in the dust Reid blurts, "And 9/11 saves the day again!"

Beulah shimmies over to him on her elbows. "You know why the ladies call you 9/11? It's not on account of any 'towering proportions' down there. It's because all the crabs in your crotch are lined up to jump to their deaths, just like those people trapped up in the WTC. You're so pathetic even your crabs can't stand you!"

She yanks down the front of Reid's trousers, exposing the ravaged skin of his groin to the wind's scalding spittle. Tides of pus eddy around clumps of dying pubic hair on his lower abdomen. Even in the darkness they can all plainly see his inner thighs and tattered genitals are alive with micro-movement.

Reid rolls away from the glare of the others and sobs quietly. A gurgle of contentment chirps from the baby's lips, followed by uproarious laughter from the rest of the group.

CHAPTER THIRTEEN

Pittman convinces the others that there must be a decent reward for information about the heart of Humanzee activity. It is decided they should go straight to the top, bypassing any other law enforcement agencies who could horn in on their credit. On the way into the nation's capital they pass by the local suicide pit and are overwhelmed. Bodies in the tens of thousands overflow its borders, adding to contaminated winds already foul with the smell of things dead and dying. Rampaging hordes of Humanzees work around the clock to haul away the dead for their own nefarious uses.

Pittman licks the baby's misshapen nose, shaking his head at the spectacle. "Fuckers are gonna take—"

"Yeah, WMD it, we got the message!" Javier can only take so much repetition.

Reid hasn't said anything during the ride. He sulks over a quintuple toe-cheese burger "value added" meal, including cedar chips and sweet piss. There was a time when people were able to choose better ingredients, or so the literature says, but Reid can't understand what they mean by "better." *If they don't like it*, he tells himself, *they can get out!*

Beulah cranes her neck. "Anybody see Hog Heaven yet?"

"It's a'comin', bloodclot!" Pittman pounds the steering wheel. "Mother may I! What is it with you people? All you ever want to do is party!"

"You're full of grace today," Beulah replies.

In the distance the Statue of Liberty looms high in the air, lighted from below, menacing a series of smaller monuments and attractions. It was relocated after the fall of New York City in order to protect its chastity. On the cracked monitors that litter the foreground news mongers shriek about the serial killer suicide rate reaching an all time high. Between the destruction of the clone factories and the insult of *Rape is a Girl's Best Friend* serial killers may soon become extinct.

Pittman turns to face Javier. "You might have the greatest kill record of any serial killer on record. Even better than your

dear ol' great-grandpa." Thadiana is lost, so he adds, "It was her that wrote the book!"

Thadiana looks Javier up and down, saying "Kid tested, mother approved!"

"Whatever," Javier says, pointing at something ahead. "Not only did I *not* kill all those people, but we're here."

Indeed, Hog Heaven is directly ahead. Pittman realizes this too late and crashes into one of the police barricades directly outside the main entrance. For some reason the entire area is devoid of activity.

Reid leans out and shouts vigorous greetings and profanity, neither of which illicit a response. Inside, things are distressingly clean. The marble floors are cracked here and there, but not a speck of dust is visible.

Deeper inside Hog Heaven they are confronted by an even more disturbing sight: the congressional chambers are all empty. They enter, unsure what will happen next. No police or special forces drag them away, and there are no sessions to interrupt. "Do Me" by Bell Biv Devo is the national anthem and the group feels compelled to sing the song, despite the fact the place is a ghost town. Seeing that Javier hasn't joined in, Pittman draws his gun and cocks it. She gets the hint and sings along; the words are barbed dog shit on her tongue.

Penetrating further into the empty congress the group finds no trace of life, not even a stray senator or two hiding beneath their chairs. There is a note pinned to the microphone: "Gone to the suicide pit. Take care of things for us, thanks. P.S. Fuck you all!"

"When do you think they'll be getting back?" Thadiana wonders, finger absently twirling her cornrows.

Javier snickers, "I don't think they went on a field trip, sweet meat."

"Every last one," Reid nods, impressed. "Every last member of congress was a serial killer."

Their mission is a failure. There's nobody around to report the Humanzee lair to. Instead, while the others investigate the empty congressional chambers Javier busies herself with drafting a change-of-name bill, proposing the USA be called Jackass, Incorporated. Taking a vote she notes with pride the bill goes unopposed.

Beulah takes a break from playing with her voodoo dolls long enough to notice something. "Hey, I wonder what this does?" She pulls a massive chord, unveiling an enormous chalkboard over to the side. It carries a running tally for the country's various ongoing conflicts:

The Zero Degree War
Darkness People 17
Iron People 13

The Darwiniwar
Humans 64
Humanzees 5

World War IV: Armageddon It
Kaballahryans 7
Normal Folks 3

The War On Terror
Us 0
Terror 100

The baby giggles. Pittman smacks it a few times, then grunts, "I didn't realize there was another World War on."

Javier tickles under his chin, cooing, "You say that as if you mean it."

"I'll show you what a girl's best friend is right here and now!" Pittman fondles his gun, but is restrained by Reid.

Thadiana throws her arms around Beulah and Javier. "Just like mother used to make," she laughs.

CHAPTER FOURTEEN

At the Honkey Pad the situation isn't any less grim. The building is devoid of tourists, interns, advisors, Secret Service, even South American slaves. If the Congress is wiped out, surely at least the Presidency is still intact. Otherwise, that would mean there was nobody at the top, no method, only chaos.

They enter the Ovular Office, expecting a spray of bullets or a hail of grenades. Instead they are met by eerie silence. The Secret Service has become, perhaps, a little *too* secret. Behind an enormous desk made of authentic wood is an overstuffed chair, facing away from the door. Nervous glances run through the group. The baby starts to make a sound but Pittman clamps his hand over its mouth.

Reid, hoping to regain some of his lost esteem, steps forward and spins the chair around. He is greeted by pickle juice sloshing in a jar. The jar contains a brain. A makeshift turban covers the lid, and a label across the glass reads, in almost illegible writing, *Osama*. Corroded wires snake from the top, worming away to shaded crevices that leak vermin and screams. A "Go Vegan!" bumper sticker and a "Have A Nice Day, God Made It!" sticker have been slapped on the bottle's side. Reid looks to the others, then back at the bottle, then the others again. "What's it mean?"

Thadiana clears her throat. "It means that God, as *creator* of the universe, *made* this day and, like, *everything* that happens during this day. So, in order to give Big G props you have to not only accept what happens, but be happy about it." She flashes the bottle to see if the brain will get scared; it doesn't.

Reid pounds the desktop. "I meant, what does this blar-hah about bin Laden have to do with anything?! Is he in charge? Does this mean the Kaballahryns have won?"

Thadiana is too busy flashing the baby to reply. Instead of being scared or awestruck the baby just seems to get hungry.

"Maybe they're all the same person in the end," Beulah ventures.

Javier snorts, kicking the jar to the floor where it shatters.

"Move over Sizzlean!" Thadiana gushes. "There's a newwww girl in town, and she's feel…in'…good! Got a smile, got a song for the neigh…bor…hood—"

"This isn't a sitcom about some white trash waitress," Pittman barks, thrashing her with his gun. While Thadiana grovels on the floor spurting blood and tears, Pittman stomps on the purple velvet of her booty shorts, ensuring she'll feel his kicks every time she sits down for the next week.

"*Now with gel…*" she sobs.

Javier searches the desk, finding only used condoms and a well-read copy of *Sex a Baller*, before digging out the presidential seal. She stamps her change-of-name resolution and faxes it to whatever news outlets she can think of.

"I do believe it's getting better," Pittman tells the baby while surreptitiously sniffing its privates. "It's getting better all the time."

CHAPTER FIFTEEN

Thadiana and Javier are watching television. Pittman is passed out in the corner surrounded by dozens of Pabst Blue Ribbon cans; the baby busies itself attempting to suckle through Pittman's shirt. They are in the Honkey Pad's mad theater set up for personal entertainment. On screen a weather forecaster sits in a broken office chair, shirt half untucked, tie loose, hair on strike, so unwashed he gives your eyes sweat stains. "Do I have to?" he sighs.

The sound of a shotgun being loaded can be heard from somewhere off camera.

"Well then…ahem…it looks like lower Jackass, Incorporated is in for more of God's Dander. If you can, try to stay indoors. For all the good it'll do you. P.S. NASA, send that fucker some Head And Shoulders already."

God's Dander is collecting faster than it can melt. Nobody can remember this ever happening before. Lightning continues to arc across turbulent clouds in the dark sky as gray chemical flakes swirl on the wind. Most areas are reporting several inches worth of accumulation, while others are dealing with twice as much. The temperature has jumped by five degrees overnight, and most people attribute that to the unusual amount of God's Dander lying around.

Calls from state governments across the nation pour in at the Honkey Pad. Everyone seems to think the government should do something. "Aren't there any fun calls?" Javier asks Honkey Pad operators. "Only send through fun calls!" And just like that the incessant ringing stops.

Thadiana remembers something and brings in a DVD that arrived earlier. "Check it, check it, check it!"

"What is it?" Javier sees that it bears her name and shrugs. She pops it in and waits.

A dark room fades in on the screen. The first thing she notices is the bright red paint covering the walls, only illuminated in small patches. A figure sits in shadow on the bed, launching into a half-hour tirade using voice distortion filters. After it's over Javier thinks about what she has seen, then starts it again. She pauses the video after only a few seconds and uses the zoom function. She focuses on the bed's water-warped headboard. Etched in the wood is "Labor not as one who is wretched."

"So," she says. "The profiler-serial killer tracked us down, eh?" She looks to Thadiana, who flashes her, earning only a disgusted shake of the head before Javier leaves. Perhaps Beulah will shed some light on the killer's video.

Instead she bumps into Reid as he exits one of the executive washrooms. For the first time since Beulah's 9/11 revelation he seems no longer withdrawn, instead full of nervous energy. "What's up with you?"

she asks.

"Nothing."

He starts away but she grabs his arm. "What's that—the window cleaner we saw at the Nerd House?"

In Reid's hand is an empty test tube. "No, I was just…ah…you know, trying to help out with your sperm donor thing."

"Couldn't get it up, huh? I shouldn't have bothered asking a limp-wristed stroker like you."

He retreats into the shadows further down the hall, punching his groin and mumbling violent nothings all the while.

Beulah has taken leave of duty to have her voodoo doll collection imported. It has taken her decades to make them all. Hundreds of people doomed never to exist now line the halls, the furniture, the beds, defects of fate with nowhere else to go. Their tiny pin-riddled forms summon to mind Abu Ghraib infants.

Pittman, when conscious, pleasures himself by sitting on a window ledge and firing at the vague forms moving about under cover of God's Dander. The fact that his gun shots wrack the baby with horror only serves to increase Pittman's fun.

Thadiana, as the new Press Secretary, spends much of her time battling the media. Semi-functional children from the Defective Canteen crawl into the ring between rounds to mop blood up from the mat. "The administration's decision to let profilers partner with other profilers is entirely sound," Thadiana rages while body slamming Matt Drudge, Junior. "With virtually no serial killers left how is the species supposed to thrive?" she growls while drop-kicking an Associated Press correspondent. When she isn't doing battle with the media she compulsively flashes the mirror to see what effect she'll have on herself.

Reid is barricaded in the Jefferson Room. Occasionally shouts of "Left, right, left!" and "Attack!" can be heard through the door. Like Pittman and Beulah he no longer feels connected to the police force, or the responsibilities associated with his job.

When Javier catches a headline about the murders he shares the news with the others. It would seem the serial killer-serial killer and profiler-serial killer have stopped their killings.

"Yes," Pittman and Beulah say in unison, too quickly.

Thadiana pops some bubble gum in her mouth. "Maybe they, like, killed themselves and shit like that?"

CHAPTER SIXTEEN

The Iron People have loosed their ultimate weapon on the unsuspecting Darkness People: Poontangutans swarm out of hidden bunkers, wave upon wave of Women of Mass Destruction crashing against the society's teetering fortifications. Covered in stringy orange hair, faces boasting fatty growths, tin cups over their swaying breasts, these new monstra sapiens tower over their Humanzee counterparts.

Watching Poontangutans rampage across the television screen Javier snorts. "This thing between your Darkness People and your Iron People, it's some cold-hearted stuff."

"Zero degrees," Beulah mumbles.

"I can't wait to become a naturalized citizen. Wanna marry me? I've got my own sperm supply, so we could even have kids."

"I'm not into marriage," Beulah replies, looking her up and down. "I just want to ball you."

In the distance something the populace refers to as "Mount Chimpmore" is being erected. Thousands of human corpses have been piled up in enormous bonfires to illuminate the audacious Humanzee work: the visage of the first great Humanzee leader's profile is being engraved on the metal palate that is the Statue of Liberty. On her posterior.

Next to it the Humanzee God is being engraved. It is the deformed baby Pittman carries, now immortalized in all its bugshit glory. Jackass, Incorporated has yet to formulate a response to this outrage.

God's Dander hasn't hindered the Poontangutans and Humanzees in the least. They use their underground network of tunnels and crumbling military corridors to pop up wherever they please. Their human counterparts aren't as fortunate. The dander drifts are as deep as five feet in some places, bringing all travel to a halt and making people wonder, *How can that fucker have any scalp left?*

Things are going very poorly for the country. A message from the Humanzees, recorded in their dimly-lit underground layer, has arrived. Specialists believe they have broken the code; the message is: "The Baby Freakus weeps. Turn over the Baby Freakus to us and you won't be harmed. Otherwise we shall declare Holy War against your infidel tribe."

On top of that, the profiler/profiler match-ups aren't working out. It turns out that when you pair two profilers neither one gets to be the good guy all the time. They just sit around staring intently at each other, trying not to let anything on while attempting to figure out what the other is thinking.

Desperate for action, the populace demands an explanation from the Honkey Pad. Pittman has no interest in dealing with the issue, unless it means a chance for him to randomly kill more people. Reid won't even deign to answer the door in the Jefferson Room. Javier is only worried about ending the incessant phone calls—lewd grunts and groans that could originate either from Langston or a Humanzee with a cell phone. Thadiana has been missing for quite some time, and Beulah is beginning to get suspicious.

Isolated reports start to come in from fringe communities—tales of primate rage, empty homes awash in blood, nightshift workers fending off Humanzees with whatever

weapons are under the counter.

"What did I tell you?" Pittman puts his feet up, smoking his cancerettes three at a time. "Do I need to say I told you so?"

Javier decides to boost security, then remembers there is none. Instead she takes comfort in going to the basement to visit the National Treasury. There are hundreds of coolers here loaded with tumors of every kind. She gropes their slick membranes, licks them, stuffs them in her armpits to relieve the itching. It's still not enough to forget all the videos she has been receiving from the profiler-serial killer. Climbing into a refrigerator, wrapped in a cancer cocoon, she can finally imagine a world in which she doesn't exist. She's never slept better in her life.

CHAPTER SEVENTEEN

Javier has been spending more and more time in the Treasury, the darkness of sleep obscuring piles of unwatched DVDs sent by the profiler-serial killer. Eventually, though, she has to come up for air.

Pittman eyes the bits of lymphoma clinging to her dark hair. "You doing something different with your look lately? Maybe trying to disguise yourself to avoid prosecution?"

"I can't believe you're still on about that. Have you been paying attention to what's happening out there? Nobody cares about a few murders when the whole world is coming apart!" Although Pittman offers no arguments Javier knocks over a vase and kicks the wall. "Even the Kaballahyrans have stopped attacking Jackass, Incorporated! They know we've had it. It's obvious to everyone!"

Her tirade is interrupted by a phone call. Heavy grunts and moans wait on the other end. After smashing her phone on the floor she picks at a crusty melanoma in her nostril.

Pittman watches the display with a smirk, then flicks at the baby's genitals. "Looks like our profiler-serial killer is getting more and more unstable all the time."

"Oh, up you, mother." Javier storms out.

Cabin fever is getting to them all. God's Dander is now twenty feet deep, pouring from the heavens with no end in sight. The good news is the condensed chemical flakes have cleaned up the sky enough to cause vague differentiation between day and night. Iron People with windows more than twenty feet off the ground are bugged out by the lighter shade of charcoal gray referred to as "day" by the news mongers. For the generation struggling to rebuild after the war, the words "night" and "day" were merely substitutes for "awake time" and "sleep time." Those words shouldn't have to actually *mean* something after all these years.

There hasn't been any contact with citizens in rural communities or A-bomb slums for days. Either they've revolted and broken off to form a new nation, or they've succumbed to subhuman hordes. The Humanzees now roam free, inheritors of one nation under God's Dander. People aren't even safe in the metropolitan areas any more.

Javier raids the armory, appropriating small knives, grenades, a shotgun and ammo, whatever she can carry. She even finds a space age tomahawk and hooks it through her belt. This is not in anticipation of conflict with the Humanzees and Poontangutans, no. She is simply tired of Pittman's nipple-twisting ways.

The sound of gunfire and screams ends her trip to the armory. She rushes to the source of the disturbance, where Pittman is engaged in battle with Humanzees. The baby is struggling to reach them but Pittman keeps it firmly headlocked under his left arm. Javier scans the chaos—an alcove formerly boasting a moss-covered bust of Lincoln is now home to a hole in the ground. Poontangutans hang back near the hole barking orders at Humanzees as they emerge from the depths.

Without hesitation Javier tosses a grenade, but instead of exploding it releases a smoke cloud.

"Great!" Pittman yells. "Now they can attack from under cover!"

"You whine more than that baby! Just get to killing, already!" Javier fires her shotgun into the billowing smoke at random, and the resulting cries of primate pain send a shiver across her thighs.

Oblivious to these developments Beulah stalks through the Honkey Pad's empty corridors. She locates Thadiana under the desk in the Ovular Office. With the God's Dander situation being what it is, the press can no longer make it to the White House, so why bother with news conferences? It's time to return to her old profession. She hasn't been put to use yet because nobody ever sits at this desk anymore.

"There you are. I've been all over the Honkey Pad looking for you!"

"Thought somebody stole these?" Thadiana has Beulah's voodoo doll collection under the desk with her, the cavernous space a snapshot of the daily hustle and bustle of voodoo doll life. Gang wars, Thanksgiving feasts, the diorama is both extensive and amazing.

"Geez...how many interns was this desk designed to hide?"

"I dunno. I counted over a hundred fifty names, then I stopped. I mean, that was only on one side of the desk alone!"

Beulah scoots in close, shoulder-to-shoulder with Thadiana, stroking her cornrows and thigh. "Are you really a serial profiler?"

"Uh-huh!"

"That means you what...profile people in a compulsive and ritualistic manner?"

"Uh-huh, uh-huh, uh-huh!"

"How about you and I make our own personal Auschwitz?"

"Gee," Thadiana says, surveying the diorama. "I just finished putting it all together!"

Beulah knocks away a cluster of dolls. "No, I mean *you* and *me*...oh, never mind." She pushes Thadiana to the floor and climbs aboard.

Thadiana exclaims, "The San Francisco treat!"

CHAPTER EIGHTEEN

Pittman only has two clips of ammo, and Javier is down to her last two shotgun shells. She's holding onto the final grenade in case they are overrun by the Humanzees and Poontangutans—she will ensure they all go out in a blaze of glory. A Poontangutan swings across the ceiling tiles, a pair of Humanzees dangling from her hand-feet. Javier empties the shotgun into them and tosses it aside. The tomahawk hooked in her belt comes out to play as Pittman unloads bullet after bullet into the horde.

"This isn't your style," Pittman shouts over the noise. "I'm surprised you can get it up for non-profilers."

"*I don't kill profilers!*" A smattering of Humanzee blood and skin lands in her mouth.

Just when all hope seems to be lost a massive arm knocks both Javier and Pittman aside. Reid has finally hit the scene, radiating power like never before. The primates sense something is different about him too, and they wait to see what the deal is. Neither side makes a move for what feels like ages, giving the Poontangutans enough time to drag their wounded below ground.

"I'm not into stupid school yard stare-downs," Javier says. She steps forward brandishing her tomahawk.

"Get back," Reid orders, "I've got it under control!"

"Huh?"

"I've trained them! Now they are thunderbolts loosed from my loins!" So saying, Reid yanks down his pants. What at first appears to be a fine mist of blood spraying from his nether regions is, in fact, a multitude of living things. "Armageddon it!" Reid shouts over the fray. "Armageddon it now, you crotching cock blockers!" Countless crabs spring forth from the glorious wounds that are his genitals, each anchored by a gossamer strand of spider silk. The electroshock collar has been latched around the base of his penis, its electrodes glimmering in the light.

Reid's armada of airborne crabs makes quick work of the enemy. By the thousands they latch onto Humanzee faces and start shredding. Several of them stumble blindly into their brethren clutching the raw mass that is their heads, desperate to hold in the face-jelly seeping between their knobby-knuckled fingers. Seeing this display drains the last drops of courage from the Humanzees and Poontangutans. The final few turn tail and disappear into the chemical steam. Javier tosses her grenade after them for good measure, caving in the entrance.

Pittman thrashes the baby around. "What'd you do that for, you Nazi slutbucket?! We have to go after them! Right Reid? Reid?"

They look and find that Reid's militant STDs are not content to stop their maneuvers simply due to a lack of enemies. They have launched to the ceiling and are burrowing a hole in the weak foam board tiling.

Obviously, the master is no longer in control. Reid whips the remote from his pocket and presses a large red button. Instantly the electro-collar crackles with devastating voltage. Unfortunately for him Reid is the only one adversely affected. The crabs continue as before, dragging his body ever higher. The current running through his body forces his limbs to go rigid, keeping the red button depressed, therefore continuing his slow electrocution. Chimp-like noises escape between his clenched teeth, along with foamy vomit. Cooked pus drips from him in pudding-like dollops. The others watch as he is hauled out of sight, faint wisps of smoke trailing from between his legs, the smell of over-cooked hot dogs causing their stomachs to growl.

Javier nods. "Well, I guess that does that."

"Let's go find those other two wenches," Pittman says, stalking away with the baby hanging limp at his side. "I wanna know what excuse they have for not being here when we needed 'em."

Javier follows, positive she can convince the other women to help her get rid of Pittman. They check Beulah's room—she has redecorated it with red paint and dark curtains. The words "Labor not as one who is wretched" are carved into the water-warped headboard of her bed. Across the room a video camera is mounted on a tripod. They look at each other and shrug.

"She has a profound method," Pittman says. "She can really get into the head of the person she's profiling."

They continue on, a bit unnerved by the silence permeating the Honkey Pad. Still, with Reid out of the picture things are looking up. The tables seem to be turned, though, when their search leads them to the Ovular Office.

Thadiana is sprawled out on the floor, several stab wounds in her back. The blood has turned her bikini into an interesting maroon and purple tie-die. She struggles to lift her head, and when she does there is a glimmer of pained recognition in her eyes. The presidential seal has been stamped on the wall dozens, perhaps hundreds of times to form the words: "Do not despise death, but be well content with it, since this too is one of those things which nature wills."

They stand over her leaking body as she intones, "I do believe...it's getting better...it's getting better all the time..." Phlegm and bits of collapsed lung spew from her mouth, then she goes still.

Pittman stoops, clunking the baby's head against a wall, and checks her pulse. "She fucked up, all right."

CHAPTER NINETEEN

Beulah is sitting cross-legged on a hand-carved mahogany table in the dining room. She is surrounded by plastic fruits and vegetables, a wax boar's head with an apple stuffed in its mouth, artificial potatoes, salads and soups. Her hair hangs in her face as she concentrates on the task at hand, which is the creation of a Beulah Faye Nieran voodoo doll. When she is applying the final touches she feels two pairs of eyes on her. "Hey," she says without looking up from her work. "You guys seen Thadiana around? I've been looking all over for her."

Moving closer Javier asks, "How do you know she's not here? You didn't look to see who it is."

"Touché, Jitlé, touché." Finished with the Beulah Faye Nieran doll she lays it on the table. Then, before Javier can stop her, she hammers a nail through it.

Pittman finishes urinating in a vase and faces them, shaking the baby at the women like a talisman. "What's all this voodoo hubbub about? You have a lot of explaining to do!"

Beulah produces her service revolver and, smirking, pulls back the hammer. "Honestly, how many videos did I have to send you?"

Pittman quietly calculates his shots fired during the fight with the subhumans. His brow furrows—the numbers don't look good. If he throws the baby at Beulah it might prove enough of a distraction for him to slip in an old-school tackle and punch combo, T.J. Hooker style.

"It doesn't have to end this way." Javier takes a furtive step forward, palms facing Beulah. "What about you balling me? There's plenty of ways this could go."

"There's no point in sticking around. I mean, come on...there's only Poontangutans and Humanzees left out there. What's the point in killing something that's hardly alive to begin with?"

The baby snorts several times, and Pittman rubs its head. "What's your major malfunction anyway, beeotch?"

Beulah's smile contains a thousand razor-edged threats. "I'm a philosophile living in a dour and depressing world that has no use for my joyful absurdity. The worst of it is all the skulls. It's so expected."

"What skulls?!" Javier snarls.

In response Beulah sinks her fingernails deep into the flesh of her own face, ripping it away from the underlying bone. Even in these times this is a ghastly sight, and the others cringe while blood spurts from her torn muscle and skin. Beulah's lipstick adds an unnatural slash of color across her crimson mask. Her eyes, lids torn away, bulge out as she cries, "That's comedy!" Her ecstatic proclamation is cut short by the discharge of her service revolver going off in her mouth.

Pittman, Javier, and the baby stare down at Beulah's deflated head for some time. Its contents are spilled on the table as if it were a melon dropped from the top of the Washington Monument. Warm brain tissue dribbles onto the carpet, making Pittman's stomach growl. Now that her body has moved from its original position on the table her parting words are visible on the tabletop: "P.S. Fuck you all!"

Javier lets out an extended sigh. "Obviously she was the killer all along. Happy now? It's all over..." She faces the window and stares into God's Dander, wondering if it will ever melt.

Pittman chuckles. "You not only got everyone to kill themselves, but you tricked Beulah into committing murders for you. I've got to admit, you certainly are the craftiest serial killer I've ever seen."

He fires his final bullet into her back. She manages to turn slightly, not quite enough to confront him, trembling as she uses the wall for support. Slowly she falls to her knees, then her hands and knees, then finally her face smacks against the floor. Javier's last act is to raise her hand and give Pittman the finger. Within seconds her hand waivers and falls to the carpeting.

Pittman is all smiles as he holsters his weapon. This is his ultimate accomplishment. After all, he is the "serial killer-serial killer."

Pittman returns to the Ovular Office, determined to position Thadiana's corpse under the desk in order to celebrate.

"Hey, she ain't *that* dead yet—if ya know what I mean!" he tells the baby.

He hesitates just outside the Ovular office door, considering the pale, wheezing thing in his clutches. What reason is there to keep it alive now? As the functioning president he won't have to answer to his old superiors at the police department, and with his companions all dead he no longer has to worry about their judgments.

"Sorry little buster. It's you or me, and I'm pickin' me this time. Enough of shouldering the burden for everyone else!"

Determined to toss the baby from the Ovular Office window and skeet-shoot the fucker, Pittman strolls in with an extra bounce to his step. He freezes mid-stride, breath caught in his throat. An abundance of Humanzees and Poontangutans await, weapons in hand and teeth bared. He can hear dozens more pouring in down the hall.

Pointing at Pittman the baby laughs, and laughs.

BRUCE TAYLOR
(aka Mr. Magic Realism)

LOCATION:
Seattle, Washington

STYLE OF BIZARRO:
Magic Realism and Surrealism

BOOKS BY TAYLOR:

The Final Trick of Funnyman
Kafka's Uncle and Other Strange Stories
Edward: Dancing On the Edge of Infinity

DESCRIPTION: In the introduction to Bruce Taylor's story, "The Breath Amidst the Stones" in New Dimensions 10, the editor, Robert Silverberg, said, "The specialty of Bruce Taylor of Seattle is brief, playful, bizarre stories that occupy the mysterious middle ground somewhere between fantasy and the surreal." Since that story was published, the "fantasy" to which he referred, is more that of Magic Realism, similar to some of the work of Bradbury, and the stories that appeared on Serling's, The Twilight Zone—people leading ordinary lives suddenly caught up in extraordinary circumstances or realizing that what they thought was reality turns out not to be so.

INTERESTS: Hypnosis, remodeling, urban walks, reading, backpacking (Bruce is vice-president of Switchback, Inc., manufacturer of hard-shell backpacks— www.switchbackpacks.com) When not doing that, he enjoys travel, astronomy, remodeling, urban walks, reading, and getting artists together at once-a-month gatherings at his home (such events come under the name of FOKUS—Friends of Kafka's Uncle Society, named after Bruce's recently published book.)

INFLUENCES: H. G. Wells, Ray Bradbury, Franz Kafka, Anton Chekhov, Jack Cady, Rod Serling, Dostoevsky, Flaubert, Robert Penn Warren, Karel Capek I, George Orwell, Steinbeck.and the absolutely amazing wealth of imaginative writing of Magic Realist writers as well recent Magic Realist film.

WEBSITE:
www.pantarbe.com/mrmagicrealism

The Breath Amidst the Stones

"Foo-fra!" says the wall.

I look up from the sleeping desk. "I can't understand you. Take the plasterboard out of your mouth."

The wall sneers; the grain distorts. "I don't have plasterboard in my mouth," says the wall.

"Then what were you saying?"

"Foo-fra."

"Foo-fra?" I scratch my head. "What kind of word is that?"

"I don't know," says the wall. "I just invented it. Maybe"—and the wall stares at a picture by van Gogh—"maybe it's an expression that's halfway between *fooey* and *frampt*."

"*Fooey* I understand, *frampt* I don't."

"Huh," replies the wall. "I just made up frampt. I suppose I should define it before I use it in other words."

I nod. "It would really help."

"Skidge," says the rug.

I stare down. The blue-green rug smiles pleasantly.

"Skidge?" I say.

"Skidge. I like that word. I thought it up."

I rub my eyes. "What does it mean?"

"It's a combination of *skid* and *edge*. I'm sure it has applications to rugs in general, but I'm not sure how."

"Maybe," says the wall, "it can mean a rug that has a tendency to skid near the edge."

"Spain," says the big picture window.

"Sorry," I say, "Spain is taken. It's a country."

The glass warps in embarrassment. "Damn. I meant it to mean a soapy pane of glass. No good, huh?"

"No," I reply, "no good."

I look about me, amused and angered. Amused because all those things which we used to consider as having no life—well, now they do, and how they wrestle with their special conditions of existence is amusing. Yet, I'm angered...

"Sputz," says my pencil.

"Sputz," I repeat. "It sounds like a mispronunciation of *spuds*, which means potatoes. Is that what you mean?"

"No," says my pencil. "I meant it to mean the act of spelling incorrectly."

"Oh."

The pencil crawls across the desk and, in the border of my income tax form, it begins a game of tictacktoe with my pen. The pen suddenly makes a big black pool of ink. It whispers, "Have you any Kaopectate? I think I'm getting the runs."

I shake my head. "No." The letters on the paper run from the engulfing black tide; then the tax form stands and tries to shake the ink from itself. Then the paper lies back down, the letters rearrange themselves, and what once read "If you do not itemize deductions and line 15 is under $15,000, find tax in tables" comes out $di dte 00t yoi5t 51zeit o f do i x.

And the letters know they are in the wrong positions, but since they never learned how to spell, nor learned anything about word order, they give up and lie around, babbling incoherently. A *t* jumps up and down. A capital *A* tackles a small *z*, and they tumble across the page. I sigh.

In the background, I hear a slopping. The water is climbing out of the fish tank again. And the fish inside dart about, always very frantic when the water does this. This time I don't bother trying to put the water back in the tank. Every time I tried before, there was nothing really to grab onto. I watch the water. It is still experimenting with mobility. First it lengthens itself out like a snake and tries to inch forward. Then it rolls. As it tries new forms, it mutters, "Maybe? How do I . . . ? No . . . no, that won't work." It rolls up into a moist ball and tries to roll. "Better," it says. It rolls over to the cat, which stands with stiff fur. The animal always stares at the water with a look that must be incredulity. The water mimics the cat's form—even the tail, which it switches about as a cat might. A pregnant guppy stops its mad swimming long enough to look out from the water in the place where a cat's eye would be. The form then looks at itself and the fish inside. "Most amazing," it says.

"You're getting better," I say.

"Thank you," says the water. "Finding a convenient form is most difficult."

"Well, at the risk of making a bad pun, your options for form are indeed fluid."

"Hm! Fluid indeed. Aren't we funny." And, like a cat, the water sits on the rug, ears back.

"Move!" says the rug. "You're getting me wet."

I shake my head. "You really should be more careful. You risk being soaked up."

"True," says the water, pacing about. "Also, since more surface area of me is exposed, I guess I risk rapid evaporation."

It walks back to the fish tank, which is trying to scrub algae off its inside surfaces. It mutters, "Can't see a goddamn thing."

"Crap," says the water. "I don't really want to go back into the tank and sit there. I feel like a kitty stuck on a potty box."

I shrug. The water crawls back into the tank. I hear whispering. I look around. The books are talking among themselves. Suddenly there is a paper-thin scream. *Tropic of Cancer* has just opened its pages and exposed itself to *Jane Eyre*. Portnoy is complaining again. My abnormal psychology text is shouting theories that either drastically conflict with theories in other texts or simply do not make any sense. I sigh. Let them shout. The theories have little to do with reality, anyway. The *I Ching* is tossing

yarrow sticks, and the Bible is screaming, "Pagan! *Heathen!*" The dictionary is looking into itself and shouts words that it finds amusing: "Foregut!" Rustle of pages. "Galago!" Then, "Macronutrient!"

A wastebasket sneezes, and papers fly up.

"Willbillet, woorbillet, woobillet." The wall frowns. It looks to me. "Not all words have to make sense, do they?"

I shrug. "I don't know. It helps if they do."

"Isn't there such a thing as poetic license? Woorbillet?"

"Words are supposed to mean something," I say.

"Scoobie-doobie-doo? Twenty-three skiddoo? Ya-hoo? Don't give me that crap."

"I don't want to argue. Maybe you are right."

"Yippee-skippee. Wait! Where are you going? Are you angry at me?"

"No," I say. "I want to go for a walk. Ever since The Change, it's been awfully noisy in here."

"Ah," sighs the rug, "was not The Change wonderful? Isn't it magic to be aware? To be sentient?"

"For you," I say. "Me, I'm not so sure. Right now I guess I'm *really* pissed at the Valaslavians."

"Maybe you're pissed," says the water. "We're not."

I get my coat. "I'm glad for you. I mean, I really am. But don't forget how hard it is for us people to deal with The Change."

"You're angry," says my pencil, "because we won't be exploited any longer. We now have minds of our own. We won't be controlled by you any more."

As the pencil talks, it makes an exclamation point on the paper.

"Think what you will," I say. I limp out the door.

My inner agitation keeps me, thankfully, from remembering why I limp. As the door closes, it wishes me a nice walk. The sidewalk looks at me. I smile.

"Tread lightly, stranger," the walk says.

"Since I hurt my foot, I don't have much choice."

The walk still looks at me with wariness. I stop walking to let two rocks cross in front to me. Following behind them are seven little stones. I walk past brush and hear gasps. Looking down, I see two beer cans making love. I shrug.

"Stop!" says a stop sign. "No parking within thirty feet!"

"I'm not going to park," I reply. "I'm just out for a walk."

I continue on. And I'm angry. The Change. The goddamn Change. If we had only been more careful; Valaslavia looked so wonderful. We certainly studied the planet, the culture, and it certainly seemed that it would be a very nice addition to our Empire. And so we set our ship down near a city.

The inhabitants came out. People. They looked just like people. We had our IBM Translator, and I read the speech—a very nice speech, really, although somewhat standardized. "'Greetings,'" I read, "'in the name of Earth, you are now a subject of our Empire.'"

I was just about ready to continue with our list of expectations and various kindnesses when I heard: "Go plitz yourself."

I did not have to know the meaning of the word to know that I'd been insulted. I glowered at the Valaslavian. The Valaslavian smiled meekly and pointed down. There was a large rock by my foot. A very large, squarish rock.

I looked around to my crew members. They shrugged.

Lieutenant Arko shook his head. "The jerk doesn't understand. Try again."

"In the name—"

"Plitz you!"

I guess I got angry and grabbed the Valaslavian by his tunic, and then pain! Pain! Pain! I looked down. The rock was sitting on my foot. The rock moved in a grinding motion, and I felt the bones in my foot turn to mush. I screamed. Once. Twice.

"Respect," said the rock, "respect, respect, respect! Even though these life forms be inferior to us, respect!"

My foot was beyond hurting; it was also beyond repair. I squeezed my eyes shut and behind my eyelids saw yellow and blue and purple lights.

Lieutenant Arko looked very pale. "I think we made a mistake," he whispered.

"Uh," I replied. The rock backed off my foot.

With Lieutenant Arko and Communications Engineer Toshiba helping me, we began to back away to the ship. The rock jumped toward us. We scrambled into the great white ship. And from all over, rocks began to leap toward the ship; rocks of all shapes, sizes, colors. And we heard the message: "*All* has life. And as the Great Ones from Trixpoxya made us aware, so we make *you* aware!"

"But," I called down from the hatchway of the ship, "we are already aware!"

"Yes, yes," said Communications Engineer Toshiba.

"See?" He wiggled his thumb. "Notice how aware I am of my thumb! See? I can touch all five fingers with my thumb! Isn't that neat? I'm aware I can do that—"

"*Awake!*"

"But we are awake!" said Lieutenant Arko. "See? My eyes are open. I am aware of my awareness!"

"Awake! And we give you the power to give others what we give you!"

Our minds were filled with something—I don't know what. But I felt a presence. My mind—not my head—ached. Somewhere within me, a thin wail; something reaching forward, something reaching back, and then—then—touching.

The whole ship shuddered.

"Kabort?" I looked around. A mouth had formed in the wall. "Ka-plut?"

"Pootz!" The floor shifted.

Then a deep growl. I swallowed. We all looked at each other. I still had the translator in my hand; it self-activated, and I stared at it with astonishment. "The stars! The stars! They are mine! No longer am I controlled by sweaty, soiled fingers of the inferior flesh! I shall go where I wish to go! I shall go where no machine has gone before!"

The hatch sealed itself. The growl came again; once more the ship shook, and our minds were filled with immense power and an incredible sense of destiny!

"Hang on!" I yelled.

The ship leaped skyward at I don't know how many g's. The ship bounced around the universe like a Ping-Pong ball for I don't know how long. It was obvious that the ship was enjoying sentiency.

We all knew what we had to do. We did not dare let the ship get back to Earth. We jammed the controls. We pulled wires. We stuck chewing gum in tape heads. We blew fuses. We kicked and hit and destroyed as much of the navigational-communications systems as possible.

But the ship had a mind of its own.

And Earth appeared on the viewscreen.

And in our minds we heard the command: "Awake!"

We all looked at each other hopelessly.

I remember. I remember it well. I sigh. My jacket snuggles around me for more warmth. Such the memory. Now the reality. I shrug. My foot hurts.

I want to return home, but in order to do so, I have to cross a drawbridge. The span is up; the bridge is yawning. I look to my watch, but the little hands are folded. "Sorry," it says, "but I'm taking my rest break."

("The Breath Amidst the Stones," originally appeared in New Dimensions #10, Ed. Robert Silverberg, Harper and Row, 1980.)

A Little Spider Shop Talk

Now, I remember talking to my neighborhood spider, you know, she lives right next door and spends all her time in her apartment weaving those webs that others would not care to admit to weaving but she does it right in her living room and doesn't seem to mind that people walk by and scream at her frankness.

Me, it never bothers me. No sir. We became good friends. I always admired how hard she worked as she anchored one end of the web here and the other end there. If I worked as hard as she did, I'd be sweating in a second.

"Really," she said one day as I was visiting her, "it isn't really all that difficult to build webs, it really isn't at all." She regarded me casually with a few of her eyes.

"Huh, do tell," I replied. "It certainly seems like a task."

"Care for some coffee?" she asked. (I know she had a very complicated Latin name, so I just called her Mrs. Webb and she said that was fine.)

"Yes," I replied.

"Well, you know how to do it. Excuse me while I lay a batch of eggs."

"Certainly," I replied. And shoving a few silk strands aside, and being careful which burner to turn on (a part of her web was anchored to the refrigerator near by and I didn't want to burn the silk) I put on a pot. "I take it you'd like some?"

"Uh-huh," she said; she really didn't seem all that interested; laying eggs and all does take some concentration. So, I brewed some coffee up, ducked some silk strands and put her cup in a fairly level area of silk where she often sat, sometimes splayed like a black flower in a delicate silk setting.

And when she was through with her onerous task, she came up the web and sat right down and with her front legs, she held the cup and drank. "My, that's good," she said. "Is that the last of the Maxwell House?"

"I didn't see it," I said. "This is the Brim."

"Nice," she replied.

"How many eggs do you lay all at once?" I asked politely, not knowing if she'd be offended by such a question.

"I don't know," she said, and I think she might have glanced to the corner, to the eggs, with all her eyes, but I wasn't too awfully sure. "A few, I suppose."

And she sipped her coffee. And I sipped mine.

"I really do admire you," she said, "for being my friend. So many who walk by would like to pretend that I don't exist, but I know they are frightened. I wonder why."

"People are afraid of spiders," I simply said.

I suspected Mrs. Webb was amused but looking at her, she appeared expressionless.

"Spiders outside of themselves or the kind that dwell inside?" she asked.

"Oh, hell," I said, "maybe it's both—maybe there's a part of ourselves that so reminds us of insects that we can't stand the knowledge. Or maybe it's a fear of being ensnared in something and having no way out, or being overwhelmed by something symbolic that catches us with so many legs that we can't escape—"

And Mrs. Webb did laugh. "Oh, the fear. It's the fear, isn't it? Of being overtaken, of being unable to escape, of being held powerless by the incomprehensible."

"Maybe," I said, as I drank my coffee. "But maybe people are specifically frightened of you—"

"By my webs?" And she lowered her coffee cup. "By my silk?"

I laughed. "'Oh, the tangled webs we weave'—uh, Shakespeare, I think."

"So, I remind people of the webs they weave and they see themselves more like spiders than they want to admit?"

"Possibly. But with you, something else—"

"And that is—"

"Your name—isn't it Latin for Black Widow—"

"Oh!" And she was definitely upset, "all that folklore about how deadly I am? That I eat my mate?"

"Well, you do—you have done that—"

"Well," she said, "is it that act that I do or is it the fear people have that, if they get involved with one another, they will somehow be devoured? The sense of themselves lost to another because people will do just about anything for love? Or be slowly drained of the essence of themselves until just a shell of one remains?"

I almost choked. "That's rather good," I said, "matter of fact, your insight into the human condition is awfully astute."

"Thank you," she said, "our species has been around long enough to have quite a folklore about humans. Actually, probably more accurate than your folklore about us. But tell me, is there anything else about me—specifically—that may bother people?"

I thought for a minute and then said, "Yeah, that red hourglass design on your body."

I heard defensiveness in her voice. "Well, what of it? It is certainly distinctive and I think rather attractive—"

I laughed. "Hold it, I didn't say it wasn't attractive or bad or anything like that. I'm just stating a fact—"

"Why should it be bothersome—"

"The hourglass is the classic symbol of the passage of time," I thought. "And of death."

She sipped her coffee reflectively. She lowered it as if considering to say something—then sipped again. Quietly and with great injured pride she said, "But I'm a widow—a black widow to be sure and sometimes my appetite does get carried away I suppose—but time? Time? It's just coincidental that I have a red hourglass."

"Symbolic," I said, "maybe people fear spiders because they associate the hourglass with being overwhelmed by time." I paused. "Or the lack of it. Or the passage of it."

Mrs. Webb chuckled. "Overwhelmed by the Black Widow of Time. My, how sinister and ugly we sound—we are life forms just like you—we don't even kill for sport or blow up anyone and yet we're regarded as so horrible." She sighed, finished her coffee and simply held the mug. "More and more," she finally said, "it sounds like the attributes given to spiders—especially Black Widows—are qualities that people hate and cannot accept in themselves."

"Maybe," I replied. "A lot of it sounds like that to be sure. The term, I believe, is 'projection'." I drained my cup. "Well," I said, "as usual, it's been interesting talking with you."

"Thank you," Mrs. Webb replied. "Hope our chat didn't scare you."

"Hardly," I replied. "What is most frightening and always frightening is when things aren't said—then the fantasies, and usually the worst ones—set in."

"Indeed," she sighed, "indeed. Well, I have to get positioned in my web here to see if dinner drops in."

"Let me take your cup," I said and so doing, and dodging thick silky strands, I went to the sink, washed the cups and put them on the drainboard. Then, "Take care," I said as I walked out the door.

"Good-bye," Mrs. Webb said, "do come back; it's always so interesting talking with you."

I went downstairs thinking of many things. When I reached my apartment, I stopped by the mirror—yup, I sighed, a few more gray hairs. I shook my head and, on the way to the kitchen to fix dinner, I glanced to the table at the red hourglass and watched, drop by drop, this mortal blood pass.

Of Tunafish and Galaxies

"Tunafish," the madman said. Let me clarify that. You can't say that he was actually a madman because when you spoke to him, there was that instant of recognition of what you said and a second's pause as he decided what crazy response that deserved. Not saying he wasn't crazy. But there was, as Shakespeare so eloquently said, method. This guy could talk for hours—and he did. But dammit, to look at him, you knew that he knew that you knew what was going on: he insisted on being crazy. He had made a rational decision to be irrational—which in mental illness—is usually not the case.

His name was Mr. Stevenson. He was forty-seven, black unruly hair and when you spoke to him you sensed enormous intelligence. As near as we can figure out, he's manic-depressive. Something is depressing him so God dam much that he can't face it and handles it by being high and crazy from the anxiety.

Course of therapy? Try to talk to him. Try to establish some sort of rapport, empathy.

"Hello, Mr. Stevenson. How are you today?"

"Tunafish."

"I'm having a hard time following that, Mr. Stevenson."

"Well, you know what they say. They're always saying it. It. Always it. Tit. Haven't felt tit for ages. Tit. Tit-tat. Shall we tit-tat, you queer? Get your thoughts off me. Put out your fire; I'll not combust for you, you salad eater! You vegetarian! Nazi Germany died because you ate salads. You need a dressing down. A Thousand Island's for you, buddy!"

"Mr. Stevenson, I find it very difficult to carry on a conversation with you—"

"Carry on. That's it. Carrion. Carrion, my sweet, meet my friends."

"Mr. Stevenson, I—"

"You know what they say: a hand on the bird is worth six in the scoff."

"Mr. Stevenson, I think you're going to have to—"

"Eat shit."

"No—"

"Yes! Try it with catsup!"

"I have no desire to eat fecal—"

"Shit! Call it shit! Call it by its proper noun, you silly gerund!"

With that, Mr. Stevenson snapped his fingers and walked away.

Out there. Out there. It's happening without warning. Fire. Heat. Breaking down. Melting. Heat. Hotter. Hotter. Tighter the atoms squeeze. Heavier. Heavier and then blinding light as the center of the galaxy explodes...

"Mr. Stevenson..."

Mr. Stevenson sat hunched like a tight ball in the corner of the day room. As I watched him, he hunched himself tighter, tighter.

"Mr. Stevenson!" Gently, I touched his shoulder. His muscles were tight and as I touched him he contracted still tighter. I stepped back. I'm not exactly certain why but I felt as though something was going to happen. And it did. Oh, Lord. How do you describe a person exploding? Suddenly, he leaped up, flinging his arms and legs out and yelling, "Boom! I go boom! Boom! Boom! Boom! Whizzz! Whee! Whee! Boom! Boom! Boom! The whole God damn thing go boom!" He spun about, did a cartwheel and flipped to his back, arms, legs out straight and silently said, "Boom."

He had a silly grin on his face but his eyes showed fear. Some other patients had frozen smiles. Others looked horrified. For a long time everyone was silent. Then

Mr. Stevenson stood and began laughing. And then, talking. "Funnier than a schizophrenic cat. Blooie! Guts blow out! Wheee! The deadness of it all. All fried like sardines in sand. More beautiful than a dry fog. Dehumidified oceans; cement clouds. More fun than a windy vacuum."

"Mr. Stevenson, I really think you can be more straightforward—"

He looked at me. He looked at me for a long time and then he switched into a high falsetto. "My name is Mickey Mouse. I fuck Pluto and Donald Duck when Uncle Walt isn't looking. Yes, yes, it's true. He drew me and when he was gone I had to draw on my own talent. He cheated me, he did. Gave me gloves, four fingers and no penis. I had to erase a lot and add a few lines. And even then—even then it was all a Fantasy Land near the Frontier Land just left of Tomorrow Land but when you wish upon a star/Makes no difference who you are unless you're John Wayne—" Mr. Stevenson stopped and switched into the role of John Wayne; "Hi. I'm John Wayne. I suck off gun barrels. I grab bulls by the balls and squeeze. If you ain't American, you ain't real. And if you ain't real, why, then, I'm gonna have to shoot you." Abruptly, he switched again. He became rigid, stiff and began making mechanical movements like a robot. "Bleep! Bleep! I am—am—America—John Wayne/Fantasy Land. What does woman mean—mean to me—butt, big tits and warm, moist—buzz! Buzz! Ejaculation! Ejaculation! This is Ejaculation Command! The penis has entered! That's one small surge for man, one giant grunt for mankind!" He stopped suddenly then tilted his head as though listening. "Attention! Attention!" He turned around three times, walked back and forth six times and then turned to me. "Andromeda calling. One order for one tunafish sandwich with side order of hard boiled sand with steak sauce."

"Mr. Stevenson, I feel I should tell you that you are totally disorganized."

"Andromeda calling. Also one

chilled entropy over boiling ice."

"Mr. Stevenson... I... uh..."

He laughed and leaped and touched the ceiling. "Whee!" was all he replied. I gave up and went to a staff meeting where we were to discuss the patients. As I walked out of the day room to the meeting room, I realized that I had *no* idea what to say about Mr. Stevenson except that he came across totally disorganized. But then, everybody knew *that*.

No civilization in the galaxy knew what the ramifications of the suddenly intense radiation meant because by the time instruments detected the change, the instruments, the minds that created the electronic tools, the planet on which the tools and minds worked together—vanished. And even if minds remained intact long enough to know the change, they would realize it was happening in the nearby galaxies as well—but what could be done? Besides, if one goes by conventional space-time physics, then the explosions in nearby galaxies had occurred billions of light years ago... *if* one went by conventional space-time physics.

Dr. Leery tried hard to look comfortable. And the harder he tried, the more uncomfortable he became which made him try all that much harder and of course the staff noticed it and *they* became uncomfortable which made Dr. Leery even more uncomfortable which made the staff that much more uncomfortable until finally Dr. Leery excused himself to get a cup of coffee. When he got back, the staff was comfortable and was already discussing the patients. After Dr. Leery sneaked in the door, he leaned against the door frame, trying to look as comfortable as possible. The staff decided to ignore him.

"And so," the resident said, "James Stevenson is our next patient. Mr. Bradley, would you care to discuss him?"

I cleared my throat. "He has been on the unit two days. He came in on a police hold for directing traffic and saying that the order was breaking down. Since he has been here, his ability to interrelate to people has disintegrated rapidly—"

The resident shook his head. "Damn. This pen doesn't write. Got another one?"

I tossed him mine. "Jesus! This one doesn't write either. Someone got a pencil?"

A nurse tossed him one and we finally got on with the report.

"No diagnosis as yet," I said.

"Well," the resident said, and he paused to think of something meaningful to say, "sounds like he's a manic-depressive in an acute manic phase." The resident looked to me. "Would our astute and illustrious medical student care to say something?"

"I think you're right," I said. Actually, I wasn't sure; I didn't like the resident, but he would be a great one to write a letter of reference for me and so I wanted to be as agreeable as possible. Besides, you never but *never* say anything foolish in psychiatry. You have to be so careful lest everyone turn to look at you as though you had let a verbal fart at least and at most, you were really inappropriate and on the edge of a breakdown. Of course, that usually makes me embarrassed and self-conscious and I begin to fumble with my hands and the staff looks even closer at you which makes you even more embarrassed until finally you excuse yourself to get a cup of coffee. By the time you return, some other staffer has come under scrutiny—they're through with you, having decided, in your absence, what *your* problems are—but that's neither here nor there. Anyhow, the resident looked at me and gave me a quick nod for being as perceptive and intelligent as he imagined himself to be and he sat back and said, "What do you think of treating him with lithium to kind of even him out?" I know that he's going to treat him with lithium anyway, so I say, "Yeah, I think it's a good idea." The resident smiles. I'm going to get a good letter of recommendation. After he writes it, then I can go my own way and disagree with him and tell him what a shmuck I think he is, but right now, I'm nice, nice, *nice*.

"So," the resident says, "lithium it is. Also, when dealing with this guy, be as concrete as possible. Don't abstract. Be good role models."

I bobble my head. I glance at Dr. Leery. He's obviously uncomfortable with the idea and looks very uncomfortable, but really, he's insecure and wants to be liked by everybody, but realizes he's *not* liked by everybody which makes him more uncomfortable and the staff begins to look around, wondering where the bad vibes are coming from and in all their eyes the question is the same: is it me? You? Is someone's psychosis coming out of remission? But in Dr. Leery's eyes, he *knows* it's him and he starts shifting about and staff members begin to glance at him which makes him very uncomfortable and he quickly drains his coffee cup and goes out for another cup. The staff once again becomes comfortable and returns to business.

"Next patient," the resident says. He gives me an approving nod. It's going to be a great letter of recommendation. Dr. Bradley. Yeah. Yeah. Ohhhhh! The *money!*

"Mr. Stevenson!" I see Mr. Stevenson running about the dayroom, flapping his arms. His face is serene, even with all the exertion. He stops in front of the window, but still flaps his arms like a giant bird. The late afternoon sunlight streams in and I squint for it is almost impossible to see and in the brightness Mr. Stevenson is a dark form waving and undulating. I go over to him. "Sir."

"Casserole," he says, "it reminds me of Dresden, the days when it was a caterpillar potentially butterflying about. Pretty bird it was; yellow of bill burning, burning in the night whose broad stripes and quasars never more Crest toothpasting/And the wienies in air/mustered buns to eat there—" Mr. Stevenson then hopped upon a chair, still flapping his arms and looked down at me with a very penetrating look. "Come to the quarry and get stoned with me. We'll have a rock concert which we'll take for granite. Bring along quartz of wine and we'll marble at the sights and watch the old order pass away and the galaxies are now beyond our command/and the space-time it is de-ranging." He stopped flapping his arms. I looked at him. "I'm terribly confused," I said.

"Tunafish," he replied, jumping down from the chair. "You can tune a piano but you can't tunafish. What's a cute psychotic break like you doing in a place like this? Boom! All go boom!" Then he became very still, tensed up and let a very noisy fart. "Like that. Just like that." He flapped his arms, whistled and skipped out of the room.

I watched. I didn't even have time to be concrete. Not even asphalt. Nor gravel. I laughed. What the *fuck* am I saying! I—

...if one went by conventional physics. But it was unconventional. Civilizations did not have time to shriek. The Force had arrived. It was chaotic; born of chaos, yet it was ordered. It was total paradox. It was breaking laws and making new ones. The speed of light meant nothing. The Force itself was its own constant and set its own way. Blinding, swift, immeasurable heat and planets turned to smoke; space warped, suns changed color, became rubbery; some ran like glowing hot plastic; others popped like soap bubbles; inconsistent yet the destruction was consistent and the Force moved...

Dr. Leery and the resident read the chart. Dr. Leery was uncomfortable. He'd look at you, then look away and shift weight from one foot to the other and he'd grimace. The resident looked uncomfortable and kept flipping the pages back and forth, back and forth, forth, back and—uh—I—seem to be having trouble—consecra—concentra—oh, yes—and Dr. Leery said he'd be right back after he made a telephone call. The resident smiled. "Well, how's the lithium working, Mr.

Bradley?"

"It's not," I replied. "He's higher than ever and the personality disintegration is more obvious; I can't follow a word he says; it's like—you know—rutabaga—"I stopped. I said that?

The resident looked at me. "Like *what*?"

I opened my mouth and shook my head, not knowing what to say. I realized that I was blowing my recommendation and I tried to save my ass—"Rutabaga," I said again, "like in a salad bowl—you know—a football game—"

The resident just stared. He sat with a pencil in his hand. Abruptly the pencil softened and gently fell on the resident's wrist like a thin cord of yellow toothpaste. He looked at me and said, "Rumplestiltskin!" and then his watch exploded in a puff of metallic blue smoke.

I ran to the dayroom, passing Dr. Leery who stood in the hallway watching the walls sag and the ceiling lights melt and hang like glowing stalactites.

I saw Mr. Stevenson. He turned, smiled and shouted "Tunafish!" and waved good—

City Streets

All the cities on the Earth are the same: dark, deserted, still, lonely. The tall and gaunt man, a shadow, a mere memory of his former self, came over the top of a hill and there was another city. Just like the one before. A thin wind stirred the snow. The man kept walking and abruptly the snow ended and the pavement began. He walked slowly. It was evening. Venus was high in the sky. Over the south flank of a massive volcano, the moon rose. The man sighed; looking to Venus, he said, "You son of a bitch! You're just God damn lucky. That's all. If we were a few million miles closer, if the sun hadn't cooled, I'd give you a run for your money, you pearly bastard." The man gave the finger to Venus, then he turned and continued to walk.

The city was ancient; the buildings were not tall. They had big windows, curved at the top. Some of them had peaked roofs, others were flat. But the city itself was a perfect statement of proud architecture; somewhat ponderous, perhaps, but nonetheless stately, roomy, elegant, comfortable. For the time the city was used, it was used well; a fair of use, a carnival of creativity, a festival of delightful architecture, as though the builders, those who decided to remain behind and who knew the end was near, put as much energy into the living as they could into that great moment.

The man was proud of them. He sighed again, looked about, occasionally taking his tattered sleeve to rub the outside of shop windows to peer inside. In one building, he saw occupants sitting at tables. They appeared perfectly preserved, no signs of deterioration—like they were just sleeping—waiting to be awakened. The man scratched his head, laughed and thought, oh, how we can get carried away with ourselves. Shaking his head, he realized that this city was like all the others: dead. Dead as the rock which made up the buildings. But there was one thing that puzzled him: why *he* was not dead. And how he survived without food. And why he was so angry and hurt. He often thought there must be a reason—but what? Was there some mission for him? Why was it up to him to carry about the miserable burden of memories of a long dead planet? Why had he not left with the others? Why had he chosen to stay and die—but not die after all? The man frowned. The same questions over and over again and the same answer: some things are not known. One thing he *did* know was his constant rage at Venus.

Perhaps that anger fed him and kept him alive—but why him? He was the only one he knew of who had survived and he certainly got very lonely—yet he kept on, more than once asking himself, why? Why do I continue to trek around this snowball? This gaunt, this shadow, this memory of a former planet? Was there something that he had missed? No answers. Walking on, he was about to cross the street when he noticed something. He stopped and backtracked. A parking meter—an hour left on it. He frowned. Malfunction. Must be. But out of curiosity, he checked another parking meter and there was an hour left on it. The man was puzzled. He had not noticed this before in other cities. Meaningful? Meaningless? The man continued on.

Some time later, he realized he was getting tired; stopping, he looked about. In the thin light of the moon, the city streets were so dark; the windows looking over them like sad, lonely eyes, as though watching for something yet to come or seeing that which had passed; eyes turned in on themselves and seeing the darkness outside penetrating within to darken the soul. The man wanted to cry; looking to Venus, he shouted, "Damn you!" Shivering and walking once more, he tried the doors to buildings. He needed a place to sleep, a place comfortable, where he could curl up tight as a seed.

Unexpectedly, a door he tried opened; a gust of wind caught it and the knob slipped from his hand. *Bang!* The door slammed against the inside wall with the sound of an explosion. The man gasped, jumped back, then calmed himself and thought, outside of myself, it is the only sound that I have heard. He quieted his heart and noticed the moon shining through high and dirty windows. Slowly closing the door, he abruptly realized how *warm* it was. But then, he remembered that it had been a fairly warm day—he even saw, late that afternoon, ice melting on a cliff face. Obviously, the stone buildings soaked up the meager heat during the day and released it at night. Yet

he was still surprised at the warmth—it didn't seem *that* warm that day. He looked about. In the dim light, he saw huge wooden boxes or crates. Some kind of warehouse, he mused. All around were unopened boxes. Though the man was tired, his curiosity was aroused and, discovering a hammer on the floor, decided to look inside one of the boxes. Entertainment comes easy, he thought, as he pushed the box into a pale pool of moonlight. He began prying boards off, surprised at how much effort it took and deciding the box wasn't about to yield its secret easily. Finally, he was able to peer down inside; in the moon's light, he saw an ocean, waves, high and white, crashing against cliffs, and a blue sky. The man stood back, hurt and angry, and kicked the crate. "God damn you, you son of a bitch! What a miserable joke!" Kicking the crate again, he breathed through clenched teeth, his hands fists. "Just what I want," he whispered, "to be reminded of the past."

He abruptly wished he had not opened the box. He had tried hard to forget the way it once was; by looking into the box—it only served in opening old memories. Again, he kicked the crate. Now he was too angry to sleep. He went after another box; the wood squeaked and scuffed as he pushed it into the moonlit area. After much work, he had the top off that box and peering in, he gasped. Never had he seen anything like it: a city. A beautiful city with towers white and tall, shining in the sun and the contrast between city and sky was sharp. His heart ached to see such a city. Wanting a closer look, he took off more boards, then scrambled up the side of the box, bending double to look in. People! Yes, people! They were smiling and he heard singing. The air was fresh and clean. He pulled back out of the box, amazed; it was like no city he could even imagine. He concluded that it was a city on Venus. It must be. He had *never* seen anything like it in his wanderings. But what he could not understand was why Venus would send these boxes. He began to think it a joke. What a bastard is Venus. What an incredible, insensitive bastard! How base, boorish, crude to flaunt its good fortune before something so starved as Earth—like eating cake before a beggar and tossing a few crumbs. The man thought all of this while he dragged out from the darkness a third crate and opened up that one.

What he saw stopped his thoughts. He began to cry. Then, sitting with his back to the crate, he bawled and that changed to hysterical sobbing. Smashing the floor with his fists, he sobbed, "It's unfair! It's unfair! It's so God damn fucking unfair!" And what he saw haunted him: a rolling landscape, green of grass with so many flowers of different colors that it must be the origin of rainbows. In the distance, a broad river and beyond the river, a snow crowned volcano with majestic waterfalls pouring down high cliffs to the plain below. And the sky—ah! The sky was so incredibly blue and yes, that's the way it was and God damn it, the man doesn't want to remember it; he was then certain, beyond a doubt that it was trickery from a wicked Venus which now suddenly had so much more—suddenly he ran out to the street and, seeing Venus, he shrieked, "You son of a bitch! Not only can I not die, but you torment me with memories! Why this torture! Why remind me of what is no more!" He shook his fist—then gave in to his hopeless rage. And through his tears, he looked about: the city silent, ancient; snow moving down the street like a front of dust—he stumbled back into the warehouse to fall against the crate with the ocean inside; he sobbed as he sat in the light of the moon, sobbing then finally falling asleep.

Sometime during the night he awoke. It was dark where he lay; he shook his head, uncertain if he had heard a noise or if he had just dreamed it. Silence. He sighed, curled up on the floor again but just before he drifted off—he opened his eyes and sat up so fast that he banged his head against the crate. The man listened. The wind? He

stopped breathing. Then, faintly, faintly—yes—crying! He heard something *crying!* From the back of the building—silently, he made his way back to the interior of the vast room. Stumbling into a large box, he stopped, swore silently, waited. The light of the moon came through a high bank of windows on the other side of the warehouse, now. In the light, the man saw a cleared area; a ring of chairs circled about an old-fashioned, pot-bellied stove.

The man stopped. The crying came from within the stove! He was impressed by how lonesome a cry it was, how pathetic, how sad; thin, high and wailing. Stooping, the man opened the fire door. The crying continued.

"Hello," the man whispered, "Hello?"

The crying stopped; all he heard was a sniffling. Then a weak voice: "Who are you?"

"That makes no difference," the man said, "The question is—what is wrong? Why are you crying?"

"I don't want to die!"

The man peered into the belly of the stove, but saw nothing. "Why can't I see you?"

"I don't want to die!"

"Shh!" the man said. "Shhh! Let's not talk of that now. Where are you?"

The thin voice filled him with despair. "Look in the ashes. Blow, blow gently, stranger, for I am almost gone."

The man suddenly realized how he was trembling and frightened as well. Gently, he blew into the belly of the stove; ashes touched his face like infinitely soft fingers.

"*Gently, gently,*" came the voice, "oh, stranger, *gently.*"

And there, there, amidst the darkness of ashes, a little red ember. "Behold me," came a faint whisper, "behold me for I am dying."

The man pulled back. "Not if I can help it." He stood and frantically stumbled about the warehouse, looking for paper, wood splinters, anything that would burn. There! There by the door; something white. He grabbed it. Yes, yes, paper; an ancient cough drop box. Then, a board from a crate. In running back to the stove, he ran into another box and dropped the paper. "God damn it," he muttered, dropping to his knees and scuffling in the darkness. And in the distance, a wail, a high sobbing. Time was short. "Son of a bitch," he muttered, "Where the fuck is the paper!" He spent precious minutes looking on this side of the box, on that side. Nothing. He ran back to the stove, board in hand and knelt before the open belly.

"I am dying. I am dying." The man could barely hear the voice.

"No," he said, ripping his tattered shirt into small fragments. He placed them in a pile right down by his knee. Then, carefully, carefully, he took one fragment and placed it next to the ember. "Here," he said, "eat!"

"It's too late, too late."

"No! No, it's not! Eat!"

Oh, God, the ember was so faint. But it nibbled the fabric. "That's right," the man said, "that's right; you need strength. Eat." The little ember became brighter. "Yes," the man said, "wonderful. Wonderful. Don't stop." He placed another bit of cloth with the first. The ember began to nibble that one—the red changed to orange; he put on even more cloth. The orange became bright and yes! There! A little flame danced. More cloth. Then the man took the board, looked for splinters and, finding them, fed them to the flame. The flame grew brighter. He stood, then broke the board with his feet. More splinters. More fire. "I feel stronger," said the fire, "much stronger."

"You're going to feel stronger still," the man replied, placing larger pieces of wood on the fire; he raced about gathering more boards; soon, the fire was yellow, warm and bright in the stove. The light, flooding out of the door, pushed, pushed the darkness back. "Yes," the fire roared, "yes, yes, oh, yes."

Then the fire crawled out of the stove; it slipped down the front and then stood on two flaming legs. It walked over to the man; he was so stunned that he could not move. He was kneeling, hands on knees, mesmerized by the fire; it then reached out, touched his hand with flaming fingers—yet the man did not feel a burning heat; rather, it was a gentle warmth; the fire whispered to the man, "You have saved me. You took the time to save me."

The man did not know what to say. All he knew was that he was surrounded by warmth, light and in the warehouse, there was no darkness.

"Ah," said the fire, "ah, I was wrong. There is time after all."

The man nodded and mumbled, "There was an hour left on the parking meters…"

"Good," said the fire, "good. Good. And *what* an hour it shall be. You have certainly done your share. Now to do mine."

The fire collapsed into a ball, rose and, flashing through the warehouse, bust through the front window. The man ran after it, only to see it rise high, high into the air. He lost sight of it. And was puzzled. He waited. Dawn was coming; the sky on the horizon east of the black mass of the volcano was grey blue. Silence. Still. A suspended moment: the moment of between, of transformation. He was holding his breath; he wanted to scream. He was sweating. He could not bear the tension and gritted his teeth. He wanted to pull his hair, wanted to break things. And still, still the moment continued. He stood frozen and, not knowing why, stared at the volcano, staring at it until his eyes watered.

Suddenly, a tremor. Then, a jolt. The man was thrown to his knees. Another tremor. And then, looking up, he saw it, high, high above: a huge fire ball. A fire ball not falling, but driving, driving at incredible speed—aiming for the caldera of the volcano. The sun rose just as the fire ball struck the volcano's caldera. A brilliant explosion of light, of thunder, and the man covered his eyes. The ground trembled and shook; the buildings of the city began to crumble. The intense light faded and when the man was able to see once again, what he saw was the entire upper half of the volcano engulfed in black, heavy, dense rolling smoke. From fissures in the side of the mountain, lava gushed. Another quake; the glass of the warehouse behind him burst out, covering him with glass. More buildings toppled, but the man was too stunned to move. In the distance, the volcano roared and amidst all this fury of light and sound, he heard something else. He turned—and backed away. The crates. The crates which he had looked into the night before, were swelling, the steel bands around them snapping like thread while boards split and popped—the man turned and ran. Around him, the ancient city continued to crumble, the bricks fell, the old concrete, the rock shattered like glass and he ran. And as he did, he saw that the sky was completely dark; pumice rained down. He ran up the hill, outside the city and found, on the other side, a valley and at the bottom of it, room sized boulders. He ran to them and found two that, leaning together, formed a cave. He crawled in—to wait.

For days the sky was dark. For days he heard the thunder and felt the earth shake. He waited. Slept. Dreamed of the cities he had seen while the darkness and the rain of rocks continued. He awoke with a start. Quiet. He noticed something else: he was sweating, because it was *hot.* Looking down, he saw that he sat in mud and that the large boulders had settled, leaving just a very small exit. He clawed at the hole, pulling at the mud, the rocks and finally it was large enough for him to crawl through; once out, he stood—and stared. His mouth dropped open: there was water in the valley. He looked up. The sky was a very deep blue and the air *was* warm. He tried to think of what had happened, then realized what must have happened—the smoke, the gasses must have

trapped the sun's heat and so began melting the ice which created water vapor which further increased the temperature and so on and although he understood it, he still shook his head in disbelief. "No," he whispered, "no, no, it's not possible!" He ran up the hill and turned around; the water in the valley was an inlet, an extension of a larger body of water. Why, he thought, I must be looking out over an ocean—and not far away, he saw waves, white and shining in the sun, beat against a rocky peninsula and he was reminded of a slow and ponderous heartbeat as he listened: *Whump! Whump! Whump!* And the waves, the waves beat, beat against the rock. The spray was carried high and how it sparkled in the sunlight!

He turned again, shaking his head in amazement: the volcano: the top half of it was gone. What remained was cloaked in snow. Waterfalls cascaded down the steep flanks to join a broad and slow river that meandered easily through green, rolling meadows.

But the most wonderful thing was right before the man; downslope from him: the city. There was the city with towers, white and tall, shining in the sun. And people! People! He saw them strolling the wide streets; he heard them singing and suddenly he was running, running in the new, rich air; running and could still hear the surf. He ran through the tall grasses and flowers of purple and gold waving in wind and on the horizon, the mountain all splendid and white and he ran, yes, ran, then was leaping and laughing and running again to those people in that city with the towers so tall and, oh, God, so white and shining, yes, shining, shining in the light of the sun.

Bizarro books

CATALOGUE – SPRING 2006

Bizarro Books publishes under the following imprints:

www.rawdogscreamingpress.com

www.eraserheadpress.com

www.afterbirthbooks.com

www.swallowdownpress.com

For all your Bizarro needs visit:

www.bizarrogenre.org

BIZARRO BOOKS CATALOGUE – SPRING 2006

BB-001

"The Kafka Effekt"
D. Harlan Wilson
A collection of forty-four irreal short stories loosely written in the vein of Franz Kafka, with more than a pinch of William S. Burroughs sprinkled on top.
211 pages   **$14**

BB-002

"Satan Burger"
Carlton Mellick III
The cult novel that put Mellick III on the map... Six punks get jobs at a fast food restaurant owned by the devil in a city over-populated by surreal alien cultures.
236 pages   **$14**

BB-003

"Some Things Are Better Left Unplugged"
Vincent Sakowski
Join The Man and his Nemesis, the obese tabby, for a nightmare roller coaster ride into this postmodern fantasy.
152 pages   **$10**

BB-004

"Shall We Gather At the Garden?"
Kevin L Donihe
Donihe's Debut novel. Midgets take over the world, The Church of Lionel Richie vs. The Church of the Byrds, plant porn and more!
244 pages   **$14**

BB-005

"Razor Wire Pubic Hair"
Carlton Mellick III
A genderless humandildo is purchased by a razor dominatrix and brought into her nightmarish world of bizarre sex and mutila-tion.
176 pages   **$11**

BB-006

"Stranger on the Loose"
D. Harlan Wilson
The fiction of Wilson's 2nd collection is planted in the soil of normalcy, but what grows out of that soil is a dark, witty, otherworldly jungle...
228 pages   **$14**

BB-007

"The Baby Jesus Butt Plug"
Carlton Mellick III
Using clones of the Baby Jesus for anal sex will be the hip underground sex fetish of the future.
92 pages   **$10**

BB-008

"Fishyfleshed"
Carlton Mellick III
The world of the past is an illogical flatland lack-ing in dimension and color, a sick-scape of crispy squid people wan-dering the desert for no ap-parent reason.
260 pages   **$14**

BIZARRO BOOKS CATALOGUE – SPRING 2006

BB-009
"Dead Bitch Army"
Andre Duza
Step into a world filled with racist teenagers, cannibals, 100 warped Uncle Sams, automobiles with razor-sharp teeth, living graffiti, and a pissed-off zombie bitch out for revenge.
344 pages   **$16**

BB-010
"The Menstruating Mall"
Carlton Mellick III
"The Breakfast Club meets *Chopping Mall* if directed by David Lynch."
- Brian Keene
212 pages   **$12**

BB-011
"Angel Dust Apocalypse"
Jeremy R. Johnson
Meth-heads, man-made monsters, and murderous Neo-Nazis. "Seriously amazing short stories..."
- Chuck Palahniuk, author of *Fight Club*
184 pages   **$11**

BB-012
"Ocean of Lard"
Kevin L Donihe/ Carlton Mellick III
A parody of those old Choose Your Own Adventure kid's books about some very odd pirates sailing on a sea made of animal fat.
244 pages   **$14**

BB-013
"Last Burn in Hell"
John Edward Lawson
From his lurid angst-affair with a lesbian music diva to his ascendance as unlikely pop icon the one constant for Kenrick Brimley, official state prison gigolo, is he's got no clue what he's doing.
165 pages   **$14**

BB-014
"Tangerinephant"
Kevin Dole 2
TV-obsessed aliens have abducted Michael Tangerinephant in this bizarro combination of science fiction, satire, and surrealism.
212 pages   **$11**

BB-015
"Foop!"
Chris Genoa
Strange happenings are going on at Dactyl, Inc, the world's first and only time travel tourism company.
"A surreal pie in the face!"
- Christopher Moore
300 pages   **$14**

BB-016
"Spider Pie"
Alyssa Sturgill
A one-way trip down a rabbit hole inhabited by sexual deviants and friendly monsters, fairytale beginnings and hideous endings.
104 pages   **$11**

BB-017
"The Unauthorized Woman"
Efrem Emerson
Enter the world of the inner freak, a landscape populated by the pre-dead and morticioners, by cockroaches and 300-lb robots.
104 pages   **$11**

BB-018
"Fugue XXIX"
Forrest Aguirre
Tales from the fringe of speculative literary fiction where innovative minds dream up the future's uncharted territories while mining forgotten treasures of the past.
220 pages   **$16**

BB-019
"Pocket Full of Loose Razorblades"
John Edward Lawson
A collection of dark bizarro stories. From a giant rectum to a foot-fungus factory to a girl with a biforked tongue.
190 pages   **$13**

BB-020
"Punk Land"
Carlton Mellick III
In the punk version of Heaven, the anarchist utopia is threatened by corporate fascism and only Goblin, Mortician's sperm, and a blue-mohawked female assassin named Shark Girl can stop them.
284 pages   **$15**

BB-021
"Pseudo-City"
D. Harlan Wilson
Pseudo-City exposes what waits in the bathroom stall, under the manhole cover and in the corporate boardroom, all in a way that can only be described as mind-bogglingly irreal.
220 pages   **$16**

BB-022
"Kafka's Uncle and Other Strange Tales"
Bruce Taylor
Anslenot and his giant tarantula (tormentor? friend?) wander a desecrated world in this novel and collection of stories from Mr. Magic Realism Himself.
348 pages   **$17**

BB-023
"Sex and Death In Television Town"
Carlton Mellick III
In the old west, a gang of hermaphrodite gunslingers take refuge in Telos: a town where its citizens have televisions instead of heads.
184 pages   **$12**

BB-024
"It Came From Below The Belt"
Bradley Sands
What can Grover Goldstein do when his severed, sentient penis forces him to return to high school and help it win the presidential election?
204 pages   **$13**

BB-025

"Sick: An Anthology of Illness"

John Lawson, editor
These Sick stories are horrendous and hilarious dissections of creative minds on the scalpel's edge.
296 pages $16

BB-026

"Tempting Disaster"
John Lawson, editor
A shocking and alluring anthology from the fringe that examines our culture's obsession with taboos.
260 pages $16

BB-027

"Siren Promised"

Jeremy R. Johnson
Nominated for the Bram Stoker Award. A potent mix of bad drugs, bad dreams, brutal bad guys, and surreal/incredible art by Alan M. Clark.
190 pages $13

BB-028

"Chemical Gardens"
Gina Ranalli
Ro and punk band *Green is the Enemy* find Kreepkins, a surfer-dude warlock, a vengeful demon, and a Metal Priestess in their way as they try to escape an underground nightmare.
188 pages $13

BB-029

"Jesus Freaks"
Andre Duza
For God so loved the world that he gave his only two begotten sons... and a few million zombies.
400 pages $16

BB-030

"Grape City"
Kevin L. Donihe
More Donihe-style comedic bizarro about a demon named Charles who is forced to work a minimum wage job on Earth after Hell goes out of business.
108 pages $10

BB-031

"Sea of the Patchwork Cats"

Carlton Mellick III
A quiet dreamlike tale set in the ashes of the human race. For Mellick enthusiasts who also adore *The Twilight Zone*.
112 pages $10

BB-032

"Extinction Journals"
Jeremy Robert Johnson
An uncanny voyage across a newly nuclear America where one man must confront the problems associated with loneliness, insane dieties, radiation, love, and an ever-evolving cockroach suit with a mind of its own.
104 pages $10

BIZARRO BOOKS CATALOGUE – SPRING 2006

BB-033
"Meat Puppet Cabaret"
Steve Beard
At last! The secret connection between Jack the Ripper and Princess Diana's death revealed!
240 pages $16 / $30

BB-034
"The Greatest Fucking Moment in Sports"
Kevin L. Donihe
In the tradition of the surreal anti-sitcom *Get A Life* comes a tale of triumph and agape love from the master of comedic bizarro.
108 pages $10

BB-035
"The Troublesome Amputee"
John Edward Lawson
Disturbing verse from a man who truly believes nothing is sacred and intends to prove it.
104 pages $9

BB-036
"Deity"
Vic Mudd
God (who doesn't like to be called "God") comes down to a typical, suburban, Ohio family for a little vacation—but it doesn't turn out to be as relaxing as He had hoped it would be...
168 pages $12

BB-037
"The Haunted Vagina"
Carlton Mellick III
It's difficult to love a woman whose vagina is a gateway to the world of the dead.
176 pages $11

coming soon

BB-038
"Tales from the Vinegar Wasteland"
Ray Fracalossy
Witness: a man is slowly losing his face, a neighbor who periodically screams out for no apparent reason, and a house with a room that doesn't actually exist.
240 pages $14

BB-039
"Suicide Girls in the Afterlife"
Gina Ranalli
After Pogue commits suicide, she unexpectedly finds herself an unwilling "guest" at a hotel in the Afterlife.
100 pages $9

COMING SOON:

"And Your Point Is?" by Steve Aylett **$11**
"Not Quite One of the Boys"
by Vincent Sakowski **$14**
"Misadventures in a Thumbnail Universe"
by Vincent Sakowski **$10**
"House of Houses" by Kevin Donihe **$10**
"War Slut" by Carlton Mellick III **$10**

ORDER FORM

TITLES	QTY	PRICE	TOTAL
Shipping costs (see below)			
TOTAL			

Please make checks and moneyorders payable to ROSE O'KEEFE / BIZARRO BOOKS in U.S. funds only. Please don't send bad checks! Allow 2-6 weeks for delivery. International orders may take longer. If you'd like to pay online via PAYPAL.COM, send payments to publisher@eraserheadpress.com.

SHIPPING: US ORDERS - $2 for the first book, $1 for each additional book. For priority shipping, add an additional $4. INT'L ORDERS - $5 for the first book, $3 for each additional book. Add an additional $5 per book for global priority shipping.

Send payment to:

BIZARRO BOOKS
 C/O Rose O'Keefe
 205 NE Bryant
 Portland, OR 97211

Address

City   State   Zip

Email   Phone

Lightning Source UK Ltd.
Milton Keynes UK
12 April 2011

170789UK00001B/226/A